THEODERIC
'IMITATION OF AN EMPEROR'

THEODERIC

'Imitation of an Emperor'

The story of Theoderic Amalo,
the barbarian who wanted to be Roman

Ross Laidlaw

First published in Great Britain in 2008 by
Polygon, an imprint of Birlinn Ltd
West Newington House
10 Newington Road
Edinburgh
EH9 1QS

9 8 7 6 5 4 3 2 1

www.birlinn.co.uk

ISBN 978 1 84697 082 5

British Library Cataloguing-in-Publication Data

A catalogue record for this book is available on
request from the British Library.

Typeset by Palimpsest Book Production Limited,
Grangemouth, Stirlingshire
Printed and bound by ScandBook AB

To the memory of my old tutor, Professor Philip Grierson, fellow of Gonville and Caius College, Cambridge, who taught me the importance of thorough preparation

ACKNOWLEDGEMENTS

My warmest appreciation to Barbara Halley for unearthing many useful facts online, to Dr Alberto Massimo for helping me to get Theoderic over the Julian Alps, and for supplying me with information about Roman families and the Roman Curia, to Helen Simpson for her superb editing, and to my wife Margaret for freeing me from various domestic duties to give me more time for writing. A special word of thanks to my publishers, Hugh Andrew and Neville Moir, for their steadfast support and encouragement.

CONTENTS

MAPS AND PLANS

GLOSSARY OF TERMS AND PLACE NAMES

acta diurna	daily bulletins
acta publica	government enactments
agens (pl: *agentes*) *in rebus*	government courier-cum-spy
Alpes Carnicae	the Carnatic Alps
Alpes Juliae	the Julian Alps
andbahtos	armed retainers
Anderida	Pevensey
Anderida Silva	the Weald
Arelate	Arles
Aremorica	Brittany
Ariminum	Rimini
Arverna	Clermont-Ferrand
Arvernum	the Auvergne
Augusta Suessonium	Soissons
ballista (pl: *ballistae*)	huge catapult-like crossbow
Barcino	Barcelona
bestiarii	animal-handlers
baurg	thatched village or settlement
belagines	statutes of law
Bodotria Aesturia	Firth of Forth
Bononia	Bologna
Borysthenes river	the Dnieper
Brundisium	Brindisi
Burdigala	Bordeaux
Calleva	Silchester
Cambria	Wales
campidoctores	drill-sergeants
Caput Senatus	Head of the Senate
cardo	main street
castellum (pl: *castella*)	fortified settlement
Castra Batava	Passau
Castra Gyfel	Ilchester
cena	evening meal

xiii

centenarius	horse, winner of 100+ races
circitor	non-commissioned rank, roughly equivalent to corporal
civilitas	high-minded moral responsibility and respect for justice
civitas barbara	foreigners' section of Ravenna
classiarii	marines
Classis	Ravenna's port
codex	pupil's waxed writing-slate
coloni	tenant farmers or peasants
Comes Rei Privatae	Count of the Privy Purse
Comes Sacrarum Largitionum	Count of the Public Purse
consistorium	court dealing with Roman affairs/crimes
cubiculum	bedroom
cucullus	hooded cloak
currus	light carriage
cursus publicus	state postal system
curule chair	movable chair
Dacia Ripensis	province roughly equivalent to north-east Serbia
Dalai Nor	Lake Baikal
Deruuentis river	the Derwent
decurion	(i) junior military officer; (ii) town councillor
Dravus river	the Drava
dromon	war-galley
Dunpender	Traprain Law, East Lothian
Dyrrachium	Durrësi, Albania
Exercitus Britanniae	Army of Britain
Excubitors	300-strong bodyguard corps
Fasti	official state records, especially consular lists
fibula (pl: *fibulae*)	clasp or brooch
fliehburgen	places of refuge
foederatus	liegeman or ally
foedus	oath of allegiance
francisca	heavy throwing-axe
Fretum Gallicum	Straits of Dover
frijai	free men
gards	palace
gerulus	handyman

Gesoriacum	Boulogne
gladius	short sword
Haemus Mountains	Balkan Mountains
Herta	Roman fortress on the middle Danube
Humbri river	the Humber
Isca river	the Esk
Kärnthen Gebirge, das	the Carinthian Alps
Kuni	Amal tribal council
latifundium	large estate
Lauriacum	Lorsch
leges scriptae	legal statutes
Liger river	the Loire
limitanei	frontier troops
locarius (pl: *locarii*)	usher
lorica (pl: *loricae*)	cuirass
Magister Militum	Master of Soldiers/Commander-in-Chief
Magister Militum praesentalis	Commander-in-Chief of the main army – 'in the presence' [of the emperor]
mappa	white cloth used to start races
Mare Suevicum	Baltic Sea
Mercurii Promontorium	Cape Bon
Moesia Secunda	province roughly equivalent to northern Bulgaria
Mons Badonicus	Mount Badon
Mons Garganus	Mount Gargano
Moravus river	the Morava
munerator	producer of the Games
Mutina	Modena
nauta (pl: *nautae*)	sailor
navarchus	sailing-master
Neapolis	Naples
Noricum	West Roman province, roughly corresponding to southern Austria
noxius (pl: *noxii*)	condemned criminal
nuntius	civic official, part herald, part town crier
Oenus river	the Inn
otium	leisured scholarship

Padus river	the Po
Placentia	Piacenza
platea major	main street
pomoerium	Rome's official city boundary
paedagogus (pl: *paedagogi*)	slave who escorted children to and from school
Pons Sontii	Isonzo Bridge
Pontus Euxinus	Black Sea
praecepta	rights and traditions
praetorium	headquarters
prandium	midday meal
primicerius	non-commissioned rank, roughly equivalent to sergeant-major
protectores domestici	palace bodyguards
Pyretus river	the Pruth
quadratum	quadrangle, courtyard
Reged	Cumberland (old county)
Referendarius	Head of Security
regnator	ruler
reiks	king
remiges	naval oarsmen
retenator	governor
Rhaetia	province between the Inn and Rhine rivers
Rhenus river	the Rhine
Rhodanus river	the Rhône
saio	crown agent
Samara river	the Somme
Savus river	the Sava
Scandia	Scandinavia
Scriba Concilii	Secretary to the Council
Sequana river	the Seine
Serica	China
sica	Anatolian fighting-knife
silentiarius (pl: *silentiarii*)	gentleman usher at the imperial court
Singidunum	Belgrade
Sinus Corinthiacus	Gulf of Corinth
Sinus Tarentinus	Gulf of Taranto
Sipontum	Manfredonia
Sirmium	Sremska Mitrovica
skalk	slave
Sorus river	the Sora

Spangenhelm	segmented conical helmet
spatha	long sword
spina	barrier down centre of Circus Maximus
Stabula Diomedis (fo. 98)	city of Macedonia
Stobi (fo. 96)	city of Dacia
suffragium	covert bribe or 'backhander'
tablinum	study
Tanais river	the Don
Terginus Sinus	Gulf of Trieste
Ticinum	Pavia
Tolosa	Toulouse
triclinium	dining-room
Tridentium	Triglav
Tyras river	the Dniester
Ulca river	the Vuka
Uure river	the Wear
Vallum Hadriani	Hadrian's Wall
Vectis	Isle of Wight
veniationes	wild-beast hunts
venatores	hunters
Venta	Winchester
Viadrus river	the Oder

HISTORICAL NOTE

AD 468, when this story begins, was a critical year for the Western half of the Roman Empire; nothing less than its survival or extinction hung in the balance. How had this 'moment of truth' come about?

The beginning of the fifth century had witnessed successive waves of barbarians – Visigoths, Vandals, Suevi et al. – break through the West's frontiers and rampage through Gaul and Spain, with Britain being abandoned in the chaos. But cometh the hour, cometh the man. Just when it seemed that nothing could halt the West's slide towards disintegration, a remarkable Roman general, Constantius, took on the German invaders and forced them to settle peacefully on Roman soil as federate 'guests'. After his premature death, Constantius' work was continued and consolidated by an even greater Roman commander, Flavius Aetius. For thirty years, Aetius was able, most of the time, with the help of his allies the Huns, to maintain stability and some form of imperial control. Ironically, it was the Huns, a formidable horde of nomadic horse-archers from Central Asia who, by pressing the German tribes from the rear, had set off a chain reaction of migration resulting in the barbarian invasions. These were largely confined to the West, whose long Rhine–Danube frontier was especially vulnerable to attack by the confederations of German tribes beyond the northern banks. In contrast, the Eastern Empire – wealthy, stable, the home of ancient civilizations – had only the Lower Danube frontier to defend; also it became adept at passing on barbarian invaders, such as Alaric's Visigoths, to the West. (Persia, to the east, potentially a far greater threat than any barbarian confederation, was a civilized power which on the whole kept its peace treaties with Rome.)

The great exception to Aetius' entente with the German invaders was Gaiseric, king of the Vandals. As ambitious as he was cunning and cruel, in 429 Gaiseric had transported his tribe from Spain across the Straits of Gibraltar, wrested North Africa – the West's richest and most productive diocese – from Roman control, and set up an independent Vandal kingdom in its place. Unlike other German immigrant leaders, Gaiseric never showed the least desire for an accommodation with Rome, towards whom he maintained a stance of unvarying hostility.

In 451, Aetius' policy of forging bonds with the federates was triumphantly vindicated. In that year, his old friend Attila, king of the Huns, abandoned a long-running campaign against the Eastern Empire to launch a full-scale attack on the West. Heading a coalition of Roman troops and German confederates, Aetius defeated Attila and his Huns in an epic battle on the Catalaunian Plains – the West's greatest, though final, victory. Yet from this high point things began to go rapidly downhill for the West. Two years later Attila died, then in the following year, 454, Aetius was murdered by his jealous emperor, Valentinian III, himself assassinated in 455 by loyal followers of Aetius, thus ending the long Theodosian dynasty. (Whatever its faults, the House of Theodosius had provided a valuable measure of stability.) With the threat of Attila gone, and no general of the stature of Aetius to keep them in line, the federates took advantage of the constitutional vacuum resulting from the murder of Valentinian, and began to flex their muscles with a view to expanding their territories.

There followed in rapid succession four further reigns, the emperors virtual appointees of the new Master of Soldiers, Ricimer, the first German to fill the post for half a century. Meanwhile, the Western Empire, weakened by protracted haemorrhaging of taxes, troops and territory, was beginning to unravel, the federates held in check from an all-out land-grab only by wariness concerning possible counter-measures by the powerful Eastern Empire acting in concert with the Western government. Then, in 467, the storm-clouds gathering over the West suddenly rolled back, as circumstances combined to promise a real hope for recovery. A charismatic new emperor, the fifth since Valentinian, ascended the throne of the West, in parallel with the devising of a Grand Plan for finally driving the Vandals from Africa. (More than one abortive attempt had already been made.)

This emperor, Anthemius, seemed an ideal choice to head a Western recovery. Polished and affable, approved by Ricimer and having the full backing of his promoter, the Eastern emperor, Leo, Anthemius came with impeccable credentials. These were: successful campaigning as an Eastern general; a distinguished family background; named consul for 455 and Patrician; marriage to the daughter of the late Eastern emperor Marcian; and near elevation to the Eastern purple on Marcian's death. If anyone could restore stability to the West, that man, it seemed, was Anthemius.

He made an auspicious start. His arrival in Gaul at the head of a considerable force drawn from the Roman field army of Illyricum, cowed the federates there – Franks, Burgundians, and Visigoths – into, if not quite submission, at least acquiescence. (In set-piece battles, as the barbarians knew to their cost, properly led Roman troops would always beat them. Only overwhelming numbers had enabled them to establish themselves on Roman soil. Now, the prospect of East Roman reinforcements descending on them if they stepped out of line encouraged them to adopt a posture of appeasement.) Almost to a man, the Gallo-Roman aristocracy, whose loyalty to the centre had become eroded by the necessity of making terms with the dangerously volatile settlers in their midst, flocked to declare allegiance to their new head of state. (The *cursus publicus** we know was still functioning.)

But, as everyone knew, the main plank of any scheme to revive the fortunes of the West consisted not in tweaking the balance of power in Gaul, but in reconquering North Africa. The potential benefits were enormous. The immediate effect would be a massive injection of revenue into the cash-strapped Treasury in Ravenna. With fresh blood pumping through its fiscal arteries, the West could replenish its shrunken, decimated field armies, and begin the process of re-establishing imperial authority. Peter Heather, in his brilliantly perceptive *The Fall of the Roman Empire*, says it all: 'The knock-on effect of a decisive victory over Geiseric . . . would have been far-reaching. With Italy and North Africa united, Spain could have been added to the new western power-base . . . Then, once Hispanic revenues had begun to flow in again, . . . Visigoths and Burgundians could have been reduced to much smaller enclaves of influence [in Gaul] . . . The Roman centre would have become once again . . . dominant . . .' In addition, Britain (which had never been officially written off, and where Saxon settlement had only just begun) might have been scheduled for re-occupation.

---

* The efficient state post used relays of horses operating from postal stations 8–10 miles apart. Subject to official permit, it could be used by civilian VIPs.

Like the thinking behind the Spanish Armada, the strategy of the invasion was to disembark a huge sea-borne army on the coast of Africa, bring Gaiseric to battle, then smash him. Before enlarging on this plan, it should perhaps be asked: why was the East willing to commit its resources on a massive scale to rescue its beleaguered partner? First, Gaiseric was a thorn in the flesh of both Empires; as the only barbarian leader with a fleet (of Roman-built vessels) he had become a serious nuisance to the East, disrupting sea-borne trade by raids and piracy. Second, the Eastern emperor, Leo, mindful that Anthemius had come within a whisker of being elevated to the purple, was only too willing to have a potential rival removed as far away as possible – and kept there. (There is no evidence that Anthemius had accepted being passed over with anything other than good grace; but in the unforgiving world of Roman power politics it was best to take no chances.) Third, although East and West had in many ways drifted apart during the seventy-three years since their formal separation, there still existed an emotional attachment to the concept of 'the One and Indivisible Empire' – rather like the ties binding the British Commonwealth, and before that 'the Empire upon which the Sun Never Sets'. (The late great Peter Ustinov had a delicious story about when, arriving at his first school, he was confronted in the hall by a large painting. It depicted a Boy Scout gazing at a map of the world, beside which stood Jesus Christ pointing to the red patchwork of the British Empire!)

To finance the expedition the treasuries of both East and West were emptied, yielding one hundred and thirty thousand pounds' weight (fifty-eight tons!) of gold. Thus was raised a vast combined operation: a fleet of eleven hundred ships transporting a force, according to Gibbon's estimate (and his figures are usually reliable), upward of a hundred thousand strong. In June 468, the great armada set sail from the Bosphorus, carrying with it not only one of the largest armies the world had ever seen, but the hopes of salvation for the Western Empire.

PART I

THE COLUMN OF ARCADIUS
AD 468–488

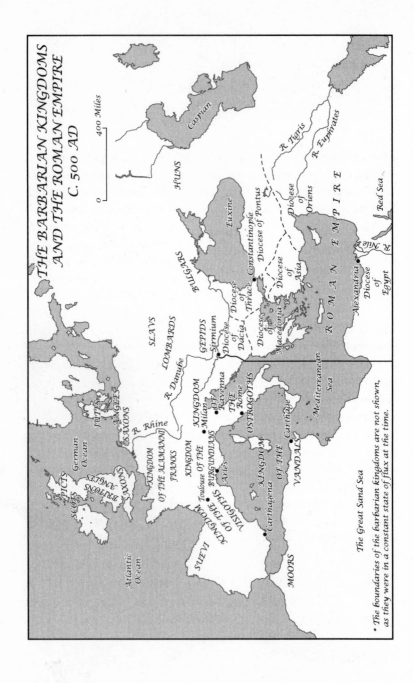

THE BARBARIAN KINGDOMS
AND THE ROMAN EMPIRE
C. 500 AD

400 Miles

0

Atlantic Ocean

PICTS

SCOTS

BRITONS

German Ocean

ANGLES

JUTES

ANGLES SAXONS

SAXONS

KINGDOM OF THE ALAMANNI

FRANKS

R. Rhine

KINGDOM OF THE BURGUNDIANS

Toulouse

Arles

KINGDOM OF THE VISIGOTHS

SUEVI

Carthagena

MOORS

The Great Sand Sea

KINGDOM OF THE VANDALS

Carthage

KINGDOM OF THE OSTROGOTHS

THE Rome

Ravenna

Milan

KINGDOM OF THE

R. Danube

LOMBARDS

SLAVS

GEPIDS

Sirmium

Diocese of Dacia

Diocese of Macedonia

Mediterranean Sea

Euxine

BULGARS

HUNS

Caspian

Diocese of Thrace

Constantinople

Diocese of Pontus

Diocese of Asia

R O M A N   E M P I R E

Alexandria

Diocese of Oriens

Diocese of Egypt

R. Nile

R. Tigris

R. Euphrates

Red Sea

• The boundaries of the barbarian kingdoms are not shown,
as they were in a constant state of flux at the time.

PROLOGUE

Like an endless row of needles, the mast-tips of the approaching fleet rose above the horizon, followed by the white flecks of sails then dark hulls – hundreds upon hundreds of them. The Vandal scout, watching from the northern tip of Mercurii Promontorium,* the monstrous headland pointing like an accusing finger from the African coast towards Sicilia, tried for a time to estimate the number of ships, then abandoned the attempt. As well essay to count the pebbles on a beach. Scrambling into the saddle of his waiting mount, he spurred off to bring the news to his master, Gaiseric, king of the Vandals.

The swirling crowds that filled the streets and squares of Carthage – from the forum crowning Byrsa Hill, to the quays beside the great twin harbours (naval and trading) and the sprawling suburbs of Megara to the west – seethed with aggressive excitement. Almost all the faces were of Romans, Moors and native Berbers. Those Vandals rash enough to venture out of doors had encountered a barrage of jeers, insults, rotten fruit, and even stones. For at last the Romans had arrived, to drive out the swaggering yellow-haired tyrants, with their harsh German voices and ugly sun-reddened skins, who for nearly two generations had bullied and oppressed the citizens of Roman Africa. Like wildfire, the news had spread that the Roman fleet – of over a thousand sail, some claimed – was even now riding at anchor less than forty miles to the north. The hour of deliverance had surely come.

* Cape Bon, Tunisia.

Seated before his council within the great basilica of Carthage, where the baying of the mobs sounded only as a distant murmur, Gaiseric, though he gave no outward sign, was worried, deeply worried. Since seizing Roman Africa forty years before, he had maintained his grip on the territory by a mixture of luck and cunning, fomenting dissension between his enemies to play them off against one another, then striking when, divided, they were at their weakest. But now, it seemed, luck, fate (the 'weird' of his ancestors in their cold northern forests), call it what you will, had finally deserted him. For let the army of the Romans, currently aboard their fleet at anchor off the western shore of Mercurii Promontorium, once disembark, and he was finished. He was certainly outnumbered, probably vastly so, and, while his Vandal warriors would fight with ferocious courage, they were no match for the armoured Romans with their iron discipline. Nor could he rely on the support of his native auxiliaries; anticipating a Vandal defeat, they would undoubtedly desert to the Romans.

The only counter left him in the game was to play for time. If only the Roman commander (one Basiliscus, so his spies in Constantinople had informed him) could be prevented from landing his army, until . . . Until the wind reversed direction, pinning the Romans against the western shore of the great promontory? Lead might float. At this time of year the prevailing south-easterly, famed for its constancy from time immemorial, could be expected to blow for weeks yet. With the wind in their favour, the Romans could sail at any time they chose, to establish a beachhead westward of their present position.

Gaiseric rose, to address his assembled war-leaders and advisers. Though stooped with age, and lame from an early riding accident, the Vandal monarch, white mane falling to his shoulders, was still an impressive figure, an aura of ruthless will and power seeming to emanate from him.

4

'Who can tell me of this Basiliscus?' the king demanded, in his deep, guttural voice.

'Sire, he is the son-in-law of Leo, the Greek who sits on the throne of Constantinople,' offered a battle-scarred veteran. Like many present, he had adopted the burnous of the local Berbers, a hooded cloak of light material affording some protection from the fierce sub-tropical sun, to which the Vandals' fair skins were especially vulnerable. 'An able general, it would seem. They say he drove the last of Attila's sons from Dacia and Macedonia when they tried to find sanctuary within the Eastern Empire.'

'Does he love gold?'

'What Roman does not, Sire?' answered a grey-haired councillor. 'But if you mean can he be bribed? Unlikely, I would say. The man is hardly poor, so why risk his reputation?'

Further discussion concerning the relative strengths of the opposing forces served only to confirm Gaiseric's worst fears. Dismissing the council, he sent for Engedda, a 'cunning man', skilled in the arts of healing, wise in the ways of beasts, and the lore of weather. When the sage arrived – a tiny shrivelled Ethiopian whose black skin hung in wrinkled folds from his ancient frame – Gaiseric put the question 'Will the wind change, and if so when?'

'*Two* questions, Mighty One,' cackled the sage. 'My fee is therefore double. Let us say . . . twenty fat kine? To great Kaiseric, who is a river to his people, such a price is nothing. As it says in our Holy Book, "The labourer is worthy of his hire."'

'You drive a hard bargain, Engedda,' growled the king, secretly amused by the little man's effrontery. With Gaiseric's hatred of all things Roman common knowledge, no one but Engedda would have dared address him as 'Kaiseric', incorporating the title of a Roman emperor into the monarch's name. As for the 'our', referring to the Bible, Gaiseric had to remind himself that the Ethiopians had been converted to Christianity even before his own people. (As Arians, however, the Vandals were heretics in the eyes of the Orthodox Romans.) 'When may I expect an answer?'

Engedda rolled his eyes portentously. 'First, I must consult the spirits of my ancestors,' he intoned. 'Tomorrow at noon, ask what they have told me.'

On being informed by Engedda, at the appointed time, that in five days the wind would begin to blow from the north-west, Gaiseric felt a stab of hope. In thirty years he had never known the Ethiopian to be wrong. (Of course, he told himself, Engedda's claims concerning supernatural assistance were just part of his persona, like his magician's rattle and the bag of bones around his neck. The sage's uncanny ability to predict the weather had to rest on a skill at reading signs, imperceptible to others, in the behaviour of birds and insects, cloud-patterns, the dryness or dampness of the air, etc.) If, for the next five days, the Romans could somehow be kept from weighing anchor, disaster might yet be staved off. Filled with renewed vigour and purpose, the old king began to lay his plans.

'For God's sake, Basiliscus, give the order for the fleet to sail!' shouted Iohannes, the commander's senior general. He banged the table in frustration, making a silver wine-jug jump, spilling ruby drops on a chart of the North African coast. They were in the great cabin of the flagship, *Perseus*, one of the *dromons* that made up the strike force of the fleet. Monster galleys, these were armed with viciously pointed bronze rams which could punch a gaping hole in an enemy vessel below the waterline, causing it to sink. 'Every hour that we delay allows Gaiseric to strengthen his resources.'

'What resources?' scoffed Basiliscus with a smile. A large man, running slightly now to fat, he was adored by his soldiers for the generosity of his donatives and care for their welfare. In return, he had their loyalty and trust. 'Look, by being in no hurry we achieve two things. First, we create an impression of Roman invincibility which should shake the Vandals' morale. Gaiseric's luck has finally run out; he knows it and his tribe knows it. Second, we allow time for intelligence of our overwhelming strength to percolate throughout the usurper's realm. This will encourage disaffection among his Roman subjects, and desertion on the part of his native levies. Meanwhile, our people have a chance to rest and recuperate after the voyage, furbish their gear, clean and repair the ships . . .' He gestured through the stern window at a scene where a relaxed, almost holiday atmosphere prevailed. Overshadowed by the beetling cliffs of the huge headland, naked soldiers and *classiarii* – marines – splashed and skylarked in the blue waters of

6

the Mare Internum, while sailors scoured the decks and scraped the hulls of sleek *dromons* and round-bellied transports.

Another advantage – although a strictly personal one, Basiliscus admitted to himself – was the receipt of *suffragium** from Gaiseric. Each day, an emissary from the Vandal king would appear on the rocky foreshore and be rowed out to *Perseus*. In addition to assurances that Gaiseric now wished to become a Friend of Rome with federate status in the empire, the messenger would bring a bag of gold. So the longer he allowed Gaiseric to hope that his olive branch might be working, the more he, Basiliscus, benefited. Where was the harm in that?

'What if the wind should change?' demanded Iohannes, his patrician features flushed with anger. 'We would lose our present great advantage of the wind-gauge. We could even be driven on to a lee shore.'

'You worry too much, Iohannes. As every skipper knows, at this time of year the south-easterly is practically guaranteed *not* to change. Why else do you think that, in the old days of a single empire, the corn fleets used to sail from Egypt to Ostia between June and September? Because delivery was always on time. An emperor's popularity, therefore security, depended on the bread dole being regular.' Basiliscus rose, stretched, and poured wine. 'Here, have some vintage Nomentan – help you relax.'

'No, thanks,' snapped the other. 'One of us needs to keep a clear head.'

'All right, all right.' Basiliscus raised his hands placatingly. Iohannes' concern was, perhaps, he conceded to himself, not unjustified. It might be wise not to tempt Providence too much. A pity to forgo his little 'bonus', courtesy of Gaiseric; but all good things had to end sometime. 'We'll do as you suggest. Anyway, in the five days we've been here, the fleet's been made pretty well shipshape. Tomorrow, I'll give the order to weigh anchor.'

Surfacing from a heavy sleep, Basiliscus was dimly aware that someone was shaking him. He sat up in his bunk, pressed hands to a throbbing head – the price of punishing that vintage Nomentan. He made a mental note to add more water next time.

---

* Payment of a 'backhander' accompanying a transaction; in effect, a covert bribe.

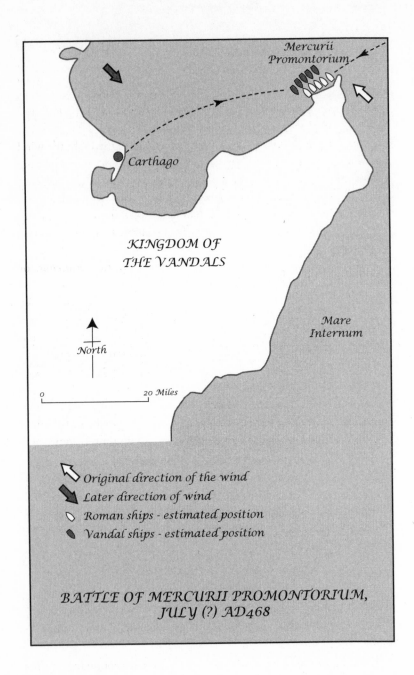

Mercurii
Promontorium

Carthago

KINGDOM OF
THE VANDALS

Mare
Internum

North

0   20 Miles

Original direction of the wind
Later direction of wind
Roman ships - estimated position
Vandal ships - estimated position

BATTLE OF MERCURII PROMONTORIUM,
JULY (?) AD468

'Captain asks if you could come on deck, sir.' His pilot's voice held a note of urgency.

Hastily pulling on shoes and tunic, Basiliscus became aware that *Perseus* was rolling violently. He followed the pilot topside up a short companionway, gasped as cold spray peppered his face and a buffet of wind slammed the breath back down his throat. The sight that met his eyes in the grey light of dawn was disturbing. In the night the wind had changed; a near-gale, blowing from the north-west, was whipping the sea into a field of tossing whitecaps, with everywhere ships plunging and wallowing as they strove to point their bows into the wind. Several transports, their anchors dragging, had been taken in tow by *dromons*, which, with their banks of crawling oars, resembled strange monsters of the deep.

Enveloped in a hooded smock of heavy wool, the *navarchus*, or sailing-master, approached the commander.

'The ships need sea-room, sir,' he shouted above the howling of the wind. 'We need to get clear of *that*.' He pointed to the towering rampart of Mercurii Promontorium looming darkly above the anchorage. 'No problem for the *dromons*, even in this sea. Harder for the transports, though – means sailing closer to the wind than they can comfortably manage.'

Driven on to a lee shore – next to fire, the mariner's worst nightmare, thought Basiliscus. The great headland which, until a few hours ago, had formed a natural breakwater could now become their graveyard.

With storm lanterns hoisted to her mast-head and boom-tips signalling other ships to follow, *Perseus* weighed anchor and began to creep jerkily away from the coast, her oars, first on one side then on the other, biting air instead of water in the choppy seas. As the light strengthened, Basiliscus breathed a sigh of relief; the fleet was slowly clawing clear of danger, the transports rolling wildly as they angled sideways to the wind to make seaway.

'Sail ho!' The cry of the lookout in the crosstrees came faintly to Basiliscus. Peering into the distance, he made out a dancing white speck, then another, and another, as the sea became stippled with sails. The Vandal fleet!

Fighting for calm, Basiliscus told himself that his command was not at serious risk. With their vastly inferior numbers, the Vandal ships, despite having the wind in their favour, could only harry, not destroy, the Roman fleet. Then his mind seemed to freeze, as a row of glowing dots sprang up along the Vandal van. Fireships!

Basiliscus watched, horrified, as the blazing hulks swept down-wind upon his ships. Fire was the worst thing that could happen at sea: canvas, sun-dried timbers, tarred cordage – so much tinder waiting for a spark. Within minutes, all cohesion in the Roman fleet was lost, as vessels strove to flee the danger. Valiantly, the *dromon*s tried to secure cables to the fireships to drag them clear but, overwhelmed by sheer numbers, could make little difference to the outcome.

Ship after Roman ship exploded into flame as the fireships got among them, becoming in their turn agents of destruction. Soon chaos reigned, with vessels piling up on the rocky shore, or scattering wildly in their efforts to escape. Now, like a wolf pack closing on a helpless flock, the Vandals struck. With the wind-gauge allowing them to manoeuvre as they chose, they picked off single vessels with several of their own. Then, boarding, they swamped the defenders with a tide of yelling warriors. After vainly trying to repulse one such onslaught, Iohannes, shouting defiance, leapt into the sea rather than surrender, his armour pulling him instantly beneath the waves.

Only a battered remnant of the mighty war-fleet that had set sail with such high hopes limped back to the Golden Horn. As news of the disaster spread throughout the Roman world, the Western feder-ates breathed a collective sigh of relief. With the treasuries of both empires exhausted, no further rescue of the West could be attempted. Gaul, Spain and Italy were theirs for the taking.

In that same fateful year, the twelve hundred and twenty-second from the Founding of the City, a fourteen-year-old hostage was receiving the education of a Roman aristocrat in Constantinople. The boy was the son of Thiudimer, king of the Ostrogoths, a Germanic tribe settled in Pannonia.* His name was Theoderic.

---

* An abandoned West Roman province in the Upper Danube region.

ONE

The poor Roman imitates the Goth, the well-to-do Goth the Roman
Aphorism of Theoderic, *c.* 500

'"Ingentem meminit parvo qui germine quercum
Aequaevumque videt consenuisse nemus",'

declaimed Demetrius to the semicircle of (mainly bored-looking) school-boys. 'He remembers the great oak as a small acorn, and sees the grove, planted when he was born, grown old with him.' The class, sons of aristocrats, generals and top civil servants, mainly from the Eastern Empire with a few from Italia and Gaul, was being held in a room of Constantinople's Imperial Palace, a jumble of splendid though ill-assorted buildings that sprawled downhill towards the Propontis.* The schoolmaster was expounding the ideas contained in Claudian's poem *On the Gothic War*.

'Bearing in mind that Alaric's barbarians had crossed the Alps and were rampaging down through Italy,' continued Demetrius, 'what do you think Claudian was trying to tell us about this simple old man from Verona?' He looked round his pupils' faces expectantly. 'Well?'

Silence, while his charges fiddled with styluses and waxed tablets, or stared out of windows at the towering bulk of the Hippodrome. Sometimes, he wondered why he bothered. Granted, for most of them Greek was their mother tongue; but they'd had Latin – Caesar, Vergil, Tacitus, Ammianus et al. – drummed into them from an early age. It wasn't the language they couldn't cope with, just the authors' concepts. Horses were the only thing that occupied the minds of these upper-class lads. Soon it would be girls. And after that? A sordid scramble for money and power, which was all that seemed to matter these days.

---

* The Sea of Marmara.

Unless, that is, you were a member of the hoi polloi, when religion and betting on the Blue or Green teams at the Hippodrome were the twin obsessions. Whatever happened to *otium* – leisured scholarship – which, with civic patronage, was once seen as the proper ambition of a Roman gentleman?

Before the pause could become embarrassing, Demetrius forced a smile and said, 'No volunteers? Well, let's start with George. Your thoughts, please.'

An open-faced boy with an eager-to-please expression rose. 'Pigs eat acorns, don't they, sir? Perhaps he was a pig-farmer. Barbarians probably like pork, so naturally he'd be worried.'

A murmured, derisive cheer rippled round the class.

'Thank you, George. An imaginative contribution, if nothing else. You may be seated. Julian, perhaps we might have the benefit of your opinion?'

A tall, stylishly dressed youth stood up. His chiselled features bore a remarkable resemblance to those of Alexander the Great when a boy. So much so that his classmates had nicknamed him 'Alexander', a soubriquet he played up to by cultivating long, carefully disordered locks.

'Perhaps the old fool hoped to hide from the Goths among his oak-trees,' drawled Julian with a smirk. 'And if they found him, well, he could always pelt them with acorns. Couldn't he, sir?'

A delighted titter greeted this sally, not on account of any humour it contained but because it laid down a challenge to the master's authority.

'Sit down!' snapped Demetrius, a spurt of anger bringing red to his cheeks. Arrogant young lout. It had been a mistake to ask him, of course – he'd simply handed the boy a chance to show off. With his wealthy family connections, subversive attitude and air of cool confidence, Julian was, unfortunately, something of a hero to many of his classmates. Aware that he must rescue the situation before it slipped out of control, Demetrius turned towards his favourite pupil, Theoderic Amalo. Though shy and awkward, the young Gothic prince could usually be relied on to come up with an intelligent answer. 'Theo, perhaps you could shed some light where all seems darkness?'

Stooping slightly, as if to avoid drawing attention to his great height, Theoderic rose. In his mind, he reviewed the lines Demetrius had quoted. The message that Claudian was trying to get across was surely to do with familiar memory. Unbidden, a vision from his Pannonian homeland flashed into his mind, filling him with a sudden, sharp nostalgia: Bakeny Forest with its scented glades of noble trees – oaks, pines and cedar; the air filled with the plash of hidden waterfalls and the cooing of rock-doves. All at once, he knew what that old man had felt: affection for the trees, contemporary with himself; and fear that he might lose them through depredation by the Goths – his, Theoderic's, own kinsmen, he thought with a pang of guilt.

'Those trees were planted as acorns at his birth,' he said, speaking slowly and with a kind of passionate conviction, something he had never before expressed. 'He had grown old with them, as they matured. They had become part of his life. Almost friends. I think he . . . loved them. So he was anxious in case the barbarians should carelessly destroy them.'

The class sat up, visibly impressed. Who'd have thought old Yellowknob could hold the floor like that? Suddenly self-conscious, Theoderic shuffled and looked down.

'Well done, Theo,' declared Demetrius warmly. 'There's nothing I can add to that.' He breathed a mental sigh of relief. With the class now quiet and receptive, the lesson could proceed on an even keel.

Then Theoderic clapped a hand to his cheek as something struck it a tiny, stinging blow. A wax pellet dropped to the mosaic floor and rolled to the foot of the master's throne-like chair.

'All of you, hold up your tablets – *now!*' thundered Demetrius. Cowed, the class promptly obeyed. Their genial master could, if pushed too far, change in a flash to a terrifying autocrat. A brief inspection exposed the culprit: Julian's *codex* showed a hollow where a lump of wax had been gouged out. Rolled into a ball and flicked from the flattened erasing end of Julian's flexible ivory stylus, it had made a highly effective missile. Punishment was duly meted out with a bundle of birch twigs, then, with discipline restored, the lesson resumed.

'I hear your pet barbarian showed up your young Roman charges,' Paulus remarked to Demetrius. The two schoolmasters were in a *taberna* off the Mesé, the capital's main thoroughfare.

'The cream of Byzantium – thick and rich,' Demetrius chuckled wryly. Nothing stayed secret for long in the palace. Probably one of the *paedagogi* – slaves who accompanied pupils to school, and who waited for them at the back of the classroom to bring them home – had spread the story. 'At times, I feel I'm casting pearls before swine.'

'Don't we all. Your Goth – a bright lad, I hear.'

'He's that all right. Somehow, having just one pupil of his calibre in a class makes it all seem worthwhile. Doesn't make him popular, unfortunately. The others tend to pick on him; that oaf Julian's the ringleader. Poor little beggar; I speak figuratively – he must be several inches taller than I am.'

'Then why doesn't he give Julian a good thumping? The rest would soon leave off.'

'Not in his nature – a gentle giant if ever there was. But if he chose to he could thrash the lot of them I'm sure. Most people tend to dismiss him as a passive ox, but I admire the lad. I feel he has an inner strength, also that he's looking for something – trying to find his destiny, perhaps?' Demetrius paused and shook his head. 'Sorry. I must sound like Aristotle on the subject of the young Alexander.'

'No, you intrigue me. What do you suppose it is he's looking for?'

'I believe it's Rome. I think he wants to identify with her, be accepted by her.'

'Rome? What's that?' Paulus grinned and refilled their wine-cups. 'After the North African fiasco, the West's finished. There won't be a second rescue attempt; Gaiseric's stronger than ever, Basiliscus terrified for his life, has taken sanctuary in Hagia Sophia, the Treasury's empty, Anthemius no longer has a role. The Franks and Visigoths'll grab what's left in Gaul and Spain, and Ricimer could well take over Italy. Anthemius might turn out to be the last Augustus of the West. What would that leave? The Senate and the Papacy. Augustus and Constantine would turn in their graves.'

'But Rome's more than just a physical empire. Rome's an *idea*. And even if the West goes down, the East's still there to pick up the torch.'

'And so the race goes on,' intoned Paulus with mock solemnity. 'Apologies; you're right, of course. And who knows? Even if it falls, the West might one day be re-occupied. But back to your young hostage. What is it about Rome that he so admires?'

'Think what an impact Constantinople must have made on him when he arrived six years ago. To an impressionable youngster from a primitive shame-and-honour society geared to a dreary cycle of petty feuds and subsistence farming, the city with its statues, paved streets, and great buildings, buzzing with cosmopolitan life and colour – it must have seemed wondrous beyond words. From the first, he showed an interest in the examples of Roman culture to be found everywhere around him: sculpture, architecture, literature, philosophy, science, law – things conspicuously lacking among his own people. He picked up Greek in no time, and was the first in his class to master Latin. He actually *enjoys* reading the classics. How many fourteen-year-olds can you say that of?'

'Sounds, then, as though he could be in for a big comedown when he returns to his own people.'

'Sadly, I have to agree. I sometimes wonder if our policy of civilizing German hostages isn't misplaced kindness. We give them a taste of something they can never really be a part of. Anti-German discrimination's rampant: intermarriage with Romans illegal, German clothes like furs and trousers banned, Germans barred from elevation to the purple . . . I could go on. Perhaps Rome only feels at ease with those she's conquered. That never happened with Germania.'

'Didn't a general called Varus try, back in the time of Augustus?'

'Yes. Got wiped out, along with his three legions.'

'And Germans have been a thorn in Rome's flesh ever since.' Paulus shrugged and drained his goblet. 'Seems that Varus has a lot to answer for.'

Trailed by his bodyguard (a necessary precaution, given his status as a royal hostage), a tough Isaurian called Timothy, Theoderic wandered disconsolately through the streets of the capital. This morning's incident was the latest in a long campaign of petty spite waged against him by Julian. The other boys were not really hostile, Theoderic knew, just willing to follow the lead of a character stronger than themselves. He was not afraid of Julian; should it ever come to a straight fight between them, he suspected he would beat the Roman easily. But that would be to betray his father's counsel, given him at eight years old on his departure for Byzantium.

'You are too young, my son, fully to understand my words now,' Thiudimer, king of the Ostrogoths, had said, 'but in time, you will. Learn all you can from the Romans – they are a great and clever people, and have much of worth to teach you. But do not forget you are a Goth – a Goth of royal lineage, who will one day be a king. That means trying to live by three things. Never use your strength against those weaker than yourself, but spend it freely for those who need your help. Deal justly with friend and enemy alike. Think long before you give your word, but, once given, do not break it. You will find these precepts hard at times to keep. Succeed, and you will return to our people a man fit to rule them.' His father had embraced him then, and he had set out for the Great City with a lump in his throat, but a heart beating faster with excitement and high hopes.

As ever, wandering among the capital's great buildings soothed Theoderic's troubled spirit. Around him, in abundance, were beauty, strength and permanence – all qualities which spoke of Rome: the mighty Walls of Theodosius before which even Attila had quailed; the stupendous dome of Hagia Sophia; the aqueduct of Valens with its soaring tiers of arches . . .

Then, finding himself in the Forum of Arcadius, his mood changed suddenly to one of puzzled sadness. In the middle of the great square rose a tall marble column, its surface wonderfully carved to depict an ascending spiral of figures in action. On closer inspection, however, the frieze took on a sinister aspect. The figures were fugitives fleeing, falling, dying, before the frenzied onslaught of a mob armed with staves and cudgels. Long and short hair differentiated Goths from Romans, respectively. The scene represented the great Expulsion of the Goths from the city, sixty years before. It was beautiful – and horrible.

Why do they hate us? Theoderic wondered. From his reading of history (written, of course, by Romans – Polybius,* Caesar, Tacitus, Suetonius, Ammianus) he knew that even the fiercest of her foes – Spaniards, Gauls, Illyrians, Dacians – had yielded in the end to Rome. Only the Caledones and the Germans had refused. Therein, perhaps, lay the reason.

'Jerry bastard!'

Theoderic wheeled. There, twenty paces off, stood Julian, at his back half a dozen of his followers holding eggs or fruit which they were clearly intending to throw.

---

* He was actually a Romanized Greek.

Theoderic began to move off; the best method of dealing with such confrontations was to avoid them, he had found.

'That's right, run away,' the group chanted. 'Yellow as his own hair. Yellow! Yellow!'

An overripe pomegranate burst on the paving beside the young Goth, splattering his legs. Theoderic halted, as something seemed to snap in his brain. This was where it ended. He would throw down a challenge, something testing, with an element of danger. What form could such a challenge take? He had barely asked the question in his mind when the answer came to him. But perhaps that idea was a bit *too* dangerous. He hesitated, but only for a moment. If that was the only way to gain their acceptance, by proving that he was their equal – in courage, at the least – so be it.

Feeling strangely calm, he walked up to the group. Something in his bearing made them fall silent and lower their throwing arms.

'If *you* are all so brave,' he said, 'I will give you the chance to prove it.'

'It speaks. Ooooh, I'm quaking in my shoes,' responded Julian, his scoffing tone not quite concealing a hint of uncertainty. 'Hear that, boys? He's going to set us a dare. Wonder what it'll be? Climbing the Golden Gate? Pinching peaches from the palace orchard?' The others sniggered dutifully, but it sounded somewhat forced.

'Come with me to hunt Cambyses.'

'Cambyses?' Julian laughed disbelievingly. 'You can't be serious.' A pause, then Julian continued, his face paling, 'My God, you *are* serious.'

Cambyses. The legendary wild boar that had killed or maimed not only several unwary passers-by but more than one hunter who had sought to make him their quarry.

'Well?'

Heads bowed, two of Julian's followers slunk away. The rest stood firm.

'We accept.' All trace of bluster had gone from Julian's voice, replaced by a note almost of wondering respect.

Theoderic's heart gave a leap. He had, he felt, just crossed some sort of Rubicon.

TWO

*With loud shouts, Herakles dislodged from a thicket the
Erymanthian Boar*

Pisander, *c.* 650 BC

Returning to his spartan little suite in the palace, Theoderic found
himself confronted by Timothy. Standing with folded arms in the
middle of his charge's *tablinum* or study, the bodyguard – stocky,
muscular, nose flattened in some ancient brawl – looked exactly what
he was: a self-reliant bruiser.

'Timothy! You wish to speak with me?'

'Indeed I do, young Deric, indeed I do. This Cambyses business . . .'
He shook his head and chortled softly. 'Lucky for you I'm an Isaurian
– agin the government. What I *should* have done is report your plan
to the Master of Offices. Then you'd have been confined to barracks,
as it were, and I'd have been commended.'

'But . . . how did you know?'

'To see but not be seen, to hear but not be heard – all part of my
job. A gaggle of schoolboys taking on Cambyses on their own. I can
think of simpler recipes for suicide.'

'I suppose it *was* a stupid idea,' Theoderic admitted, reddening. He
shuffled his feet, his expression downcast.

'Now there you're wrong. It has the makings of an excellent idea.
All it lacks is a bit of planning, preparation and expert assistance. That's
where I come in.'

'You'd help us?' Theoderic's face lit up.

'I must be crazy even to be thinking of it,' murmured Timothy
wryly, 'but the answer's yes. Having grown up in the back streets of
Tarsus, I know how important it is to establish your status in a peer
group. If you don't, they'll kick you to the bottom of the heap, and
that's where you'll stay. So old Timothy understands that you need to

18

even the score with your schoolmates. Lucky it's me you've got to lend a hand. Isaurians aren't just streetwise; most of us, and that includes yours truly, are expert woodsmen to boot. The Taurus mountains are our backyard, and they're teeming with bears, wolves, deer, wild boar – you name it. There's scarcely a cottage in Cilicia without its bearskin on the floor or pair of horns on the wall. Right, listen, young Deric, this is how we'll go about it . . .'

As arranged, the six boys – Theoderic, Julian, and the four of Julian's circle who had accepted the challenge – met Timothy outside the Charisius Gate at the second hour,* soon after the opening of the gates in the Theodosian Wall. It was the feast day of St Euphemia (so no school), a celebrated local martyr, credited with performing a miracle at the Council of Chalcedon seventeen years previously. For several miles they followed the River Lycus north-west on made roads, taking turns to wheel the handcart containing a long bundle, which Timothy had brought. Arriving at the confluence of the Lycus and a small tributary, they followed the latter north along a farm track, gradually leaving behind villas and cultivation to enter an area of rough pasture climbing towards woods. Reaching an isolated farmhouse the party halted; Timothy went off to find the farmer, while the boys flopped on the ground, exhausted by the trek in the warm September sun. After quarter of an hour Timothy returned, with four rangy mongrels on leash.

'Not much to look at,' he said, 'but the best boar-hounds this side of the Bosphorus. If any get killed, your dads'll pay the bill – except Deric's, for obvious reasons. Understood?' He looked round the circle of tense young faces; all nodded. 'Right, gentlemen, what I'm about to say I'll say just once, so listen good. In a mile or so we'll be entering Cambyses' parish. Follow my instructions and you'll be all right. Ignore them and you could end up dead or maimed – *your* silly faults but *my* head on the block. Which I don't intend to let happen.'

Exchanging the leashes with Julian, the Isaurian unwrapped the bundle on the cart and handed a short spear to each boy, retaining the last for himself. They were workmanlike affairs, with sturdy hafts and broad, vicious-looking blades with a cross-bar below where the blade

* About 7 a.m. (see Notes).

joined the handle. 'Tempered steel with razor edges; extra-wide for maximum damage. The guard's to stop the quarry getting close, if spitted. A boar's weapons are its tusks – sickles that'll rip you open from crotch to breastbone. Now, we don't want that to happen, do we, lads? So here's the plan. When we track down Cambyses' lair – which'll be in dense undergrowth – the first task is to persuade him to come out. That'll be my job. You lot stand back in a semicircle, weapons at the ready. When he comes, he'll do so in a rush. A charging boar's a scary sight, and Cambyses is a lot of boar. It's vital to keep your nerve and hold your ground; he won't charge the blades. Let the dogs distract him, then, when I give the word – and not before – move in for the kill. Above all, no heroics. There are old hunters, and bold hunters, but no old, bold hunters. Remember that. Questions, gentlemen? No? Then let's be having you.'

Deep in a thicket, Cambyses slept. At twenty years, too old for sows to feature in his reveries, he dreamt of sunlit glades carpeted by acorns, with juicy tubers just below the surface waiting to be grubbed up. Suddenly he started twitching, as something intruded on these pleasant visions. Blinking awake, he became aware of of what it was that had disturbed his rest: a familiar, hated scent. Man. His inch-thick hide seamed with scar tissue bore witness to past encounters with hunters, some of whom had suffered death or mutilation from his tushes. The scent grew stronger, stirring memories of pain and danger. Quivering with fury, the old boar raised his vast bulk from the ground and prepared to give battle.

'They've got the scent, lads. Let 'em go,' Timothy called to the three who, besides himself, had held the hounds in leash while they quartered the terrain – a soggy plateau stippled with bushes and stands of dwarf timber. Unleashed, the hounds – silent until now, streaked off, barking with excitement. They halted before a patch of dense undergrowth, their baying, an eerie chiming sound, rising to a frenzied crescendo.

Lining up the boys in a wide semicircle behind the hounds, Timothy took a handful of pebbles from a pouch at his waist, and proceeded to pelt the patch of brush. For a full minute nothing happened. Then the bushes began to shake, and a moment later the quarry burst from shelter. He was a terrifying sight: huge body covered in blackish bristles streaked with yellow, tiny red-rimmed eyes blazing with hate, long foam-flecked snout, pair of wicked tusks curving from the lower jaw.

Faced with this apparition, Theoderic was seized with paralyzing fright. The urge to run was overwhelming, but, recalling Timothy's advice, he stood firm, spear levelled – as, to their credit, did the others.

Confused by the hounds, Cambyses halted in full career, then charged first one, then another. But his tormentors were old hands at the game, and backed away from his furious rushes. At last, bewildered and exhausted, flanks heaving, the old boar stood at bay.

Julian, next in line to Theoderic, broke ranks and rushed forward, spear raised to deliver the coup de grâce.

What happened next, though lasting only seconds, seemed to Theoderic to pass as though time had slowed down. Julian tripped on a tree-root and toppled forward, to lie extended on the ground. Spotting one of his enemies prostrate, the boar, like an ox turning a mill-wheel by its pole, wheeled slowly round and made for Julian, its short legs rising and falling no faster than a galley's oars.

Then the moment passed, and the enraged brute was hurtling towards the boy like a bolt from a *ballista*. Unaware of making a conscious decision, Theoderic found himself sprinting forward, standing athwart Julian's body and thrusting out his spear to receive the boar's charge. The blade took the animal full in the throat, the impact hurling Theoderic backwards, in a spray of blood jetting from a severed artery. Closing in at once, the others quickly finished off the dying monster. Julian rose shakily to his feet.

Timothy, his face suffused with anger, struck the boy a ringing slap across the cheek. 'Glory-hunting fool!' he roared. 'You nearly got yourself killed. Worse, you put your mates in danger. If it hadn't been for Deric here . . . Now, apologize and make up.'

Trembling as reaction set in, his emotions in a tumult, Theoderic extended his hand to his erstwhile enemy. His chief feeling was exaltation: surely now they would accept him as an equal and, more importantly, a Roman.

'I'm sorry,' said Julian stiffly, Timothy's handprint livid on his face. 'I behaved stupidly. I owe you my life. For that I thank you.' He looked at the other's open hand, then turned his head away. 'But I don't shake hands with Germans. You're brave, I grant you that, but then so are all your race. For all your courage, Goth, you'll never be one of us – Roman, that is.'

Theoderic's euphoria drained away, replaced by a terrible feeling of failure and frustrated longing. Now he knew how Moses must have felt when, having led his people to the Promised Land, he alone was not allowed to enter.

THREE

That noble sentiment, love for Rome
from a letter of Theoderic recorded by
Cassiodorus in *Variae, c.* 537

'Timothy of Tarsus, Your Serenity – guardian of Prince Theoderic, son
of Thiudimer Amalo, joint king of the Ostrogoths,' announced the
silentiarius – one of the tribe of gentlemen-ushers who ensured that the
elaborate machinery of court procedure in the Imperial Palace functioned smoothly. Bowing, he showed Timothy into the reception
chamber, then withdrew.

Timothy found himself in a vast colonnaded hall, at the far end of
which were two figures: enthroned, an elderly man swathed in purple
robes which somehow created the effect of diminishing his slight form;
and, sprawled on a bench, a colossal individual wearing undress military uniform: round pillbox cap, undyed linen tunic (somewhat soiled
and worn) with indigo government roundels at thighs and shoulders.
These were, respectively, Emperor Leo and his top general, Zeno, a
tough Isaurian chieftain who had changed his name from the barbarous-
sounding Tarasicodissa to the more euphonious Zeno in deference to
the sophisticated ears of the capital's citizens.

Making what he hoped were the correct obeisances, Timothy advanced
towards the pair, halting with lowered head several paces from the throne.
'Serenity, General, your humble servant is honoured to receive your
summons, and awaits your pleasure . . . er, is desirous to know how best
he may be of service.' Despite having been on the palace staff for years,
this was the first time Timothy had been in the imperial presence. He
was, as he admitted to himself, making up the rules of etiquette as
he went along; he just hoped he wasn't committing any major gaffes.

'Tarsus, eh?' chuckled the general. 'A fellow Isaurian then. But I
could have told that from your accent.' He surveyed the other's muscular

frame appraisingly. 'There's a place in the Excubitors, my crack corps of Isaurians, if you're interested – good pay, easy service, generous donatives. Isaurians always welcome.' He turned to Leo. 'Sorry – bad form to be speaking ahead of my emperor.' He grinned in mock contrition. 'Over to you, Serenity.'

'Thank you,' snapped Leo, a flush of annoyance spreading up his neck. Addressing Timothy, he stated, 'We have just received a message from Theoderic's father, requesting the return of his son. You've had the boy daily in your sights for the past nine years. In your opinion, would you say the time is, ah, appropriate, for the young barbarian to rejoin his tribe?'

Timothy thought carefully before framing his reply. 'Appropriate' was code for 'suitable on account of the subject's posing no threat'. In other words, had nearly a decade of exposure to the civilizing influence of Roman culture been sufficient to dilute the warlike instincts natural to any Goth, while inculcating respect and loyalty for Rome, thus rendering him more likely to prove a useful ally than a dangerous foe of the empire? The 'Cambyses incident' two and a half years ago had, in order to avoid awkward consequences for all involved, been kept a strict secret. So no one suspected that the shy, studious persona that the young Goth presented to the world concealed a spirit both courageous and determined. It was best, Timothy decided, that Leo remain in ignorance of this side of Theoderic's nature. (As a result of the boar-hunt, persecution of Theoderic by Julian and his gang had stopped immediately; though shunned, he was treated with wary respect. Schooldays had ended soon afterwards, some of his classmates going, like Julian, into the army, others entering the civil service, one or two the Church. Theoderic himself continued his studies at Constantinople University, founded by Theodosius II just forty-four years previously, attending classes in philosophy and Latin grammar.)

'Theoderic's a quiet lad, Secrenity,' Timothy pronounced. 'Mild, inoffensive, a conscientious student. Overall, rather timid and ineffectual, I'd say.'

'Timid and ineffectual?' ruminated Leo. 'Excellent, excellent. Well, assuming what you say is true, I think we can safely let our young barbarian go. Probably to sink without trace. Theoderic – a name written on water, it would seem.'

'Doesn't sound like any Goth I've ever encountered,' snorted Zeno. '"Timid and ineffectual"'? You must be joking! Alaric himself could come over all sweet reason when it suited – and look what *he* did to Rome.'

Leo shook his head impatiently. 'Spare us the history lesson, Zeno. Sometimes we have to go with our instincts and take a chance on things. I'll have the release order made out straight away.' He glanced at Timothy. 'Our thanks for your advice. On your way out, tell the *silentiarius* to send for my scribe.'

In the name of the Invincible Augustus the Most Sacred Leo, four times Consul, Emperor of the Eastern domain of our One and Indivisible Empire, his Master of Offices requests that within the Prefectures of Illyricum and the East: the vicars of the Dioceses of Thracia and Dacia, and the governors of the Provinces of Europa, Haemimontus, Thracia, Moesia Secunda, Dacia Mediterranea, Dacia Ripensis and Moesia Prima, together with all officers and servants acting in their names, allow to pass freely without let or hindrance, affording him such assistance and protection as may be necessary, Prince Theoderic, the son of Thiudimer Amalo, king (jointly with his brother Vidimir) of the Ostrogoth nation which currently resides within the provinces of Pannonia Secunda, Valeria, Savia and Pannonia Prima, by gracious permission of the Invincible Augustus of the West, the Most Sacred Anthemius. Issued at the Imperial Secretariat within the Great Palace of Constantinopolis, and given into the hand of our trusty and well-beloved emissary Timotheus Trascilliseus, guardian of the aforesaid Theoderic. Pridie Kalendas Junii, in the year of the consuls Leo Augustus (being his fourth consulship) and of Probianus.*

With disbelief tinged with awe, Timothy finished reading this portentous document, Theoderic's safe-conduct, with which he had been entrusted. 'Trusty and well-beloved emissary'! Could that really refer to him, Timothy the brawler, Timothy the small-time crook, Timothy

* 31 May 471 (see Notes).

25

the humble bodyguard – a nothing, an invisible presence lurking in the shadows? But that was yesterday. Today, by some miraculous stroke of administrative alchemy, he had been transformed into a government official entrusted with an important mission, and holding the impressive title of *agens in rebus*, a catch-all job description covering anything from spy to diplomat. It felt good. With the commission in his satchel, and wearing the same undress uniform as Zeno (having semi-military rank, *agentes* were entitled to wear uniform, though not armour), he found himself walking with an extra swagger and confidence. Now palace underlings made way for him with respectful expressions, whereas formerly they had treated him with indifference or easy familiarity. All immensely gratifying.

Next morning at the first hour, mounted, accompanied by a small train of spare horses and pack-mules carrying luggage and supplies in the charge of a groom, Timothy and Theoderic arrived at the Golden Gate, where they were to be joined by the armed escort assigned to accompany them on their journey. They hadn't waited long when, with a clatter of hooves and jingle of accoutrements, a dozen horse-archers plus remounts and supply wagon approached along the Mesé. With their highly polished cuirasses of overlapping iron scales and red-crested Attic helmets of gleaming bronze, they made a brave show.

'Legio Quinta Macedonica,' observed Timothy; 'note the sunflower motif on their shields.' He groaned in sudden consternation. 'Oh no! Look who their decurion is – our old friend Julian, no less.'

A splendidly mounted young officer, scarlet cloak billowing, pulled up before Theoderic.

'*You!*' exclaimed Julian. His expression of shocked amazement swiftly changed to one of calculating malice. 'Well, Goth, this should be an interesting trip. It's a long way to Pannonia.' He shook his head in simulated concern. 'You'll need to watch yourself; a lot can happen in a thousand miles. Well, there's the gate opening. Shall we go?'

Headed by the escort, the cavalcade proceeded through the second of the triple arches in the Golden Gate, the chief entry into the city through the Theodosian Walls at their southern end. Turning in the saddle, Theoderic looked back at the city that had been his home for the greater part of his young life: the mighty double rampart of the Walls studded with massive towers, before which even Attila had quailed, and beyond them the roofs of churches, palaces, baths, and gymnasia without number, the statues crowning the columns of Constantine, Arcadius and Marcian, the topmost tier of arches of Valens' aqueduct . . .

A wave of nostalgia and sadness engulfed the young Goth. He was leaving, probably for the last time, all the things that had shaped his life and that he held dear – Roman art and architecture, Roman thought, Roman poetry and learning, Roman law with its noble aspirations linked to equity and justice. Through his education as a hostage, in outlook he had become fully Roman. Yet because of his German blood and Arian faith Rome rejected him – as Julian had once so cruelly reminded him. (It was ironic as well as unfortunate that fate had decreed their paths should rejoin, if only for a limited period. He supposed there were worse alternatives to being saddled with Julian for several weeks: a long sea voyage, for instance, tedious, uncomfortable, perhaps even dangerous. As for the young Roman's thinly veiled threat, he dismissed that as the empty rhetoric of a spiteful mind.) He should be glad, he knew, to be returning home. But what was home? A dimly remembered land of plains and forests peopled by warlike farmers, ignorant, illiterate, scratching a living from the soil, eked out by plundered goods and livestock. A world without culture, barren and violent, where enjoyment was equated with fighting and feasting, and personal worth with loyalty and courage: noble qualities, to be sure, but hardly the compass of a man's full measure. How would he be judged when back among his own people? Would he measure up? One thought alone sustained and comforted him: the memory of his father. Strong, wise and loving, Thiudimer would surely help him to make the transition from Roman to Goth.

The group had travelled only a few miles along the Via Egnatia, the great artery linking the empires of the East and West, when Theoderic and Timothy, in the rear, were alerted by a distant pattering behind them. Turning, they saw a dense mass of galloping horsemen, some way off but closing fast. Splitting into two wings, the pursuers, a wild-looking lot whooping and brandishing weapons, raced past on either side to join up again some hundreds of paces to the fore. Then, swiftly wheeling round, they charged towards the other group with levelled lances.

FOUR

The adjacent high ranges of Haemus and Rhodope leave between their
swelling hills a narrow pass, which separates Illyricum from Thrace*
Ammianus Marcellinus, *The Histories, c.* 395

Theoderic and Timothy spurred to the front of the column, where
Julian had halted the escort.

'Nock arrows and draw,' ordered a white-faced Julian in a voice
which trembled. 'Loose on my—'

'No!' roared Timothy. 'Can't you see – they're Isaurians; that's Zeno
in the van. It's just a bluff to test our nerve.'

But Julian, clearly in the grip of panic, wasn't listening. He opened
his mouth to give the order.

'Do not shoot,' Theoderic heard himself say. Unbidden, the command
– uttered with quiet authority – seemed to have come from someone
else. It was the first time he had ever given an order, he thought,
wondering. Even his bold stand against Julian over the Cambyses business had been carried through as a result of suggestions, not commands,
on his part. It was Timothy, not he, who had organized the hunt, the
boys unquestioningly obeying the Isaurian's behests. And afterwards?
He had happily slipped out of the limelight back into obscurity, content
to be left alone to pursue a life of study and contemplation. But his
countermand, however out of character, was, it seemed, effective. The
archers were letting down their bows, thumb release-catches already
off the strings.

Meanwhile, the ground began to tremble as the approaching
cavalry thundered ever closer – a terrifying frieze of yelling warriors,

---

* I hesitate to differ from the great Ammianus, but Dacia, not Illyricum, is the
diocese adjoining Thrace on the west. Perhaps he is using the term 'Illyricum' in
a loose sense for the area known as 'Illyris Graeca', the western Balkans, Greece
and Macedonia.

flashing hooves, and wicked spear-points. Theoderic felt his bowels loosen and his palms begin to sweat. The urge to flee became almost overpowering.

'Steady, Deric,' murmured Timothy beside him. 'Hold your nerve.'

With cries of fear, the escort – including Julian – broke and scattered, leaving Theoderic and Timothy alone facing the charge. Just when it seemed that nothing could halt their headlong career, the Isaurians, in a stunning display of horsemanship, reined in only paces from the pair, then, with a shout of acclamation, raised their lances in salute.

'A true Isaurian, a true Goth,' declared Zeno with an approving grin. He kneed his horse forwards to join them. 'I've brought you some of my Excubitors to see you safely to Pannonia.'

'I heard that,' cried Julian, returning with a shamefaced band. He rode up to Zeno, confronting him. 'How dare you challenge my authority? I have orders from the emperor.'

'That's all right, sonny. Just turn around and take yourself and your toy soldiers back to barracks. I'm relieving you.'

'But my orders—'

'—are from the emperor. I know; but not to worry. I'll take full responsibility.' Zeno smiled and continued in patient tones, as though explaining to a not-too-bright child. 'You see, to all intents and purposes I *am* the emperor. He may wear the purple, but it's me who pulls his strings. So off you go. Unless,' he went on, his voice hardening, 'you fancy arguing the toss with my Excubitors.'

Julian, his face a mottled red, opened his mouth as though to make an angry retort, then clamped it shut. He paused, glared at Zeno, then barked an order and departed with his troop.

'Gilded popinjay,' chuckled Zeno to Theoderic and Timothy, who had been listening dumbfounded to the exchange. 'You don't know what to make of me, right? I'll explain. It's bandit country where you're going. Security's broken down all along the Upper and Middle Danube frontier, with bands of Alan and Sarmatian raiders looting and destroying everywhere. No one to stop them, what with the Danube fleet stood down these twenty years, and the field army of Dacia confined to base except when called upon to deal with a major crisis.'

Timothy whistled. 'Things as bad as that? I hadn't realized. But what about the *limitanei* – the border troops? Aren't they supposed to keep order on the frontier?'

'Been pulled back to reinforce the field armies decimated in the wars with Attila. All things considered, I'd not have bet a brass obol on your making it through to Pannonia, not with that lot who've just left us. Don't get me wrong; the Fifth Macedonians are a good bunch. It's just that they've been trained to fight pitched battles in the field, not take on shadowy marauders using hit-and-run tactics – the sort of people you'll be up against. As for their their boy decurion, he's a callow green-horn who'd likely lose his head in a crisis and get you all killed. With my Excubitors, it's an altogether different story; when it comes to dirty fighting, they're the ones who wrote the book.'

'May I ask a question, sir?' enquired Theoderic, patting his horse's neck to calm the animal, grown restless.

'Ask away.'

'Why are you willing to help us? I don't wish to seem offensive or ungrateful, but some in my position might ask, "What's in it for you?"'

'A fair point, young man. Your question shows a Roman cast of mind: logical, rational, weighing up pros and cons, gains or losses. But I'm not Roman, I'm an Isaurian. My people have always been fiercely independent, and were never really conquered by Rome. Oh, to keep them off our backs we made a show of accepting Roman rule. In return, they've had the sense to leave us pretty well alone so long as we don't cause too much trouble. Also, we provide some of the best fighting men for their legions. But back to your question. Isaurians are ruled by their hearts not their heads – the opposite of Romans. Let's just say I've taken a liking to my fellow Isaurian Timothy here. As I've taken a liking to yourself; there aren't many would have held their ground in face of a charge by Excubitors. I admire that. A pity, I thought, should either of you come to grief because of poor protection.'

'And the real reason?'

Zeno stared at Theoderic, then let out a delighted whoop. 'By the bones of St Euphemia, there's more to you than I was led to think.' Shaking his head, he shot Timothy a rueful glance. 'All right, I'll come clean. Nothing personal, young Theoderic, but I'm no great lover of your people. Ever since they wiped out our army at Adrianople nearly a century ago, they've been a thorn in the empire's flesh. Most, thank goodness, have now moved on – the Visigoths to a new homeland in Gaul, the Ostrogoths to theirs in Pannonia. But here in Thrace, too close to the capital for comfort, a large contingent of Goths have been permitted to settle, officially as federates. Their leader's your name-sake: one Theoderic Strabo, known as "the Squinter", a formidable young man who's got the emperor's ear, thanks to General Aspar – my rival for the top army job. He admires the Goths, by the way, and to my way of thinking has allowed far too many Goths into the army. Complicated?'

Theoderic and Timothy looked at each other. 'Just a bit,' admitted Timothy.

'Bear with me. The Squinter's federates are getting restive; seems they're afraid that me and my Isaurians might displace them in the emperor's favour. To keep them in check I need a counterbalance – a group powerful enough to take them on should they become a danger to the Eastern Empire. Unless your uncle Vidimir blocks the succession, which is unlikely, you, Theoderic, are set to take over from your father eventually as king of the Ostrogoths. Given that you're willing, *you* could provide that balance of power – the Amal Goths holding the scales against the Thracian Goths. As a Friend of Rome, you'd have a lot to gain: the backing of both empires, generous subsidies, the security of a guaranteed homeland. What do you say?'

Theoderic's head whirled. Things were moving almost too fast for his mind to grapple with. At seventeen, a retiring student with no experience of ordering the lives of others, he was being invited to enter the heady world of power politics, to hold the balance between, on the one hand, the huge might of the Roman Empire – or at least of its Eastern half – and, on the other, the immense and dangerous energies of volatile barbarian nations. A challenge at which the most experienced of statesmen might surely balk. Hopefully, though, his father would reign for many more years yet, years in which his son would learn from him the arts of statecraft and the management of men. And being a Friend of Rome, well, that at least represented a form of acceptance by that glittering world of power and beauty which he admired and loved, but, as a barbarian, could never fully enter.

'What is there to say?' rejoined Theoderic. 'When the time comes for me to rule the Ostrogoths, I'll gladly take up your offer.'

'Splendid,' pronounced Zeno, making his horse perform a cara-
cole. 'If we had wine, I'd drink a toast to that. I'll leave you now, in
the care of my Excubitors. That's their captain, Thalassios.' He indicated a villainous-looking individual with a leering, scarred face.
'He'll see you safe and sound to Pannonia. You've nothing to worry
about till after the Succi – that's the pass between Dacia and Thrace.
Thrace being the Squinter's fief, and the Squinter being Aspar's ally,
no one's going to bother you this side of the diocesan border. Well,
good fortune, and may the gods—sorry, God, be with you.' And with
a wave and a grin, Zeno wheeled his mount and galloped back
towards the capital.

The first part of the journey, heading slightly north of west, was through
the central plain of Thrace, which was studded with farms and villas,
with endless fields of wheat and sunflowers rolling away on either side.
On the fifth day they reached Adrianople, near which, as Zeno had
mentioned, the Goths had inflicted a massive defeat on a Roman army
a hundred years before. The arrow-straight strap of the Sirmium road
branching off from the Via Egnatia now followed the valley of the
broad, tree-lined Maritsa river, dotted with craft of all kinds from
fishing-boats to freight transport vessels.

Eight days out from the capital, the party reached the great walled
city of Philippopolis,* founded by Philip of Macedon, father of
Alexander the Great, its Graeco-Macedonian past now subsumed by
Roman buildings. These included a vast theatre, a stadium, and a church
dedicated to Emperor Constantine. Once beyond the city, the scenery
changed dramatically, the route running between the heavily wooded
foothills of the Haemus and Rhodope ranges, to north and south respectively, with glimpses of distant snow-capped peaks etched against skies
of brilliant blue. The steadily rising terrain afforded welcome relief
from the heat, oppressive even in early June.

The approaches to the Succi were heralded by steepening slopes
hemming in the highway on either side, a dramatic V-shaped cleft on
the far horizon marking the pass itself.

'Well, Deric,' remarked Timothy, 'so far, so uneventful.' He jerked

* Plovdiv.

his chin towards the distant gap. 'Once through that, perhaps the fun will start.'

'We may not have to wait that long,' observed Theoderic drily. 'Look.' He pointed to the hillside above them to the right, where scores of men were emerging from the trees.

'And over there.' Timothy pointed to the left. All at once, the surrounding slopes were swarming with footsoldiers who, rapidly descending to the road, surrounded Theoderic's group. Big, fair-haired fellows armed with spears, they were clearly Goths. One, their leader, judging by his sword and gilded *Spangenhelm* – the conical, segmented helmet favoured by Teutonic warriors – approached Theoderic and Timothy. 'You will come with us,' he announced in passable Greek.

'What's all this about?' asked Theoderic, striving to sound calm despite his pounding heart. 'We were promised safe passage through Thrace.'

'You will come with us,' the man repeated stolidly. 'Now, surrender your weapons.'

Theoderic looked at Timothy and Thalassios. They shook their heads in unison. 'Better part of valour, I think, sir,' said the captain, shrugging. 'No choice, really; as you see, we're heavily outnumbered.'

After handing over their arms, Theoderic's group dismounted and, leading their horses and pack-animals, accompanied the strangers two abreast along a steep path snaking up the hillside to the south. All questions to his captors being met with silence, Theoderic gave up, to share his speculations with Timothy. Neither could think of any reason to explain their abduction.

That night they camped in a forest glade, the Goths issuing their captives blankets and strips of dried meat. Next day the trail led high into the mountains, past tarns, rushing streams, remote villages and occasional stone keeps, to enter a strange and silent world of sandstone pinnacles carved by wind and water into fantastic pyramids and columns. Once, they passed a line of figures performing a processional dance, dressed bizarrely in the skins of animals surmounted by the heads – bears, wolves and bison.

Not long past noon, a turn in the path suddenly revealed to Theoderic an arresting view. Ahead, the terrain fell steeply away to a verdant cup enclosed by tall spruce-clad mountains rising to spires of naked rock and seamed by silvery waterfalls. In the middle of the hollow rose an extraordinary building, or rather a complex of connected structures – something between a fortress and, with its peristyle and outer courtyard, a typical Roman villa. There followed a difficult descent, the path continually looping back on itself to accommodate the gradient. The great doors in the gateway of the surrounding wall swung open and the column entered a courtyard hung with long wooden galleries and dominated by a massive tower. Grooms led away the horses and baggage-mules, and Theoderic's party were conducted through an open colonnaded square into a long hall. This was filled with noisy Goths, seated on benches or reclining on pallets, drinking, furbishing gear, playing dice or board games. At the chamber's far end, seated, very still, on a throne-like chair, was a young man perhaps six or seven years older than Theoderic. In contrast to the others in the hall – they were bearded and attired in belted tunics, some with cloaks fastened at the shoulder with chip-carved *fibulae* – he was clean-shaven and wore a Roman dalmatic of fine but plain material. The most singular thing about him, and the obvious source of his nickname, was a marked squint in one eye, which however did nothing to detract from his air of authority and calm self-confidence. A hush spread throughout the great chamber as Theoderic's group was led towards him.

'Welcome to the monastery of St Elizabeth the Miracle-Worker, Theoderic, son of Thiudimer,' the young man said in a quiet voice, beneath whose apparent friendliness there was an edge of hostility. 'The monks have graciously granted us the temporary use of the cloisters and this refectory. I am Theoderic Strabo, son of the great Triarius and king of the Thracian Goths; also *Magister Militum*, Master of Soldiers, of the diocese on behalf of the emperor. When we heard that you were on your way, we thought it only proper to arrange that you be met by a reception committee at the Succi.'

'Is that what you call it?' responded Theoderic. 'Then why do we find ourselves treated as prisoners? Before we left Constantinople, I was assured that we would be given safe passage through Thrace, under your protection.'

'And so you would have been,' replied Strabo equably, 'had the situation in the capital remained unchanged. Events, events,' he murmured. Then, casting aside the mask of mocking affability, he said with icy menace,

'The Isaurian troops in Constantinople, no doubt jealous of what they see as preferential treatment of his Goth soldiers by General Aspar, have risen in revolt. In the course of the disturbance, Aspar and a number of his Goth bodyguards were murdered by order of his rival, General Zeno. Natural justice demands some evening of the score. Do you not agree?'

Theoderic's heart seemed to turn to a block of ice. This was appalling news. Strabo, as a barbarian leader, could not afford to let such a situation rest. To avoid a loss of prestige which would inevitably endanger his position as monarch, he must act overtly to avenge the deaths of his fellow-Goths, and of Aspar, his people's protector and champion. 'Some evening of the score': the words had an ominous ring which hardly bode well for Theoderic or his companions.

'What happened is regrettable – extremely so,' Theoderic conceded. 'But surely no blame can attach to my Isaurian escort. The things you mentioned happened after our departure from Constantinople.' Even as he uttered them, the words sounded hollow in his ears. In a barbarian society's simple code of justice, someone always had to pay – if not the transgressor, a member of his kin or following.

'I could have your party slaughtered on the spot,' declared Strabo. 'My men here would certainly approve. But I am not quite the lawless savage some Romans no doubt think me to be. As perhaps do you, being Roman-bred. Nine Goth soldiers were slain by Zeno's men. Therefore nine of your Isaurians must die. You yourself will remain here as my ... 'guest', shall we say, until the situation in the capital resolves itself. Your men will now draw lots to decide who are the ones to die. Sentence to be carried out immediately thereafter.'

Theoderic's brain seemed to spin. Nine deaths – that was half his entourage! Their deaths would be for ever on his conscience. Moreover, the chances of his party completing the journey to Pannonia safely would be thrown into jeopardy, even should he be released. And that was unlikely to happen any time soon. As Strabo's hostage, he would be far too valuable a bargaining chip in any negotiations with Leo (or rather with Zeno, his puppet-master) to be readily set free. Perhaps he was destined never to succeed his father. And that would mean the ending of a cherished dream, Theoderic, the Friend of Rome. These reflections flashed through his mind in seconds, to be succeeded by a sudden thought which offered, perhaps, a ray of hope.

'Wait,' he cried. 'There is another way.'

Strabo smiled indulgently. 'Convince me.'

Raising his voice so that all in the chamber could hear, Theoderic declared, 'Single combat, a duel between a champion of yours and one of ours. The condition: should your side lose, my party be permitted to continue our journey unmolested.' The suggestion stemmed from Theoderic's recollection of something he had learnt at Constantinople University. The institution boasted two famous chairs of law. Although the subject was not one for which he was formally enrolled, Theoderic had sometimes attended law lectures, especially those touching on the laws of Germanic nations, as contained in tracts such as *Lex Gothica*, *Leges Visigothorum*, and the recently enacted *Codex Euricianus*. Written statutes known as *leges scriptae* or *belagines* often referred to the time-honoured practice of settling disputes by combat, with God (or, in the recent pre-Christian past, gods such as Thor or Odin) the arbiter: a tradition with which even kings meddled at their peril.

A charged silence throughout the great hall followed Theoderic's words, witness to the interest they had aroused. An enthusiastic murmur arose among the assembled Goths, gradually swelling to a roar of approval, with weapons being banged on the floor or benches. Watching Strabo's face intently for any sign of reaction, Theoderic hoped against hope that the other would be swayed by his followers' mood. A German king – *reiks* in the Gothic tongue – was not like a Roman emperor whose orders commanded unquestioning obedience. A *reiks* ruled strictly by consent and force of personality. Once perceived to be weak, unsuccessful, or acting against the interests of his people (or at least of those that counted), he would swiftly be replaced. The Goths present were probably Strabo's *andbahtos*, his personal following of armed retainers. Such men would belong to the top rank of Goth society, *frijai* or free men, the other orders being freedmen, then slaves. Should they approve the duel (something members of a warrior society in which a man's status was linked to his prowess as a fighter might be expected to endorse), could Strabo, as no more than *primus inter pares*, afford to ignore their collective will? Theoderic had read in the *Histories* of Ammianus Marcellinus, that eminent Roman soldier-turned-historian, that German kings often found great difficulty in controlling the martial ardour of their warriors.

'Very well,' at last pronounced the Squinter, his face impassive. 'It shall be as you suggest.' He leant forward, yellow hair swinging about his shoulders, to look intently into the other's face. The squint was unsettling, disconcerting, and lent a chilling weight to the king's next words. 'However, by your terms, should my champion win we would have no advantage over and above the status quo. That is hardly fair. I therefore add this rider: should your champion lose, *all* your party, yourself excluded, will suffer death.'

The thunderous applause that greeted Strabo's verdict made Theoderic's blood run cold. The ingenious 'solution' he had sprung upon his namesake had backfired, creating a situation with implications too nightmarish to contemplate.

FIVE

A Goth, Valaris by name, tall of stature and most terrifying . . . challenged
all the Romans, if anyone was willing to do battle with him.

Procopius, *History of the Wars, c.* 550

A tense hush spread throughout the mass of Goths packing the cloister's
pillared walkways. Facing each other across the grass-covered central
enclosure, stripped to the waist, were the rival champions: the Goths'
a flaxen-haired giant armed with a great two-handed sword; Timothy,
the choice of the Isaurians, with a slender knife. (Thalassios had reluctantly given way to Timothy, who had persuaded the rest of Theoderic's
party that his background of no-holds-barred street fighting gave him
the edge.) On the face of it the pair were unevenly matched. The Goth's
huge stature, powerful physique and formidable weapon appeared to
give him a distinct advantage over the short, stocky Isaurian with his
puny blade.

The umpire stepped into the middle of the arena. 'No gouging, no
backstabbing,' he announced, 'the contestants to fight until one is killed
or surrenders, in which event his life is forfeit.' He glanced at Strabo,
who was seated on a specially erected dais. The king nodded, whereupon the umpire called, 'Begin,' and exited the courtyard.

His sword a whirling silver blur, the Goth charged at Timothy, who
waited till the man was nearly on him then skipped nimbly aside, just
avoiding a ferocious cut which, had it landed, must have split him from
neck to navel. Forged by master-swordsmiths and edged with razor-
sharp steel, such blades were lethal. Time and again the Goth repeated
the manoeuvre, on each occasion Timothy's deft footwork proving his
salvation.

'I see what Timothy's game is,' Thalassios murmured to Theoderic's
party, huddled in a tense knot apart from the Goths. 'He's letting the
big chap wear himself out, then he'll go in for the kill.'

38

'Risky,' demurred another Excubitor. 'If he spins things out too long, chances are the Goth'll score a hit. Just one would finish Timothy.'

Which is what almost happened. With his opponent's next rush, Timothy fractionally mistimed his avoiding action and the sword-tip flickered down his rib-cage. A scarlet thread tracked the point's passage, widening instantly to a ribbon pouring blood. Timothy staggered, flung himself clear as a second blow parted the air inches from his head.

A collective sigh, like wind in a cornfield, rippled round the audience, followed by a gasp of horror from the Isaurians as Timothy appeared to slip on grass made treacherous by dripping blood, to measure his length on the ground. With a roar of triumph his adversary swung the great sword above his head.

Suddenly, in a sequence almost too rapid for the eye to follow, Timothy doubled forward from the hips, tucked his legs beneath him, then sprang upright with the speed of a striking adder. His knife, a wicked-edged Anatolian *sica*, insignificant to look at but deadly in close-quarter fighting, flashed across the other's throat. The Goth, sword still raised aloft, blood jetting from a severed artery, swayed, then, with a look of surprise, collapsed, shuddered, and lay still.

The ensuing silence, born of shocked amazement, seemed to stretch out interminably, then was broken by a storm of cheering. Rough and violent they might be, but the Goths admired two virtues above all others, even when displayed by an enemy: martial skill, and valour.

'Farewell, then – for the present,' Strabo told his namesake at the monastery gate. 'You turned the tables on me,' he admitted, a note of wry respect entering his voice. 'This time. When next we meet – as the Norns who weave the web of men's lives have surely decreed we shall – Theoderic Thiudimer will be the one to lose.'

SIX

In the banqueting hall . . . these bold fighting-men took their seats.
A servant. . . performed the office of pouring out the sparkling beer.
From time to time a clear-voiced poet sang

Anonymous, *Beowulf,* seventh century(?)

Five days after crossing the boundary between the empires into Pannonia (nominally a province of the West, but long abandoned by a weakening Rome first to the Huns then, following their collapse and dispersal after the death of Attila, to the Ostrogoths), Theoderic and Timothy, having parted with their escort at the border, approached Thiudimer's 'capital'. This was a straggling *baurg*, or townlet of thatched huts, in a forest clearing north of that great inland sea the Lake of Balaton.

Thanks to the presence of Thalassios' Excubitors, the remainder of the journey, from the Succi on, had been comparatively uneventful. Isaurians had a formidable reputation far beyond their homeland, and the sight of a well-armed band of these ferocious hillmen was sufficient to deter all but the most foolhardy of marauders. Only once did they encounter any trouble, when a party of mounted warriors sallied forth from Singidunum* and attacked them. This imperial city had recently been taken by one Babai, a Sarmatian petty warlord who fancied himself a second Alaric or Attila. Stripped of most of its garrison to replenish the distant field army, the place had fallen to a surprise attack in which luck had played a greater part than skill. Those assailing Theoderic's group had paid dearly for their temerity, being swiftly put to rout, leaving several of their number dead on the ground.

Word of the party's coming had preceded them; Theoderic and Timothy were still some distance from the baurg when a richly attired figure on horseback, accompanied by two retainers, appeared round a

* Belgrade.

bend in the path. Theoderic's heart swelled; apart from greying hair and beard, Thiudimer was just as he had been all those years ago: tall, broad-shouldered, with a strong yet kindly face.

Father and son embraced with exclamations of joy. 'What a fine young fellow you've grown to be,' declared Thiudimer, pretending to remove a mote from a watery eye. 'Those Romans have looked after you well, then?'

'Very well indeed, father,' enthused Theoderic. 'I can speak Latin as well as Greek, have read the works of all their famous authors, studied their philosophy and law. You should see their buildings; why, a score of our villages could fit inside their Hippodrome—' He broke off, seeing a frown crease the other's forehead. 'Still, it's good to be back home,' he finished lamely, embarrassed by his tactlessness.

'I'm glad to hear it.' Thiudimer glanced at Timothy. 'And who's this lowborn-looking fellow? A *skalk* – a slave – perhaps?'

'This is Timothy, father,' said Theoderic stoutly, 'my bodyguard and friend. To save the lives of all my escort, he killed a man in single combat.'

'He is welcome, then,' said Thiudimer stiffly. 'But why are we wasting time gossiping here like old maids?' he went on, his face clearing. 'A great feast is preparing, to welcome home my son. Come.'

Thiudimer's *gards* or palace consisted of a great timber hall surrounded by outbuildings – kitchens, smithies, stables, store houses, etc. Inside the hall, the chief feature was a long trestle table flanked by benches. Near the entrance, temporary fire-pits had been set up; above them spitted carcasses of oxen, boar and deer gave off delicious smells. On the side of the board nearest the wall, in the centre, sat the king, with Queen Erelieva at his side, Theoderic to his right. Beyond, on either side, were Thiudimer's chief retainers and their ladies.

Thiudimer rose; all followed suit.

'Friends, fellow Amali,' announced the king, his voice vibrant with emotion. 'This is indeed a joyous day for me and for our nation, as we welcome home my son, your future king. As you know, he has spent the greater part of his life among the Romans. This was a great sacrifice for me, but one which, because it sealed our friendship with the Empire, I made willingly. Our gain is twofold: today, I have my son again; and our people have as ally, the greatest power in the world. I give you – Theoderic.'

'Theoderic!' echoed the guests. Goblets and drinking-horsn were raised, and the toast drunk to the young prince. Seated beside him to his right, Timothy nudged Theoderic. 'I think you're supposed to reply,' he whispered.

Theoderic was gripped by panic. This was something he should have foreseen and prepared for. To strike the wrong note, could, quite conceivably, compromise his position as Thiudimer's successor. With these people – *his* people now – to be accepted as a leader you needed more than inheritance. You had to look, sound and act like a leader. Desperately combing his brain for inspiration, he rose to his feet. The faces of his audience – fierce and proud, intensely curious – swam before his eyes.

'As my father says, I have lived as a Roman for more than half my life,' he began haltingly, nervousness making his rusty Gothic even rustier. 'But I hope I have not become too Roman. At heart, you see, I am an Ostrogoth [too late, he realized he should have said 'Amal', their clan name within the tribe] and will do my best to become like one of you.' His mind went blank and he could think of nothing more to say. He sat down amid a scatter of half-hearted and perfunctory applause. He had made a wretched start, he thought miserably. His 'speech', if you could call it that, had been feeble and apologetic when it needed to be bold and confident. His father must be deeply disappointed.

A young man to Thiudimer's left leant forward. 'Congratulations, brother,' he said. 'At least your life among the Romans has given you the gift of eloquence – something you may have need of on the day you claim the throne.' And he sat back with a malicious smirk, forestalling any intervention by Thiudimer.

The speaker must be his brother Thiudimund, whom he remembered only dimly, Theoderic realized. Did his words imply that Theoderic's succession was somehow invalid? But how could that be? Thiudimund was his *younger* brother. Was there some dark secret here, or had the lad spoken merely out of spite and the eternal jealousy of the younger sibling passed over in matters of inheritance?

Any jarring of the atmosphere produced by Thiudimund's words was soon forgotten as the feast progressed. Gold arm-rings were distributed by the king for feats of valour in raids against the Sciri or the Gepids; beer flowed copiously, with endless toasts proposed and drunk;

vast quantities of pork, beef and venison were consumed; jokes (mostly simple puzzles such as 'What is the cleanest leaf?' Answer: 'Holly.'*) did the rounds, to gales of merriment; a harper sang of the deeds of Goth heroes from legend and history, of Amal, the founder of their clan, of Fritigern, who had smashed a Roman army at Adrianople, of Alaric, who had taken Rome itself . . .

Self-conscious in his Roman clothes, ashamed of his poor showing in his speech, Theoderic found himself unable to join in the revelry, becoming increasingly tense and silent. The never-ending toasts (which he was compelled to drink or risk giving offence) were making his head swim and his stomach rise. The plentiful but greasy and monotonous meat dishes – unrelieved by sauces, fruit, and puddings, such as he had known in Constantinople – grew cloying, and the tales of battles and heroic exploits wearisome. He had nothing in common with these valiant boors, he told himself. A tide of longing for the life of Roman culture and refinement he had left behind washed over him. (In contrast, Timothy, who had acquired a fair amount of Gothic during drinking sessions with Aspar's troops, was proving a great success, regaling those around him with tales of brawls and drinking bouts in Tarsus and Constantinople.)

After hours that seemed interminable, with the torches guttering and guests slumped snoring on the benches or the floor, the king turned at last to Theoderic and laid a kindly hand on his shoulder. 'Go to bed, my son. Things will look better in the morning.' The pity in his voice made the young man burn with shame as he stumbled to the curtained alcove reserved as sleeping quarters for Thiudimer's family.

Awakening in broad daylight, Theoderic picked his way over sleeping bodies to the entrance of the hall. Outside, he breathed in grateful lungfuls of morning air, which helped a little to clear his pounding head. Despite his father's words of reassurance, things didn't look any better; in fact, in the cold light of day they looked considerably worse. Deciding to take a solitary ride in order to sort out his thoughts, he made his way to the stables and asked a groom to saddle his horse. As he was about to mount, he was accosted by Thiudimund.

---

* Barbarians used leaves as lavatory paper; Romans employed sponges on sticks.

'Good morning, brother – or should that be "Crown Prince"?' Thiudimund sneered.

It might have been the combination of an aching head, nervous exhaustion, humiliation at the feast, and his younger brother's renewed provocation, but a red rage he had never before experienced swept over Theoderic. He took a step towards the other, fist raised. 'Guard your tongue!' he shouted.

Thiudimund stepped back, eyes widening in alarm. Then, noticing an interested knot of stable-hands gathering nearby, he recovered his courage. 'Why should I, brother?' he retorted. 'My claim to the throne is better than yours. Our father was married to *my* mother, not yours. Your dam, Erelieva, is his concubine, not his wife, which makes me his rightful heir and you a royal bastard.'

His mind reeling, Theoderic was too shocked to react to Thiudimund or notice him depart. Mounting, he rode off in a daze. Could the words of his brother – his half-brother as it now transpired – be true? He had always assumed that Erelieva was the mother of them both.

Two hours at a canter, through wooded hills where saker falcons flew, took him to the tree-lined shore of Balaton lake. The ride in the bracing upland air had helped to clear away the cobwebs from his mind. He could now see where his future lay. If Thiudimund had the better claim, let him have the throne. He, Theoderic, was a misfit here. He would return to his beloved Constantinople and resume his studies. There, a pleasant life of *otium* awaited him, beckoning to a scholarly career, perhaps a lectureship at the university . . .

These reveries were broken by the clip-clop of approaching hooves; he looked up, to see a familiar figure riding towards him.

'Timothy! How did—?'

'To see but not be seen, to hear but not be heard,' broke in the other with a grin. 'Remember?' He shot Theoderic a quizzical glance. 'Anything you want to tell old Timothy? A trouble shared, and all that?'

Glad of the chance to unburden himself, Theoderic let it all spill out: his feeling of inadequacy as a reclusive scholar among rude fighting men, his nostalgic longing for the culture and refinement of Roman life, the fact that his succession might be dubious. 'My father's people would soon see through me – if they haven't done so already,' he concluded. 'I'd become an embarrassment to everyone, myself included.

44

My future's in Constantinople, not Pannonia.' He looked at the tough Isaurian appealingly. 'I'd like you to come with me. Say you will.'

Timothy shook his head. 'No, Deric, I'm not going back. And neither are you. You're angry, disappointed and confused. Quite natural; but those feelings'll pass. You know your trouble? You put yourself down too easily. You say they'll see through you. Not the case. What they'll see, if you give them time, is what I've already noticed. One: courage – you showed that with Cambyses, and the charge of the Excubitors. Two: decisiveness – you challenged Julian and won, and did the same with Strabo. Three: authority. Either one has it, or one doesn't. You do, although you may not know it yet. Look how Julian's archers snapped to it when you told them not to shoot.'

'But . . . what Thiudimund says about my claim, suppose it's true. That would mean my staying on was pointless, anyway.'

'Why? Among the Goths, I think you'll find that primogeniture has never been the deciding factor regarding the succession. Take Fritigern and Alaric: successful warlords who became kings despite not having royal blood. Besides, your father's named you his successor; it's unlikely the tribal council would disagree. If it comes to a choice between you and that spiteful little whelp Thiudimund, I know who I'd put my money on. As for your own people, don't let their lack of polish put you off. They may be rough and simple, but their hearts are true. Once they've accepted you, as I'm sure in time they will, you'll have their total loyalty. Roman sophistication – that's just the stamp on the obol piece; it's the man, Goth or Roman, that's the gold.' He pointed to an imperial eagle stooping above the waters of the lake to take a fish. 'Forget Constantinople, Deric. There's your destiny.'

All Theoderic's doubts and fears, which a short time before had filled his mind's horizon like dark thunderheads, seemed to shred and dissolve to a few wispy clouds in a clear sky. He looked at the Isaurian with renewed affection and respect. 'Thanks, Timothy. I needed putting straight.' He smiled sheepishly then, after a pause, asked, 'What must I do?'

'I can't answer that, Deric. Only you can. But you'll find the solution; of that you may be sure.'

As they rode back towards his father's *baurg*, the answer suddenly came to Theoderic, and he knew what it was he had to do.

45

SEVEN

With nearly six thousand men, he [Theoderic] crossed the Danube and
fell upon Babai, king of the Sarmatians

Jordanes, *Gothic History,* 551

From his hiding-place on an island at the confluence of the Sava and
the Danube, Theoderic surveyed the walls of Singidunum, and felt his
heart sink. Massive, striped with reinforcing layers, bristling with
towers, they were typical of the thickened shells that Roman cities
everywhere had grown in the age of insecurity ushered in by the battle
of Adrianople. Towering above them rose the citadel, a mighty complex
of bastions and ramparts. In vain he scanned the visible defences for
weak points – cracks or bulges, crumbling mortar between blocks of
ashlar; the place looked utterly impregnable. Maybe this wasn't such a
good idea, after all. His mind flashed back to when the plan had been
conceived . . .

On Theoderic and Timothy's return to the *baurg,* Thiudimer had told
his son he must be absent for some time. Under their leader, Hunulf,
the Sciri had invaded the territory of his third brother, Valamir, to the
north; in the fighting Valamir had been killed, and his people had
appealed for assistance.

'Take my place here while I'm away,' Thiudimer had told his son,
adding, 'If you need help, just ask Videric.' Videric, a grizzled veteran
of many raids, was head of the assembly of the Kuni, the Amal tribal
council. Though the king spoke with kindly tact, the implication of his
words was clear: he didn't trust Theoderic to run things in his absence,
and was really leaving Videric in charge.

Theoderic had said nothing to his father about the idea that had
come to him as he journeyed back from Lake Balaton: he would lead
a raid against a Scirian settlement, returning hopefully with plunder

and renown sufficient to dispel any doubts about his fitness to succeed Thiudimer. But, with his father's announcement, a more ambitious plan had sprung to mind. He would raise a force from among the warriors not accompanying Thiudimer on his northern campaign, and recapture Singidunum from Babai. Such a feat would do more than impress his father and the Amali. Singidunum being an imperial city, returning it to the Eastern Empire's fold would earn the gratitude of Leo and Zeno. Then truly could he call himself a Friend of Rome.

Once his father had departed for the north, Theoderic set about implementing his plan. With the approval of the Kuni, he summoned a meeting of the clan's young warriors. Tentatively at first, then with growing confidence, he expounded his idea, which was received with an enthusiasm far exceeding his expectations. He discovered, to his pleasure and surprise, that he had a natural gift for leadership, based on an ability to fire others with his own enthusiasm. Giving orders came easily; in fact, it didn't feel like telling others what to do, more like making requests to friends, who would then carry them out because they wished to please you. In a heady moment of epiphany, he realized that here lay the secret of command: those you led became your comrades – a band of brothers united by common fellowship, like the men who followed Alexander, Caesar or Aetius, saviour of the West from Attila's hordes. Even Thiudimund appeared to have come round and accepted his brother's authority. Theoderic's next step was harnessing the wild energy he had tapped into.

His main problem would be keeping his force together. Unlike Roman armies (at least, East Roman armies, the West being increasingly reliant on fickle and unruly federates), which operated under strict discipline, barbarian armies could not be kept in the field for long periods. Strictly, they were not armies at all, more mobs of individual warriors on holiday from labour at the sickle or the plough, and motivated by desire for plunder and glory, or hostility to an invading enemy. Battles were settled swiftly: a charge, followed by a shoving-match between the opposing lines, with victory going to the one that didn't break. Siege warfare was out; glory-hunting heroes lacked the patience or resources to undertake protracted enterprises. Even the great commander Fritigern had declared, 'I have no quarrel with stone walls.' So, for his plan to succeed, Singidunum must be taken quickly.

But it was one thing to conceive a bold plan, quite another to prepare its execution, as the young leader was discovering. A hundred matters, which previously had not occurred to him, suddenly clamoured for urgent attention: supplies, equipment, strategy, tactics . . . Timothy proved a tower of strength. At his suggestion, each man would carry a bag of dried meat and hard biscuit sufficient for a month. This would obviate the need to live off the country – a time-consuming alternative, which would moreover antagonize local populations, who might prove useful allies in the future. To save valuable time, it was decided to cut directly across country south-east to Singidunum, rather than head south to the Sirmium* road, then east along that highway to the destination. The preferred route, by avoiding the dog-leg created by the great bend in the Danube, would form the hypotenuse of a triangle and thus be much shorter than the alternative. Its main drawback, apart from taking the six-thousand-strong force across broken and largely trackless terrain, was that they would end up on the wrong side of the river. To remedy this, Timothy, with a small picked group, would leave ahead of the main party and requisition enough craft from local fishermen to ferry the rest across the Danube, on arrival.

Thus far, everything had gone smoothly, according to plan. (Perhaps too smoothly, if you believed in hubris – Theoderic had seen a performance of Euripides' *The Bacchae* in Constantinople.) The men, all young and hardy, had made light of the forced march to the Danube, Timothy had done a sterling job ensuring transport, and the little army was now encamped in woods a few miles upstream of Singidunum. Now, through one glaring omission, the whole enterprise might fail, Theoderic reflected bitterly. If Babai – whom everyone he had spoken to dismissed as nothing more than an opportunist land-pirate – could take the place, its recapture should surely be feasible. However, this, his final reconnaissance, had convinced him him that nothing short of storming the ramparts stood any chance of success. But that, apart from being costly in lives, might well fail. The thought of returning home with his tail between his legs, instead of surprising his father with a triumph, made him shudder. Babai, he decided, must have gained entrance to the city

---

* Sremska Mitrovica – not to be confused with Kosovska Mitrovica, much further south.

by bribing some in the garrison to open one of the gates, but that trick could hardly be repeated now that the Sarmatian's own men were in charge.

'Any ideas?' he asked Timothy, who lay beside him in a concealing stand of willows.

Timothy gave a wry chuckle. 'The words "Trojan" and "horse" rather come to mind. Sorry, Deric. Not a jesting matter.'

'You know, I think you might have something,' murmured Theoderic after a pause. Then he went on excitedly, 'A Trojan horse – that's the answer!'

At dawn, the two great half-sections of Singidunum's north gate swung open to admit the first of the carts that daily brought produce to the city from surrounding farms. Filled with grain or vegetables, a stream of vehicles flowed slowly through the entrance, then halted as a great tented wagon lumbered to a stop directly beneath the arch. Cursing, sleepy sentries in Sarmatian scale armour emerged from the flanking towers to investigate the problem. Suddenly, headed by Theoderic and Timothy, armed Goths poured from the wagon, dispatched the sentries, and rushed for the towers – but too late to stop those within from releasing the portcullis. Down crashed the massive iron grille, only to be checked in its descent by the stout sides of the wagon. Spears bloodied, several Goths emerged from the towers.

'The diversion – what's happened to it?' exclaimed Theoderic to Timothy. 'We should have heard the signal by now!'

'I tried to warn you, Deric. It was a mistake putting your brother in charge. You'd best send word for our lot to come in.'

'You're right – we've got no choice. God, what a mess!' Grim-faced, Theoderic dispatched runners to summon the main force.

Awaiting its arrival, Theoderic cursed his ill-advised generosity in entrusting Thiudimund with the diversion, a gesture intended to reconcile his brother over the grievances he harboured. The plan had, like all the best plans, been simple, and had seemed foolproof. Under cover of night, two-thirds of the army – some four thousand men – would hide in a stretch of wooded parkland between the Danube and the northern section of the city walls. The rest, under Thiudimund, would take up concealed positions near the city's south gate. At dawn, when

49

the gates were opened to admit supply carts, Thiudimund's section would begin a mock attack, with plenty of noise, on a southern stretch of the walls, sounding horns to advise Theoderic that the diversion had begun – the signal that the 'wooden horse' (the wagon) could be activated. Babai's men, as observation had confirmed, were ensconced in the citadel. When aroused by the tumult of the diversion, it could safely be assumed that they would sally forth to repel the 'assault', whereupon Theoderic's contingent would enter the city by the north gate and fall upon them from the rear.

That part of the plan affecting Theoderic had been carried out to the letter. But now, owing to the diversion's inexplicable failure to materialize, everything had been thrown into jeopardy. Babai and his men had only to remain in the citadel, and the Goths would be faced with either having to mount a siege – a recipe for certain failure – or trying to take the fortress by direct assault. The latter would inevitably result in many casualties; probably, against such a strong position, to no avail. But there was no alternative, Theoderic decided. If they were not to lose the element of surprise completely, they had to act at once.

The towers had been secured and the portcullis raised, as the van of Theoderic's force arrived at the north gate. Sending messengers to urge Thiudimund to join him, Theoderic, accompanied by Timothy, led his men to the nearby eminence on which loomed the citadel. Confronting them was its gate, two massive slabs of timber between a pair of mighty bastions projecting from the curtain wall. The Goths were greeted by a volley of arrows, and hastily pulled back out of range.

'What a brute!' exclaimed Timothy, sounding far from happy, as he surveyed the entrance to the citadel. 'D'you really think it's worth it, Deric? We'd need ladders.'

'Or *a* ladder.' Theoderic's brain was working furiously, as a memory of something he had witnessed in the Eastern capital flashed into his mind. A troupe of entertainers performing tricks, one of which featured a woman strapped to a board, a man hurling axes which slammed into the wood all round her . . . Turning to his men, he began issuing orders. Doors ripped from neighbouring buildings, and with battens quickly nailed to them for handling, were pressed into service as screens. Propelled by willing volunteers, an arrow-proof wall was soon advancing towards the gate; behind the screens a party of Goths wielding heavy throwing-axes called *franciscas*, most popular among the Franks and Alamanni but also used by many Goths. Came a ripple of thuds and a 'ladder' of axes raced up the face of the gate. Seizing the grapnel someone thrust towards him, Theoderic, giving himself no time to reflect, began to climb the rungs provided by the wooden helves. No arrow-slits faced inwards from the bastions, so he was screened from enemy fire, and in moments reached the overhang of the walkway extending, via passages through the bastions' upper storeys, to the curtain wall on either side.

He swung the grapnel; the hooks clanged against the parapet, bit home, and with a heave and a scramble he was on the walkway, to be joined moments later by others swarming after him. Heading a stream of Goths, he raced, sword drawn, down the staircase of the nearest bastion. The lightly armed archers on the various floors were no match for the tide of yelling warriors and died where they stood, skewered by spears. The gate was opened from inside and the Goths surged through. The battle in the citadel's courtyard was swift and bloody. The Goths' blood was up; their huge stature, strength and battle-frenzy made them truly fearsome opponents. Outnumbered (Thiudimund's men were at last arriving on the scene) and outfought, the Sarmatians were slaughtered to a man.

At one juncture, Babai, a giant in glittering carapace of silvered scales, tried to stall the momentum of the fight by calling for the issue to be decided by single combat – a ruse calculated to appeal to the Amal. It almost worked. Shouting for Theoderic, the Goths began to draw back, creating a space for the combatants to face each other. Caught up in the madness of the moment, Theoderic found himself stepping into the arena – to be rudely pushed aside by Timothy.

'Sorry, Deric, but I'll handle this,' muttered the Isaurian, stepping in front of him. Whipping out his deadly *sica*, Timothy sent it flashing through the air to find its mark in Babai's throat. 'Snakes like that you don't allow to bite,' he remarked, as Babai writhed in his death-agonies on the ground. 'You scotch them first.'

With their leader's death, the Sarmatians lost heart and the battle was virtually over.

Singidunum's Roman citizens were overjoyed to be rid of the Sarmatians, who had abused or tortured many to force them to reveal their wealth. That night the city's decurions, or town councillors, held a great feast to honour the triumphant Goths.

After effusively thanking the Amal for freeing them from Babai's yoke, the chief decurion turned to Theoderic and asked, 'May I assume that, as of this moment, Singidunum is returned to Roman rule?'

About to rise to give his assent, Theoderic felt a restraining tug on his sleeve. 'If what you're going to say is what I think it is, don't,' whispered Timothy. 'The Romans are masters of intrigue; when dealing with the empire, it always pays to do so from a position of strength. Keep Singidunum for the moment. It'll make an excellent bargaining counter for you in any negotiations with Leo. Remember, you want to extract as many concessions as you can for the Amal, your people now, regarding any future settlement.'

When informed that, for the time being, Singidunum would remain in Amal hands, with its taxes going to Pannonia (as just reward for the Goths) instead of Constantinople, the smiles on the faces of the Roman hosts became somewhat strained.

Before the Amal departed for Pannonia, Theoderic took Thiudimund aside. 'Well, brother,' he demanded, 'I think you owe me some explaining. Why did you fail to warn me, and to implement the diversion?'

'Why did *I* fail?' blustered the other. 'It was you who failed, not I. I waited for your signal but it never came.'

Misunderstanding or deliberate malice? Theoderic could not be sure. He knew, with total certainty, that he had told Thiudimund to sound the horns as a signal that the diversion had begun. It was possible – just possible – that his brother could have confused their respective roles. But never again, he decided, would he involve him in his plans.

'Very well,' he replied, 'we will leave it there. For now.' He paused and gave Thiudimund an appraising stare. 'But take care, brother. There is one thing among our people that can never be forgiven: disloyalty. Remember that.'

EIGHT

*Our lord and master [Euric], even he, has but little time to spare
while a conquered world makes suit to him*
Sidonius Apollinaris, Carmina, c. 475

To Gaius Lampridius, esteemed author, and adviser to the most
noble Euric king of the Visigoths, greetings.

My dear old friend, *tempora mutantur*, as they say. When last
I wrote to you, from Arverna,* I was organizing that city's resistance against its annual summer siege by the Visigoths, while still
nurturing the hope that Anthemius, our late Augustus, could
bring Gaul, or Septem Provinciae† at least, back within the
Imperium Romanum of the West. (Our new Augustus, little
Romulus, is of course only a front for his father, General Orestes,
one-time envoy of Attila. It's too early yet to know what Orestes'
plans are; but we live in hope. God willing, he might even prove
a second Aetius and restore the fortunes of the West.)

Since then, as all the world now knows, Arverna has fallen.
Considering I've long been a thorn in the flesh of our new masters,
I got off pretty lightly. I was carted off to exile here in Burdigala,‡
where the worst I have to endure is the drunken screeching of
two old Gothic crones, next door in the draughty tenement where
I presently reside. No matter how hard I try, I don't think I'll
ever get used to barbarians: their smell, disgusting manners,
outlandish appearance – furs and trousers, long hair smeared with
rancid butter . . . How do you, living in their midst at Euric's
court, manage to put up with them?

---

* Clermont-Ferrand in the Auvergne.
† The southern of Gaul's two dioceses.
‡ Bordeaux (in Aquitaine, the homeland granted to the Visigoths in 418).

Now, you'll remember, I'm sure, that some time ago I lent you my treasured copy of *Mosella* by Ausonius? No thought then, of course, of any quid pro quo; but perhaps that time has come. The enclosed is a little poem I've written in praise of Euric. I've laid it on a bit thick but, being a barbarian, he's sure to lap it up. I'd be for ever in your debt if you could show it to him, with a view to his revoking my exile. I've heard that (for a Goth) he's quite a reasonable fellow, so perhaps he might be willing to let bygones be bygones. If you think it would help, you could say that I'd be willing to put whatever literary talent I possess at his service – perhaps as a species of court poet? (Panegyrics to order!) There must be worse fates. I trust this finds you in good health and spirits. I know you'll do your best for your old friend and fellow-scribbler, Sidonius Apollinaris. Vale.

Written at the Insula Marcella, Burdigala, III Nones Decembris, in the year of the second consulship of Zeno* (no Western candidate this year!)

To Sidonius Apollinaris, poet, former bishop of Arverna, greetings.

Good news, old friend. As requested, I showed your poem to Euric; I think he was more amused than flattered by your (shameless) attempt to butter him up. But he's not the sort to bear grudges, and I think he's rather taken with the idea of having a famous Roman poet in his entourage – along with jesters, cooks and grooms! Anyway, the outcome is that you're forgiven, your exile is revoked, and your estates in Arvernum (which could easily have been forfeit) returned to you. So you see, 'barbarians', as you call them, are not perhaps as dreadful as you seem to think. At least they're capable of generosity and fairness, which is more than can be said of many Romans.

A friendly word of caution. The world has changed and we'd be wise to accept the new realities. Whether we like them or not, the Goths are here to stay. Whatever adverse views you have of them, I must urge you to *keep them to yourself*. On the whole, they're open, friendly types, but they have quick tempers and

* 4 December 475.

54

don't easily forgive a slight. I'd hate to hear of the distinguished author of *The Panegyric of Avitus* coming to an untimely end because he'd offended 'a smelly, trousered savage, with rancid butter in his hair'. They're the masters now, and must be shown respect, if only for reasons of self-preservation.

Which brings me to another point. You seem to cherish hopes of some sort of recovery for the West. Well, let me disillusion you; it's not going to happen. Even so recently as seven years ago, I might have conceded that you had a point. But the failure of the East–West expedition to recover Africa from Gaiseric has put paid to any chance of a Western revival. Now no Eastern army's going to intervene to save the West. And the Army of Italy, composed of federates, is hardly likely to take up arms against the Franks, Visigoths and Alamanni – all fellow Germans, who are taking over Gaul and Spain. Anyway, what would be the point? Romulus is emperor of . . . what, exactly? Italy, and a small enclave of south-east Gaul! The old Rome that we both knew and loved is passing and will soon be gone. The future lies with the German kingdoms that are taking its place. How will they fare? Maybe only the Sybils would have known the answer. But they, like Rome, belong to yesterday. With hopes that we may meet soon, perhaps at Euric's court, your friend Gaius Lampridius bids you farewell.

Written at the Praetorium of Tolosa,* postridie Natalis X̄P̄Ī, in the eleventh regnal year of Euric, king of the Visigoths.†

---

* Toulouse.

† 26 December 475. ('X̄P̄Ī' is a contraction, using modified Greek letters, for 'Christi'. 'X', as a symbol for 'Christ', lingers on in 'Xmas'.)

NINE

The garrison of Batavis, however, still held out. Some of these had
gone to Italy to fetch for their comrades that last payment
Eugippius, *The Life of Severinus*, 511

Striding over the flower-spangled meadows of the Oenus* valley,
Severinus wondered if the detachment – from the last Roman garrison
that Castra Batava was ever likely to see – had made it back from Italy.
He had warned them not to go.

For more than sixty years, Noricum† had witnessed the barbarian
tides roll past it to the north and south – and had been miraculously
preserved on account of its being a rustic backwater, off the main
routes into Italy and Gaul. But lately things had changed. Raids by
Alamanni, Heruls and the northern branch of the Ostrogoths led by
Valamir had year by year become more savage and destructive. From
experience gained in Britain he, Severinus, had shown the Noricans
the best way to resist. This was to retreat to *castella* – fortified settlements (contemptuously called *fliehburgen* by the German marauders)
– garrisoned with citizen-militia stiffened by the remnants of Roman
units which, so recently as the Attila campaign, had amounted to a
considerable military presence.

Seating himself on a boulder for a breather (though still hale and
active, he *was* eighty, Severinus reminded himself), he filled his lungs
with the pure mountain air. Around him stretched a vista of majestic
peaks, lakes and limpid streams – the most beautiful land he had known
in his travels to every corner of the Roman Empire: Britannia with its
mists and rain, the burning sands of Africa and Egypt, the forests of

* River Inn.
† West Roman province, roughly corresponding to southern Austria – *Sound of*
Music country.

the northern frontier. His mind drifted back to his early childhood in Britannia, where his father had been a *primicerius** in the great military base at Eboracum.†

He was born in the final year of the reign of the great Theodosius, when, for the last time, Rome had been a single empire and was still the mightiest power in the world. When the self-styled 'emperor', Constantine III, had taken the field army of Britannia with him from the island in a doomed bid for the purple, little Severinus had accompanied his family with the legions, to Gaul. But, in the meantime, following the death of Theodosius and the 'splitting of the Eagle' (as the soldiers had termed the final division of the Empire into East and West), catastrophe had struck. On the last day of the year 406, a vast barbarian confederacy of Vandals, Sueves and Alans had crossed the frozen Rhine; they later swept through Gaul and into Spain.

In the chaos of Gaul, his father had been killed fighting the Vandals, his family had become dispersed and, aged twelve, Severinus had found himself a homeless refugee. Sustaining himself by begging and stealing, he had made his way to Aremorica‡ in north-west Gaul, an enclave run by the Bagaudae. These were 'outlaws' (as the state termed them), refugees from oppressive landlords and the crushing demands of the Roman tax machine, who had banded together to form their own self-governing communities, with strict laws and People's Courts. Severinus had lived among these tough and independent-minded folk for several years, absorbing many useful skills, from woodcraft to healing.

When quasi-stability was restored in Gaul by the great general and co-emperor Constantius, Severinus had made his way south in stages to Italy, earning a living by practising the medical skills he had learnt among the Bagaudae. So much in demand did his craft become in Rome that he had been able to live in enough comfort and security to attend classes in law and philosophy at the university. Crossing to Roman Africa, he had continued his studies at the University of Carthage, and conversed with the famous scholar Augustine, bishop of

---

* A non-commissioned rank roughly corresponding to sergeant-major.
† York.
‡ Brittany.

Hippo. When the Vandals crossed the Pillars of Hercules* and seized the diocese, he had moved to the Eastern Empire, first to Egypt, where he had studied medicine at Alexandria – Galen's alma mater – then to Constantinople, at whose university he had attended lectures in philosophy and rhetoric.

And so, in an unplanned Odyssey as a wandering scholar-cum-healer, he had completed the whole vast circuit of both empires, returning to Britannia (now abandoned to its own defences) as part of Germanus' second mission to combat the influence of the Pelagian heretics. Here, he had met and befriended Ambrosius Aurelianus, son of a Roman senator and resistance leader against the inroads of the Saxons. After helping Aurelianus to organize a system of self-defence among the island's cities, he had returned to imperial soil. Finally, these fifteen years past, he had made his home in Noricum where, to his amusement, he had become venerated as a 'holy man' and sage.

When at last the barbarians came, Severinus had slipped naturally into the role of leader, organizing the defences of Castra Batava, Lauriacum† and a dozen other places. Apart from an intermittent trickle of pay for the few surviving Roman units, no help from the central government had been forthcoming. When that, too, ceased, some Roman soldiers based at Castra Batava had volunteered to make the journey to Ravenna and bring back the funds themselves. Severinus had tried to dissuade them; the way was long and arduous, beset with danger. Moreover, the political situation in Italy was in a state of melt-down. The latest wearer of the diadem and purple, one Julius Nepos, having murdered the previous incumbent, Glycerius, and proclaimed himself emperor, was in conflict with the commanders of the Army of Italy. (Severinus had actually met one of them, Odovacar, of the old Scirian royal line. En route to Italy to seek his fortune, Odovacar had sought out the famous holy man of Noricum. Severinus remembered being impressed by the big German's intelligence and self-confidence, predicting Odovacar would go far.) Despite Severinus' warnings, the Batavan soldiers, brave and stubborn, had insisted on going. Two months having passed since their departure, the old man was now making his way to Castra Batava, to find out if they had returned.

'Nearly home, lads!' At the rear of the straggling line of soldiers and pack-mules laden with coin, the *circitor** pointed ahead to a dramatic gash in the saw-toothed crest of the Alpes Carnicae.† The men, travel-stained and weary, raised a ragged cheer and quickened their pace. A few hours later they reached the summit of the pass and began the descent into Noricum.

They had found Ravenna, the imperial capital and terminus of the outward journey, in a state of confusion, with harassed heads of state departments rushing about like so many headless chickens. No one seemed to know who was in charge of anything; the latest emperor, Julius Nepos, had apparently quarrelled with his top general, Orestes, and sailed for Dalmatia – abandoning the Roman West and creating, in effect, an interregnum. After endless requests, the Batavans were eventually granted an audience with the two chief financial ministers, the *Comes Rei Privatae* and *Comes Sacrarum Largitionum* – the Counts of the Privy and Public Purses respectively.

'Until I get the emperor's permission,' the Privy Purse, a thin, intense man, had bleated, 'I cannot issue funds. And as the emperor is – not forthcoming, shall we say, my hands are tied, completely tied.' The Public Purse, a plump, jolly individual clearly sympathetic concerning their predicament, had proved more accommodating. 'I think we can, ah, "liberate" a small amount from the pay chest of the Army of Italy,' he said with a conspiratorial wink. 'After all, they're federates – barbarians, not Romans like yourselves. Anyway, everything's going to hell in a handcart just now; I doubt if I'll ever be called to account. Best assume, though, that this'll be your final pay instalment.'

Now, relaxed and carefree to be nearing journey's end, the Batavan soldiers abandoned their usual caution. Helmets and heavy hauberks loaded on the pack-mules, they made their way beside the sparkling Oenus, eagerly anticipating the welcome that awaited them in Castra Batava, which was expected soon to come into view.

---

* A non-commissioned rank roughly equal to corporal.
† The Carnatic Alps.

They followed the riverside path into a wood. Suddenly, spears thrusting, axes hacking, armed Alamanni raiders burst from the trees and fell on them. Unarmoured, taken by surprise, the Romans could put up only token resistance. In seconds it was all over; the soldiers' lifeless bodies were tumbled into the stream, and the killers departed, delighted with their spoils.

When Severinus reached the Oenus and observed the threads of scarlet in the current, he had a premonition of disaster – soon to be confirmed, as the first body bobbed in sight. Tears flowing down his face, the old man hastened to break the news to the Batavans.

TEN

All their inhabitants [of British towns] . . . were mown down, while swords flashed and flames crackled

Gildas, *The Destruction of Britain*, c. 540

'Saxons, Sire – a mighty host,' gasped the scout, reining in his lathered mount before Ambrosius. 'As thick as blowflies on a week-old corpse.'

'Numbers? Distance?'

'My guess is ten thousand at the least, Sire. Now about five miles off, I'd say.'

More than thrice our strength, thought the other grimly. Ambrosius Aurelianus: *Dux Britanniae et Saxum Britannorum* – Duke of Britain and 'the Rock of the British' – son of a Roman senator and leader of the British resistance against the blue-eyed heathens from across the German Ocean. Within two hours, his rag-tag army, the *Exercitus Britanniae*, could be locked in battle with the Saxon host. Less than three generations ago, he reflected, when Britannia was still a diocese of Rome, the 'Sea Wolves' had come as raiders only. Now, with the legions long gone and the forts of the Saxon Shore abandoned and crumbling, they arrived each year in ever greater numbers, driving the Britons from the land to seize it as their own. Already, the great province of Maxima Caesariensis* had fallen to the North and South Folk and the East and South Saxons, the native Britons fleeing to the west or across the sea to 'New Britannia' in north-west Gaul.

Turning in the saddle, Ambrosius surveyed his force: civilian volunteers stiffened by *limitanei* – second-rate frontier troops, all that remained of the Army of Britain after Constantine, self-styled 'the Third', had taken the legions with him to Gaul in a doomed bid for the purple.

---

* It covered most of south-east England, from East Anglia to Hampshire, and was governed from London.

Desperate appeals for help against the Saxon menace had been sent to Aetius, the greatest general of the Western Empire – appeals perforce ignored by a Master of Soldiers struggling to save the West from extinction by barbarian insurgents. Now, any hope of help from Rome had long vanished; Aetius was dead these twenty years, slain by a jealous emperor, and the West itself was tottering towards its end. With the aid of a remarkable man, one Severinus – scholar, healer, natural leader, a member of Germanus' second mission to counter the Pelagian heresy in Britain – he had encouraged the British to organize defence centres. These were fortified strongpoints within whose walls the local populace could gather and be safe whenever Saxon war-parties approached. It was his efforts in this field that had earned Ambrosius his nickname, 'the Rock of the British'. For a time his scheme had proved successful, but of late the increasing frequency of attacks had begun to make such centres appear like islands in a raging Saxon sea.

Of Ambrosius' troops, the *limitanei* alone had proper armour – battered ridge-helmets and mail hauberks issued by the Roman government many years before and since patched up times without number; the volunteers made do with caps and cuirasses of boiled leather. Each man carried a long spear and oval shield, the *limitanei* also bearing swords. The cream of the army consisted of the cavalry, positioned at either end of the three-deep line of infantry. Handpicked, sons of Romano-British aristocracy, these were natural horsemen, needing only some basic training to weld into a formidable fighting machine.

Until this year, the Saxon conquest had been a matter of slow attrition by separate war-bands. This present threat was on an altogether different scale, a mass invasion which suggested a concerted plan, perhaps masterminded by a single leader. A century before, Britain had faced a comparable danger, when a Barbarian conspiracy of Saxons, Picts and Scots, had overrun the island. But Rome then had a mighty army, and within a year Count Theodosius, father of one of Rome's greatest emperors, had cleared the land of the invaders. Now that army was gone, replaced by federates as fickle and greedy as they were ill-disciplined and violent, ready on a whim to turn upon their masters.

To meet this new and terrible Saxon threat, Ambrosius had hastily assembled a scratch militia, organizing instruction in elementary drill and tactics by officers drawn from the all-but-vanished landowning and administrative class. On first news of the route of the enemy's advance, using the terrain to maximum advantage he had drawn up the Romano-Britons on the crest of a low ridge flanked by woods, to negate as far as possible any Saxon superiority in numbers. Far away across the plain, the trilithons of the ancient Hanging Stones appeared as a faint tracery of concentric rings.

The hot summer afternoon bled away, the army standing down to snatch some rest before the coming encounter. At last, a swirling haze on the horizon, accompanied by a sound like breakers on a distant shore, announced the approach of the Saxon host. As the dust-cloud rolled nearer, a myriad of tiny specks interspersed with glints and flashes appeared at its base, while the noise swelled from a murmur to a muted roar. The Britons stood to arms, the ground beneath their feet beginning to tremble.

'Is there no end to their number?' breathed the young cavalry officer beside Ambrosius. 'They blacken the earth like the locusts in the Bible. We'll never hold them, surely?'

'True,' the general replied to his second-in-command. 'But we can sting them, teach them that the price of British soil's a heavy one – in blood.'

Like an incoming tide, the Saxon host – flaxen-haired giants, un-armoured and on foot – flowed across the plain, lapped the foot of the ridge, surged up it to break against the British shield-wall with an ear-shattering crash. For a time, the two armies swayed back and forth, the British footsoldiers holding the ridge while their cavalry mounted charge after charge to carve bloody swathes deep into the enemy mass. Forced to fight on a narrow front, the Saxons were at first unable to bring their overwhelming strength to bear. But, inexorably, sheer weight of numbers began at last to tell. The British line thinned from three deep to two, then one, while the cavalry returned from every charge diminished. His horse killed under him, Ambrosius fought on foot until brought down by a Saxon javelin. Rushing to the general's side, his second-in-command dragged him behind the battle-line and made to pull the shaft from his leader's armpit, where the opening in the antique Roman cuirass left it unprotected.

'Leave it, Artorius,' gasped the general. 'I'm finished. Now it is you

who must carry on the fight. We've done all we can here. Given
them a mauling they'll not readily forget. Withdraw with what's left
of the army, and regroup. Cambria, the mountains of the north, the
moors and uplands of the west – that's the terrain we can best defend.
Raise and train a force of heavy horse; strike them hard and often,
using hit-and-run tactics. You saw today the damage cavalry can
inflict.' Ambrosius forced a grin. 'Your sword's broken, I see. Well,
at least that means a few less Saxons. You'd best have mine.' He handed
to Artorius not the customary long *spatha* of Rome's late armies, but a
bloodstained *gladius*, the short stabbing sword with which the legions
had won an empire. This one had been handed down from father to
son of the Aureliani for two centuries and more, since the days when
the dynasty of Severus had worn the purple. Struggling to hold back
tears, Artorius took the venerable weapon from the dying 'Rock'.

Out of such fleeting moments, mythologies can grow. Thus did
Arthur take the Sword from the Stone.

ELEVEN

Are you ignorant that it is the constant policy of the Romans to destroy the Goths by each other's swords?
Jordanes (quoting Strabo taunting Theoderic),
Gothic History, 551

Entering the foothills of the Haemus range,* Theoderic looked back at the long, long column snaking behind him almost to the gates of Novae, his base in Moesia Secunda.† First came the host, fit men aged sixteen to sixty, mostly on foot and armed with spears; then the train of baggage – mules and ox-drawn wagons accompanied by women, children and the elderly, with nursing mothers, the sick and the feeble carried in the vehicles. To his left and right, now invisible because of intervening spurs, marched two similar columns, one under Soas, his trusted second-in-command, the other led by Thiudimund, to whose care he had entrusted both their mothers. (Reasoning that the circumstances hardly gave scope for Thiudimund to effect any mischief, also unwilling, for the sake of appearances, to advertise any family disharmony, Theoderic had decided, albeit reluctantly, to give his brother the charge.) Barring those Goths who had migrated with Vidimir, brother of Thiudimer, to Italy (and ultimately Aquitaine to join their Visigoth cousins), the three columns together comprised the entire Amal nation. Fixing his gaze on the formidable mountain chain looming above them, Theoderic reflected on the highs and lows of his career these last ten years: from his homecoming in Pannonia, to this new beginning, which a wonderful offer by the Romans had made possible.

Returning in triumph from Singidunum, a hero to his people, also to his father – who was overjoyed (and secretly relieved) that his son had

* The Balkan Mountains.
† Equivalent to Bulgaria; Novae is now Sistova.

proved himself a worthy successor – he had accompanied Thiudimer with the Amal soon after to Moesia. There were two reasons for the migration (undertaken without imperial permission): starvation and the Squinter. Year after year, the harvests of Pannonia, its soils exhausted through abuse and over-tilling by successive waves of migrants since its abandonment by Rome, had proved increasingly inadequate to feed the Amal nation. Meanwhile, in Thrace, Theoderic Strabo had become a growing menace not only to the Eastern Empire, but also to the Amal, owing to his ambition to assume the hegemony of all the Ostrogoths, not just those of Thrace. By repositioning the Amal close to Strabo's heartland, Thiudimer (allied to the East) could more effectively contain this double threat, as well as feed his people in the rich and fertile Eastern province. Not long after the great trek to Moesia, Thiudimer had died, whereupon, honouring the late king's will and spurning Thiudimund's rival claim, the Amal had proclaimed Theoderic their king and warrior-ruler,* raising him on a shield according to tradition.

True to his verbal pact with Zeno (who had succeeded Leo in the same year that Theoderic became king), Theoderic had championed the new emperor's cause: curbing the Squinter's aggressive moves against the empire in a series of skirmishes and armed confrontations; also helping Zeno to regain his throne, following a short-lived usurpation by Basiliscus, the incompetent general responsible for the disastrous North African campaign against Gaiseric. However, despite proving himself a loyal Friend of Rome ('Rome' now consisting of the East alone, little Romulus, the last Western emperor, having been sent into exile by Odovacar just two years after Theoderic's accession), official sanction of Moesia as the Amal's new homeland had been withheld, with promised subsidies in gold arriving only intermittently and below the amount stipulated. In consequence, plagued by insecurity and diminishing resources, the Amal had seen their fortunes steadily decline, while those of Strabo (able, thanks to his Thracian power base, to blackmail and intimidate Zeno) year by year increased. In the darkest days, Timothy had proved a rock to Theoderic, ready with advice and encouragement whenever the king's morale flagged.

* In 474.

Then, just when the plight of his people was starting to look desperate (and therefore constituting a potential challenge to his kingship), a Roman envoy had arrived from Constantinople bearing marvellous tidings. If Theoderic were to cross the Haemus with his people, he would find awaiting him north of Adrianople not only the arrears of subsidy but an enormous force of Roman soldiers. Together, the Amal and the Romans would then advance into the Squinter's Thracian heartland, and crush him. Thereafter, Theoderic would assume his rival's forfeited titles of *Patricius* and *Magister Militum*, Patrician and Master of Soldiers, and his people's grant of homeland would be officially confirmed. At last, after years of frustration and uncertainty, Theoderic saw his dream of proving a worthy leader of his people, and achieving recognition by the Roman state, on the point of becoming a reality.

Gradually the terrain steepened, open uplands, stippled with flocks of grazing sheep, giving way to forested slopes. Dense stands of spruce, beech and oak closed in on the rutted trail; within their cool dimness, the column proceeded in a sepulchral hush broken only by the occasional call of birds, the shuffle of feet, and the creak of wagon wheels. That night the column made camp in a huge clearing. By noon of the next day the trees had begun to thin out, being replaced by rock and gravel as the Amal broke out of the forest onto a boulder-strewn wilderness hemmed in by stony walls – the mouth of the famous Shipka Pass, scene of an early victory by Alexander the Great. Away to his right, Theoderic could see Soas' column keeping pace with his, but of Thiudimund there was no sign. Theoderic experienced a momentary prickle of anxiety, then dismissed his fears; a vast body of people, led by experienced Roman guides, could hardly get lost. Could it? He and Soas would wait for Thiudimund at the summit, the designated rendezvous for the Amal to meet and rest before beginning the descent of the range's southern flank. But, as the two columns entered the throat of the pass, an unpleasant surprise awaited them.

In a scene eerily reminiscent of a long-ago ambush in the Succi Pass, thousands of armed men sprang up from among the boulders where they had been hiding, surrounding the Amal on both sides and to the fore. Then, amplified by the ravine's containing sides, a familiar voice boomed out: 'Greetings, Theoderic, son of Thiudimer. You remember, perhaps, our farewell conversation at the Monastery of St Elizabeth the Thaumaturge? I promised then that when next we met the score between us would be evened. That time has come.'

Switching his address to the Amal, Theoderic Strabo declared, 'Fellow Ostrogoths, your leader is a loser.' 'Loser . . . loser . . .' came the mocking echo, reverberating from the canyon walls. 'You, who left Pannonia with two or three horses apiece, now go on foot like slaves. He promised you gold by the bushel; now you can barely find two nummi to rub together. But, even worse than failing you, is this: your king is a traitor to his race, ready to shed the blood of other Goths whenever his Roman masters snap their fingers.' Turning back to Theoderic, he shouted, 'Well, namesake mine, here's your chance. Come on, if you've the stomach for a fight.'

Shaken and bewildered, Theoderic looked around for the guides who had led him to this spot; they were nowhere to be seen. 'Timothy, what's happening?' he cried.

'It looks as though the Romans have made fools of us,' replied the burly Isaurian. 'We took their bait – hook, line and sinker. Let's face it, Deric, there's no Roman army waiting for us on the other side of these mountains, no subsidy, no homeland. We've fallen for the oldest trick in their book: playing off one set of barbarians against another – in this case, engineering a confrontation between ourselves and Strabo, in the hope that we'll destroy each other. Which would suit them nicely; a final solution to their Gothic problem.'

'Where in God's name is Thiudimund?' exclaimed Theoderic. 'If only he were here, we could take on Strabo. Without him, we're outnumbered and would probably lose, especially as Strabo holds the advantage of the ground.'

'I'm not sure "taking on" Strabo is an option, anyway. Listen.'

From all around, a swelling murmur was arising from the Amal: 'Strabo's right – we shouldn't fight each other . . . We have suffered enough; give us bread and land, not graves . . . Together, we can force the Romans to grant us food until the harvest, extend our settlements . . .'

'Can you hear what your people are telling you, Theoderic?' resumed Strabo. 'If so, I suggest you listen. Order them to fight me, and they'll mutiny. But I have another plan,' he went on, in tones of seeming magnanimity. 'Why don't we all meet and discuss how best to get the Romans to grant concessions to *both* our nations. Agreed?'

Fury, bitter humiliation and betrayal engulfed Theoderic, as his dream collapsed in ruins. But he retained sufficient grip on reality to appreciate that he had been comprehensively outmanoeuvred, and had no choice but to comply. The words sticking in his throat, he heard himself call out, 'I agree.'

His anger and frustration were compounded when Thiudimund eventually turned up – plus the two mothers, but minus the wagon train. This, he explained, he had been forced to abandon when his column had been threatened by a Roman force led by one of their top generals, Sabinianus. Misfortune, incompetence or treachery? Theoderic could not decide. But, for the second time, he found himself vowing that never again would he entrust his brother with responsibility.

In time-honoured fashion, the two Gothic kings drew up their peoples facing each other across a river, and entered into an agreement. From now on, they would present their demands jointly to the imperial government, the details to be supervised by Roman officials – as only Romans possessed the know-how to implement such things efficiently. With concord apparently established, the two great branches of the Ostrogothic nation broke camp and went their separate ways – Strabo eastward to Constantinople, to parley with the emperor, Theoderic westward to Stobi in the diocese of Dacia, which city he sacked and whose garrison he massacred, in revenge against the Romans for their perfidy.

TWELVE

Then came Fenge to Amleth and spoke him fair, but with a false smile: 'I have brought a horse for you and would have you ride it'
Saxo Grammaticus, *Gesta Danorum*, c. 1190

Approaching the coast of south-east Macedonia, Timothy rode through an enchanted landscape: meadows thick with poppies, interspersed with noble stands of beech and oak, their silence broken only by the chatter of squirrels and the call of grouse, while inland rose pine-clad mountains streaked by waterfalls. Occasionally, a deer or boar would dash across the path ahead, and, once, he glimpsed high above him an imperial eagle, moving through the air with majestic flaps of its great wings. There had been a magic moment during his journey from Epirus, when his attention had been caught by a strange-shaped white cloud far to the south; on its remaining immobile, he had realized that in fact it was the snow-capped peak of Mount Olympus.

Skirting the battlefield of Philippi where, five centuries before, Antony and Octavian had smashed the legions of Brutus and Cassius, Caesar's murderers, he headed south and in a few miles picked up the Via Egnatia, the mighty Roman highway linking Constantinople to Epidamnus on the Adriatic. Turning to his left, westward, he cantered along the verge of the paved road, running parallel to the Aegean, Homer's 'wine-dark sea'. Breezes from the offshore isle of Thasos carried a tang of cypresses and olive trees – the very smell of Greece.

Several paces behind his mount, connected to Timothy's hand by a lead-rope, ran a beautiful dapple-grey horse, his muscles rippling like silk beneath the glossy coat. This was no ordinary steed. An enormous stallion, a cross between a Hun great horse and a chunky Parthian (the type beloved of Roman stablemasters), and a full twenty hands in height, he was the biggest horse that Timothy had ever known. He had bought him for a song from a Gothic horse-coper who had purchased him as a reject from the Roman cavalry. For, although beautiful, Sleipnir – as his Gothic owner had named him after Odin's terrible eight-legged steed – was evil. No one had succeeded in riding him; of those who tried, a legacy of smashed limbs and broken backs bespoke their failure.

No one, that is, until Timothy. For Timothy, the breaking of horses had, from an early age, been a passion, an obsession almost. The method favoured by most Roman riding-masters – bending an animal to one's will by harsh treatment – he despised. By a system based on rewarding and praising co-operation, balanced by withholding attention in response to bad manners or aggression, he had never, thus far, failed with any horse. Sleipnir had proved his severest test; but a challenge was something Timothy relished, and with patience and consistency he had eventually won the creature over. But woe betide anyone else foolhardy enough to try to mount him.

An hour's easy ride from where he'd joined the Via Egnatia brought Timothy to the edge of Strabo's camp outside the Macedonian town of Stabula Diomedis. Having failed to forge an alliance with Zeno advantageous to himself, Strabo had launched a full-scale assault on Constantinople. Repulsed (predictably), he had resolved to switch his attack westward and was en route to invade Epirus, hoping to co-opt Amal support, as Theoderic's new base at Epidamnus was in that very province.

Timothy's entry into the camp made an immediate impression. Unlike their Visigothic cousins, the Ostrogoths had long been familiar with the use of horses, first as steppe-dwelling herdsmen, then as allies of Attila, when their cavalry had severely tested, though not broken, the Visigoths' shield-wall at the epic battle of the Catalaunian Fields. Though only the wealthy could afford them, all Ostrogoths shared an appreciation of horses. An animal of Sleipnir's appearance inevitably caused a huge buzz of interest, and he was soon the focus of an admiring, and growing, throng.

A lane parted in the mass of warriors and Strabo, yellow hair swinging about his shoulders, strode up to see what the excitement was about. He gazed at the dappled stallion with ill-disguised cupidity. 'We know you,' he declared, turning to Timothy. 'You're the one who defeated our champion in single combat at the Monastery of St Elizabeth.'

71

He fixed the other with a squinting stare. 'But the fight was fair; we bear you no ill-will. What brings you to the camp of Theoderic of Thrace?'

Dismounting, Timothy knelt and said, 'I come, Sire, with a gift from the king of the Amal. He hopes you will accept this horse as a token of the amity that now exists between our peoples. His name is Sleipnir, and he is without peer among his kind.'

'Sleipnir? A strange name for a strange beast.'

'A mount fit for a god, Sire. Or a king. Let me demonstrate how perfectly he responds to a rider's will. The lightest touch of heel or bridle, the merest hint of pressure by the knee is all the guidance he requires.'

Oddly enhanced by the squint, the glint of avarice in Strabo's eyes was plain to see. 'Show me, then.'

Timothy vaulted nimbly onto the back of Sleipnir, whose tack was already in situ. Without once touching saddle-horn or bridle, he proceeded to put the stallion through his paces – the old, old moves going back to Xenophon, which all war-horses must learn if they were to be of any use to a rider whose hands were occupied with shield and lance. With consummate grace and apparent ease, Sleipnir performed a series of evolutions: the high trot on the spot; rising up with hocks bent and forelegs pawing the air; and, hardest of all, static leaps, a feat accomplished by only the very best of mounts. Alighting, Timothy bowed to Strabo and extended a hand towards the horse. 'Your turn, Sire.'

Matching the Isaurian's agility, the king sprang onto the saddle – whereupon the full wickedness of Sleipnir's nature manifested itself. Feeling the weight of a stranger on his back, the stallion, eyes rolling, ears laid back, immediately began to rear and plunge, obliging Strabo to hang on grimly to the two front saddle-horns. A gasp of horror arose from the scattering onlookers as Sleipnir bounded in the air, then landed with a jarring thud that sent Strabo flying from the saddle, to crash onto a rack of spears outside a tent. Several blades drove through the king's back, their bloody points emerging from his chest. Strabo gave a choking cry, a fount of blood gushed from his mouth, and he lolled lifeless, suspended from the spears.

Before the Goths could react, Timothy had mounted Sleipnir and was galloping from the camp. A spear whistled past his head; a warrior who tried to bar the way went down, skull stove in by an iron-shod hoof. Then they were clear and speeding eastward along the Via Egnatia, at a pace no other steed could hope to emulate. The plot – intended by Theoderic and Timothy only to humiliate Strabo before his followers, and thus hopefully reduce his standing – had succeeded beyond their wildest imaginings.

The results of Strabo's accidental death were immediate and far-reaching. Theoderic had proved himself stronger than his rival. Therefore (according to the Gothic mind) he was worthy to be the leader of Strabo's followers. Thus the hegemony of all the Ostrogoths fell to Theoderic, who thus became, almost at a stroke, a major potential threat to Zeno. Unable now to play off one Gothic bloc against another, the Eastern emperor sought to win over Theoderic by a series of gestures. He connived in the murder of Strabo's son Rekitach, thus eliminating the only serious challenge to Theoderic's supremacy; he granted the Amal Goths land in Dacia Ripensis* and Moesia Secunda; he appointed Theoderic *Magister Militum praesentalis*, the highest post in the Roman army; and he designated him (along with one Venantius) consul† – an unheard-of honour for a barbarian. Through an unexpected turn of fortune's wheel, it seemed that all Theoderic's tribulations had been smoothed away, and his dream at last fulfilled.

---

* Roughly equivalent to north-east Serbia.
† For 484.

THIRTEEN

The divine inspiration of his [Severinus'] prophetic mind
Eugippius, *The Life of Severinus*, 511

As he neared his destination, Lauriacum, Theoderic's pleasurable anticipation at the throught of meeting the famous holy man of Noricum, Severinus, was tempered by a deep sadness. Everywhere throughout the former West Roman province, ruined farmsteads and the fire-blackened remains of villages made a stark and ugly contrast to the beautiful landscape of mountains, lakes and Alpine meadows. The devastation had been wrought only in recent years by bands of Alamanni, Heruls and, sadly, the northern Ostrogoths under his brother Valamir, now dead. (The Sciri had ceased their raids, banned by Odovacar of the royal house of that tribe and now king of Italy. For all that he was a barbarian ruler, Odovacar was a just and enlightened one, doing a far better job than his recent predecessors who had worn the imperial purple.)

Keen to capitalize on the power-vacuum created by the death of Strabo, and anxious (secretly) to know what the future held in store, Theoderic had decided to visit the famed sage and reputed seer to seek advice and prognostications. Forced to leave Thiudimund nominally in charge of the Amal during his absence (but with Timothy and Videric, the aged but able head of the Kuni, primed to take over at the first hint of disloyalty), Theoderic had travelled by ship from Dyrrachium* up the Adriatic coast and out of the empire, to the port of Tergeste† (Aquileia, which would have been nearer his destination, having been destroyed by Attila thirty years earlier). He had completed the remainder of his journey via the route over the Alpes Carnicae, in

* Durrësi, Albania.
† Trieste.

the guise of a wandering monk – sure defence against the attentions of raiders or bandits, such was the universal veneration in which these anchorites were held.

At the town's main gate, Theoderic was searched and questioned by two guards in imperial-issue helmets and mail hauberks – reminders of a Roman government now defunct. Theoderic didn't object, accepting that in these times of insecurity, strangers, especially those of Germanic appearance, were understandably regarded with suspicion. Enquiring as to the whereabouts of Severinus, he was given directions but warned that the sage was dying, and might be too ill to receive him. Outside a mean dwelling in a back street he found a throng of people, some openly weeping, waiting their turn to see the great man.

'No more today,' a man in the doorway called to some visitors approaching the line. Then, spotting Theoderic's tall form among them, he added, 'Just one more,' and signalled him to join the end of the queue. Two hours later, when the last of those before the king had been ushered out, the porter, a spare man with a wise and pleasant face and the tallest forehead Theoderic had ever seen, admitted him to a bare lower room, then shut and barred the door behind him. Showing Theoderic to a settle, he seated himself on a stool.

'My master is exhausted and must rest a while, but will see you by and by, Sire,' said the doorkeeper with a smile. 'I could hardly send away such a distinguished visitor as the king of the Amal.'

'But, how—' began Theoderic, amazed.

'—did I know who you were?' finished the other. 'Not magic, I assure you, Sire. Merely observation, a faculty I've practised and developed all my life. Despite your monkish garb, your bearing, fair colouring, and blue eyes bespeak a German warrior of high rank. Among that race and class, how many have attained such a great height as yourself? You see, already the field has narrowed to a few. Your habit is worn, and ragged at the hem, besides bearing traces of salt, suggesting you have made a long journey by land and sea. Which fits the circumstances: all the world has heard that the squinting king is dead, and now waits to see what his great rival, Theoderic, will do. What more likely than that the king of the Amal should seek counsel from the sage of Noricum – as did Odovacar, on his way to Italy? The clues all point to just the one conclusion, Sire.'

'Well, when you put it like that, it seems obvious enough,' said Theoderic. He shook his head and laughed. 'Still, I'm impressed. Not many would have spotted those tell-tale signs, let alone deduced anything from them.' He went on gently, 'I'm sorry to hear that your master is sick.'

'His days draw peacefully to a close.' The man paused and blinked back tears. 'Excuse me, Sire. We should celebrate rather than grieve; he has had a long and wonderful life, full of service and achievement, and is assured of a heavenly reward. But where are my manners? You must be tired and hungry; let me offer you some repast – only poor fare, I'm afraid.'

While Theoderic gratefully partook of a bowl of thin soup, with bread and a wrinkled apple from a store-cellar, the other told him a little about himself. Named Myrddin, from Cambria in Britain, he had become, while scarcely more than a boy, an eager acolyte of Severinus when the latter visited the island as part of Germanus' second mission, during the wretched reign of Valentinian III. When the sage stayed on to help Aurelian organize the Britons' fight-back against the Saxons, Myrddin had become part of his team. He had returned with Severinus to the empire, eventually settling with him in Noricum as the old man's factotum, as well as friend.

A monk appeared on the stairs leading to the upper part of the house, and said, 'If there are any more visitors, the master will see them now.'

'Thank you, Eugippius.' Myrddin turned to Theoderic. 'Severinus' mind and memory are as sharp as ever, and you'll find him willing to listen, and discuss any topic you wish to raise. But bear in mind he's very weak, and will unselfishly overtax his strength if allowed to.'

'It will be *ave atque vale* with but two questions in between. You have my word.'

The group of monks surrounding Severinus moved to a far corner of the chamber. Theoderic seated himself on a bench beside the bed on which the patient lay, propped up by pillows. Long white hair and beard reinforced the aura of authority and dignity emanating from the strong features. Though the old man was gaunt and pale, his breathing shallow, the eyes in the kindly face glittered with a fierce intelligence.

'Greetings, Theoderic,' said the sage, in a faint yet clear voice. He seemed, by some strange mental osmosis, to be aware of Myrddin's observations to the king. 'For some time now, I've been expecting you – and at last you've made it. But only just,' he added with a wry chuckle. 'Is there anything you wish to ask me?'

'I have arrived at my own Rubicon, and am uncertain what my next course of action should be. Also, I would know what the future holds for me, if that is possible.'

'As to your first point: the death of Strabo, while appearing to have solved your problems, has in fact created one much greater. As long as Strabo lived, you were useful to the Eastern emperor as a counterbalance to the Thracian Goths. Now that he is gone, and with all the Ostrogoths united under your rule, Theoderic has become a far more serious threat to the Empire than either he or Strabo were separately, as rivals. Oh, I know that you yourself are well disposed to Rome; but the people you lead are too warlike, their energies too violent, ever to co-exist peaceably within the empire. But if you were to try to fight that empire, you would lose; it is simply too strong. So, for you, the status quo is not an option: you must remove your people from imperial soil. Where, I cannot say. Bleak tidings I'm afraid, but all I have to offer.' Severinus gave a wan smile. 'However, you are wise and strong, I think, Theoderic. I have no doubt that you will find a way.

'Now, regarding the second matter that you raised, I fear I cannot help you. My reputation has become somewhat inflated, you see. I am credited with the power of prophecy, would you believe, a power which I simply do not possess. But try Myrddin. He is said to have what they call the 'second sight' – a gift peculiar to the Celts, I believe. It comes to him only at certain times; but who knows, you might be lucky.' The old man drew a wasted hand from beneath the coverlet and laid it on Theoderic's. 'Thank you for coming, my friend. Farewell, and God's blessing be upon you.'

Saddened and dispirited, Theoderic took his leave and descended to the lower room.

'I see two eagles,' intoned Myrddin, 'one living, and one dead: the living in the East, the dead in the West.' The seer sat upright in a trance-like state, his eyes open but seeming to look at something far beyond the confines of the chamber. 'A horse comes from the land of the live eagle to that of the dead one, where he fights and kills a boar which has come there before him. After many years the horse dies, to be followed by eight others of his line. The final six of these the eagle of the East attacks, killing the last. The vision fades; there is no more.' Myrddin stirred and blinked, seeming to return to the present.

'Don't question me about what I've seen, or ask me to explain it,' he said. 'I have no memory of anything. The meaning is for you alone; in due course it will reveal itself to you.'

'That's good to know, for I confess I can make nothing of the menagerie that you've described. Eagles, boars and horses!' Theoderic shook his head, giving a wry smile. 'But I'm grateful nonetheless. Tell me, what are your plans now, Myrddin? Stay on in Noricum, perhaps, to continue the work begun by Severinus?'

'Hardly that, Sire. There is only one Severinus – "the latchet of whose shoe I am not worthy to unloose", as it says in the Gospel of St John. Besides, his work here is done. As a province of the former Western Empire, Noricum comes under the jurisdiction of Odovacar, who has proved himself a strong and able king. In the six short years of his reign, he has done more to solve the problems of the Noricans than all the petty emperors who wore the purple following the murder of Aetius. Severinus has suggested that I return to Britannia. He says that there I will find work fully to engage my hands and brain, in helping Artorius.'

'Artorius?'

'The successor to Aurelian, the *Dux Britanniae* who fell in battle against the Saxon invaders seven years ago.'

'Then I wish you good fortune, Myrddin. I fear you will need it. I've heard the Saxons are a hard and cruel foe, still clinging to the fierce old gods that we Goths abandoned a century ago for a kinder faith.'

'I've no doubt the struggle will be long and bloody, Sire. But I've had a vision of my own in which two dragons fight, a red against a white. In the end it is the red dragon which prevails.'

'Make it the symbol on your pennant, then. A red dragon fluttering in the breeze before the host – now *there's* a flag to inspire your fighters.'

FOURTEEN

If, with the Divine permission, I succeed, I shall govern in your name
Anonymous Valesianus (paraphrasing Theoderic's reply to Zeno, on being
commissioned to invade Italy), *Excerpta: pars posterior, c.* 530

From the battlements surmounting St Barbara's Gate, Julian watched
the flotilla creeping across the Bosphorus from Chrysopolis on the
Asiatic shore. Licking his lips nervously, he glanced at the array of
brazen tubes poking between the crenellations. 'These things had better
work,' he snapped at Menander, the engineer in charge of a revolutionary new weapons system intended to counter Theoderic's assault
on Constantinople.

'Don't worry, General,' replied the other calmly. 'They performed
perfectly during the trials yesterday. Those chaps have a nasty surprise
coming to them.' And he nodded towards the fleet of impounded vessels
crammed with Ostrogoths, the van of which was already grounding
on the narrow strip of shore below the city's sea-walls.

Should Menander's contraptions prove ineffective, he, Julian, would
be in serious trouble. Sourly, the general reflected on the events leading
up to this crisis – events for which he was being made to shoulder the
blame. It all went back to the confrontation between Strabo and
Theoderic at the Shipka Pass. Julian had engineered the clash, but
unfortunately it had backfired badly. The empire had paid dearly for
his miscalculation. Full of fury and resentment, his trust in the word
of Romans shattered, Theoderic had gone on the rampage, sacking
Stobi and slaughtering its defenders, then embarking on a campaign
of devastation and pillage throughout Thrace. The death of Strabo and
the consequent unification of all the Ostrogoths under Theoderic made
the latter a doubly dangerous foe. However, Zeno's attempts to mollify
Theoderic – heaping him with gold and honours, making him a 'Friend
of the Emperor', consul and *Magister Militum praesentalis*, the top post

in the army – had been largely successful. (Julian, a career soldier who had come a long way from his first appointment as a lowly decurion of horse, had been especially resentful of this last preferment. He had expected to be appointed to the post himself, but had been fobbed off with the lesser assignment of *Magister Militum per Thracias*.) And then, just when it seemed that fences had been mended with Theoderic, this wretched business of Illus had blown up.

Illus, an ambitious general and, like Zeno, an Isaurian, had at first supported Basiliscus in his short-lived usurpation ten years previously. However, realizing in time that he had backed a loser, he had switched his allegiance to Zeno – temporarily, as it transpired. In the year of Theoderic's consulship he had made his own bid for the purple, coming out openly against the Eastern Emperor. To meet this fresh threat, Zeno had turned to the old ally who had helped him regain his throne from Basiliscus: Theoderic. With a mixed force of Gothic warriors and regular Roman troops (including Thracian units under a seething Julian), Theoderic loyally set out for Isauria. The army had advanced no farther than Nicomedia, the first major city in Asia, when a messenger came secretly to Julian in camp. The man revealed that he had come from Theoderic's brother Thiudimund, with this warning: the Amal king was planning to join forces with Illus; together they would then overthrow Zeno and replace him with his rival Isaurian. Julian couldn't believe his luck. If he acted swiftly, he could bring about the humiliation, perhaps downfall, of his old adversary. At the same time, he would be ingratiating himself with the emperor, and no doubt the coveted post of *Magister Militum praesentalis* would soon be his. Minutes later, a dispatch rider was posting westward for the capital; within hours rather than days, Theoderic would surely be receiving the order – written in purple ink and bearing the emperor's seal – for his recall . . .

And so it had transpired. In bitterness and fury, Theoderic had returned to his base at Novae, whence he had vented his feelings of betrayal in a series of devastating raids on Thrace. Within these last few weeks, he had escalated his offensive by launching a major assault on Constantinople itself: pillaging suburbs, cutting the Aqueduct of Valens, the conduit to the city's main water supply, and now mounting this sea-borne attack on the capital's soft underbelly, unprotected by the great landward-facing Walls of Theodosius.

The expected imperial gratitude for divulging Theoderic's reported treachery had not been forthcoming. To Julian's consternation, when he told Zeno that the source of his information was Thiudimund, the emperor had reacted with rage and disbelief.

'Thiudimund slanders his brother – and you believe him!' Zeno had stormed. 'Good God, man, everyone knows that their relationship is poisonous, and that Thiudimund wouldn't overlook the slightest opportunity to do his brother down. Everyone but Flavius Julianus it would seem. Well, thanks to you, we've got the most powerful barbarian nation in Europe in a state of war against us. For your sake, you'd better pray that Theoderic's assault on the capital doesn't succeed.'

'Jacite!'* On Menander's command, the stubby tongues of flame wavering from the mouths of the row of tubes were suddenly transformed into roaring jets, as his team began to work the pump-handles of the reservoirs containing a mixture of bitumen, sulphur and naphtha. The leading Goths swarming up the ladders propped against the sea-walls were engulfed in a fiery blast. Human torches, they dropped, screaming, to the beach; water flung on them by their horrified companions had no effect. Relentlessly, the flames continued to burn – through skin and muscle to the very bone.

The success of the new weapon was instantaneous and total. Witnessing the fate of the first to scale the ladders, the Goths – individual warriors who, unlike Roman troops, couldn't be ordered into battle against their will – refused to press on with the attack, and the fleet retreated to the Asiatic shore. Soon afterwards, Theoderic called off the investment of the city, and marched his host back to their Moesian heartland.

'Well, thanks to your new weapon, this "Greek fire", as the Goths are calling it,' Zeno reluctantly conceded to Julian, 'we've now got a breathing-space from the attentions of Theoderic. For the moment.'

---

* 'Fire!' (Literally, 'Hurl!'; orders in the East Roman army were still given in Latin.)

The pair, together with Thalassios (now *Magister Excubitorum*, commander of the crack Isaurian unit from which was drawn the emperor's personal bodyguard), were holding a council of war in the capital's Great Palace. 'But we can't allow things to drift. After that débâcle at the Shipka Pass, and more recently his recall from the Illus expedition' – Zeno paused, to glare meaningfully at Julian – 'Theoderic's never going to trust us again. We now have to treat him as a permanent enemy – one who's going to continue blackmailing us, by beating up the Balkans, into granting more and more concessions of land, and subsidies in gold. Any suggestions, gentlemen?'

'Serenity, let's not keep on appeasing Theoderic,' declared Julian. Playing up to his nickname of 'Alexander', bestowed on account of his uncanny resemblance to the famous Macedonian, Julian was tricked out in Ancient Greek-style armour, which had the effect of making him appear both formidable and faintly ridiculous. 'The Goths, after all, are just barbarians. If we were to mobilize a big enough Roman army, we could take him on and destroy him.'

'And risk another Adrianople?' sneered Zeno. 'I think not. I suspect that, if pushed, Theoderic might prove to be as effective a tactician as Fritigern.'

'What we need is another Strabo,' put in Thalassios. 'Pitting one barbarian against another – that's a game the Romans have long been masters of.'

'"*Divide et impera*" – good point,' replied Zeno. 'Trouble is, my friend, the Ostrogoths are all united now, and, inconveniently, we haven't any rival barbarians within the empire.'

'But *outside* the empire . . .' murmured Julian, as an idea formed in his mind. Enthusiastically, he began to expound his plan.

Alone in a reception chamber, Zeno rose from his throne as Theoderic entered. 'Greetings, my dear old friend,' he declared, with a warmth that was only half simulated. Despite the bad blood that now flowed like a river between them, he liked the tall German with the frank blue eyes and thoughtful, slightly troubled expression – this man who, in the past, had proved himself a loyal Friend of Rome, and to whom, indeed, Zeno owed his throne. 'We have a proposition which may interest you,' he continued, waving the other to a chair.

'Your "propositions" I have heard before, Zeno. I would remind you that my bodyguard of loyal Goths is just outside this palace, and ten thousand of my warriors are encamped beyond the city walls.'

'Well, no one can blame you for taking precautions.' Dropping the imperial 'we', Zeno continued, 'I confess that in our dealings in the past, I may sometimes have allowed myself to be swayed by wrong advice. But let's try to put such misunderstandings behind us. I need someone to take over in Italy as my vicegerent. Who better than my friend and former ally Theoderic Amalo?'

'But, Odovacar—' exclaimed Theoderic, stunned.

'—has shown himself to be a renegade, threatening to send warriors to help Illus in Isauria, against me. Why, I can't imagine, except that power must have gone to his head. Granted, he's made a reasonable fist of running things in Italy, but he can't be allowed to flex his muscles in the East. He must therefore be removed. The last claimant to the imperial throne in the West, Julius Nepos, died eight years ago.* So, this is where you come in. Interested?'

Theoderic felt himself drowning in a tide of conflicting emotions. Vicegerent of the Eastern Emperor! It was a heady thought – next to the purple and the diadem, no higher role existed in the Roman world. His ambition to be accepted by the Roman state, an ambition which had been cruelly manipulated and thwarted in the past, would be fulfilled beyond his wildest dreams. And why had Zeno thrown in that remark about Julius Nepos, unless to suggest to Theoderic that the imperial throne was still vacant, and that therefore . . . ? Resolutely, he banned his thoughts from pursuing such intoxicating speculation – for the moment, anyway. Then, inside his mind, Theoderic seemed to hear the voice of Timothy urging caution: 'He's using you, Deric, employing the old, old trick of setting barbarian against barbarian – finally to rid the Eastern Empire of those troublesome Ostrogoths. Odovacar's just an excuse; the Scirian's posture over Illus is little more than sword-rattling, a reminder that, in the sphere of power politics, he can't be overlooked. Anyway, what's the vicegerency? An empty title which it costs Zeno nothing to bestow. A fiction devised to preserve

---

* In 480 – i.e., *after* the deposition of the last Western Emperor, but still leaving open the possibility that the throne could, in theory at least, be occupied again.

the comforting illusion that the "one and Indivisible Empire" still continues in the West, under the aegis of the Eastern Emperor. Remember, Deric, the ABC I taught you when dealing with the Romans. A: accept nothing; B: believe nobody; C: check everything.'

But the pull of Rome (which also held out a solution to the problem of his remaining within the empire, which Severinus had pointed out to him) proved too strong. Seduced by glittering images of semi-imperial status – riding in state through the venerable City; saluted by senators from ancient noble families; acclaimed by throngs of cheering Romans . . . He heard himself reply, 'I accept.'

Then, unbidden, the opening words of Myrddin's prophecy rang in his head: 'A horse comes from the land of the live eagle to that of the dead one, where he fights and kills a boar that has come there before him.' The meaning was suddenly clear. The eagle, the enduring symbol of Rome. The live one – the Empire of the East; the dead, the now defunct Western Empire. A horse, long the totem of the Ostrogoths. A boar, the motif of the royal house of the Sciri. The Ostrogoths would come from the Eastern Empire to Italy, where they would defeat Odovacar. Wonder tinged with dread swept over Theoderic.

The sheer immensity of the enterprise to which he was now committed began to dawn on him. The task was staggering in its implications: the migration not just of the warrior host, but of a whole people, to the number of two hundred thousand souls, involving the organization of transport, food supplies, equipment, planning and following a route of nearly a thousand miles through sometimes hostile tribal territory and difficult terrain. The challenge called for someone with the vision and authority of a Moses. Thus far in his career, he had proved himself a successful warlord: good at plundering, sacking cities, holding his own (just) against rival Goths, and Romans – hardly a glittering record. Now, at thirty-four, the call upon his leadership was of uncharted, infinitely greater dimensions. Would he prove equal to the test?

PART II

EXODUS
AD 488–493

FIFTEEN

*Cold is the way to Miming, hidden and perilous, and it lies over icy
mountains and frozen seas*
Saxo Grammaticus, *Gesta Danorum, c.* 1195

In his dream, Theoderic saw the ancestors of his people, the Gothones,
in countless galleys crossing the Mare Suevicum* from Scandia – a cold
land of fiords, forests and tall mountains – to Germania. There, under
a great leader, Filimer, they began the long, long journey that ended
only when they reached the northern shores of the Pontus Euxinus.†
In two great clans, the Balthi, and the Amali of divine descent, they
travelled with their herds and wagons, between the valleys of the
Viadrus and the Vistula, across a mighty watershed, and so to the great
southward-draining rivers, the Pyretus, the Tyras, the Borysthenes and
the Tanais,‡ that led them to the Euxine.

That had been a time of gods and heroes, long ages before their
kinsman, the missionary Ulfilas, persuaded the Gothones to adopt the
faith of gentle Christos, a 'king' who sacrificed himself not only for his
people (who rejected him), but for all mankind. Folk then believed in
Odin the mighty, in Balder the good and gentle, and in evil Loki who
brought about the death of Balder, and so hastened the coming of
Ragnarok, the dreadful day when gods and evil beings shall destroy
each other, and when Yggdrasil, the Tree of Life and Fate, shall be
consumed by fire along with Earth itself. In those far-off days, a hero
was the only man who mattered, brave deeds alone worthy of
recounting, and a king's self-sacrifice for his people the noblest act a
leader could perform. And then...

And then had come the Huns, thought Theoderic, awaking. Like a

* The Baltic Sea.
† The Black Sea.
‡ The Oder, Vistula, Pruth, Dniester, Dnieper and Don.

storm of angry locusts, the *Hunnensturm* had burst upon them from the east. True nomads, unlike the farming Goths, the Scythian* horse-archers – squat, powerfully built men with yellow skins and flat Oriental faces – had conquered or driven out all who stood in their path. The Balthi, who later became the Visigoths, had sought refuge within the Roman Empire; the Amal had stayed, becoming subjects of the Asiatic horde. In a heroic gesture, redolent of the ancient tradition of kingly sacrifice, Ermanaric, the Amal king, had taken his own life, hoping thus to placate the old gods, who might then help his people prevail against their oppressors. If so, the hope was vain, and the Amal – as the nation of the Ostrogoths – were destined to become the ally of Attila in his campaign against West Rome. Following the Hun king's death (which occurred the year before his own birth, Theoderic recalled) and the disintegration of his empire, the Amal had remained for a time in Pannonia, the territory allotted to them by their Hun masters. And the rest, thought the Amal king, is history – my own and theirs, intertwined.

His dream had been extraordinarily vivid and was slow to fade; Theoderic experienced an unaccountable, sharp longing for the home-land of his ancestors – those icy mountains, fiords and forests he had seen in his sleeping thoughts: a fitting stage for mighty deeds of valour, from where fallen heroes were translated to Valhalla. But perhaps such feelings were nothing more than childish nostalgia. Could the things his forebears had seen and felt really be transferred across the genera-tions to himself? Anyway, was not Italy, sunny, rich and fertile, a more appealing vision? Of course it was, Theoderic told himself sternly, banishing northern fantasies to a dark corner of his mind. This was the real, the Roman world, where a man's status was measured in wealth and property, a world which had no place for gods or heroes.

He shaved (a Roman custom he refused to abandon), dressed and, munching a hunk of bread dipped in wine, left the house in Novae he had commandeered. Resentful Romans making way for the tall German, Theoderic strode through well-paved streets to the Amal camp outside the city walls. Here, preparations were under way against the day of departure for the great expedition. Wagons, gear and

* Scythia: an imprecise term, roughly equivalent to the steppes of Central Asia.

weapons were being furbished, carts were bringing in the harvest (Theoderic had promised Zeno not to live off the land while travelling within the empire – a promise which, because of the residual affection and respect he harboured towards the old fox, he knew he would keep) – a scene replicated countless times throughout all lands assigned to the Amal in Moesia Secunda and Dacia Ripensis.

Suddenly, a huge weight of depression seemed to settle on the king's shoulders. He must say goodbye to the old freebooting past that had occupied his youth and young manhood – a colourful past of skirmishes and raids, when pitting his wits against Zeno and Strabo had made life seem at times like an exciting game. Granted, a life not lacking in hardship and privation, but with an edge and zest which would surely be lacking in the years that stretched ahead. Middle age beckoned, and with it the massive responsibility of getting his people to Italy: a prospect full of toil and tribulation, with each day presenting a remorseless tally of problems to be solved, grievances assuaged, and plans formulated. Even when they reached journey's end, there was Odovacar to be dealt with. The bold Scirian, who had risen to be king of Italy through cunning and resolve, was hardly the man to surrender his realm meekly to another. In a trial of strength between them, could Theoderic be sure the Ostrogoths would prevail? He could give no guarantee, he admitted. Perhaps the two barbarian peoples would end up destroying each other? Which of course might be the result that Zeno had planned all along – a necessary prelude to bringing back Italy within the imperial fold.

He longed for Timothy, the steadfast and resourceful friend who always knew ways to lighten his blackest moods. But Timothy had gone to Olbia on the Euxine, hopefully to bring back one Callisthenes, a famous merchant with a trading empire throughout Scythia, who should be able to provide expert advice regarding provisioning and transport for the epic trek.

Looking up, Theoderic felt his heart sink. Bounding towards him was young Frederick, the son of the Rugian king whom Odovacar had captured and murdered, after annihilating many of his people. Theoderic sighed; like all relations between the empire and Germanic peoples, the Rugian Question was complex, with far-reaching repercussions. He reminded himself of the facts. To counter Odovacar's threat to support

Illus in Isauria, Zeno had enlisted the Rugians – whose territory adjoined Noricum – to block any force the Scirian king might send eastwards. Odovacar's response had been swift and brutal; descending in strength on the Rugian kingdom, he had wreaked devastation and slaughter on such a scale as to destroy it utterly. Frederick, however, had escaped, and with a band of pro-Ostrogothic followers had managed to join up with Theoderic in Moesia, where he had offered his services in the inevitable campaign to wrest Italy from Odovacar.

Theoderic liked the young Rugian, with his open friendly manner and boyish enthusiasm; but at this moment, sunk as he was in gloomy introspection, hearty Frederick was the last person he wished to encounter. Forcing a smile, he greeted the prince with a polite, if unenthusiastic, 'Good morning.'

'And the same to you, Sire,' boomed the young man. He glanced about him at the busy scene with an approving eye. 'Looks as if we'll soon be ready to begin the march.'

'Just as soon as the harvest's in,' agreed the king. 'We need to break the back of the journey before the onset of winter.' Now that Frederick *was* here, Theoderic decided he might as well make use of him by picking his brains as to the route. In his flight from Odovacar, the young Rugian must have covered virtually the same ground that the expedition would be following for the first half of the journey.

'Nothing to worry about, Sire, until we reach the Ulca,'* replied the Rugian in response to Theoderic's query about possible hazards. 'That's the river forming the boundary between the Empire and Pannonia.'

'Pannonia, the Amals' old homeland,' observed Theoderic. 'But that was many years ago. We abandoned it to become . . . "guests", let us say, of the emperor.'

'"Guests" – I like it,' chuckled Frederick. 'Well, Pannonia's since been taken over by the Gepids, a brutish bunch allied to Odovacar. Their orders were to wipe out me and my Rugians following our escape from the attentions of the last-named gentleman. There not being many of us, we managed to detour round them undetected. No way can you hope to do the same, unfortunately, Sire. But my guess is you won't

---

* River Vuka. The town of Vukovar has become familiar from the 1990s' Balkan conflict. On 18 November 1991, it fell to the Serbs after enduring a terrible siege.

have any trouble; you'll only be passing through their territory, after all. They'd be mad to pick a fight with so formidable a nation as the Ostrogoths.'

'Let us hope you're right.'

SIXTEEN

And the children of Israel . . . about six hundred thousand on
foot . . . and flocks and herds, even very much cattle . . . went out
from the land of Egypt
Anonymous, *The Bible: Exodus, c.* 900 BC
(referring to an event some four hundred years earlier)

'You expect to get to Italy in *that?*' screamed the merchant, adminis-
tering a savage kick to the side of the wagon. His single eye glittering
with simulated rage, the diminutive Greek advanced towards the
vehicle's owner, a huge, tow-headed Goth, who backed away in alarm.
'Well, I, Callisthenes of Olbia, whose wagons have forded the Borysthenes
and traversed the Altai Shan,* say that you'll be lucky if this apology
for a donkey cart gets as far as the Alps, which it stands as much chance
of crossing as an icicle in Hades. Those spokes – they're oak, hard but
dense – like your head, my friend. They should be of ash, tough yet
springy, yielding instead of cracking when the going's rocky.'

Enjoying the performance from the sidelines were Theoderic and
Timothy. 'The man's a treasure,' chuckled the king. 'Remind me how
you found him.'

'He's from Olbia, an old Greek colony and trading-centre on the
opposite side of the Euxine from Anatolia – my home turf, you'll
remember. Everyone in Anatolia – a Greek sphere of influence since
long before Alexander – knows of Callisthenes the famous trader. He
claims in his youth to have guided Attila to the shores of Dalai Nor,†
to confer with the seer Wu Tze.'

On meeting the tiny Greek, who was one-eyed, aged and voluble –
especially concerning his own alleged exploits – Theoderic had not at
first been impressed, being inclined to dismiss him as a bombastic

---

* A range of mountains in central Mongolia, to the north of China's Great Wall.
† The 'Holy Sea' of the Mongols, Lake Baikal.

blowhard. However, within an hour of Callisthenes' arrival at Novae, the king changed his mind. Without waiting for explanations or introductions, the little merchant had begun buzzing round the camp like an angry gadfly, examining wagons and draught oxen, poking into stores, quizzing Goths in their own tongue . . . After completing an exhaustive inspection of the site, he had delivered his verdict.

'Half your transport isn't fit for purpose, King,' he snapped (eschewing the usual respectful 'Sire'). 'Many of your oxen are in poor condition or require their hooves treated; gear's often defective or lacking; a lot of grain and foodstuffs badly stored – which means it'll spoil. I could go on. All in all your expedition's anything but ready.'

'But half our lives, we Goths have been on the move.' Theoderic protested mildly. 'So far we've managed to cope, without—'

'Oh, yes – inside the Eastern Empire!' cut in the little Greek, with a dismissive snort. 'Good roads, tamed countryside. What happens when you reach what used to be the empire's Western half? Roads in disrepair, tillage and pasture reverting to wasteland, above all the crossing of the eastern Alps to face. A journey of a thousand miles, part of it over some of the hardest terrain in the whole of Europe. I tell you this, King: if your transport and provisioning are defective, you may not make it.'

'What must I do?'

'Nothing. Put me in charge, and be willing to see that my instructions are carried out – to the letter, mind.'

'To the letter.' With difficulty, Theoderic suppressed a smile.

Like a miniature tornado, Callisthenes swept through the encampments in Moesia Secunda and Dacia Ripensis, the two provinces assigned to the Ostrogoths: observing, questioning, assessing, taking notes. His lightning tour completed, he returned to Novae, armed with a lengthy list of Things to Be Done. First, transport. To be 'fit for purpose' (the merchant's favourite expression), each wagon must be eighteen feet long by four wide, the body constructed of hard-wearing timber such as oak or hornbeam. The wheels (two pairs, bound with iron tyres fitted when white-hot so as to shrink and grip securely, the front ones with pivoted axle for steering) must be of tough, flexible wood such as ash or some species of walnut;

connected to the front axle, the drag pole must be sturdy and long enough to inspan twelve draught oxen by a system of yokes, yoke-pins, and rawhide ropes. Attached to the body by iron staples, there would be green-wood boughs to support a canvas tent against hot sun or foul weather. At the front there should be a large chest stretching the width of the wagon, providing seating for the driver and storage space for personal belongings, also iron hooks inside and underneath the body to support pots and pans, tools and other heavy gear. Stores must include sacks of flour and grain (plus hand querns for milling) and bags of dried meat – sufficient to feed each family as far as the edge of the Empire; also drums of fat to grease the wheels hubs, spare ropes, yokes, yoke and linch-pins; rolls of canvas and rawhide for repairs; bars of iron; tools such as augers, spokeshaves, chisels, tongs, hammers, drawing-knives to trim hooves; spare horseshoes (for those wealthy enough to own a mount), and a hundred other items. All livestock (especially draught animals) to be rigorously examined and if necessary treated, to ensure they were strong and healthy enough to cope with the rigours of the long trek.

Regarding implementation of these specifications, Callisthenes was utterly inflexible. '"Intolerance" is my middle name,' he told the king. 'To get your people to their destination safely and securely, you can't afford any weak links in the chain. One single broken wheel or axle could bring the expedition grinding to a halt.' Fortunately, a seemingly inexhaustible stream of funds from the Treasury in Constantinople ensured that even the poorest Gothic household could afford to meet Callisthenes' stringent requirements. (This heightened Theoderic's suspicion that Zeno was only too willing to part with however much gold it took, to be rid of 'guests' whose presence had become unwelcome.)

Regarding weaponry, Callisthenes had nothing to say, declaring that he was a trader, not an arms dealer. Theoderic had few worries on that score. As a warrior nation, the Ostrogoths were probably equipped as well as or better than any other tribes they might encounter. The great mass of the host, some forty thousand warriors, was armed with spears; a few – leaders or the wealthy – might also possess helmets, swords, and ring-mail hauberks.

With the last of the harvest in, and all items on Callisthenes' list of Things to Be Done ticked off, the great migration finally began on the

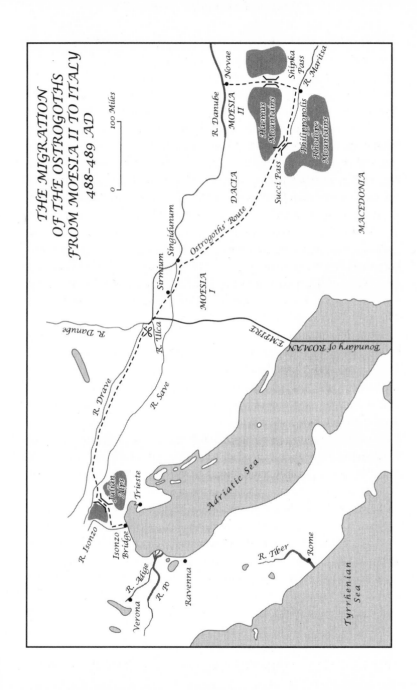

THE MIGRATION
OF THE OSTROGOTHS
FROM MOESIA II TO ITALY
488–489 AD

0 — 100 Miles

last day of September in the year of the consuls Dynamius and Sifidius.*
Headed by Theoderic's party, then Frederick and his Rugians, the wagon
train set off in sections of a hundred vehicles, there being two hundred
sections altogether. In charge of each section was a wagonmaster, handpicked by Theoderic and Timothy for reliability and leadership.
Conspicuous for not being chosen to fulfil such a role was Thiudimund.
(Theoderic's suspicions of treachery on his brother's part had been aroused
too many times for the king to risk entrusting him with such a key
responsibility.) Predictably, Thiudimund had protested, then, his brother
remaining adamant, had raged and sulked, but in the end been forced
reluctantly to accept the king's decision.

Like a long, long snake, the column of wagons wound slowly south,
covering ten to fifteen miles per day. This first part of the journey was
over familiar terrain: through the Shipka Pass to the Maritsa Valley,
where the train picked up the great Roman highway leading them west
to Philippopolis; then north-west through the Succi Pass, scene of
Theoderic's ambush by Strabo; and after a further three hundred miles
to Singidunum, where, all those years ago, he had defeated Babai.
Knowing that in all likelihood he was viewing these scenes for the last
time, Theoderic felt a keen nostalgia as the train rolled steadily north-
westwards through the diocese of Dacia. Ablaze with the reds and golds
of autumn, a succession of achingly beautiful landscapes moved slowly
past: forests, majestic mountains, lakes and waterfalls. Beyond
Singidunum the scenery changed abruptly, rolling hills clad in woods
of oak and chestnut giving place to tillage and meadow, as the Roman
road led them down into the broad valley of the Danubius.

Some fifty miles beyond Sirmium, as the wagon train, with supplies
now running out, approached the River Ulca (where the empire ended),
outriders, who had been scouting ahead, came galloping back.

'We can go no further, Sire,' gasped the leading scout. 'The way is
blocked. Gepids, Sire – they've barricaded the far bank of the Ulca.'

* 488.

SEVENTEEN

Set ye Uriah in the forefront of the hottest battle . . . that he may be smitten, and die
Anonymous, *The Bible: Samuel, c.* 500 BC
(referring to an incident some five hundred years earlier)

Spotting Theoderic, who had ridden out to scout their position, the Gepids broke into a chorus of derisive catcalls. Contrary to Frederick's optimistic prediction, it was obvious that the Gepids were not putting on a show of bravado, but were determined to deny passage to the Ostrogoths. The king's heart sank. The Gepids were entrenched in force behind a system of barricades surmounting the steep western bank of the Ulca, below which the river flowed sluggishly, more marsh than stream, its course delineated by a series of pools and reed-beds – the worst possible approach from which to mount an assault. Half concealed as they were behind their defences, it was hard to estimate the Gepids' strength, but Theoderic thought they must number many thousands of hostile warriors. It was going to be extremely difficult to dislodge them from such a strong position. But unless they were removed the consequences for the Ostrogoths would be serious. With food supplies virtually exhausted, any delay would spell starvation.

What on earth had caused the Gepids to get fired up? Theoderic wondered, as he cantered back to the encampment through pasture overlooked by vineyards. To put on such a show of force, they must consider the Ostrogoths a threat – which made no sense at all. By now, all the world must know that the Ostrogoths' objective was Italy and not Pannonia; armed confrontation must inevitably result in a bloody battle with enormous casualties. Why would the Gepids risk that, when all they had to do was wait until the Ostrogoths had passed beyond their territory?

*

97

On reaching the Amal camp, Theoderic was accosted by a concerned-looking Timothy.

'Your brother, Deric – have you seen him recently?'

'Well, no, but what of it? A day or so back, he rode off on his own, as he often does. Said something about a spot of hunting.'

'Hunting?' Timothy shook his head. 'Does that seem likely? Since Singidunum it's been all fields and vineyards. Normally, I suppose one wouldn't pick up on a little inconsistency like that. It's just that . . .' Timothy paused, and looked uncomfortable.

'Get to the point, man.'

'It may be nothing – I wouldn't wish to stir up trouble needlessly between yourself and your brother. But last night when, as is my habit, I was snooping round the wagon lines – you know me: "To see and not be seen" etc. – I spotted Thiudimund sneaking back into camp from the direction of the Ulca. I use the word "sneaking" deliberately; he was leading his horse and clearly anxious not to be observed. But I thought no more about it – until I heard that the Gepids had blocked the route ahead.'

Theoderic's brain whirled. Suddenly it all made sense. Singidunum, the Shipka Pass, Illus, and now the Gepids. Past suspicions crystallized into certainty: Thiudimund had made contact with the Gepids and told them something. Whatever it was, it had had the effect of turning them from passive unfriendliness to active hostility.

'Thank you, Timothy. You were right to report this.' And the king strode off towards his brother's wagon.

'You will tell me about your meeting with the Gepids,' Theoderic demanded. Concealed from outside view within a clump of alders beside the Danubius, the brothers faced each other. Something in the king's grim expression had prevented Thiudimund from arguing, when summoned to accompany his brother to this isolated spot.

'What meeting?' Thiudimund protested.

An ungovernable fury swept over Theoderic. 'Liar!' he roared, and he sent his brother spinning to the ground, as the back of his hand smashed into his cheek. Mastering himself with a huge effort, he went on, 'The truth, brother – or I swear you will not leave this grove alive.'

'I told you, I was hunting,' blustered Thiudimund, picking himself up. Then, something in his brother's look made him change his stance. 'All right, all right,' he pleaded, as the king drew a dagger and advanced towards him. 'I – I'll tell you everything.'

It all came out, the words tumbling pell-mell from the lips of the terrified man, in his haste to avert Theoderic's threat. At Singidunum, he had deliberately failed to give the signal for the diversion to begin; he had colluded with the Romans to bring about the confrontation with Strabo at the Shipka Pass; he had sent a message to Zeno misinforming him that Theoderic planned to join Illus in a coup to overthrow him; and, yes, he had secretly visited Thrapstila, king of the Gepids, warning him that the Ostrogoths intended to make war on his people. The reason: the Gepids had allied themselves with Odovacar, the foe of Theoderic and the oppressor of those friends of the Ostrogoths, the Rugians.

'I'll do anything – anything you want – to make amends, brother,' babbled Thiudimund when he had exhausted his list of confessions. 'Only spare my life.'

'I will not stoop to take your worthless life,' sighed the king, regarding him with weary contempt. 'But others may. Tomorrow, you will lead the Forlorn Hope in an attempt to breach the Gepids' barricades. It's unlikely you'll survive. But, no matter if you live or die, you'll be regarded as a hero.' He gave a bitter smile. 'Never say your brother is ungenerous.'

About to ask Thiudimund what had prompted his treachery, the king desisted. What would be the point? The reasons were obvious: resentment fuelled by jealousy, stoking up malicious spite which had spiralled out of control.

Their ranks thinning steadily as they came within javelin range, the Forlorn Hope, headed by the tall figure of Thiudimund, struggled through the boggy shallows of the Ulca towards its western bank. Whatever the risk, there was never any shortage of volunteers for this most dangerous of roles, spearheading an attack on the enemy's defence in order to create a weak point which those who followed could exploit. With half their numbers down, the Hope reached the father side, then, stabbing and hacking like men possessed, began to clear a passage through the mass of Gepids who swarmed to meet them. A few, a very few, made it to the top of the bank.

Heading the host across the stream, Theoderic watched the swirling knot of warriors – a chaotic mêlée of struggling bodies and flashing blades – surge back and forth before the barricades. Then, suddenly, a gap appeared in the defences: the Hope had broken through! A great cheer burst from the Ostrogoths as they waded the last few yards to the shore. Knowing that death from hunger would soon begin to harvest their people unless they prevailed, and inspired by the example of their king – a heroic figure in the gilded Roman armour that was Zeno's parting gift – they fought grimly step by step up a slope grown slippery with blood. Cutting a gory swathe through the press of foes with sweeps of his great sword, Theoderic formed the tip of an advancing wedge which gradually forced a salient in the Gepid line. A final push and they had gained the crest, then in a bloody rush the barricades were carried. Perhaps daunted by their opponents' ferocious valour, the Gepids broke and fled, to be cut down in their thousands by the triumphant Ostrogoths. Among the slain was later found the corpse of Thrapstila, their king.

Also recovered was the body of Thiudimund, pierced by twenty great wounds, all to the fore. As befitted a hero, he was buried in his armour with his weapons by his side, the host filing past his open grave to honour this most valiant warrior who had secured them victory against the Gepids. It was ironic, thought Theoderic without rancour, that his brother's glory should eclipse his own. In dying a royal hero who had sacrificed himself for his people, Thiudimund had exemplified, like Ermanaric before him, the highest tradition of the legends of his race. At least in death, the king reflected, he had made a kind of reparation.

Theoderic himself had crossed a great watershed in his life, he realized. By masterminding the migration of his people, and taking them successfully beyond their journey's halfway point, he had proved himself a great leader. And his victory against the Gepids had achieved for him the status of a hero king. When he faced Odovacar in the spring, it would be at the head of a united, strong and confident nation.

*

With supplies replenished from the Gepids' harvest – enough to see them through wintering in camp – the train pushed on up the valley of the wide, slow-moving Dravus,* through a gentle landscape of low hills crowned by woods, with vineyards terracing their lower slopes. The frosts of early December were riming the grass in the mornings, when the wagons parked for the final time against the crossing of the Alps in spring.

* The River Drava, in modern Slovenia.

EIGHTEEN

Appoint the day and field of battle
Message of Clovis to Syagrius, 487

At the time when Theoderic was laying siege to Constantinople, Myrddin, true to his resolve to join Artorius, was nearing the city of Augusta Suessionum* in north-east Gaul, en route to Britannia. Armed with both safe-conduct and letter of introduction from Odovacar (who, cherishing warm memories of his meeting with Severinus, was pleased to help his acolyte), Myrddin had travelled from Noricum through northern Italy to the adjoining kingdom of the Visigoths. Although their powerful king, Euric, had died three years previously, to be succeeded by his infant son Alaric, the friendly relations established by Odovacar during Euric's reign still obtained. Accordingly, Myrddin was able to travel in perfect security up the valley of the Rhodanus,† then west and north through Arvernum to the Liger,‡ which river formed the boundary between the Visigothic realm and that of the Salian Franks – that is, Gaul to the north of the Liger.

Within this recent and somewhat tenuous kingdom existed a surviving island of *romanitas*, the area corresponding to the former province of Belgica Secunda. This territory was ruled by one Syagrius, a Roman landowner who had revived the province's name, and whose subjects – both Roman and Frankish – had accorded him the astonishing and incongruous title of 'Rex Romanorum'. It was the capital city of this 'king' that Myrddin was approaching. The guards at the main gate, wearing imperial-issue armour, after scrutinizing his documents waved him through, with directions to the *praetorium*.§

* Soissons.
† The Rhône.
‡ The Loire.
§ Headquarters building – either a palace or municipal offices.

Myrddin proceeded through well-maintained streets to an imposing public building where, after waiting his turn in a queue, he was ushered into a pillared council chamber. Swathed in an archaic toga, the affable-looking man reclining on a couch waved Myrddin to a chair.

'Britain – bad choice,' declared Syagrius after scanning Myrddin's papers. 'Place is crawling with those ghastly Saxons. Unlike Gaul, it'll never be reoccupied by Rome.' He smiled, charmingly. 'I see Odovacar describes you as a healer. In that case, why not stay on here? Medics are always welcome – especially as it looks as though I'll have to use force to see off this young puppy Clovis. Calls himself king of the Franks, after taking over – at the age of fifteen! – from his father Childeric, who died six years ago. Childeric knew his place – never aspired to anything more than client-king status, even after the Imperium Romanum in the West came to an end eleven years ago. A *temporary* end,' he added, rising and beginning to pace the mosaic flooring energetically.

'Temporary? Surely not, Highness.'

'"O ye of little faith"!' exclaimed the other. Whirling round, he pointed an admonitory finger at Myrddin. 'Look how long Sidonius held out in Arverna – and that was against the mighty Euric. Now that Euric's gone, who's to say it won't fall into Roman hands again? Look at my own fiefdom, Belgica Secunda; no reason why other Roman magnates shouldn't follow my example.' Syagrius resumed his pacing. 'Zeno's just waiting till the time is ripe, to replace Odovacar with a Western emperor. That should have been Julius Nepos, of course – still the legitimate, if exiled emperor when he was assassinated seven years ago, after Odovacar had taken over. Plenty of candidates waiting in the wings.' He paused in his perambulations, then went on in musing tones, 'Should the offer come my way, I wouldn't be averse myself to donning the purple.' He turned his head sideways to Myrddin's gaze. 'My profile – suitable for a new imperial coinage, do you think?'

Murmuring polite platitudes, Myrddin acknowledged to himself that the other's profile – eagle nose, lofty forehead, determined chin – did indeed add up to everyone's ideal image of a Roman emperor. What drove the man? Syagrius, son of Aegidius, a general of the great Aetius who had defeated Attila at the Catalaunian Fields, was living in a fantasy world, he decided. All this talk of 'reoccupation by Rome', 'client kings', 'Belgica Secunda', 'donning the purple', 'new imperial coinage', suggested that the man was acting out a dream in which the barbarians were a temporary nuisance who, in the course of time, would surely be removed. Everyone – except Syagrius, it seemed – knew that the Western Empire was finished,* a fact tacitly acknowledged by the Eastern Emperor, Zeno, by not contesting Odovacar's usurpation. (Although Odovacar had seemed to hedge his bets at first, by having Julius Nepos' head stamped on his coinage.) Even Sidonius, who had heroically defended Arverna against the Visigoths, had accepted that the game was up, and was now living amicably among the barbarians he had once despised.

During the next few days, while enjoying Syagrius' hospitality (Myrddin was waiting to join an armed party who would escort him to Gesoriacum† on the coast when they went there to pick up supplies), the Briton's sense of inhabiting a strange dream world grew ever stronger. In 'Belgica Secunda', Syagrius had succeeded in creating a Roman mini-state which somehow worked. Everything ran on Roman lines: administration, taxes, law. Even the Frankish war-bands who, under Childeric, had penetrated the region in a rather haphazard way, seemed to have accepted the authority of their Roman 'governor'. They were apparently happy to be judged by Roman rather than by Salic law – an exception to the situation obtaining in the rest of Gaul, where barbarians and Romans adhered strictly to their own separate legal codes.

   The glue holding the whole tenuous fabric of the 'province' together appeared to be nothing more substantial than charisma – a quality Syagrius possessed in overflowing measure. Like Aetius before him, he had the ability to establish a rapport with barbarians, chatting easily with the Franks in their own tongue, tempering their natural ferocity with tact and humour, and persuading them to integrate peacefully as part of the Roman *'communitas'*. Under the mild and just regime established by Syagrius, whose vast estates covered much of the area

---

* It wasn't – quite. In the next century, much of it, though not Gaul, *was* restored (temporarily) by the generals of the Eastern Emperor, Justinian (see Notes).
† Boulogne.

he claimed to rule, the machinery of society ran smoothly: the economy flourished, roads and public buildings were kept in good repair, and law and order maintained – with the help of veterans from the old Roman Field Army of Gaul.

It was all *too* perfect, Myrddin told himself. Sooner, rather than later, the bubble had to burst. And in fact, on the very day he departed with the 'cohort', there came a hint of cold reality waiting to intrude. Syagrius was visited by a messenger from Clovis, bearing a challenge to meet the Frankish king in battle on a day and at a place of Syagrius' choosing. The latter seemed to relish the prospect, cheerfully remarking to Myrddin that he would teach young Clovis, an upstart scarcely out of his teens, a lesson he wouldn't forget. He would show the presumptuous pipsqueak that a disciplined Roman force was more than a match for a rabble of disorderly barbarians.

'Sin', sin', sin'-dex'-sin',' chanted the *campidoctores*,* as – with ancient titles resurrected from the glory days of Rome, Syagrius' 'legion' marched to meet Clovis's Franks outside Remi.† The force, arrayed in antique ridge helmets and ring-mail hauberks dug out of storage and patched up, and with dragon standards streaming, made a brave show. Someone had even managed to find a battered old legionary eagle; now, burnished till it gleamed like gold, it swayed proudly at the head of the column. In the van, together with his senior 'centurions' and 'tribunes' – young Gallo-Roman aristocrats – rode the 'legate', Syagrius, looking every inch the Roman general.

The mood, as evidenced by the soldiers' singing as they marched, was confident, even carefree. Training in tactics and marching evolutions had been thorough; weapons and equipment were sound – certainly superior to those of the Franks, who mostly went into battle unarmoured and armed only with spears. The older officers alone, many of them old sweats who had seen service under Aetius against Burgundians and Huns, harboured reservations. They knew how the guts shrivelled up with fear when you faced a screaming wave of barbarians, and only the

---

* Sin' – sinister ('left'); dex' – dexter ('right'). *Campidoctores* were drill-sergeants.
† Reims – where Clovis along with his chief followers was baptised in 496 as a *Catholic*, not an Arian, Christian, an act which did much to reconcile the Catholic Gallo-Romans to Frankish rule.

knowledge that disciplined steadiness would usually guarantee survival and victory kept you from throwing down your shield and turning tail. If enthusiasm alone were enough to win battles, a Roman victory was assured. If. The young Gallo-Romans, mostly *coloni** and artisans, who had flocked to the standard of Syagrius were commendably eager. What they lacked was that important element, experience. Only the test of battle would discover if that lack would prove fatal – or otherwise.

The three-deep Roman line presented a formidable appearance: an ordered mass of armoured men, protected by a triple wall of shields topped by a frieze of glittering spear-blades. Facing their opponents across a rolling plain, some of Clovis's veterans who had fought against Rome in the old days, and seen a Frankish charge break in red ruin against a Roman line, were for caution. 'Better, Sire, to make honourable terms with Syagrius now,' one greybeard warrior advised the young king, 'than see many thousand widows made this day.'

'There's just one thing you're forgetting, old Look-before-you-leap,' smiled Clovis, clapping the aged veteran affectionately on the shoulder. 'The last of Rome's armies was disbanded years ago. Those fellows over there may look like Roman soldiers, but they're not. They're unblooded boys dressed up in Roman armour, who'll break and scatter when we charge them. Mark my words.'

And so it proved. Before the tide of yelling fair-haired giants had closed with them, panic had begun to spread among Syagrius' troops. In twos and threes at first, then in groups, they dropped their weapons, turned and ran. In vain the veterans railed, pleaded, threatened; there were simply not enough of them to stop the rot. With horrifying speed the army lost cohesion, then suddenly disintegrated and became a fleeing rabble, to be cut down in their thousands by the pursuing and triumphant Franks.

Being mounted, Syagrius escaped. Making his way to Tolosa, he threw himself on the mercy of the Visigoths. Had Euric still reigned, he might well have afforded the 'Rex Romanorum' protection. But the Council of Regency who ruled the kingdom in the name of his son, the boy-king Alaric, was divided and irresolute. They hesitated to

---

* Tenant farmers; peasants.

offend Clovis, whose name was already inspiring respect, even fear, far beyond the boundaries of Frankish territory. When Clovis threatened war, the Goths surrendered Syagrius to the Franks, who promptly had him executed.

Thus was extinguished the last flickering light of Imperial Rome in Gaul.

NINETEEN

In this year Aelle and Cissa besieged Andredesceaster and slew all the
inhabitants; there was not even one Briton left alive there
The Anglo-Saxon Chronicle, ninth century (the entry for 491)

Scudding through a choppy Fretum Gallicum,* the little ship, with a
stiff sou-wester blowing on the quarter, approached the landing-stage
of Anderida† the last of the forts of the Saxon Shore to remain in British
hands, thus providing the only safe entry to Britannia along her southern
shore. Beyond the pebble beach loomed the fort's mighty ramparts,
studded with huge projecting bastions ribbed with bonding courses of
red tile.

The fort's main gate opened, and a stream of people, mostly anxious-
looking families clutching possessions, crowded on to the jetty. 'Poor
devils,' the skipper muttered to Myrddin, as the sailors prepared to lower
the gangplank. 'Refugees from the Saxons, hoping to re-settle in
Aremorica. Best I can do is dump them in Gesoriacum; after that they're
on their own. Some of them may make it – if they can avoid being killed
or enslaved by Franks en route. 'Course, they'll have to pay me. Most
do in kind, occasionally in coins, but there are precious few of those left
in Britannia – mostly old nummi of Honorius, from the last issue ever
sent.' Turning from Myrddin, he roared, 'Get back there!' as the gangplank thumped on the pier and a swarm of desperate passengers tried
to rush it – to be beaten back by burly seamen wielding belaying-pins.

Saddened by the sight, Myrddin, clad in his monk's black robe, with
satchel over shoulder and walking-staff in hand, hurried ashore and
sought admission at the gate before it closed.

*

* Straits of Dover.
† Pevensey.

'Keep to the ridgeways* and you'll be all right,' Meurig, the fort's commander, told Myrddin. They were in the former's quarters in one of the twin towers surmounting the main gateway. The commander – a tough-looking grizzled veteran – was in charge of a four-hundred-strong garrison, the Numerus Abulcorum. This was the island's last surviving unit of *limitanei*, the frontier troops left behind when Rome's Field Army of Britannia had been withdrawn eighty years before. Since their profession was hereditary, with land being granted on discharge, the *limitanei* became bonded into the local community, continuing from one generation to the next. 'The Saxons – lowland farmers to a man – seem to hate the hills,' Meurig continued. 'So far, they've settled only in the plains and valleys. You want to reach Artorius, you say? Let's see; last I heard, he'd set up his headquarters near Castra Gyfel.† That's on the great Roman road running from Isca to Lindum – a hundred and fifty plus miles due west from here; say a week to ten days' walking.' He glanced at Myrddin quizzically. 'Beats me why you'd want to come to Britain, when anyone who's able to seems anxious to get out. Still, no business of mine. Whatever your reasons, I expect they're good ones – especially if they're connected with Artorius. What a man! If it wasn't for him, the Saxons might have pushed us Brits back to Cambria by now.' He smiled at his visitor. 'You'll stay the night of course; can't let you go without a proper Anderida send-off. Seeing we protect them, the locals keep us well supplied – boar and venison from Anderida Silva,‡ washed down with home-brewed ale. At least you'll be setting out with a full stomach.'

Striding along the ancient ridgeway cresting the chalk downs west of Anderida, Myrddin felt his spirits lift on this glorious autumn morning. Below him, to the right, stretched the vast expanse of Anderida Silva, a sea of reds and golds, while before him, starkly beautiful, the sculpted hills rolled to the horizon, the nearest with an arresting figure cut

---

* Prehistoric tracks along the crests of the chalk downs of southern England. Parts of some of them are popular with walkers today.
† Ilchester (see Notes). The Roman road is the Fosse Way, connecting Exeter and Lincoln.
‡ The Weald.

through the turf to the bare chalk, showing a giant holding a staff in each outstretched hand.*

Sleeping at night in shepherds' huts, or among the banks and ditches of hill-forts which had been old when Roman legions stormed them, his thick wool robe proof against the worst of the chills, Myrddin made good progress westward. The ridgeways took him through a magical landscape: huge rounded hills like frozen billows, some with chalk-cut figures of giants and horses adorning their bare flanks; strange mounds like bells, inverted bowls, or upturned longboats – tombs from ancient times when men had only tools of flint or bronze; concentric rings of standing stones, one such overlooked by a tall hill so perfectly conical it could only have been raised by man – but why or when was something only to be guessed at.

On the eighth day, spotting far below the settlement of Castra Gyfel on a Roman road running arrow-straight towards the north-east, Myrddin descended from the ridgeway he was walking, to the plain – a land of streams and water-meadows, yet unconquered by the Saxons. Given directions to Artorius' headquarters by a farmer who spoke glowingly about the British leader, Myrddin found himself, after a pleasant walk of a few miles, approaching an extraordinary edifice, an ancient hill-fort from its earthen banks and ditches, reinforced with recent defences of stone and timber.† Presenting himself before a crude but massive timber gateway, Myrddin got ready to produce his documents.

'This says you helped Aurelian, and that now you wish to help me. Should I feel flattered?' Artorius, a flame-haired giant, clean-shaven in the Roman manner, and with a hint of humour about the shrewd eyes and the decisive mouth, handed back Myrddin's letter of introduction. 'Subscribed by Odovacar no less, I see,' he went on with mock reverence. 'We *are* impressed.' He shot the other an appraising look. 'Well, my friend, if you really are what you claim to be – a healer, not a quack – we might, I suppose, find some use for you. Let's put you to the test. As it happens, a man of mine's just come in from hunting, with a dislocated shoulder. Our own sawbones seems to be having a spot of bother putting it to rights.

* The Long Man of Wilmington (for this and other features mentioned in Myrddin's itinerary, see Notes).
† Cadbury Castle/South Cadbury hill-fort (see Notes).

Perhaps you'd care to have a try?' They were in a great timber hall (the largest of the many buildings – barracks, stables, kitchens, workshops – within the fort's vast courtyard), its roof supported by a double row of pillars made from tree-trunks, the walls hung with weapons and trophies of the chase: antlers, skins of deer and wolf. A dozen men, retainers of some consequence from their gold arm-bands and neck-torques, lounged on chairs or settles, chatting, drinking ale, playing dice or board games.

On Myrddin's nodding in response to the question, Artorius went to the hall's entrance and bellowed a command. White-faced with pain, a man entered the hall, his shoulder-joint projecting in an ugly lump. Accompanying him was an elderly personage, who skipped around him, fussing.

'Get this torturer away from me,' growled the man.

'How can I help him, Sire, if he won't keep still?' bleated the old man.

'I'm sure you've done your best, Camlach,' Artorius replied soothingly. 'But you won't object to a little help, surely?' And he signalled to Myrddin.

'I'll need two assistants, sir.'

'Cei, Bedwyr, give our friend a hand.'

Two young men arose and joined Myrddin. Following his instructions they held the patient securely, while Myrddin gripped the affected arm. He gave a sudden pull and twist; with a click, the joint slipped home.

A spontaneous burst of applause broke out, blending with the patient's thanks.

'It was nothing,' murmured Myrddin, feeling quietly elated. He couldn't have asked for a more opportune way to demonstrate his skill. What he had done looked (and sounded) impressive, but was really just a trick, easily mastered given a modicum of training and experience. Had he been asked, say, to treat a fever or internal injury, that would have called for a far greater degree of skill, without, necessarily, the bonus of success.

But it would take more than such a facile feat to impress Artorius, Myrddin realized, as the leader whispered in his ear, 'First time lucky, eh? You can stay – for now. Just remember, you're on probation.'

As the weeks passed, with autumn slipping into winter, Myrddin quietly consolidated his reputation, by treating with skilled efficiency a variety of ailments among Artorius' followers. These ranged from petty injuries such as cuts and broken bones to agues, boils, coughs and toothache – the last invariably 'cured' by drawing the affected item, an operation calling for a degree of dexterity and strength. His stock-in-trade consisted of – besides surgical tools such as probes, scalpels and suturing needles – salves based on extracts of plants: henbane, St John's Wort, poppy and comfrey. With a combination of tact and patience, Myrddin gradually won over old Camlach, whose pride had suffered as a result of the other's preferment, from jealous aloofness to valued partnership.

This was a happy time; the campaigning season over, the days were spent in hunting and martial exercises and contests, the evenings in feasting, storytelling and song. Drawing on his experience of travel within the Roman Empire and beyond, Myrddin became popular as something of a raconteur. In addition, he discovered a certain talent for diplomacy and problem-solving. For instance, at meals or conferences held at the high table with the *Dux* (as Artorius was addressed, inheriting the title from Aurelianus) and his dozen chief retainers, there was often a certain amount of jockeying for position, those finding themselves at the table's ends tending to feel diminished in status. Myrddin's suggestion that a *round* table be substituted was put into effect, and harmony prevailed.

With spring came the news that more than one large Saxon war-band was pushing towards Calleva and Venta* – the farthest west the Saxons had yet penetrated – and that they seemed to be acting in concert. This was worrying. Hitherto, bar in a single case, the Saxons had operated as small independent parties, each carving out a piece of territory then settling in it, without the help of other bands: a process of slow attrition which, if it could not be halted, could at least he slowed down and, to a certain extent, contained. But should the Saxons start co-operating, the effects might spell catastrophe. Haphazard occupation could quickly escalate into all-out invasion, as had happened with the Western Empire when hostile German tribes coalesced into confederations powerful enough to smash through the frontiers. Only once, years before, had Saxon forces combined. On that occasion, Aurelianus, aided by Artorius, had fought a mighty Saxon host to a standstill, deterring further westward incursion until now.

* Silchester and Winchester.

In response to this ominous intelligence, Artorius summoned a council of war at which, besides his twelve lieutenants (mostly grandsons of landowners or decurions from the days of Roman rule), was also present Myrddin, now a respected member of the team, thanks to his insight and sound judgement.

'According to my scouts' reports, the Saxons are advancing in two columns – each about two thousand strong,' announced the *Dux*, when all were seated round the new, circular high table in the great hall. 'Our strategy, it seems to me, must be at all costs to prevent the columns joining up.'

'Why, *Dux*?' inquired an open-faced young man, distinguished by a shock of hair so fair as to be almost white. 'If we attack them both together, we can end this threat at one blow, surely?'

'Simple arithmetic, old Gwyn,' smiled Artorius, addressing the other by his nickname.* 'Our total force is five hundred heavy horse, enough – just – to take on and defeat two thousand men on foot, provided we have surprise and terrain in our favour. But four thousand? Work it out.'

'Oh.' Gwyn paused, then added, 'See what you mean, *Dux*.'

When the laughter had subsided, Myrddin put forward a suggestion. 'I know in theory it's dangerous to split one's force. But suppose we were to try to keep the columns from converging by luring one of them away; letting them spot a small dismounted party. If the Saxons took the bait and followed, our main force could then lie in ambush . . .' He glanced enquiringly round the table, to be rewarded by a buzz of interest.

'I like it,' declared Artorius at length. 'I think I like it very much. Anyone disagree? No? Then that's what we'll do.'

Perhaps made over-confident by easy pickings further east, the Saxons advanced boldly up the valley, where at last the exhausted Britons had turned at bay to face them. With a triumphant shout, the Saxons broke into a trot.

Hidden in the woods crowning a hill which formed one side of the valley, the British horsemen waited for the signal. Clad in old imperial armour salvaged from the *limitanei*, long, cutting *spathae* in hand,

* 'Gwyn' is Welsh for 'white' (hence 'Gawain'?).

they sat mounts descended from Roman cavalry stock – big, powerful beasts, bred more for weight than speed.

High and clear, a trumpet note rang out.

A solid mass of mailed cavalry, red dragon banner streaming in the van, burst from the woodshore, swept down the slope and drove through the Saxon host as a sledge-hammer smashes through a rotten door. Re-forming on the valley's farther side, the horsemen charged again, before the Saxons could recover and form a defensive shield-wall. Time after time the tactic was repeated, until at last the Saxons broke and fled, to be cut down almost to a man, by the pursuing Britons.

Learning of their fate, the other column, putting discretion before valour, retreated to the east. Britain to the west of Vectis* was safe, for another year at least.

Looking out to sea from one of the towers surmounting the gatehouse of Anderida, Meurig experienced a twinge of concern. A shimmering wall of white obscured the coastline – perfect cover for a Saxon sea-borne attack. His anxiety was groundless, he told himself. Since Artorius' great victory at Mons Badonicus† three years before, the Saxons had lain low, licking their wounds presumably. And yet . . . All Meurig's instincts suggested that this spell of inactivity was but the calm before the storm. By nature ruthless and persistent, the Saxons were not the sort of people to be permanently knocked back by one defeat, however costly. Well, whatever happened elsewhere on the island, Anderida was secure. Nothing could penetrate these massive walls – ten feet thick by thirty high, of solid concrete faced with stone, reinforced by twelve great bastions from which a deadly enfilading fire could be directed against any enemy who reached the curtain. The fort was utterly impregnable. Wasn't it?

What was that? Straining his ears, Meurig picked up a faint sound, a low susurration which slowly grew in volume. Suddenly, as was wont with these seasonal sea-frets, the mist began to thin and shred, then in a twinkling had dissolved away. The commander stared in consterna-tion at the sight that met his eyes: a forest of sails bearing down upon

* The Isle of Wight.
† Mount Badon (see Notes).

the beach. Beneath the towering squares of canvas, banks of oars dipped and rose – the source of the sound that he had heard. This was no ordinary raid, such as Anderida had seen off scores of times in the past. This was a full-scale offensive which bore the hallmarks of concerted planning. All at once, the fort's invincibility seemed less assured.

Before the longboats grounded on the beach, the garrison had manned the walls. The great *ballistae* – new when Theodosius was emperor a century ago, but kept in good repair – were rushed from store and hastily assembled on the bastions. Meanwhile, the Saxons, pouring from their craft, formed up, thousands strong, on the narrow beach. Then, giving a savage roar, they rolled forward in massed formation.

'*Jacite!*' The order to shoot rang out from the *ballista* platforms on the nearest bastions. Their connecting cords released by a trigger mechanism, the arms of the huge catapults, powered by the enormous stored-up energy of their springs of twisted sinew, flew forwards. A storm of iron-headed bolts smashed into the Saxons, tearing great gaps in their ranks. These were immediately filled up, the enemy advancing without pause to the foot of the walls, to be subjected to a deadly hail of javelins and arrows. Despite incurring terrible losses, the Saxons pressed on. Scaling-ladders were raised, sent crashing to the ground, scattering their human loads; but more and more thudded on to the parapet until at last the Saxons gained a growing foothold on the walkways, and the balance swiftly tilted in their favour. Knowing no quarter would be given, the garrison, by now reduced to a shrinking knot of *limitanei*, fought on grimly in the fort's great courtyard until the last man was killed.

'Let us leave their bodies for the kites and crows,' said Aelle to his fellow leader.

'No,' replied Cissa, resting on his bloodstained sword. 'They were brave men. We will give them honourable burial.'

So disappeared from Britain the last reflected rays of Rome's imperial sunset.

TWENTY

The gods favour the bold

Ovid, *Metamorphoses, c.* 5 AD

Suddenly the mist, which had plagued the Amali almost from the moment of striking winter camp ten days before, began to thin. In moments it had gone, revealing a world utterly changed from the one in which they had wintered. The Dravus, then a wide and placid river flowing gently through a fertile valley, had become a rushing torrent confined by steep slopes, where stands of pine and hazel alternated with slabs of naked limestone. Ahead, a jagged wall of mountains loomed on the horizon. 'Das Kärnthen Gebirge,'* the guide (one of several Boii,† hardy mountaineers recruited for their knowledge and experience) informed Theoderic. 'Tomorrow we change route, head south towards the Savus.‡ All right, Herr König?'

Theoderic concurred, mentally reviewing the plan. They would cross from the Upper Dravus to the Savus where, at a prearranged spot, they would rendezvous with Timothy. The Isaurian had gone ahead, a) to reconnoitre a possible southern route into Italy via the Vipava valley, through the foothills of the Alpes Juliae§, and b) to discover, if possible, what Odovacar's movements were. Depending on what Timothy reported, a decision would have to be taken as to which route to follow: the southern, longer, but almost certainly much easier; or a short cut straight across the Alpes Juliae, which was bound to prove difficult, possibly dangerous to boot.

Next morning, the wagons, heading south and a little west, began to crawl round the southern flanks of the Kärnthen Gebirge, on the

* The Carinthian Alps.
† Bavarians.
‡ The River Sava
§ The Julian Alps.

tenth day descending to the Savus river at its junction with the Sorus,* the rendezvous. Here, they found Timothy awaiting them.

'The Vipava valley route's an easy one,' Timothy, gratefully chewing a slice of roast chamois, told Theoderic in the latter's wagon. 'Broad, well-used trail, no gradient steep enough to cause a problem for wagons. I followed it right through to the Italian border, which is demarcated by the River Sontius. Posing as a trader, I crossed the river at Pons Sontii† and did some snooping. Odovacar's there, waiting for you. Clearly, he expects you to come via the Vipava, the route favoured in the past by almost all invaders. According to the gossip, he's mustering an army "from the kings of all the nations" – whatever that means; but so far, not that many have turned up. If there *is* a viable route directly over the Alpes Juliae, I'd say take it. You'd then have the element of surprise, and likely catch Odovacar before he's had time to assemble all his force.'

Theoderic spent the next few hours agonizing over which route to take. If he opted for the short cut, he might end up losing half his wagons, or getting stuck in the mountains – when his people would be faced with slow starvation. But, if he chose the longer route, he might find himself eventually facing an Odovacar to whom he had gifted time sufficient to assemble an army of such overwhelming strength as to prove invincible. He thought of holding a council of war, but rejected the idea immediately; this responsibility belonged to him alone. That night he fell into an exhausted sleep, the problem still unresolved. Before unconsciousness claimed him, he found himself hoping that perhaps in dreams a sign might manifest itself.

When he awoke he discovered that, although no sign had come, his mind was made up: the short cut it would be.

The wagons pushed westwards beside the narrowing Savus, the distant blue mass of the Alpes Juliae looming larger by the day. A week after rendezvous-ing with Timothy, they arrived at a great side valley coming in from the left, above which, in the distance, dominating the surrounding sea of snow-capped mountains, rose a vast and snaggled

---

* The River Sora, near Ljubljana, in Slovenia (see Notes).
† Isonzo Bridge.

peak: Tridentium,* the Three-Fanged One, the highest summit of the Alpes Juliae.

Ordering the word to be passed down the line for the wagons to halt, Theoderic, accompanied by the Boiarian guides, entered the mouth of the valley to reconnoitre the route which the guides had already recommended as offering the most direct passage through the range. The prospect presented by the valley was a daunting one indeed: a vast stony trough, its upper slopes a field of scree and boulders, leading steeply up to a narrow col. This connected, on the left, the beetling cliffs of Tridentium's north face, with, on the right, a ferocious line of sawtoothed crags ascending to a dramatic peak, Spica.

'*Es geht nicht* – impossible!' exclaimed Theoderic, aghast, immediately regretting his choice of route.

'Not so, Herr König,' demurred the guides' leader. 'With care, and preparation, and perhaps a little luck, it can be done. You see that stream?' He pointed to a barely discernible rivulet bisecting the great cirque. 'There is a track beside it, just wide enough for a wagon, which will lead us to the summit of the pass.'

At first, the going was fair – far easier than it had seemed during Theoderic's inspection the day before. The wagons rocked and rolled along the stony trail, with grassy patches and stands of stunted beech and larch relieving the monotony of the ubiquitous bare limestone. At one point the track passed *beneath* a waterfall spouting from an over-hanging crag – an unforgettable phenomenon. All too soon, however, such pleasant sights were displaced by a grim testing-ground of unfor-giving rock. From a point where the stream mysteriously disappeared, presumably flowing underground from its source far above, the trail steepened brutally, becoming increasingly littered with boulders, which had to be laboriously manhandled out of the path of the wagons. As they gained height, slippery scree and lying snow combined to create a serious problem, denying traction to the wagon wheels with their smooth iron tyres. Drag-ropes, hauled by everyone except the very young, had to supplement the efforts of the oxen, folk and beasts labouring for breath in the thin mountain air. Others strained to push the wagons at the rear, ready at a moment's notice to jam boulders

* Triglav (see Notes).

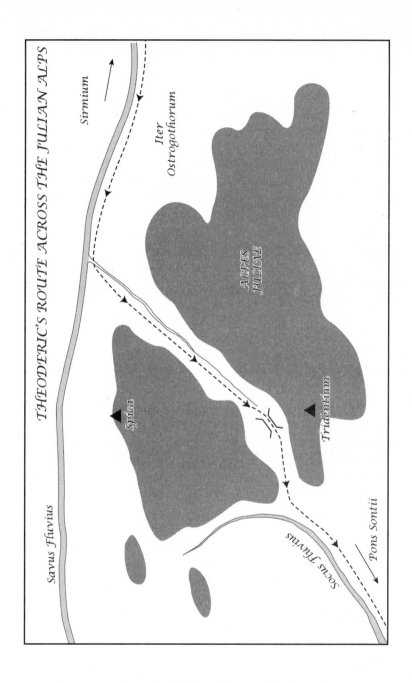

THEODERIC'S ROUTE ACROSS THE JULIAN ALPS

Sirmium

Iter
Ostrogothorum

ALPES
JULIAE

Spica

Tridentium

Savus Fluvius

Socus Fluvius

Pons Sontii

beneath the rear wheels should they start to slip, brakes alone being insufficient to stop the heavy vehicles sliding backwards.

Halting further progress, nightfall found the leading wagons well below the summit, a long, long snake of vehicles winding back down the corrie and along the valley of the Savus. What with the effects of cold at such high altitude, and anxiety lest their vehicles start to slip on the steep upper slopes, those in the foremost wagons spent a sleepless night. But dawn brought no relief.

As the wagons began to move again, dark storm-clouds rolled up from the south, discharging volleys of hailstones as big as sling-shot, accompanied by cracks of thunder, and lightning bolts that struck the mountain all around, leaving dark smoking patches in the snow. The oxen panicked, becoming almost unmanageable, taxing the drivers' skill to the uttermost to prevent the wagons overturning and tumbling to destruction. Then, as suddenly as it had worsened, the weather cleared; the oxen quietened, the train proceeded without further incident, and by noon the first wagons were trundling through the pass.

Riding beside his wagon as it started the descent, Theoderic felt a surge of relief and euphoria. Thank God, he told himself, that he had after all made the right decision as to the route; and thanks to Fortuna for sending him Callisthenes, without whose advice the expedition would probably not have got this far. Further lightening his spirit, the terrain on the far side of the pass was a welcome contrast to what had gone before: grassy slopes, dotted with trees and grazing chamois, dropped gently to a fast-flowing stream of the purest aquamarine blue, the Socus.

With the most critical part of the route now pioneered, an endless line of wagons rolled over the pass and down to the Socus valley. The train followed the winding river through a landscape of stunning beauty – grassy meadows studded with stands of pine, beech, and rowan, with a backdrop of dramatic snow-capped peaks, their flanks seamed by gorges, waterfalls and precipices. Parting at last from the Socus as from an old friend, an easy traverse took the column to the headwaters of the Sontius, which they followed to the river-crossing at Pons Sontii, above which the Sontius emptied its waters into the Terginus Sinus.*

---

* The Gulf of Trieste.

Beyond the far bank, all seemed strangely quiet and deserted: no ranks of tents nor smoke of cooking-fires, no stir and bustle of a mighty host.

Feeling a little like Moses who had brought his people to the Promised Land, but, unlike the patriarch, not forbidden entry thereto, Theoderic rode across the bridge – and into Italy, where surely Destiny awaited him. The freshly trampled earth and squares of bleached grass told their own story. Learning of his rival's unexpected advance from the north, Odovacar, his army not yet fully mustered, had withdrawn, to await confrontation at some later date.

TWENTY-ONE

Have pity on me!
Cry of Emperor Zeno from within his tomb, allegedly reported by
citizens of Constantinople, 491

Zeno stirred, as his mind returned to consciousness. He opened his eyes: blackness. He tried to sit up; his head banged against an unyielding surface. He extended his hands, which encountered what felt like cold stone. Where was he? With mounting alarm, he recalled his last memory: himself lying on a sick-bed surrounded by courtiers and physicians, the Patriarch of Constantinople leaning over him, intoning the last rites.

Terror engulfed the emperor as he realized the awful truth. Through some appalling misdiagnosis, perhaps while in a cataleptic state, he had been pronounced dead, then entombed – alive! Filling his lungs with stale and fetid air, he began to shout for help.

'Simmer down, you ghastly bunch!' bellowed the choirmaster with mock severity. The choirboys, high spirits coming to the fore on being released from rehearsing the paean for the new emperor, desisted from larking about. They were inside the vast church of Hagia Sophia in Constantinople. 'That wasn't bad,' the choirmaster conceded. 'Not bad at all.' The choirboys grinned at each other smugly. 'Not bad' was high praise from their preceptor. 'Early night, remember; tomorrow's the big day. Off you go, now.'

'Listen!' called one chorister urgently, holding up a hand for silence. 'I think I heard someone calling.' All froze, straining their ears.

Faint but distinct, there came a muffled cry from the direction of the apse, 'Help me, for pity's sake!'

'It's coming from the sarcophagus,' whispered one of the boys.

The group hurried to the great marble tomb resting on its catafalque where, only the day before, Zeno had been laid to rest. From within, the cry – desperate, terror-filled – was repeated.

'We'll get you out, Serenity,' called the choirmaster, placing his mouth to the crack between the lid and the walls of the great stone coffin. 'Can you hear me?'

'Yes, yes!' came the reply, charged with anguished hope.

'I'll get help, Serenity,' the choirmaster assured the imprisoned emperor, after he and the twelve boys had vainly tried to shift the massive lid. Clearly, nothing short of a team of workmen armed with crowbars and lifting-gear was going to move that heavy slab. 'Try to stay calm – you'll soon be out of there.'

Dismissing his charges with a strict injunction not to breathe a word to anyone, the choirmaster hurried to the palace.

'The poor man!' exclaimed Anastasius in horror. The Master of Offices had repeated the choirmaster's news to him and his bride-to-be, Ariadne – not, after all, Zeno's widow, but, it transpired, still his wife. Aged sixty-one, an undistinguished if conscientious palace official, Anastasius had, for want of a more suitable candidate, been chosen to succeed Zeno, who had expired (it had been thought) suddenly, following a massive stroke. 'We must get him out at once.' He turned to the Master of Offices. 'Summon the palace masons.'

'Wait,' said Ariadne. A woman of overweening ambition and iron will, she had agreed to marry Anastasius in the event of Zeno's death, expected since the emperor's being taken gravely ill, some weeks before. Such a wedding between May and December was acceptable to both, allowing, as it did, Ariadne to maintain her imperial status and Anastasius to inherit royal lineage through marriage to the emperor's widow. The arrangement was not without precedent. Zeno himself, an Isaurian outsider, by marrying Ariadne, daughter of the emperor Leo, had thereby acquired membership of the royal line, as had Marcian, forty years ago, by marrying the Augusta Pulcheria, sister of Theodosius II.

'Think carefully,' continued Ariadne. 'What would be the consequences were my husband to be resurrected? You, Anastasius, would of course relinquish any claim to the purple. Worse, you would be marked for death – or blinding, at best.* The throne can prove a *damnosa haereditas*. Through no fault of your own, you would have become a rival for the diadem, a potential usurper who must be eliminated. Such, unfortunately, have always been the rules of the imperial game. As for myself, it's no secret that my marriage to Zeno has been one strictly of convenience; his death means little to me. Were he to return, his days would anyway be numbered, given his health of late.' She looked hard at Anastasius. 'But you, alas, consigned to prison or condemned to die, would no longer be my suitor. I confess I value my role as Augusta too much to relinquish it willingly.' Addressing the Master of Offices, she continued, 'You too, *Magister*, should have a care. Implicated, as inevitably you would be, in what, I imagine, might become known as "the Lazarus Affair", you would be tainted by association and suffer a fate similar to Anastasius'. All totally unjust and unreasonable, of course; but that's what would happen.' She looked enquiringly at the two men. 'Well?'

'Your silence implies consent that we take no steps to liberate my unfortunate husband,' Ariadne pronounced when, after a lacuna lasting many seconds, no one had spoken. 'Good. This, then, is what we do. In case he should start circulating awkward rumours, that choirmaster must be told that Zeno was rescued, but unfortunately succumbed to shock. The cathedral must be locked immediately, for, let us say, a week. Long enough for . . .' She paused, and shrugged. 'Even though it means postponing the coronation, it will be easy enough to fabricate a convincing reason – urgent repairs to a weak wall, say.'

'It's done, Serenities.' Via a *silentiarius*, the Master of Offices set in train the machinery for closing the cathedral.

'It's monstrous – *monstrous*,' whispered Anastasius, his mild face furrowed in distress.

'Dreadful,' concurred the Master of Offices. 'But have we any choice? Of course, we may not be able to keep a lid on things. There's no way of guaranteeing that those choirboys will keep quiet.'

'Isn't there?' murmured Ariadne. 'We *can* take steps to ensure their silence.'

---

* Serious disfigurement was held to debar accession to the purple. Hence blinding, or amputation of the nose, was sometimes inflicted, as an alternative to execution, on those deemed unacceptable as Eastern Emperor.

'Enough!' roared Anastasius, suddenly red with uncharacteristic fury. 'Good God! This is Constantinople, not Ravenna – let us behave like Romans, not barbarians. With the utmost reluctance, Augusta, and to my eternal shame, I am prepared to go along with your proposal as to Zeno. But I draw the line at anything more. If I hear that one hair of those boys' heads has been harmed . . .' He glared at the empress.

'Oh, very well,' conceded Ariadne. 'Even if the story gets out, it probably won't matter much.'

'How so?' objected Anastasius. 'Zeno's been a most effective emperor. The way he's played off the Goths against each other has been masterly. And at last, by persuading Theoderic to go to Italy, he's finally got rid of the barbarians. He's succeeded, where every other emperor since Adrianople has failed.'

'True, no doubt. But there's one thing you're forgetting: Zeno's an Isaurian.'

Ariadne had a point, Anastasius admitted. The inhabitants of Isauria – wild mountain tribesmen, always ready to raid their neighbours or rebel against the government – were deeply unpopular with almost all East Romans. Sadly, the reaction of those same Romans, should they learn of Zeno's fate, would more likely be indifference than consternation.

When he heard the distant, muffled clang of the church's great bronze doors closing, Zeno knew no help was going to come. Alone, in the blackness of the tomb, despite having abandoned hope, the emperor began to scream . . .

TWENTY-TWO

Where is God?
John of Antioch (quoting Odovacar's protest as
Theoderic prepared to murder him, 15 March 493),
Fragmenta Historicorum Graecorum, seventh century

'We who are Rome pledge our lives for her peace, our strength for her own, and our honour for her citizens.' With the other standing senators, dignified in their archaic togas, Magnus Aurelius Cassiodorus chanted the words of the oath – old, old words which had echoed here down the long centuries of the republic, then the empire, and now, even when the empire was no more, in these strange new days of the *Regnum Italiae* under German kings. Barbarians might reign, but without the co-operation of the Senate – that repository of power, expertise and influence – they could not rule.

Recently enough elected to the august assembly to be awed by the atmosphere of Rome's Senate House, Aurelius, young for a senator, resumed his seat. This building was charged with the weight of history: it had witnessed speeches which had changed the course of world events. Here, in Rome's darkest hour, the Senate had resolved to carry on the fight against Hannibal even when the flower of her manhood had perished on the field of Cannae. Here had been voted the funds enabling Rome's legions to build an empire extending from Hispania in the west to Persia in the east, from Caledonia in the north to Aethiopia in the south. In this spot, Christianity had been confirmed as the official creed of Rome. In the days of chaos and uncertainty following the murder of the great Aetius, who had held the crumbling fabric of the West together, the Senate alone had kept the machinery of state functioning. And now, with the fate of Italy being decided by rival barbarians in far-off Ravenna, this same assembly must decide which of the two to support.

The *Caput Senatus*,* Flavius Rufius Postumius Festus, venerable consul from imperial times, and fresh from a mission to Constantinople to argue the legitimacy of Theoderic's claim, rose stiffly to address the House. Banging his staff of office on the marble floor to command attention, he announced in a reedy quaver, 'The first and principal motion to put before you, this Nones of Februarius in the year of the consuls Eusebius and Albinus, and from the Founding of the City the twelve hundred and forty-sixth,† concerns the future rule of Italy. Its substance is known to you all: whose cause shall we decide to champion, Theoderic's or Odovacar's? Theoderic arrived in Italy with Zeno's backing, but Zeno's successor, Anastasius, perhaps because he was preoccupied with insurgency in Isauria, declined to commit himself when I pressed him for his views. Gentlemen, the floor is yours.'

First to speak was Anicius Acilius Aginantius Faustus *albus*, consul ten years previously, and a member of the powerful family of the Anicii. He, like Festus, had recently returned from a mission to the Eastern capital, ostensibly on behalf of Odovacar. A swarthy individual despite his cognomen, he looked round the packed marble benches with an ingratiating smirk. 'The choice is obvious,' he drawled, with the easy confidence bestowed by generations of wealth and privilege. 'We back the winner.'

'Do, pray, enlighten us,' sneered an elderly senator. 'Clearly you must have contact with the Sibyl – unlike the rest of us benighted souls.'

'Do I really have to spell it out?' sighed Faustus, raising his hands in a calculated gesture of exasperation. 'It's Theoderic, of course. Anyone with a smidgen of perception can see that. You've only to look at the man's record. Through a mixture of persistence, leadership and sheer guts, he's managed to unite all the Goths in the Eastern Empire, transforming them from a collection of squabbling marauders to the most powerful nation in Europe. As the hereditary monarch of an ancient royal house – one, moreover, with the backing of the late Eastern Emperor – Theoderic has the sort of influence and personality that attend success. What does Odovacar amount to? An adventurer from a minor tribe whose rise owes more to luck them ability, elected king

---

* The Head of the Senate – in Westminster terms, his role would be something between those of the Speaker and the Father of the House.
† 5 February 493.

by a rabble of rebellious soldiery, whose allegiance is precarious at best. His rule was never recognized officially by Zeno, just not contested, as being the least bad option. Then there's the question of age. Odovacar's a worn-out old man in his sixties; not yet forty, Theoderic's in his prime. If you've any sense, like me you'll vote for Theoderic.'

A ground-swell of approving murmurs – loudest from the Anicii and another leading family, the Decii (normally their rivals, but in this instance allies) – arose from all across the benches, drawing angry protests from those supporting Odovacar.

A tall senator with patrician features rose to his feet and pointed an accusing finger at the Anician. This was Quintus Aurelius Memmius Symmachus, Roman patriot, one-time consul and City Prefect, from the most illustrious family of Rome, whose great-grandfather had in this very Senate House led the campaign against the removal of the (pagan) Altar of Victory by Bishop Ambrose of Milan and his Christian zealots. That fight might have been lost, but the honour of the family had gained immeasurably, the name of Symmachus coming to stand for freedom of speech and thought, against bigotry and intolerance.

'Shame on you, Faustus!' declared Symmachus. 'You went to Constantinople to plead Odovacar's cause. Now you stab him in the back and tell us we should do the same.'

Faustus smiled, and shrugged. 'Political necessity,' he murmured.

'Cynical expediency, more like!' shouted Symmachus. His gaze swept round the assembly, now tense and expectant. 'Has it come to this: that we, the Senate, the very voice of Rome, stand for nothing more than cowardly self-interest? There was a time when senators were not afraid to speak out for what was right. Odovacar has proved himself a good and just ruler – a great deal better than many of our emperors. He rewarded his soldiers, which he was compelled to do, with public land as far as possible, keeping confiscation from Romans to a minimum, something for which we should be eternally grateful. We owe him loyalty, not betrayal.'

'Hear, hear!' This from Marius Manlius Boethius,* another former consul from a rich and famous family, who had risen from a sick-bed to attend the meeting.

---

* The father of Anicius Manlius Severinus Boethius, then a boy, who was to become the friend and adviser of Theoderic, and author of *The Consolation of Philosophy*.

Speaker after speaker rose to express their views, most siding (some shamefacedly) with Faustus. When the vote was taken, it was overwhelmingly in favour of Theoderic. The names of those who, like Boethius and Symmachus, supported Odovacar were noted, as were those abstaining. Among the latter was Cassiodorus, who was genuinely confused. Instinctively, he sympathized with Symmachus' stance defending Odovacar, yet he was reluctant to believe that so many of Rome's great and good could be wrong.

Exactly a month later, the Porta Aurea, Ravenna's main gate, opened to admit Theoderic. Bishop John, his features gaunt with hunger from the long siege, came forward, smiling and uttering assurances that Odovacar now wished only to be friends with the Amal king and hoped that, from this moment on, they could rule jointly in amicable concord. Kissing the bishop's hand, Theoderic gladly concurred, telling himself that this was perhaps the best possible outcome of the bitter four-year struggle.

It had been a hard war, Theoderic reflected as, accompanied by the captains of his host together with the bishop's train, he made his way to the Imperial Palace, where Odovacar had his headquarters. In his mind he reviewed the sequence of events: a series of bloody clashes in the Padus* flood-plain, with fortunes swinging like a wild pendulum between the opposing sides. Gradually, however, the initiative had passed to Theoderic, with Odovacar pinned down in Ravenna – thought to be impregnable behind its screen of marshes and lagoons. But by capturing the port of Ariminum,† thus preventing supplies getting through to the besieged capital, Theoderic was able to tighten the blockade dramatically. With famine imminent, Bishop John at last came forth to make terms on behalf of Odovacar.

In the course of the campaign, one unfortunate incident had occurred which was to cast a cloud over Theoderic's mood for many months to come. Frederick, the young Rugian prince, had proved unable to control his followers. They had gone on the rampage, mistreating the local Roman population. On hearing about this, Theoderic had taken it upon

---

* River Po.
† Rimini. For details concerning the war, see Appendix I.

himself to discipline the offenders and take Frederick to task, probably, in hindsight, speaking more harshly than intended. Angry and humiliated, the young man had stormed off and switched allegiance to Odovacar, only to be killed in a subsequent engagement. Theoderic, who had felt a strong affection for the young prince, regarding him almost as a son, took the news badly – both hurt by his betrayal and deeply saddened by his loss.

Meeting the Scirian king, Theoderic was put in mind of a sick old lion. Thin and hollow-eyed from the privations of the siege, the grizzled monarch greeted the Amal courteously, and with as much warmth as the situation allowed. Theoderic liked him immediately, this impression being confirmed when, on further acquaintance, he found him to be frank, down-to-earth, and not without a sense of humour. They discovered, to their mutual surprise, that they had more in common than dividing them. Apart from being fellow Germans, though from different tribes, both had fought for Rome, been commended by the venerable Severinus, and, at different times, received the backing of the Eastern Emperor.

Here was a man he could work with, Theoderic decided, finding Odovacar's suggestion of co-rule increasingly attractive. Together, they would govern Italy efficiently and well. With supplies now flowing into the city, he planned a feast to set the seal on their burgeoning friendship. For too long Germans had allowed Romans to divide and manipulate them. It was now obvious that, in sending him against Odovacar, Zeno had hoped they would wipe each other out, thus clearing the way for Roman re-occupation. That Anastasius had so far failed to renew Zeno's mandate reinforced this conclusion. Well, this time things would be reversed. Instead of destroying each other as Rome hoped, the two German peoples would show the Romans that together they could rule in peace and concord. It would be sweet revenge for the slights and rejection that, as a despised barbarian, he had suffered at the hands of Romans from his schooldays on.

'It won't work, Deric.' Timothy and Theoderic were seated in the latter's spacious quarters assigned to him by Odovacar, in the Imperial Palace.

'I don't see why it shouldn't,' objected Theoderic, realizing that he sounded angry and defensive. 'Odovacar's a good man. We like and respect each other, as well as seeing eye to eye about many things.'

'I daresay, but that's irrelevant. I don't doubt you could be bosom friends with Odovacar, but as for ruling with him . . .' Timothy shook his head emphatically. 'In any group there can only be one boss. It's a basic law of nature. You'll never find a wolf pack with two leaders, or a herd with two herd bulls. Your mandate from Zeno said nothing about power-sharing, and it's doubtful if Anastasius would take a different line. I'll tell you a story from my own past; you're the first to hear it. And since you're offering, yes, I will have some of that local vinegar they call wine.'

The two men sipped in silence for a time, then Timothy resumed.

'As you know, I grew up as a street kid in Tarsus. My grandfather was head of the family, and he ran the family business with a rod of iron. I guess some would call that business extortion – 'protection' for a fee, although my grandfather did make sure that no outsider ever fleeced his clients. He died handing over to his sons, my father and my uncle. My father, as the elder, was supposed to be the boss. Although a crook, he was at heart a decent man, and bent over backwards to involve my uncle in decision-making and the running of the business.

'But, as well as being lazy and incompetent, my uncle was jealous. One day he picked a quarrel with my father. Tempers flared, then my uncle drew a knife and stabbed him to death. It was judged a fair fight by the neighbourhood, who made sure no word leaked out to the authorities; in the Tarsus back streets, society makes its own rules. But *I* knew it was murder, callous and deliberate: my father would never have pulled a knife on his brother.

'My uncle continued to run things – badly – on his own, while I bided my time. He never suspected that the quiet lad who went round collecting the subscriptions was secretly planning revenge. Then one dark night, my uncle had, let's say, an "accident". They fished his body out of the Cydnus two days later – the victim of a desperate client fallen behind with his dues, so everyone said.

'Not wishing to be the focus of a family vendetta if anyone became suspicious, I left home to set up my own concern, an import/export business. At sixteen, I was running an empire: handling all the portering of goods coming into and out of Tarsus, the chief emporium for traffic between Syria and Anatolia. I was the boss, and I made sure everyone knew it. No one got a job as a porter or a middleman without my say-so, plus the down-payment of a "registration fee", as it was known. Anyone trying to muscle in got warned off. Broken fingers for a first offence, smashed kneecaps for a second. That normally worked, but if it didn't... Well, we won't go into that.'

Timothy held out his cup and, when Theoderic had refilled it, continued, 'You see, I'd learnt my lesson. I'd seen what happened to my father. From the best of motives, he'd tried to share the running of the business, and ended up dead.' He gave the king an earnest look. 'Listen to old Timothy; and don't make the same mistake.'

All at once, Theoderic's euphoria drained away; as with Paul on the road to Damascus, the scales fell from his eyes. Timothy was right. He could see that now. You had only to look at history: Caesar and Pompey, Octavian and Antony, Caracalla and Geta, Constantine and Maxentius. Each pair had started out as partners, but only one ever survived. He realized what the reason was for his welcoming Odovacar's proposal: exhaustion. He was tired to the marrow of his bones. The accumulated strain of organizing the great expedition, of fighting a major battle en route, then finding a passage through the Alps, the treachery and death of both his brother and Frederick, four long hard years of war – all these had taken their toll, draining him of energy and clarity of purpose, so that, above all, he wanted to rest, to lay down the burden of responsibility; or, if not that, to share it with another.

'I know,' murmured Timothy, as if reading his thoughts. 'It's lonely at the top.'

'What must I do?' whispered Theoderic.

'I think you know the answer,' Timothy replied gently.

Ten days after Theoderic had entered Ravenna, the feast to mark the concordat between the two German kings began.* In the palace's great hall of state, where Roman emperors had entertained, rows of long tables groaned with food – predominantly meat to suit Teutonic taste.

---

* Theoderic entered Ravenna on 5 March 493. The feast was held on 15 March, the Ides of March – fateful day!

Attendants with jugs of ale and flagons of wine hovered at the ready to replenish (which was often) drinking-horns and goblets. The guests, Sciri and Ostrogoths, most in German tunics, a few in Roman dalmatics, were in festive mood, becoming noisily relaxed as the evening wore on, with toast following toast in increasingly swift succession. Then a hush spread round the tables as Theoderic, Odovacar beside him in the seat of honour, rose with wine-cup in hand. The moment had arrived for the kings to toast each other, marking the bond of amity that now united them, together with their peoples.

But instead of calling for a toast, Theoderic set the goblet down and drew his sword. At the same moment, two attendants rushed forward and grabbed Odovacar by the wrists, while from a side entrance armed Ostrogoth warriors poured into the hall, surrounding the tables and the unarmed guests.

'Where is God?' cried Odovacar in stricken disbelief.

'God is with the stronger!' shouted Theoderic, and ran him through. His action was instantly copied by the Ostrogoths, and in a few moments all the Sciri lay dead or dying, their blood staining the fine linen table-cloths and puddling the mosaic floor.

Swift and brutal, a stream of orders from Theoderic effected the immediate extinction of Odovacar's family and the slaughter of as many of his followers as could be found. As for the Romans, those who had supported Odovacar were proscribed, their rights as citizens revoked, their property forfeit. Sequestered in his quarters in the palace, Theoderic raged and wept, overwhelmed by black depression. Where was God, indeed? All his high hopes and aspirations seemed hollow and worthless, like those fabled Apples of the Hesperides which turned to ashes in the mouth. Seduced by a glittering but empty title, 'Vicegerent of the Eastern Emperor', he had been persuaded to remove himself to Italy. For what? Zeno must be laughing in Heaven. The Romans might, reluctantly, tolerate him as their ruler, but they would never allow him to assume the mantle of '*Romanitas*'. To them he would always be a barbarian outsider – and a bastard, to boot – condemned by his German blood, despite his Roman education, never to enter the magic circle of those who belonged, were part of Rome. Indirectly, because of Roman machinations he had lost a brother, lost, in young Frederick, almost a son, and been forced to murder a good and honest man who could have been his friend.

Gradually, though, the darkest clouds lifted from his mind, replaced by gloomy resignation, and eventually Bishops Epiphanius of Pavia and Laurentius of Milan, who had been waiting nervously for an audience, were admitted to his presence. Experienced negotiators skilled in the arts of diplomacy, they succeeded, through a blend of tact, sympathy and reason, in prevailing on Theoderic to moderate his stance. Provided the Sciri accepted him as their legitimate ruler, amnesty would be granted to them; and Romans who had stood by Odovacar would not, after all, be punished. Only those obdurate enough to reject these generous terms would be proceeded against. Such was the fiat issuing from Ravenna; it was carried post-haste by heralds to every part of Italy.

Surrounded by anxious crowds filling the Forum Romanum, the *nuntius* unfurled his scroll and began to read, in a stentorian voice, the latest proclamation from the capital. His minions, meanwhile, pasted up copies on walls and pillars, in the process obscuring obsolete *acta diurna* and *acta publica*.*

'Well, at least our new ruler's shown that he's no Sulla,' remarked Faustus to Symmachus, who was endeavouring, without complete success, to hide his huge relief. 'Congratulations. It seems you won't, after all, be forced to surrender your new summer villa at Baiae. I suppose we have to allow that Theoderic's made an encouraging start – for a barbarian.'

---

* A *nuntius* was a cross between a herald and a town crier. *Acta diurna* and *acta publica* corresponded, respectively, to daily bulletins and government enactments.

PART III

'IMITATION OF AN EMPEROR'
AD 493–519

TWENTY-THREE

Pope Symmachus, and the entire senate and people of Rome amid
general rejoicing met him [Theoderic] outside the city
Anonymous Valesianus, *Excerpta: pars posterior, c. 530*

Observing the awe on Theoderic's face as they came in sight of Aurelian's
mighty walls surrounding Rome,* Timothy's heart sank. Moments later
his fears were confirmed when, making the sign of the cross (an
unheard-of gesture on the part of an Arian), the king murmured,
'Behold: the Mistress of the World.'

Assembled before the Flaminian Gate, the city's main entrance from
the north, the vast throng – senators in togas, leading citizens in brightly
coloured dalmatics, robed clerics, plebs in working tunics or holiday
attire – burst into spontaneous cheering. As the royal party approached
the great arch flanked by white marble-clad towers, two men stepped
forward. One was toga-draped, ancient, stooped and bald, but with an
air of stern authority; the other was youngish, almost effeminately handsome, with the face of an Adonis carved by Praxiteles, and clad in
floating, diaphanous robes of coloured silk. The first would be Festus,
the *Caput Senatus*, Timothy thought. But the second? With a shock, he
realized that (assuming the briefing was correct) this must be the new
Pope, Symmachus.†

'The Senate and the People of Rome, together with His Holiness
the Monarchical Bishop of the See of St Peter,' announced Festus in a
voice trembling with age and dignity, 'give greeting to Theoderic Amalo,
king of the Ostrogoths and vicegerent of Italy in the name of His
Serenity Anastasius, Emperor of the East Romans.'

Dismounting, Theoderic made an appropriate response, then, with

---

* Built in the late third century against incursions of the Alamanni, they stand,
for the most part, impressively intact today.
† No relation to the senator of the same name.

his bodyguard and chief councillors, accompanied by the senatorial and papal parties and surrounded by exuberant and noisy crowds, entered the Eternal City by the Flaminian Way. 'Remember thou art only a man,' murmured Timothy with a grin; it was the ancient caution that a slave whispered in the ear of a Roman general entering Rome to celebrate a triumph.

But the jest fell on deaf ears. 'I believe the Romans love me,' said Theoderic, turning a rapt face to Timothy as they passed beneath the arch of Marcus Aurelius. 'They seem to be accepting me as one of their own – perhaps even as their emperor.'

This was extremely bad news, thought Timothy, muttering something vague but tactful in reply. Staring at the man who was his friend as well as master – also still, in some unaccountable way, his charge – Timothy decided that Theoderic looked ridiculous. To please his own people, whose identity was at risk of being swamped, living as they were among the numerically far superior Romans, the king – in contrast to his previous short Roman-style haircut and clean-shaven face – had grown his hair long in the German fashion, and allowed a moustache to adorn his upper lip. The image accorded ill with the robes of imperial purple he had affected for the occasion. In consequence, he looked neither Goth nor Roman, more a freakish hybrid. Things had changed in the time since Theoderic, by eliminating Odovacar, had made himself undisputed ruler of Italy. Timothy's mind drifted back over the past seven years.

They had been years of astonishing, solid achievement, Timothy reflected, resulting in an Italy that was (to all outward appearance) well run, stable and prosperous – as in the best days of the Caesars. Faced with the daunting and immensely difficult task of providing for his people in a foreign and potentially hostile land, and doing so without antagonizing the new Italian subjects over whom he must establish his rule, Theoderic had, thought Timothy, risen superbly to the occasion. Administered by one Liberius, a senator, a careful sale and redistribution of land had satisfied the great majority of Ostrogoths without bearing too hard on their Roman 'hosts', a settlement facilitated by the fact that the Romans vastly outnumbered their 'guests'. The two peoples were to live strictly under their own laws as separate communities, with distinct functions: the Goths (concentrated mainly in the strategically important north-east of the country, between Pavia and Ravenna) to man the army, the Romans 'to cultivate the arts of peace', and to run the administration. This last, purged of corruption for almost the first time in its long history, functioned efficiently under the Master of Offices and the Praetorian Prefect, assisted by a shadowy tribe of ubiquitous officials known as *agentes in rebus*.

Theoderic himself fulfilled a double role. To the Goths, he presented the assiduously nurtured image of the successful war leader – not difficult, considering his proven record as victorious hero-king, Timothy told himself. To his German compatriots in the Ostrogothic heartlands of Venetia et Histria, Aemilia and Flaminia et Picenum, Theoderic was 'Dietrich von Bern' – Theoderic of Verona (his favourite residence). To the Romans, he tried to appear a worthy successor to the best of their emperors, wise, strong, and even-handed: a stance which seemed to work, as the Romans increasingly compared him to Trajan or Valentinian I. As for the Church, Theoderic was content to act as impartial arbitrator when disputes arose, a position traditionally adopted by emperors from Constantine on; here, his Arianism was actually an advantage, his judgements being perceived as unbiassed. The fact that the Churches of the West and East were in schism also benefited Theoderic by allowing him to appear, if only to a limited extent, as the champion of Rome versus Constantinople.

Preoccupied with implementing these demanding policies, prior to this first visit to Rome Theoderic had had little time to speculate about his constitutional position. The status quo he had achieved would have satisfied the ambition of most rulers – men of, say, Odovacar's stamp, Timothy reflected. And yet he sensed that for Theoderic it was not enough. The Amal king's dream of becoming accepted by the Romans as one of them had never been abandoned, only put on hold while he dealt with the pressing practicalities of getting his people to Italy and establishing his rule there. The recent, tardy confirmation of his status as vicegerent by Anastasius had wrought an immediate (and, to Timothy, misplaced) change in Theoderic's priorities. Hence the visit to Rome.

To Timothy, the king's re-awakened ambition was an unfortunate development. He had seen it all before with successful gang leaders. They acquired delusions of grandeur, craving acceptance by respectable

society, striving for status, titles, above all that most Roman of acco-
lades, *civilitas*.* Almost invariably with such climbers, pride came
before a fall – exposure and disgrace by contemptuous members of the
class they aspired to join, a knife in the back by an ex-colleague in
crime with a score to settle. Take Zeno, a perfect example of a small
fish swimming in a big pond: his Roman subjects had despised him
as a barbarian who had got above himself. If he'd stuck to being warlord
of a tribe of savage hillmen, instead of vying for the purple, he would
never have endured that most horrible of deaths. Would Theoderic
make the same mistake? Was he capable, Timothy wondered, of seeing
himself as he really was: a barbarian leader who, by an extraordinary
combination of luck, personality and circumstance, had made it big
on the world stage? For his own well-being and peace of mind, he
would do well to put aside any dreams of becoming Roman. That way
lay disillusion.

The Romans, Timothy believed, were an arrogant and fickle race,
with long and unforgiving memories stretching back to the massacre
of Varus' legions by Arminius, the German freedom fighter. In the
infancy of some ancients yet alive, one of the greatest of Rome's generals,
Stilicho, debarred from the purple by reason of his Vandal blood, had
perished at the hands of a Roman executioner. For all his Roman
upbringing, Theoderic was still German, a fatal barrier to acceptance
by the Romans. He should remember that. But would he? As much
chance of that happening, Timothy admitted gloomily, as of a camel
going through the eye of a needle.

With the vast expanse of the Campus Martius, studded with theatres
and great public edifices such as the Pantheon, stretching away to the
right, the procession proceeded beneath the huge aqueduct called Aqua
Virgo, passed the Forum of Trajan, skirted the Forum Romanum overlooked by the Capitol, crossed the Tiber by the Aemilian Bridge, left
the city by the Aurelian Gate, and ascended the hill called Vaticanus to
the Basilica of Peter, built by Constantine over the apostle's grave. Here,

---

* A term defying exact translation. High-minded self-control linked to a sense of
justice and respect for law perhaps comes close. The quality was displayed par
excellence by the Roman emperor Marcus Aurelius; witness his noble *Meditations*.

Theoderic went into conclave with the Pope, to settle an ongoing and furious controversy arising from a challenge to the papal succession, and the questionable status of lands gifted to the Church. Timothy found himself wondering how a people who had raised such mighty works, could have allowed themselves to be conquered by illiterate barbarians.

En route, he had been amazed by the numbers of infatuated women who had crowded round the Pope, calling out endearments and fondling his garments – attentions which Symmachus appeared to enjoy, or at any rate did nothing to deter. Particularly brazen was the behaviour of one young female whom the others called 'Spicy',* whose propositions to the Holy Father bordered on the obscene.

Next on the royal itinerary was the Senate House, where Theoderic had been invited to speak before the august assembly. Approaching the rostrum, the king had a sudden, unexpected and extremely disconcerting attack of nerves. Confronting the rows of white-clad senators, their faces for the most part hard, proud and fiercely critical, Theoderic quailed. These Romans were men whose ancestors had ruled a goodly portion of the known world for the better part of a thousand years. And here was he, a mere barbarian, presuming to address them; the purple robe he wore all at once felt like the garb of an imposter. The scene swam before his eyes, and for a terrible moment his mind went blank. Fighting for control, he gripped the rostrum's edge in an effort to restrain the trembling of his hands.

The moment passed; the interior of the great hall came back into focus, the faces of his audience were no longer threatening but politely attentive, if slightly puzzled by the long pause. With confidence flowing back, Theoderic announced, 'Senators of Rome, I am honoured to be asked to speak to you in this historic spot.'

The speech progressed smoothly, consisting essentially of a routine confirmation in office of the great posts of state – the Praetorian Prefect, the Prefect of Rome, the Quaestor, the Master of Offices, the Private and Public Purses, et al. (with compliments about the holders' diligence in carrying out their duties), and the announcement of the names of their successors when the present holders' terms of office should have run their course.

* Sic (see Notes).

'Furthermore,' declared Theoderic, sensing that his speech had so far gone down well, 'I am pleased to express my complete confidence and satisfaction in the Synod's choice as to who should occupy the Bishop's throne of Rome: Symmachus. In consequence, the rival candidate, Laurentius, must abandon his claim to the See of St Peter, but in recognition of his good service he will be permitted to retire from his present post of Bishop of Nocera to a villa on the estates of Festus, which the *Caput Senatus* has graciously made over to his use.* In conclusion, I see no reason to reverse the grants of land formerly made to the Patrimony of St Peter.'

Mistaking the frosty silence that followed for a respectful hush, Theoderic again thanked the Senate for inviting him to speak, and departed from the building.

As soon as the great bronze doors had closed behind the king, uproar broke out. In vain Festus banged the floor with his rod and called for silence, while angry exchanges (the vast majority hostile to Symmachus) flew back and forth among the benches: 'The man's a disgrace – a womaniser who consorts with females of the lowest sort.' 'Symmachus squanders the wealth of the Church on the plebs, to be sure of mob support.' 'Most of those grants were never legally ratified – we've as much right to that land as the Church.' 'My estates in Gaul and Spain were lost to the Franks and Visigoths. If I can't recoup my losses from Saint Peter's Holdings, I could face ruin.' 'He can't even get the date of Easter right.' 'The only reason the Synod chose him was because he was able to back his claim with forged documents.'†

At length, the senators having shouted themselves out, Festus was able to make himself heard. Calling the assembly to order, he declared, 'Clearly, our new lord and master has no conception of the problems arising from confirming Symmachus as Pope, especially that concerning land grants to the Church. As you all know, I myself, like most of you, am strongly opposed to any settlement which favours Symmachus. Quite apart from the man's being morally unfit to sit on the throne of St Peter, the lands that might have been set aside, for the purpose of alleviating the distress of many of you who have lost estates to the

* See Appendix II: The Laurentian Schism.
† The charge was correct (see Notes).

barbarians, are to remain in Church hands. That situation is compounded by the compensation we've all had to pay out for Odovacar's soldiers and Theoderic's Ostrogoths. We must therefore make the king aware of our dilemma and, if possible, get him to reverse his decision.'

'Speak for yourself,' called a florid-faced senator, Faustus *niger*, known to be Symmachus' main champion. This Faustus was a member of the powerful Anicius clan, and notorious for intrigue and shady dealings. 'Surely Theoderic's edict settles the matter? I'd have thought the subject closed for good.'

'Yes, that would suit you splendidly, wouldn't it?' retorted Probinus, next to Festus the leading opponent of Symmachus. 'I expect you've come to a cosy little arrangement with the Pope whereby some of that nice Church land devolves miraculously to yourself.'

After a few more recriminations had been hurled against the numerically insignificant pro-Symmachus party, Festus declared the session closed, with, for the moment, no decision taken as to further action re the Church lands controversy. The assembly broke up in an atmosphere of rancorous bile, knots of senators muttering ill-temperedly among themselves as they left the Senate House.

'In this year of the consuls Patricius and Hypatius and from the Founding of the City the twelve hundred and fifty third, being also the five hundred and first from the birth of Our Lord Jesus Christ,' intoned the Master of Ceremonies, 'His Majesty Theoderic, king of the Amal and vicegerent of Italy, bids you all welcome.' In the great audience hall of Domitian's Domus Augustana on the Palatine were assembled, together with their wives, the great and good of Rome at a reception hosted by Theoderic. Senators and scholars mingled with bishops, senior civil servants, and the papal entourage; the vast chamber was ablaze with polychrome marble and adorned with enormous statues. Slaves bearing trays of delicacies or flagons of wine wove among the throng from which arose a buzz of animated conversation.

Theoderic circulated among his guests, chatting easily in excellent if rather rusty Latin, and even being given the chance to air his Greek when introduced to two scholar-aristocrats, young Anicius Manlius Severinus Boethius (son of the recently deceased Marius Manlius Boethius,

City Prefect and Praetorian Prefect), and Quintus Aurelius Memmius Symmachus, a senator from Rome's most distinguished family. With these two the king felt an immediate rapport, also a rekindling of interest in intellectual pursuits which, of necessity, had been forced into abeyance since his youth in Constantinople. He decided there and then to invite them to join his inner circle of councillors and advisers. He felt instinctively that these were soul mates who would be of use not only in helping him to frame his policies, but also in realizing his dream of being accepted as a Roman – perhaps even (Tell it not in Gath) in taking the ultimate step of becoming Roman emperor. Then he remembered: seven years ago, Symmachus and the father of Boethius had been among those voting for Odovacar. Well, at least that spoke of courage and loyalty, qualities especially admired by his own people, and rarely enough found among today's Romans. He would not hold the past against them. Excited and happy, Theoderic continued to mingle. After the long years of struggle and hardship, his ambitions seemed at last to be moving smoothly towards fulfilment.

The climax of the evening arrived: the presentation to his guests of medallions to celebrate his *tricennalia*, the thirty years that had elapsed since his capture of Singidunum from Babai, king of the Sarmatians. The beautiful discs, each a triple solidus in weight, showed on the obverse a frontal picture of Theoderic with long hair and moustache, clad in imperial robes, right hand half raised, the left holding a globe surmounted by a figure of Victory. On this side, the legend round the edge read: '*REX THEODERICUS PIUS PRINC I S*'.* The wording had been chosen with the utmost care, so as not to offend his Roman subjects. Theoderic was '*Rex*' only to the Goths, the title still anathema to Romans a thousand years after they had rid themselves of their own kings. '*Princeps*', the title chosen by Augustus in preference to '*Imperator*', implied (by a polite fiction designed by Rome's first emperor to soothe republican sensitivities) first among equals, rather than absolute ruler.

The distribution of the medallions proceeded amid exclamations of surprise and pleasure from the recipients. However, with some senators – those most bitterly opposed to Symmachus over the issue

---

* Expanded, this becomes: *Rex Theodericus pius princeps invictus semper* – King Theoderic Dutiful Leader Ever Unconquered.

concerning Church lands – this was a mere façade behind which, taking
care not to be overheard, they expressed their true feelings among themselves, in whispers: 'Barbarian locks and moustache, yet he has the
effrontery to have himself represented wearing an emperor's robe.' *'Pius
Princeps* indeed – who does he think he is, another Hadrian perhaps?'
'If he thinks a pretty bauble's going to shut us up, he can think again.'

Then one of them floated an idea: 'Why don't we take the opportunity to put him straight about the Church lands? He's in a good mood
– we may never get a better chance than now. Probinus, you're the best
one to put our case; would you approach him on our behalf?'

Emboldened by collective resentment, the others, after minimal
discussion, agreed to the suggestion, Probinus volunteering to be
spokesman.

'Majesty, a moment of your time, if it pleases you to spare it.'

Theoderic turned, to find a tall, distinguished-looking senator
smiling at him.

'Speak.'

'It's this business of Church lands, Your Majesty. Perhaps you may
not be fully aware of all aspects of the matter. If I may be permitted
to elucidate?' Taking Theoderic's silence for assent, the other pressed
on. 'When our ancestors made these grants, in many cases before the
invasions of a century ago, it was not intended that they should belong
to the Church in perpetuity. They were merely temporary loans to
enable the Church to raise money by short-term leases or the sale of
produce. Unfortunately, many of the documents which would prove
this have been, ah . . . "lost", as Pope Symmachus maintains. Others,
we think, have been deliberately falsified. If Your Majesty would care
to review the facts behind the case, you would be assured of our most
heartfelt gratitude.'

'And who are "we"?' Theoderic enquired, his tone deceptively mild.

'Almost all the senators of Rome, Your Majesty. Hardly one of us
but has lost lands to the barbarians – to the extent that many of us are
struggling to survive.' Probinus' heart sank, as he suddenly realized his
gaffe in using that charged word 'barbarians'.

Theoderic regarded him with rising anger and contempt. Smooth-
tongued hypocrite. He knew the type: self-serving aristocrats, like the

fathers of his school fellows in Constantinople, whose chief concern was to preserve their privileges, men who would close ranks the moment the interests of their class were threatened. Red rage exploded in his brain.

'You disgust me!' roared Theoderic. 'My edict stands. Get out of my sight!'

'As Your Majesty commands.' Probinus bowed coolly and backed away, the great hall suddenly falling silent.

Shaking with fury and humiliation, Theoderic knew that the reception was ruined past repair. He signalled the Master of Ceremonies to make the appropriate announcement.

'Well, at least we know now where we stand,' sighed Probinus as his group made its way towards the Forum. 'For all that he speaks Latin and doesn't scratch his arse, the fellow's an out-and-out barbarian.'

'And an Arian to boot,' fluted old Festus. 'Anthemius would never have behaved like that.' He was referring to the last emperor of any substance whom most of them could still remember.

'Nor would Odovacar,' declared Faustus *albus*, one of the strongest pro-Laurentians, despite his kinsman Faustus *niger* being Symmachus' patron. 'He'd just have laughed in your face, and told you to go to hell. So what do we do now? Ideas, anyone?'

'We bide our time,' pronounced Probinus. 'With Pope Symmachus able to whistle up the plebs against us, and Constantinople playing hard to get, we've no choice. For the moment, we keep our heads down and bend with the wind. Our time will come.'

As come it surely would. For these were patient, cunning men, who knew, above all, about survival. Their families, many of which went back to the Republic, had seen imperial dynasties come and go, Rome itself rise and fall, yet were themselves still here. One barbarian ruler more or less was hardly going to make a dent in their long-term fortunes.

TWENTY-FOUR

In celebration of his 'tricennalia' he [Theoderic] ... exhibited games in
the Circus for the Romans
Anonymous Valesianus, *Excerpta: pars posterior, c.* 530

During the next few weeks, Theoderic endeavoured assiduously to restore his image, which had been seriously damaged by his outburst at the palace reception. Such displays of unrestrained fury were, like drunkenness, regarded with indulgence (sometimes even admiration) by his own people, but among the Romans could result in a serious loss of *dignitas* – the very quality that distinguished Romans from barbarians.* *Dignitas* implied self-control, living according to a code in which passions were always subordinated to reason – a code (according to Roman received opinion) conspicuously absent among barbarians.

Acceptance by the Romans (and ultimately any prospect of becoming their emperor) depended, Theoderic knew, on his being accepted by their representative assembly, the Senate. Despite the Senate's apparent lack of political power, Theoderic knew it would be a grave mistake to dismiss it as a merely passive body, whose only function was to legitimize the policies of whatever ruler was in power. In the past, emperors who had continued to flout the accepted mores of SPQR† never died in their beds. The outrages of a Nero, a Caligula, a Commodus, a Heliogabalus, or a Valentinian III, ensured their violent removal. Even in the empire's dying days, the Senate's disapproval was enough to ensure the execution not only of Arvandus and Seronatus, Prefect and Deputy Prefect of Gaul respectively, but of Emperor Avitus, for the crime of making terms with the barbarians – the very people about to take over the Western Empire.

---

* See Appendix III: Romans and Barbarians.
† *Senatus populusque romanus* – The Senate and people of Rome.

As ruler, Theoderic could not apologize for his loss of temper *tricennalia*, nor for depriving the Laurentian senators of Church l. But he did the next best thing: made himself regularly attend sess. of the Senate, where he comported himself with respectful attentiv ness bordering on meekness. (Shades of Theodosius I doing penanc before Ambrose, Bishop of Milan.) And, employing a tried and tested gesture guaranteed to attract popularity from plebs and patricians alike, he decided to hold Games in the Flavian Amphitheatre.* (Normally, this would have been the dubious 'privilege' of the Western consul, but this year both consuls were Eastern appointees.)

Compared to the 'good old days' of high empire, Games had become a rarity in Rome. Disruption of trade routes resulting from barbarian invasions, centuries of depletion of wildlife stock, with shrinkage of state and aristocratic wealth, had made the capture, transport and maintenance of large animals an extremely difficult and prohibitively expensive business. Nevertheless, the recent thawing of relations between the Vandal and Ostrogothic kingdoms, combined with substantial disbursements from Theoderic's treasury, ensured ships laden with crates, containing savage beasts from north Africa, unloaded at the quays of Ostia.

Outside the amphitheatre, a huge and noisy crowd was building up. 'Ticket-holders only,' bawled a burly security guard, whereupon those fortunate enough to possess a bone slip marked with seat, tier and entrance numbers poured into the great building through seventy-six of its eighty entrances. (Of its remaining four, two were for royalty and aristocracy, the other two, which opened directly into the arena, were the Doors of Life and Death, for the entry of contestants and the removal of dead bodies respectively.) Once the ticket-holders had been shown by *locarii*, ushers, to their seats in the lowest three of the four tiers of stands, divided horizontally by flat walks and vertically by flights of stairs, the guards at the entrances stood aside, and non-ticket-holders dashed in to find a seat in the aisles or a standing-place in the topmost tier. Directly below the lowest tier, encircling the arena, ran a fifteen-foot wall, its smooth

---

* i.e., the Colosseum – a popular name, bestowed not on account of the building's size but because of its propinquity to a colossal statue of Nero.

marble surface topped with revolving cylinders of bronze, denying purchase to any beast attempting to climb it.

Inside, a soft glow filled the stadium – sunlight diffused through the awning which covered the vast oval's open top. This was the responsibility of *nautae*, sailors, who alone possessed the skills necessary for securing the enormous sheet by means of a complex system of ropes and pulleys to a ring of masts projecting from the topmost tier. Now the aristocracy – almost all senators in their traditional togas, accompanied by their wives – filed into the first thirty-six rows of seats reserved for the upper classes. Next came the privileged guests – Pope Symmachus surrounded by a coterie of leading clergy and female admirers; members of Rome's top families: the Symmachi, Decii and Anicii. These seated themselves in the podium on *curule* chairs, movable to allow their occupants to get up and stroll at will. Finally, with a flourish of trumpets, the royal party, consisting of Theoderic with his bodyguard, accompanied by Symmachus and Boethius, now his chief advisers, and the *editor* of the Games, Probinus, entered the royal box raised above the podium, from the rear. In a gesture of appeasement to the Laurentian senators, Theoderic had invited their leader to become the Games' organizer, a position which carried enormous prestige, but also normally enormous cost – however, in this instance it was being borne by the king as *munerator* or producer.

To Theoderic's shocked amazement, a barrage of rude comments was hurled by the plebs at the patricians in the podium and privileged seats: 'Hi, there, Spicy. What's the Holy Father like in bed?' 'Antonia, is it true you've worn out three new boyfriends, and you old enough to be their grandmother?' 'Basilius, you old goat, that little slave-girl keeping you warm at night?' The recipients of the taunts, though doubtless raging inside, made no response, for to do so would be a breach of *dignitas*.

A trumpet-blast announced the entry of the *venatores* or huntsmen, lean, muscled men, armed variously with spears, daggers, swords, nets, and bows. Animal-fighting alone survived of the arena's blood sports: gladiatorial combats had been ended by Emperor Honorius ninety-six years previously, after a frenzied mob had torn to pieces a monk, Telemachus, for intervening in a fight; and a generation prior to that, Valentinian I had stopped the practice of condemned criminals, *noxii*, being savaged to death by wild beasts. Nevertheless, the *venationes* or wild-beast hunts still provided enough gore and excitement to whip the mob into a frenzy of blood-lust. After circling the arena to wild applause, the procession formed up before the royal box and saluted Theoderic and Probinus in turn, before departing.

A moment's hush, then again the trumpet sounded, and a tide of wild animals began to pour into the arena. Until this moment, they had been kept in cages deep in the bowels of the amphitheatre; the cages were hauled by a system of lifts and pulleys to passageways leading to the arena, then opened.

Thrasamund, king of the Vandals, had done him proud, thought Theoderic, looking in wonder at the multicoloured mass of swarming animals: antelopes, jackals, hyenas, ostriches, leopards, lions, cheetahs, buffaloes, a rhinoceros, even several elephants. The marriage alliance he had forged with the Vandal widower (just one example of the good relations established with other barbarian leaders in the West) – sending him his widowed sister Amalafrida as prospective bride – had paid off handsomely. Thrasamund's Berber and Moorish hunters had done a magnificent job; they must have penetrated deep into the continent's interior to have been able to bring back such an astonishing variety of wildlife. Fights continually broke out among the animals, but the arena was so crowded that the contestants were swept apart as the stampeding throng frantically sought for means of escape.

At a signal from Probinus, the trumpet sounded and the *venatores* rushed into the arena through the openings the animals had used. The air filled with brays, roars and bellows as the huntsmen set to work, despatching their quarry with incredible speed and skill, some leaping from back to back delivering fatal thrusts in motion, or loosing volleys of arrows, each shaft finding its mark. The mighty elephants were among the easiest to slaughter – killed instantly by a chisel hammered between the cervical vertebrae, or hamstrung to immobilize them, then their trunks slashed off when they quickly bled to death. When at last the crowd of animals began to thin out, the trumpet sounded for the end of the hunt. The *venatores* now made way for the *bestiarii*, animal-handlers. These, armed with lead-tipped flails and blazing torches, drove the surviving beasts back into the passageways, whose gates had been opened, with basins of water placed inside to attract the exhausted animals. When the carcasses had been dragged out through the Door of Death, and with the arena once more empty, the crowd hushed in anticipation of the next show. Word had got around that this was to be something special . . .

A team of slaves carrying a long stake hurried to the middle of the arena. Some scraped away the covering of sand to reveal the planking beneath, a section of which was removed, disclosing a hole into which the stake was fitted. Two more slaves led out a struggling young woman and chained her by the waist to the stake. A huge, heavily muscled man was then conducted to the spot, and released. Shaking his mane of red hair, he glared defiantly around at the vast audience.

Probinus moved his *curule* seat to be directly behind Theoderic. 'The woman's a murderess,' he murmured. 'Stabbed her master when he tried to rape her. The man's a Celt, a runaway slave from the sulphur mines. When he was recaptured he disabled three men so badly that they'll never work again. It should be interesting to see how long he can protect her against the assault of wild beasts.'

'*Damnata ad bestias!*' exclaimed the king. 'But that's unlawful, surely?'

Probinus shrugged. 'Technically, perhaps, Your Majesty. However . . .'

He was interrupted by the trumpet's brazen clang. Into the arena walked a huge white bull with massive forequarters and long, wickedly pointed horns. The creature's skin slid and rippled like silk above its muscles as it moved. This was Europe's great wild ox, which the Romans called *Urus* and the Germans *Aurochs*, noted for its implacable ferocity when roused.

A gasp of excited admiration arose as the great beast trotted round the arena, establishing its territory. Spotting the woman and the huge Celt, he turned to face them and began to paw the sand. Immediately, the woman started shrieking and struggling – her cries and frantic movements providing the very stimulus to trigger an attack. With shocking suddenness the aurochs launched itself towards her.

Gripping the arms of his *curule* seat, Theoderic leant forward in an agony of suspense, willing the Celt to try to save the woman. But surely it could only be a doomed attempt. An unarmed man, no matter how powerful, could be no match for an enraged bull. As the ton of white destruction hurtled towards its victim, the Celt ran forward to meet it and grabbed its horns by their tips. At first he was borne along helplessly by the creature's impetus. Gradually, however, his churning feet found purchase on the sand, until, yards from the stake, he managed to bring the monster to a halt. Legs braced like tree-trunks, biceps bulging with titanic effort, he strained to twist the creature's horns.

A roar of incredulous delight burst from the spectators. Almost imperceptibly, the great bull's head was beginning to turn. The movement gradually accelerated – now the neck was sharply angled to the body; an agonized bellow, a loud *crack!* like a snapping branch, and the animal slumped to the sand.

For a moment the audience was silent, then it broke into wild, sustained applause.

'They await your decision, Majesty,' prompted Probinus.

Startled, Theoderic collected himself. From his readings of Roman history, he knew the correct response. Rising to his feet, he extended his right fist. To ecstatic cheering from the crowd, he raised the thumb. Turning to Probinus he commanded, 'Have him brought to me.'

'You are a brave man,' declared Theoderic, his voice warm with admiration, when the Celt – chest heaving as he fought for air, body dripping sweat – stood below the royal box. 'What is your name?'

'I am Conall Cearnach, a Scot from Dalriada in Caledonia. But my forebears came from Hibernia; that's the island—'

'—to the west of Britannia,' finished Theoderic with a smile. 'I am not entirely ignorant of geography, you see. The Scots are a brave and loyal race, I've heard. My bodyguard could use such men. What would you say to joining them?'

'Anything is better than the sulphur mines.'

'Have this man taken to the palace,' Theoderic told Probinus, 'with instructions that he be fed, allowed to wash, then clothed.'

'The man is still a slave, Your Majesty,' objected the senator. 'A slave, moreover, who has inflicted grave injury on several men.'

Fury filled Theoderic. About to roar a reprimand to the *editor*, he remembered – just in time – to check himself. *Dignitas*. 'See to it,' he snapped.

'Very well, Majesty.'

A growing impatient buzz alerted the king to the fact that the crowd was growing restive. Looking up, he was amazed to see the woman still secured to the stake.

'Why has she not been freed?' he demanded. 'I raised my thumb.'

'Surely, Majesty, your gesture indicated that mercy be shown to the man alone,' Probinus pointed out.

Again, rage threatened to overwhelm the king. Was he to be balked at every turn by this arrogant aristocrat? With a huge effort, he controlled his anger. 'Free her,' he ordered, forcing himself to speak evenly.

Seated to his right, Symmachus turned to speak. The great senator's face was furrowed in concern and sympathy. 'Serenity, would that be wise?' he cautioned. 'Your instinct is a noble one; it does you great credit. But to free the woman would be to disappoint the crowd. That might be' – he paused, searching for the right word – 'let us say, impolitic.'

'Impolitic?'

'Serenity, *seditio popularis* is easily aroused and can have terrible consequences.' The patrician's voice held a note of urgency. 'Only last year the Pope himself was injured in a riot, and several priests were killed. And many present can remember the lynching by an angry mob of the emperor Petronius Maximus.'

All Theoderic's nature, with its German sense of honour and reverence for women, rose in revolt against the idea of having to appease the Roman mob. Now he could see clearly what that snake Probinus' game was: to box him into a corner, forcing him to act against his nature, in a demonstration that it was the Senate, not the king, who held the reins of power. Well, he was Theoderic, the warrior king of a heroic race, who ruled by right of conquest. He would show these Romans who was master. Then something tugged at his memory, cooling his indignation. Symmachus had addressed him as 'Serenity', a title used for emperors alone! Conflict raged within the king: desire to act honourably, according to his principles and conscience, versus a new emotion, a heady exaltation that his dream, acceptance by the Romans as their emperor, could be on the point of being realized. But that acceptance was conditional, he knew; an emperor must please his people.

Meanwhile, the clamour of the crowd had risen to a rhythmic, thunderous chant: '*Ad bestias! Ad bestias! Ad bestias!*'

Like an enormous weight, Theoderic seemed to feel the force of fifty thousand wills pressing against his own. Guilt and shame welled up within him – to be suppressed by the promptings of ambition. Again, his fist came forward, but this time the thumb turned down, in the gesture of *pollice verso*. A roar of triumphant approval burst from the throats of the mob.

A great spotted cat padded into the arena.

TWENTY-FIVE

Whatever deceives seems to exercise a kind of magical enchantment
Plato, *The Republic, c.* 350 BC

Concerned about his master's growing obsession with what was bound
to be a mirage, Timothy decided to find out for himself what the
Romans thought of the idea of Theoderic as emperor. With his richly
varied background, which had seen his career progress from streetwise
gangster to royal minder to *agens in rebus* with an imperial commission, Timothy was well placed to move freely between the different
strata of Roman society – from its dregs in the Subura, the city's poorest
quarter, to the rarified world of Domitian's Palace populated by (menials
apart) civil servants, *silentiarii,* and a select band of senatorial aristocrats who constituted a kind of unofficial council for Theoderic while
he was in Rome. (The king's permanent council in Ravenna consisted
of Roman officials of middle-class background, along with high-ranking
duces or army commanders – almost all Goths – and a very few Goths
of proven ability, sufficient to enable them to hold administrative posts.)

Timothy commenced his research beneath the arches of the Circus
Maximus, the vast U-shaped stadium where chariot races were held.
Known as 'Under-the-Stands', this was an amazing world of its own,
a labyrinth of interlocking passages formed by the hundreds of arches
supporting the tiers of seats above, and populated by a colourful under-
class of fortune-tellers, astrologers, ready-meal vendors, souvenir sellers,
pimps, prostitutes, jugglers, conjurers ... The answers to Timothy's
question about Theoderic as emperor, though varied in style of
expression, were remarkably consistent in content: 'A Jerry emperor?
You've got to be joking!' 'We don't want none o' them Tedesci* bastards
wearing the diadem.' 'Theoderic's all right – gives us bread and circuses

* From *Lingua Theodisca,* the Roman name for the Goths' language.

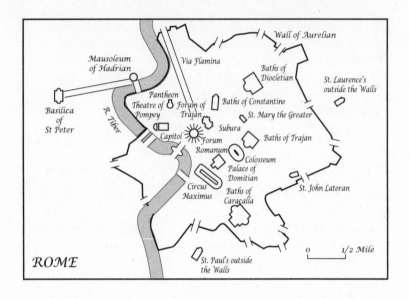

ROME

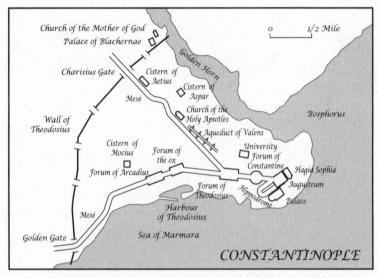

CONSTANTINOPLE

ROME AND CONSTANTINOPLE c. 500 AD

don't he? But emperor? Nah, wouldn't be right, would it? 'E's German, see.' He got similar responses in the stinking alleys of the Subura, in Chilo's Tavern near the Porta Appia – famous as an emporium of news and gossip – and in the crowded flats of that monstrous tenement the Insula of Felicula, Rome's tallest building, home to the families of tradesmen living just above the poverty line.

From the top of the great high-rise building – which had become almost as famous a tourist attraction in Rome as the Pyramids were in Egypt – Timothy looked down two hundred feet to the vast city sprawling away to the confining circuit of Aurelian's Wall. Northwards, to his left, between the Tiber and that great arrow-straight artery the Via Flaminia, stretched the level expanse of the Campus Martius; to his right, on the spurs of the Quirinal and Viminal hills, reared the Baths of Constantine and Diocletian. To the south, between the Baths of Trajan and Domitian's Palace, rose the mighty oval of the Colosseum with, beyond, the pale oblong of the Circus Maximus, fully half a mile in length. Directly below, a forest of pillars extending from the foot of the Capitol to the Sacred Way, lay the city's venerable heart, the Forum Romanum. In all directions, striding on tall arches above the roof-tops and the new basilicas everywhere replacing the ancient temples, marched the aqueducts, a network of stone suspended above the huge metropolis. Once again, Timothy found himself wondering how it was that a race capable of creating such marvels had been laid low by primitive tribesmen from the northern forests.

From comments gleaned in the palace, Timothy got the impression that the prejudice against the idea of a German emperor was even stronger among the middle and upper classes than among the plebs, although articulated with more sophistication and some attempt at reasoned argument. Germans were irredeemably wild, treacherous and unpredictable, unfitted by blood to hold the most prestigious office of all. Properly led, they could admittedly make good soldiers; some had even risen to the highest ranks of the army – witness Stilicho, the great Vandal general. But even he had proved untrustworthy, his Teutonic heritage showing through when, having spared his fellow German Alaric, Rome's great enemy, and preoccupied with plans to invade the Eastern Empire, he failed to stop a huge German confederation crossing the Rhine and overrunning Gaul and Spain.

So ran the special pleading. Timothy, however, suspected that the real reason was much more atavistic. Barring the wastes of Caledonia and Scandia,* Germania was the only part of Europe that Rome had failed to conquer. Her one attempt to do so had ended in disaster – three legions slaughtered in the depths of the Teutoburger Forest. The horror of that event had inflicted an enduring trauma on the collective mind of Rome, something never to be forgotten – or forgiven. And in the end, Rome had endured the ultimate humiliation: being conquered by the very German tribes she feared and hated above all. Small wonder, then, that, alone of almost every race within the empire and beyond, Germans had never been permitted to wear the imperial diadem.

Although his rank of *agens in rebus* enabled him to mingle on the fringes of the upper class, Timothy could hardly approach the senatorial aristocracy directly. But from conversations with the *silentiarii*, the highest rung of the social ladder he had access to (and one that did have contact with blue-blooded patricians), he discovered some disturbing facts. Boethius and Symmachus, the very pair who commanded most influence with the king, were the leading lights of a coterie of intellectuals centred in both Rome and Constantinople. The circle also included the Greek-speaking Petronius Cethegus, son of the Probinus who led the Laurentian faction and a major thorn in Theoderic's flesh; the young senator and historian Cassiodorus; and Priscian, a Constantinopolitan member of the African diaspora that had followed the Vandal invasion. (Priscian had met and befriended Symmachus when the latter visited the Eastern capital. He was also an enthusiastic apologist for the Eastern Emperor, Anastasius, whom he described in a panegyric as welcoming refugees from old Rome to his court in new Rome.) These were men, in constant touch through letters and mutual visits, whose views counted throughout the Roman world (rather as, three or four generations previously, had those of Augustine, Jerome, Ambrose and their circle), to the extent of being able to influence the attitude of leading Romans in both Italy and the Eastern Empire. What worried Timothy was the suspicion, ground out by the busy rumour mill of palace intrigue, that these men, all champions of Nicene orthodoxy, were strongly anti-Arian – the branch of Christianity to which Theoderic belonged.

* Scandinavia.

Even more disturbing was the suggestion that they regarded a barbarian king of Italy as merely the head of a caretaker government, until, in the words of Priscian, 'both Romes would come to obey the emperor alone'. This might be nothing more than windy rhetoric, Timothy thought, an intellectual nostalgia for the days when the empire had had a Western as well as an Eastern half. Or, taken out of context, it could be interpreted as highly treasonable. That word 'refugees' in Priscian's panegyric implied that some Romans, at least, were unhappy with Ostrogothic rule, and therefore might in the future challenge Theoderic's authority. Understanding (and caring) nothing about the theological aspects of the Laurentian Schism, Timothy nevertheless knew that its effect had been to cool relations between Rome (and by extension, Italy) and Constantinople. Therefore anything which fervently extolled the rule of Anastasius, as Priscian's panegyric had done, could, by implication, almost be held to denigrate that of Theoderic.

Unwelcome though he felt the news would be, Timothy knew he would be wanting in his duty if he failed to lay his findings before Theoderic. It was with a heavy heart that he approached the king's quarters in the palace.

Theoderic had never been so happy. Sequestered in a small *tablinum* or study-cum-library which he used as a council chamber, he began discussing the schedule for the day with his two new friends and chief advisers, Symmachus, the wise and cultured senator, and young Boethius, a brilliant scholar whose mind displayed the grasp and judgement of someone far beyond his years. Thanks to the assistance of this gifted pair, those early years of consolidating his rule following the overthrow of Odovacar, were being crowned by ambitious plans which were already beginning to spread his fame and influence far beyond the confines of Italy, and bidding fair to make Theoderic the mentor and unofficial leader of all the German peoples. And when the business of the day was done, it was an unalloyed pleasure to discuss, sometimes in Greek, the literature and philosophy of Greece and Rome: something for which his soul had hungered ever since he had been forced to abandon his studies in Constantinople.

Already accepted by other barbarian kings (even the ferocious Vandals) in the former Western Empire as a ruler too powerful to tangle with,

Theoderic had only one real problem: his brother-in-law, the Frankish monarch, Clovis. Twelve years younger than Theoderic, the ambitious Clovis, whose marriage to a Catholic princess, Clotilda, was followed by his own conversion from Arianism, had embarked on plans to extend his rule over the whole of Gaul – plans which threatened Theoderic's Visigothic kinsmen and allies in Aquitania, and had led to a pre-emptive strike by Clovis against the Alamanni on Gaul's eastern border. The cynical cover for these aggressive moves was a professed desire to bring the light of Catholicism to those benighted heretics living in Arian darkness – a ploy which had succeeded with the late Pope Anastasius, leading him to confer on Clovis the title of 'Most Christian King'. Boethius and Symmachus were at present engaged in helping Theoderic devise a policy aimed at curbing Clovis' expansionist designs.

'A firm but tactful stance might be the best approach, Serenity,' suggested Symmachus; 'a hint of iron hand in velvet glove.'

'Reinforced with a "sweetener" perhaps,' added Boethius with an innocent-seeming smile. 'The man loves music, especially songs accompanied by the harp. Why don't we send him an expert harpist, one who can make up songs extolling Clovis' martial feats? That's sure to go down well; our Frankish friend is not impervious to flattery.'

'Excellent,' laughed Theoderic, clapping the young man on the shoulder. 'Quintus,' he said to Symmachus, 'time to put your epistolary skills to use.'

'"Theoderic, king of the Ostrogoths,"' Symmachus read aloud, some time later, '"to his esteemed brother-in-law, Clovis, king of the Franks, greetings. The husband of your beloved sister appeals to you for help in resolving the delicate situation in which he finds himself. For I am between Scylla and Charybdis.* The Alamanni, against whom you recently won a great and glorious victory, and who have now sought refuge within my own realm, have appealed to me to intercede with you on their behalf. I beg you, take the advice of an older man whose experience has taught him that successful wars are those brought to completion with moderation. I ask you, in the name

---

* In Greek legend, two sea-monsters believed to drown sailors navigating the Straits of Messina. In popular parlance, the expression would translate as 'between a rock and a hard place'.

of friendship, to desist from further hostile action against your former foes. Likewise, I urge you to end your campaign against the Visigoths. As his friend as well as kinsman, honour would compel me to come to the assistance of King Alaric II, should he request it. But I trust it will not come to that. Restraint and good sense on your part will, I am sure, prevail.

"'As a token of my goodwill and continuing friendship, I am accompanying this letter with a gift, which will, I hope, prove a source of pleasure and solace in the manner of Orpheus.'"

Symmachus looked up with a dubious smile. 'I wonder if perhaps I haven't laid the flattery on a bit too thickly in parts, Serenity?'

'Not at all,' enthused Theoderic. 'You've hit the right note exactly. Subtlety's not one of Clovis's strong points. I'd be surprised if this doesn't get results. Now to find that harpist.'

Observing Theoderic's expression as he concluded his report, Timothy's heart sank. The king's face, which at first had reddened, was now pale.

'Where did you get this information?' The voice was ominously quiet.

'From all over Rome, Deric – from the slums, the taverns, even from the palace.'

'The idle gossip of the mob, backstairs chit-chat among palace underlings. You give credence to such malicious drivel?'

'It can't all be dismissed, surely? Sometimes it's one's painful duty to tell a friend what he doesn't want to hear.'

'You dare to call yourself my friend! Symmachus and Boethius, whom you choose to smear, they are my friends – *true* friends.'

'They're *Romans*, Deric!' cried Timothy, becoming desperate. 'Of course they're going to go along with you, agree with everything you say. It's in their interest to do so. It's all smiles and flattery – for the present. But times can change. Suppose this rift between Rome and Constantinople gets healed, and the East wishes to recover Italy for the Roman Empire? Do you really think that Symmachus and Boethius wouldn't drop you in a moment? Open your eyes.'

'Enough!' roared Theoderic, raising his fist.

'Strike me if you must, but I'll finish what I have to say. Forget these dreams of becoming Roman emperor; you can never be

"Theodericus Augustus". But you *can* be "Dietrich von Bern". That's your true role, Deric, a German ruler of a foreign land. Be content with that, as all the other German kings have been, from Gaiseric and Odovacar to Clovis and Alaric II. There, I've done.'

'As I've done with you.' The king's voice was now level, but with an edge of cold fury. He scratched a message on a pair of waxed writing-tablets – the diptych with exquisitely carved ivory covers presented to him on his consulship, sixteen years before. 'Go back to Constantinople, Timothy,' he said, handing him the tablets. 'This message will enable you to draw funds sufficient for the journey from the *Comes Rei Privatae*. You may keep the diptych – a memento of a friendship which is now no more.'

The lump in his throat prevented Timothy from speaking. Nodding in acknowledgement, he turned and headed for the door, half blinded by tears – the first he had known since his mother's death, when he was a child.

TWENTY-SIX

Another Orpheus, who by his singing and playing will bring delight to the glory of your power

Cassiodorus, *Variae*, c. 537

As the little ship approached the island in the Sequana* fringed by the concrete ramparts of Parisia (formerly Lutetia Parisiorum), Connal was surprised to hear the skipper order the helmsman to steer towards the wharves on the southern bank. The skipper pointed to a complex of impressive-looking buildings looming through the late-autumn drizzle half a mile distant, beyond a scatter of mean huts and muddy fields. 'Palatia Thermarum, the old HQ of the provincial governor under the empire. That's where you'll find the king – if he's not off hunting or campaigning.'

The ship having docked, Connal paid the man off and disembarked his escort plus harpist, with whose delivery to Clovis Theoderic had entrusted him. Following his manumission at the Colosseum, Connal had been recruited into the king's household guard, a small corps of warriors handpicked for loyalty and courage. With his formidable physique and natural authority Connal had quickly risen to become their captain, creating such a favourable impression on Theoderic as to make the Celt an ideal choice of emissary to send to Clovis, with Symmachus' letter accompanied by 'gift'.

The group had travelled by sea from Ostia, the port of Rome, to Massilia,† thence north along the Roman road through land controlled by the Visigoths up the Rhodanus valley on foot (in preference to river travel made hazardous by the rapid current and shifting sandbanks), as far as Lugdunum.‡ Here the Rhodanus veered sharply to the east, the road now following an affluent flowing from the north. This route

* River Seine.
† Marseilles.
‡ Lyons.

163

they took for a further hundred miles through Burgundian territory, then struck overland north-west past the site of Alesia (where, five and a half centuries before, Julius Caesar had finally crushed the Gauls led by their valiant young chief, Vercingetorix), to the headwaters of the Sequana in the kingdom of the Franks. There, they had taken passage on a supply vessel heading for Parisia.

As the vessel progressed along the winding river through rich champaign country, Connal reflected on the strange twists of fortune that had brought him to his present position.

Connal's grandfather, a chieftain in the kingdom of Dalriada (at that time located only in Hibernia), had been converted to Christianity by Patricius when the latter arrived from Gaul to begin his mission to his native homeland, in the reign of the emperor Valentinian III. The seed the holy man scattered fell on fertile soil indeed, and he was soon consecrating bishops, ordaining vast numbers of priests, and blessing many monks and nuns, while through his influence a culture of piety and learning quickly took root throughout the island. This same culture Connal's father had taken with him to Caledonia, when Dalriada created an extension of itself across the Oceanus Atlanticus. Born in the final years of Rome's Empire in the West, young Connal had grown up learning (besides his Gaelic mother tongue) to speak and read Latin, to become versed in Vergil as well as St Jerome, and skilled in the playing of the harp besides the arts of war.

Then, at the age of twenty, he had been snatched by pirates (very active along Britannia's western shores), and bought by Gaulish slavers who had sold him to a Roman senator. Condemned to an existence of brutal toil on the Roman's *latifundium*, or large estate, he had contrived to escape, almost killing the overseer in the process. Deemed *ferox et indocilis* at his recapture, he had been sold on to the sulphur mines, where life expectancy seldom exceeded five years. At the time of his escape from the mines followed by recapture and sending to the Colosseum, he had survived for six, thanks to an iron constitution and his will to live.

Meeting the Frankish king, Connal seemed to be confronting his mirror image. Apart from being a few years older, and with a tawny mane rather than a red, Clovis (despite being German and the other Celtic), might have been the Scot's twin brother: similar features, identical height of some six and a half feet, same massive breadth of shoulder and powerfully muscled frame. The remarkable resemblance struck both men immediately, causing Clovis to utter a delighted whoop and give Connal's arm a playful punch. After introducing himself and the harpist (a diffident lad of eighteen) and handing over Theoderic's letter, which Clovis quickly scanned, Connal, together with his group, was conducted through the maze of halls and peristyles comprising the palace, which was complemented by an enormous bath-house – now merely ornamental, the heating system having broken down. The king seemed boyishly pleased to be able to show off the splendours of his residence to one who was obviously capable of appreciating them. The effect, however, was somewhat spoiled by the indifference to their surroundings of the Frankish warriors who, clad in the close-fitting and brightly coloured garments by which the tribe was known, thronged the place, cooking meals and allowing dogs and horses to defecate freely on exquisite mosaic floors.

The Frankish king came over to Connal as a larger-than-life figure, filled with restless energy and enthusiasm. Shouting convivialities at his soldiers, who responded in kind, declaiming over murals or the wonders of the hypocaust (even though it no longer worked), the king led the party on at a relentless pace, barely stopping long enough in one spot for Connal to appreciate its features. The persona of rumbustious bonhomie masked, Connal felt, a sharp and calculating intelligence.

The whirlwind tour completed, Connal asked the king what answer to his letter he should convey to Theoderic, on returning to Italy. They were now alone in a neglected and overgrown formal garden, the escort and harpist having been dismissed to mingle with the Franks.

'You may tell my brother-in-law, *Doppelgänger* mine, that I thank him for his gift, and promise to be most conscientious in heeding his advice. Say also that his comment as to Orpheus isn't lost on me,' the king added with a chuckle. 'My Franks could certainly do with a spot of taming.'*

*

---

* In Greek legend, with the music of his lyre Orpheus was able to tame savage beasts.

In honour of the occasion, also officially to acknowledge the visit of one Apollinaris – son of the great Gallo-Roman aristocrat and bishop Sidonius Apollinaris, who for years had gallantly defended Arvernum against the Visigoths – Clovis held a feast in the palace's great audience chamber. Apollinaris had arrived a few days earlier from the court of Alaric II, to plead for a cessation of hostilities against the Visigoths, whose rule, faute de mieux, the Gallo-Romans had come to accept, even loyally support against incursions by the Franks.

Connal had heard that the Franks were generally despised for their barbarism – even among barbarians; he now discovered that this reputation was not undeserved. Vast quantities of beer and meat were consumed amid a deafening hubbub of shouted conversation, quarreling and rowdy horseplay. At one point, someone's idea of a jolly diversion was to make the unfortunate Apollinaris stand against a door, while diners hurled knives and throwing-axes into the wood all round him. Luckily, the marksmen were skilled, creating on the door a perfect outline of the Roman, without harming him. Clovis seemed oblivious of all the rough-and-tumble, carrying on an animated discussion with Connal concerning religious observance, in which he displayed all the zeal of the converted. 'Time you Celtic Christians recognized the authority of the Pope and importance of the saints,' he lectured his guest.

'The sole authority we need is in the Scriptures,' Connal replied mildly. 'By diligent study therein, a man may discover the meaning of God's Word. Why does he need the Bishop of Rome or the example of holy men to find it, when he can do so for himself?'

'Heresy, my friend, blind heresy!' shouted Clovis, ramming a forefinger into the other's chest. He appeared to be enjoying himself enormously. 'Tell him, my dear,' he said, turning to his wife, Clotilde, the Catholic Burgundian princess whose creed he had adopted in preference to his own Arian faith.

'Give our guest a little peace, Lewis,'* she replied fondly, laying a hand on her spouse's. 'Your brother-in-law has been kind enough to send us a harpist. Should we not hear him demonstrate his skill?'

---

* 'The *ch* expresses only the German aspiration; and the true name is not different from *Luduin* or *Lewis*' (Gibbon).

Summoned, the young harpist – awkward and taciturn till this moment – began to sing in a clear voice, accompanying himself on his instrument. True and sweet, the notes rang out, filling the great chamber and silencing the noisy revellers. The musician sang of the great deeds of the Franks: of Clodion, who wrested from the Romans the lands between the Rhenus and the Samara* of Merovech, and of Childeric, the father of their present king; of the victories of Clovis over the Alamanni and the Visigoths. His rapt audience banged the boards in appreciation of feats of valour, or blubbered into drinking-horns over the death of heroes.

The young harpist retired to thunderous applause, whereupon the Franks returned to the serious business of drinking, boasting and competing with each other in feats of strength and skill such as raising a barrel of ale above the head, or throwing a knife in the air then catching the descending blade between one's teeth. Not to be outdone, Clovis performed a trick for which he had become famous. The fire needing replenishing, a servant led in a donkey loaded with firewood and began to throw on logs. Thrusting the man aside, Clovis lifted both the donkey and its load and hurled them into the flames. The screams of the dying animal were drowned by the roars of approbation from a delighted audience.

Next morning, Connal, accompanied by Apollinaris, took his leave of Clovis and, with pounding head and parched mouth, set out on the long journey back to Italy.

Pacing the weed-grown suites of the deserted bath-house, his favourite retreat, Clovis mulled over his immediate plans. Let others – Gundobad of the Burgundians, for instance, or even Thrasamund the Vandal king – jump when Theoderic snapped his fingers. He, Clovis, would follow his star irrespective of his brother-in-law's approval or otherwise. That star? Nothing less than the conquest of the whole of Gaul. Everything north of the Liger was already his. The main barrier between that frontier and the Mare Internum† was the kingdom of the Visigoths. In south-east Gaul, the Alamanni had been already crushed, and the

* The Rhine and the Somme.
† The Mediterranean.

Burgundians were his allies – for the moment; they could be picked off later. But the Visigoths were no longer the mighty power they had once been, their king, Alaric II, a mere shadow of his father, the great Euric. For the time being Clovis would stay his hand. Then, when the Visigoths had been lulled into a false sense of security, he would launch his strike against them.

TWENTY-SEVEN

My ancestors, the Western Roman emperors
[quoting a remark of Theoderic], *Cassiodorus Variae, c.* 537

'Ave Petronius Rufius,' Symmachus greeted the cloaked and hooded figure that the porter had just shown into the *vestibulum* of the senator's house in Ravenna. He instructed the porter to see to the stabling of the visiter's equipage of *currus* (light carriage) and pair, and to arrange for the driver to be looked after in the domestics' quarters. 'How was the journey?'

'Ave Quintus,' replied Cethegus, allowing the porter to divest him of his dripping *cucullus*. 'Journey? Vile weather but apart from that it could have been worse, considering that the old *cursus publicus* has finally packed up. A few way-stations still operating along the Flaminia, though.'

'Come and meet the others,' continued Symmachus, when his guest had bathed and changed. 'We're all agog to hear this news you wrote to us about. Must be important, for you to have come all the way from Rome.' Symmachus conducted Cethegus, son of Probinus, the leader of the Laurentian faction in Rome, to the *triclinium*, where lamps had been lit and couches and tables made ready for dinner. Here, already waiting, were the young Boethius, who had recently married Symmachus' daughter Rusticiana, and Cassiodorus, Theoderic's *Scriba Concilii*,* whose quaestorship was virtually guaranteed within the next few years. The four men were key members of *Anulus*, the Ring, an influential group of aristocratic intellectuals centred in Rome and Constantinople, who kept in touch and exchanged ideas through regular letters and visits.

---

* Secretary of the Council.

During the meal conversation was light, consisting mainly of mutual compliments – congratulations to Cethegus on being appointed consul for the current year,* praise for Boethius' recently published treatises on music and astronomy, and for the first instalment of Cassiodorus' *History of the Goths*, an ambitious project undertaken with the approval of Theoderic and planned to be in twelve volumes. Also given due plaudits was the fare provided by their host, sows' udders in tunny sauce, followed by sucking-pig in a casserole of *garum* (fish sauce) and wine, washed down with vintage Falernian.

After dinner the four retired to the *tablinum*, where Cethegus, whose good-humoured, somewhat battered-looking features bore an astonishing resemblance to those of the Flavian emperor, Vespasian, announced without preamble, 'Fastida has made contact with Thrasaric,' a statement which was greeted with polite bemusement.

'You make it sound like, "Caesar has crossed the Rubicon",' observed Cassiodorus with a puzzled smile. 'Forgive our ignorance Rufius, but who are these gentlemen? Barbarians I take it, from their names.'

'My apologies, gentlemen,' grinned Cethegus, enjoying the others' reaction. 'My warped sense of the dramatic. Don't blame yourselves if you've never heard of them – not one in a thousand has. The only reason I know about them is that fossicking about in the tangled undergrowth of foreign affairs has long been a hobby of mine. The pair I've named are involved in something I'll call "the Sirmium question" – which is going to be very, very big in the coming months. That's why I've decided to speak to the three of you in confidence. As Theoderic's most trusted advisers, you're the ones best placed to influence his policy. Quintus, would you think me rude if I suggested we pass round another flagon of that excellent Falernian? What I've got to say may take a little time.'

The Gepids, who, fifteen years before, had tried to block Theoderic's expedition to Italy, had recovered from the thrashing they received on that occasion, Cethegus explained, and were flexing their muscles once again. Under their king, Thrasaric, son of Thrapstila, who had been killed in Theoderic's victory at the River Ulca, the Gepids, always a

---

* 504. There being no Eastern nominee, Cethegus was sole consul for that year.

troublesome lot, were growing in confidence, their embassies to Ravenna behaving with an arrogance bordering on insolence. However, on their own they were a minor irritant rather than a major threat.

The trouble was that there existed a second group of Gepids living north of the Danubius outside imperial territory, and the two Gepidic subtribes were making dangerous efforts to unite. Should that happen, the Gepids – traditional enemies of the Ostrogoths – might, just conceivably, become a threat to Theoderic's kingdom. The Praetorian Prefect's *agentes* had recently confirmed that Thrasaric had been in conclave with Fastida, king of the northern branch of the Gepids. The meeting had taken place at Sirmium, the old capital of Pannonia Secunda, the long-abandoned Western frontier province, occupied after Roman withdrawal first by the Huns, then by the Ostrogoths prior to their migration into Eastern imperial territory, and now homeland to the southern Gepids.

'I think I know what you're going to say next,' put in Boethius. 'Theoderic's about to launch a pre-emptive strike, to prevent the Gepids joining up. Correct?'

'Absolutely, young Anicius Manlius. He hasn't actually said so yet, but he will. Of that you may be certain.' He took a sip of wine and looked at the others appraisingly. 'We all know about Theoderic's imperial ambitions. He hasn't yet dared to don the diadem, but the Gepids have provided him with a perfect casus belli to achieve the next best thing, the recovery of Roman imperial territory.'

'That might prove controversial.' Cassiodorus' mild face took on a worried cast. 'Pannonia Secunda *used* to be part of the Western Empire – technically. But since it was abandoned it's become a grey area, a sort of Debatable Land, which the East has long regarded as coming within its own sphere of influence. There's a general understanding that the empire's western boundary is now the Ulca river, where Theoderic defeated Thrapstila. That's well to the west of Sirmium, whose capture, I imagine, will be Theoderic's main objective.'

'Precisely.' Again Cethegus looked round the circle of faces – now all intent and anxious. He smiled and raised his eyebrows, inviting comment.

'Anastasius isn't going to like it,' observed Symmachus. 'Relations with the East are bad enough already. Another source of friction is the last thing we need at this juncture. Theoderic must be persuaded to try diplomacy before declaring war.'

'Hear, hear,' echoed Cassiodorus and Boethius.

'Your concern is understandable, gentlemen,' Cethegus went on. 'However, there's another way of looking at the situation – one which takes a long perspective. Now, what I'm about to say must go no further than these walls. If the wrong people got hold of it, we could find ourselves facing a charge of treason.' He paused, amid a prickling silence, to make sure of everyone's full attention. 'There are moves afoot – in Constantinople, in Rome, even in Ravenna – to bring about the eventual reintegration of Italy and the West into the Roman Empire. Already the East regards Italy as pretty well its fief, hence Theoderic's status of vicegerent, a title which implies, in theory at least, eventual direct control of Italy by the emperor. So I say, let events take their course. Let Theoderic recover as much territory as he can for the West, then, when the rift with Constantinople is eventually healed, the task of building a reunited empire will be that much easier.'

'Theoderic – imitation of an emperor,' murmured Cassiodorus to no one in particular.*

Boethius felt as though someone had touched his spine with an ice-cold finger. What Cethegus had said surely belittled Theoderic and all he had achieved, reducing him to, at best, a stand-in for the Eastern Emperor, at worst a mere caretaker, expendable once his role had been completed. That role was to preserve Italy, like a fly in amber, as a Roman state, until a Roman emperor could once again take over the reins of power. It was one thing to discuss ideas of reviving the *Imperium Romanum* in the rarified and scholarly ambience of *Anulus*. Such talk, though flavoured with a heady spice of danger, never ventured beyond the theoretical. What Cethegus was proposing went far beyond that – amounting almost to a blueprint for a change of regime.

'Surely we owe Theoderic some loyalty?' Boethius protested. 'He's brought stability and good government to Italy, and been even-handed in his treatment of Goths and Romans. My father and Symmachus here

---

* The remark is adapted from a statement of Cassiodorus (in *Variae*), comparing Theoderic's realm to that of the East Roman Emperor.

were proscribed for backing Odovacar, and all of us supported Laurentius. Yet Theoderic's never held any of that against us.'

'Our first loyalty must be to Rome,' said Cethegus gently. 'I don't deny that Theoderic has admirable qualities – as an individual. But what we would be foolish to forget is that he's a barbarian. That means that at bottom he's unpredictable, and in the last resort untrustworthy. We trusted Stilicho, remember? And look where that got us.'

'I think we can safely assume that – unlike Stilicho's legionaries – Theoderic's warriors would see off any barbarians who tried to invade,' countered Symmachus.' He smiled. 'Any *other* barbarians, that is. All in all, I'd say we're lucky to have Theoderic as *"Regnator"** – to use his latest title.'

Cethegus shrugged, and spread his hands. 'Then think beyond Theoderic. A Gothic dynasty: is that really what you want? Believe me, they'll soon revert to type: small-minded, quarrelsome, vindictive, and incompetent. Theoderic's the exception; his successors will never match up to his standards. And where will Italy be then?' He smiled and rose. 'And now, my dear Quintus, perhaps you'd be kind enough to point me to my bed. I'm somewhat travel-weary, as you'll understand.' He looked round at the others. 'Expect to be summoned by Theoderic any day. Remember my advice – it's for the best. And now I must bid you all Vale. By cock-crow tomorrow I shall be heading back to Rome. As consul, I'm not supposed to leave the City during my year. So, if anyone asks, you haven't seen me.' And with a friendly wave he slipped out, ushered by his host.

Sure enough, two days later came the summons that Cethegus had predicted. Walking through the streets towards the palace (not the old one that Honorius had built when he moved the capital from Milan a century before, but a bigger, grander structure ordered by Theoderic) from his rented town-house near the Ariminum Gate, Boethius was struck by how different Ravenna felt from Rome. Neat and compact, cocooned in its ring of marshes and lagoons, the little city totally lacked the cosmopolitan buzz and glamour of the ancient capital. Ravenna was a working city, above all a *government* city, filled with bureaucrats

* Ruler.

and civil servants, and with a strongly Gothic ambience. This stemmed not just from the fact that you heard German almost as much as Latin spoken in the streets, but from the number of Arian churches that everywhere were popping up like mushrooms, filled with mosaics in the new flat semi-abstract style that would have been inconceivable in Rome.

One mosaic in particular troubled the young man deeply. It showed Theoderic wearing, besides a purple cloak (implying royal, though not necessarily imperial, status) a diadem, the jewelled crown exclusively reserved for emperors. Thus far, the king – perhaps subconsciously fearing a hostile reaction – had held back from actually donning this definitive imperial symbol. But the mosaic clearly indicated in which direction his ambitions lay. Though Boethius liked and greatly admired Theoderic, he felt that these imperial dreams could become a dangerous distraction, even to the point of destabilizing his regime. Julius Caesar had been the greatest and most successful administrator in history, until Antony had offered him the crown. Although Caesar had refused it, the very fact that he had been tempted precipitated a series of crises which had rocked the world. What had happened to Timotheus, the king's bodyguard? the young scholar wondered. Now, more than ever, his presence might have been beneficial. Down-to-earth and full of common sense, at times the tough Isaurian had seemed the only person capable of bringing Theoderic back to the ground in his more 'Icarus' moments.

Boethius sighed. The summons – assuming it was issued for the reasons Cethegus had given – couldn't have come at a worse time. Helping Theoderic's administration on an occasional basis with suggestions and initiatives – such as setting up an enquiry into the payment of the palace guard, or overseeing the construction of a water-clock and sundial as diplomatic gifts for Gundobad of the Burgundians – provided stimulating challenges which complemented rather than crowded out the chief business of his life: writing and research. But this wretched Sirmium crisis would inevitably involve endless meetings of the Council, at which attendance would be obligatory, seriously interrupting the project he was working on. This was an ambitious work (perhaps to be entitled *De revolutionibus orbium*), attempting something which had never been achieved before, nothing less than a synthesis between the ideas of the Aristotelians and those of the Pythagoreans (some of whom had advanced the radical idea that the earth and planets might revolve around the sun!), involving the interrelationship of three separate disciplines: music, mathematics and astronomy, and touching on that most elegant of intellectual constructs, the Music of the Spheres. Well, all that was probably going to have to be put on hold, the young man thought with a stab of weak resentment – of which he felt immediately ashamed. After all, the philosopher-emperor Marcus Aurelius (his favourite role model) had written his *Meditations* in moments snatched in camp, while campaigning against the formidable Marcomanni and Quadi.

Arriving at the palace – an immense fortress-like rectangle, with guard-turrets and gateways in the middle of each wall, based on the one Diocletian had built two hundred years earlier at Spalato on the other side of the Mare Adriaticum – Boethius was passed through a long peristyle to the imperial apartments. The vast scale and grandeur of everything constituted, it seemed to him, the strongest hint yet, after the mosaic showing the king wearing a diadem, of Theoderic's imperial ambitions.

'Sirmium, gentlemen.' Theoderic, eyes alight with enthusiasm, rapped his pointer against a scarlet dot, situated roughly in the middle of the map. This depicted, to Symmachus' astonishment, not the real Europe plus the lands to the south and east of the Mare Internum (Visigothic Spain and southern Gaul, Frankish northern Gaul with the Burgundian wedge between these two kingdoms; Ostrogothic Italy; Vandal Africa; the great bloc of the empire looming beyond the Adriatic) as they existed today, but the entire Roman Empire as it had been before the West's demise. It was as if the barbarian kingdoms had been somehow magicked out of existence, as though they were nothing more than a temporary aberration. He glanced in turn at the fellow Anulars flanking him, Boethius and Cassiodorus. A look of concern flashed between them, plainly saying, 'Paranoia?' Barring their own threesome and the king, the only other persons in the Council chamber were Pitzia, a veteran Gothic commander, and Count Cyprianus from an old Roman military family – proof that there were exceptions to the rule that only Goths should staff the army.

'With the capture of the city,' the king continued, 'not only do we frustrate Thrasaric's plans to unite the two nations of the Gepids, but we can use it as a base from which finally to crush the tribe, and, in the manner of my ancestors, the Western Roman emperors, restore Pannonia Secunda to the empire. Are you with me?' he went on, looking at the Anulars with, Symmachus thought, a note almost of pleading in his voice.

Mindful of Cethegus' advice, and aware that, like Agag, he must tread delicately, the senator, acting as spokesman for his two friends, forced himself to smile and declare enthusiastically, 'All the way, Serenity.'

'Excuse me, Sire,' broke in Count Pitzia, his scar-seamed face, framed by a bush of yellow hair, breaking into a frown. 'But what empire are we talking about? There's only one that I know of, and that's the East.'

'As whose vicegerent, it is my duty and my mission to restore the West.'

'Let's hope Anastasius sees it that way!' exclaimed Cyprianus. He looked directly at Theoderic, his strong Roman features creased in exasperation. 'Your Majesty, while I agree that it's important to nip this Gepid threat in the bud, it would be folly to ignore other political realities. Firstly, any move to reclaim Pannonia Secunda as part of the Regnum Italiae might annoy the Eastern Emperor, who sees it – rightly or wrongly – as coming under his aegis. Secondly, your "mission to restore the West": a noble aim, no doubt, but it ignores the inconvenient fact that Clovis, Gundobad and Alaric are hardly likely to co-operate. That would be like expecting pigs to vote for the Festival of Romulus.'* He shot a glance at his three fellow Romans. 'You, at least, can surely see that?'

Though wholeheartedly agreeing with Cyprianus' objections, Symmachus shrugged and forced himself to remain silent, as did his two companions.

'I see.' Cyprianus' voice was thick with contempt. 'Then I have nothing more to say.' He turned to Theoderic. 'I await your orders, Majesty.'

---

* At the Festival of Romulus and Remus to celebrate the Founding of the City, in 753 BC, free pork and wine were (and still are!) issued to the citizens of Rome.

'Your points are noted Cyprianus, my noble Roman with a Gothic heart,' said Theoderic warmly. Though your fears are unfounded, I do not hold it against you for expressing them. I know that you did so only in my interests, as a true friend.' He turned to the other commander. 'You, Count Pitzia, with Cyprianus as your second-in-command, will lead the army by the Vipavus Valley route to Sirmium; the city to be taken and the Gepids crushed. Those who surrender treat with leniency, but show no quarter to any who resist. King Thrasaric to be taken alive, if possible. Even should Anastasius object, there's not much he can do, his hands being full at present with a campaign against the Persians. Questions, gentlemen?'

When the last of the five had filed out, Theoderic began to pace the chamber in excitement. Pannonia Secunda/Pannonia Sirmiensis – that would be but the first step. Next, Clovis's expansionist plans must be halted. After that, the rest should prove relatively straightforward. Gundobad and Alaric would soon come to heel, their status in a resurrected empire redefined perhaps as federates, or even 'client-kings' – to recycle a convenient label from the past. Even Vandal Africa might one day follow suit; already Thrasamund acknowledged Ostrogothic hegemony. With gifted Romans like Boethius and Symmachus to help him shape his plans, who knows what limits could be put on his success? He had been right not to heed Timothy's slanderous calumnies against them; their conduct today showed them to be loyal and devoted friends, as well as useful colleagues.

As for Pitzia and Cyprianus, the army could not be in better hands. His own fighting days were over, he reflected with a twinge of regret. No matter. It was fitting for a ruler of mature years to send others to wage war on his behalf, as Roman emperors had done, just so long as they were loyal and efficient. On that score, he had no fears.

TWENTY-EIGHT

*By the power of the lord king Theoderic the Bulgars were defeated
and Italy regained Sirmium*

Cassiodorus, *Chronica*, 519

'Well, that was almost *too* easy,' Cyprianus chuckled to Pitzia as the
two leaders, after supervising the dispositions of the Gothic camp outside
the walls, returned to their improvised command post in the basilica
of Sirmium, the once-mighty Illyrian city where the great Theodosius
had been proclaimed emperor more than a century ago. Thrasaric and
Fastida had proved to be parchment tigers. At the approach of the
redoubtable Gothic host, who clearly meant business, the Gepids had
produced a great deal of noise, shouting and banging spear-butts against
shields. But when this tactic had signally failed to intimidate their
opponents, they broke and scattered before the steady advance of
their traditional foes. Fastida had fled back beyond the Danube,
Thrasaric had disappeared without trace, his mother's capture a pledge
against his future good behaviour, and his force had meekly laid down
their arms on being told that their lives would be spared if they surrendered. With the restitution of a *retenator* or governor and the return of
their *praecepta* (rights and traditions) to the indigenous Roman population, the machinery was set in motion for the reinstatement of Pannonia
Secunda as a fully functioning Roman province. (A Roman province
incorporated into the Ostrogothic realm!) Mission accomplished, or so
it seemed to Pitzia and Cyprianus as they made ready to return to Italy.

However, on the order being given by Pitzia to break camp, the
Goths assembled in marching order – facing eastwards! Fired up by
their near-bloodless victory, which had aroused but not satisfied their
martial ardour, and unwilling to pillage their Sirmian hosts, whom
they had just delivered from the Gepid yoke, the Goths – by one of
those strange collective decisions which can suddenly infect a mass, had

determined to press on into imperial territory in a quest for glory and plunder.

'Madness!' exclaimed Cyprianus to a desperate-sounding Pitzia, when the latter informed him of the situation. 'Sheer madness!' Forcing himself to stay calm, the Roman tried to assess the crisis objectively and come up with a rescue plan. He should have seen this coming, he thought grimly. This was what happened when you put a barbarian army under a leader who was not up to the (admittedly difficult) task of imposing discipline. Strictly speaking, such a force was not an 'army' at all, just a mob of individual warriors, all ferociously brave but basically motivated by a thirst for loot and personal glory. Pitzia – generous, and valorous to a fault – they would follow into battle anywhere. But Pitzia was not strong enough to control them when their will needed to be curbed. For that, you needed a Theoderic. And Theoderic, now middle-aged, was happy, it would seem, to delegate the responsibility to others.

The situation was potentially disastrous, Cyprianus reflected. The Goths were embarked on what was technically an invasion of the Eastern Empire, the most formidable power in the world. Success against the Gepids was one thing; taking on a disciplined Roman army quite another. The best that could be done, he thought (and it seemed a very poor best), was for him and Pitzia, accepting the fait accompli, to put themselves at the head of the host and hope that some easy pickings would soon come their way. Hopefully, reward enough to satisfy the Goths and persuade them to to turn back for Italy before the full wrath of Anastasius descended upon them.

A bizarre, almost surreal atmosphere seemed to surround the expedition as it marched downstream along the Danube. The men, fortified by copious supplies of food and drink transferred wholesale from the Gepid commissariat, were in a relaxed and happy, almost holiday mood, as they tramped at a leisurely pace through a beautiful landscape of water-meadows, wooded hills, and vineyards, all bathed in golden summer sunshine. Bypassing Singidunum (scene of Theoderic's youthful victory against Babai), whose massive ramparts were defended by a strong Roman garrison, the Goths pressed on towards Margus, where a shameful treaty had been imposed by Attila on the East Romans more than sixty years before. Near the latter city, as the Goths were pitching camp for the night,

Pitzia's scouts (detached from the small body of cavalry accompanying the host) came posting in with the news that a Roman general, Sabinianus, was approaching at the head of a large force of Bulgar mercenaries.

'This Sabinianus, what do we know of him?' queried Pitzia, as the two leaders conferred in the commander's tent.

'Only that he's one of the East's top soldiers,' replied Cyprianus. 'Son of a famous general of the same name, who once ambushed a column led by Theoderic's brother Thiudimund, capturing all his wagons.'

'And the Bulgars?'

'A Turkic tribe of mounted nomads, originally from Central Asia. Not, thank God, horse-archers like the Huns. The only saving grace is that, with the East's field armies fully committed on the Persian front, we won't be facing a Roman force.'

'We should be all right, then.'

'Should we now?' snapped Cyprianus, infuriated by the other's groundless optimism. 'May I remind you that our army amounts to the grand total of two thousand men on foot plus five hundred riders. We'll probably be facing a much larger force made up of Bulgar cavalry – among the finest in the world. There's only one way to see off cavalry: forming a defensive shield-wall. And that, my dear Pitzia, calls for steadiness and iron discipline, qualities which even you must admit the Goths conspicuously lack. Oh yes,' he concluded bitterly, 'we should be all right.'

'What do we do?' Pitzia now sounded sober and concerned.

'Well, we can't retreat, that's for sure. Being cavalry, they'd soon overtake us. So we have to offer battle. That means choosing a defensive position with as many advantages of terrain as possible. Ideally, a narrow front on rising ground between woods or marshes, so that we can't be outflanked, while they're prevented from bringing their full strength to bear. After that, as I've said, everything depends on discipline – our Achilles' heel, unfortunately.'

'We're going to lose – is that what you're saying?'

'Not necessarily,' mused Cyprianus, as he recalled a codicil to their orders. It granted them permission to ally with Mundo, a renegade warlord whose stronghold, Herta, was only a few miles distant, at the confluence of the Danube and a large tributary, the Moravus.*

---

* River Morava.

'Mundo? That leader of thieves and cut-throats?' exclaimed Pitzia in horror, when the other had reminded him of this option. 'We can't possibly accept help from such scum.'

'Then we'll probably all die!' shouted Cyprianus, losing patience. 'Wake up, man. This is war. We don't have the luxury of choice. If the Devil himself offered to help us, we'd have to accept. Mundo's a nasty piece of work, I don't deny it – boils his prisoners alive, I've heard. But, as far as we're concerned, the only thing that matters is: will he make an effective ally? You *can* see that, can't you?'

Chastened, Pitzia nodded.

'Good. Now we have to move quickly. Herta's less than ten miles from here; if I set off now on a fast mount, I can be there by sundown. Assuming I can persuade Mundo to join us, we should be back here sometime in the morning – hopefully before Sabinianus shows up. Mundo and his followers are Huns and therefore almost certainly cavalry, which is where we're weakest. They're a remnant of Attila's horde. Stayed behind when most of the tribe drifted back to Asia, following the collapse of Attila's empire. Right, I'd best be on my way.'

'Just one thing: why would Mundo want to help us?'

Cyprianus groaned to himself. Getting through to Pitzia could be hard work at times. 'Because the man's living on borrowed time. At present, Anastasius has bigger fish to fry – Isaurian rebels and a hostile Persia. But Mundo knows the day of reckoning is bound to come. And that day could dawn very soon. After ourselves, Sabinianus' next target – being conveniently close – would almost certainly be Mundo, who's become a serious challenge to the maintenance of local law and order. By joining us, he'd be helping to keep Sabinianus off his back. And now, I really must be off.'

'Shall we go to the rescue of this Roman and his beleaguered Goths?' boomed Mundo to his chief retainers, assembled in the *praetorium* of Herta – an abandoned Roman fortress perched on a bluff above the Danube. Cyprianus smiled to himself, prepared to indulge this game of saving face. Although Mundo needed the help of the Goths as much as they needed his, he must be allowed to appear to be conferring a favour, in order to maintain his status among his followers.

The scene had a kind of barbaric splendour, Cyprianus reflected, the great chamber's Roman austerity relieved by colourful tribal rugs, and weapons plus trophies of the chase hanging on the walls. Mundo was a mountain of a man, whose slitted eyes, deep-sunk in the beardless Mongol face, betrayed his Hunnic origins. His huge head showed the curious flattening and elongation caused by binding the skull to a board in infancy, a characteristic deformation practised by the tribe.

The chief and his kaftan-clad retainers conferred noisily for a time in Hunnish, then Mundo turned to Cyprianus and declared, 'We agree to help you; but our help will not come cheap. Twenty solidi apiece for my warriors, twice that for my captains, and let us say a hundred for myself. In addition, I desire to take the *foedus*.* If I am a *foederatus* of your king, Theoderic, he and I will have a mutual obligation to aid each other should the need arise. Those are my terms, Roman. Take them or leave them.'

The demands were, of course, preposterous, thought Cyprianus. As well as acquiring, at a stroke, a fortune which would otherwise take years to garner, as a federate Mundo would change his status from outlaw to respected ally under the protection of western Europe's strongest ruler. Well, needs must when the Devil drives, as Augustine (or was it Jerome?) said. And the deal was not all one-sided: the financial payout could probably be adjusted later to a more realistic level; also, as a federate Mundo could be a useful buffer against the East, should a state of war develop.

'I accept,' said Cyprianus, whereupon the pact was sealed by mutual toasts of *kumiss*, a beverage concocted from fermented mares' milk.

'Friends and fellow warriors,' Cyprianus – mounted, in order to be seen and heard more easily – addressed the Gothic host, 'today we face a Bulgar army commanded by a Roman general. Let us not deceive ourselves: the odds are great. They outnumber us; they are well-led, brave and skilled, mounted while we must fight on foot. But we can win – of that have no doubt. Only, however, if we behave as Theoderic would wish us to. You remember the Ulca where you defeated Thrapstila, the Addua where you turned the tide against Odovacar? Those victories were won because of discipline, because you allowed

* Oath of allegiance.

your warlike ardour to be tempered by obedience to the orders of your king. Though he cannot today be present in the flesh, Theoderic will be watching you in spirit from Ravenna. Remember that, and we shall win the day.' The thunderous banging of spear-butts on shields that followed his speech told Cyprianus it had gone down well. But would it prove enough to make them hold the line?

Shaking with reaction, his tunic below the padded cuirass soaked with sweat, the Roman stood down the host, with instructions to eat and rest until the enemy was sighted. To his credit, Pitzia had, without demur, allowed his second-in-command to supersede him as regards the ordering of the coming battle – no doubt conceding that the Roman's ability to persuade the Goths to accept discipline was superior to his own. Cyprianus had chosen the ground carefully: a declivity, flanked by great stands of oak and chestnut, and sloping down to a flat grassy expanse, the Plain of Margus.

Early in the afternoon, scouts reported that the Bulgars, numbering, they estimated, some five thousand horsemen, were close at hand and should arrive within the hour. Soon after, a growing cloud of dust on the horizon heralded the approach of the enemy van. The Gothic war-horns boomed and, following prior instructions, the host took up position along the ridge, a three-deep line of warriors bearing shields, and armed with spears plus various subsidiary weapons – daggers, throwing-axes, javelins, etc. The Bulgars, big, swarthy fellows armed, to Cyprianus' relief, with lances and sabres, not with bows, drew up a few hundred paces in front of the Gothic line. To one side, surrounded by his staff, Sabinianus, resplendent in muscle cuirass and crested Attic helmet, sat his horse.

A trumpet clanged, and the Bulgar cavalry began to trot forward; the trot became a canter, then a gallop, and the lances swept down, presenting a terrifying sight to the waiting Goths: a solid wall of flashing hooves and foam-flecked muzzles fronted by a line of deadly points. This was the first time Cyprianus had faced a head-on cavalry charge. Till now, his military experience (in the wars with Odovacar) had been limited to campaigns largely fought on foot, with cavalry action confined to skirmishes, scouting, and hit-and-run raids. His father, who had fought under Aetius at the great Battle of the Catalaunian Fields, where the Romans and the Visigoths had defeated Attila's Huns and their

Ostrogothic allies, had told him that cavalry would never press home a charge against a line of spearmen as long as the line held firm. You could persuade men, his father had said, to commit themselves to destruction, but never horses; they had too much sense. Well, he was about to find out if the theory was true, Cyprianus thought, his mouth dry with fear and his palms sweating.

The ground began to tremble as the Bulgar horse swept nearer. It seemed that only a miracle could save the Gothic line from being shattered and destroyed. At a signal from the war-horns the Goths, in a blur of movement, swung up their shields, each man planting his right foot firmly forward and presenting his spear between his own shield and that of the man to his right. Then the miracle happened. A few yards from the Gothic shield-wall, the Bulgar charge stalled; for a few moments the horsemen milled about in apparent confusion, then they wheeled about and trotted smartly back to their original position. A ragged cheer – of relief as much as triumph, thought Cyprianus – arose from the Goths.

That the line had held was due to the matchless courage of the Germans, he knew. As long as they retained formation, they would be safe. The danger lay in their warlike instincts prevailing, causing them to break ranks to attack the enemy.

Which nearly happened. Time and again the Bulgar cavalry charged, only to retreat when confronted by that rock-steady wall of shields with its row of glittering blades. Then, after the sixth charge had failed, the Bulgars' morale seemed to break; instead of withdrawing in good order, they turned and fled in confusion, uttering cries of despair.

'They flee! They flee!' exclaimed Pitzia a few yards down the line from Cyprianus, and, before the latter could restrain him, he rushed forward, followed by a section of the Gothic front.

Cursing, Cyprianus spurred his horse into motion and galloped down the line, which was beginning to lose cohesion as the warriors, the light of battle in their eyes, began to move forwards. 'Back! Get back! he shouted. 'It's a trick! Remember Theoderic – his eyes are upon you!' The reminder of their revered king's expectations cut through the fog of fighting-madness that had begun to cloud the warriors' minds. They halted, sense returning, then quietly resumed their shield-wall formation.

A terrible object lesson in how close they had come to disaster was now played out before the Goths' eyes. Halting their headlong flight, the Bulgars wheeled and galloped back, swiftly surrounding Pitzia's group. In moments the party was slaughtered to a man, cut down by sabres or skewered on lance-points.

Their ruse having failed, the Bulgars resumed their tactic of trying to break the Gothic line with repeated charges. To no avail; they could make no impression on the Goths, who now knew, from hard-won experience, that as long as their discipline held, they could see off the enemy indefinitely. At last, their horses blown, their resolve faltering, the Bulgars ceased attacking. At a trumpet-signal ordered by Sabinianus, they turned and began to move off – this time in good earnest.

Now Cyprianus sprang the surprise he had prepared. A special call on the war-horns boomed out, and from the enclosing woods there issued on one side the Gothic cavalry held in reserve until this moment, and on the other Mundo's Hunnic horse-archers. Exhausted, caught unawares, the Bulgars reeled before the double onslaught, falling in scores to Gothic spears and Hunnic arrow-storm. The enemy being too numerous to defeat decisively, Cyprianus called off his horsemen before the Bulgars could start to counter-attack, allowing Sabinianus to leave the field and lick his wounds.

TWENTY-NINE

What can be hoped for which is not believed?
St Augustine, *On Faith, Hope and Charity, c.* 421

Rumours concerning the Sirmium expedition reached Timothy (who, hoping for a change of heart on the part of Theoderic regarding his banishment, had spun out the date of his departure for Byzantium) at Brundisium, as he was about to board a trading-vessel bound for Corinthus. Thanks to the powerful state-sponsored guild of shippers, the *navicularii*, which, because of the benevolent and conservative administrations of Odovacar and Theoderic, had survived the passing of the Western Empire to maintain trading links with the Eastern, and even with southern Gaul and parts of Spain, the voyage back to Constantinople had posed no problems. As the ship sailed down the coast of Epirus and on into the Sinus Corinthiacus,* Timothy had time aplenty to consider his future plans.

Since his dismissal from the king's service, he had felt slack and useless – like an unstrung bow. What would he do now? The future stretched before him, grey and drab, like those mist-shrouded flatlands of the Padus valley round Ravenna. For the first time in his life he felt old. At sixty-three – twelve years older than Theoderic – he *was* old, he supposed. Old enough to draw his pension as an *agens* of the Eastern Empire when he returned to Constantinople – assuming that his commission from Leo, granted all those years ago, was still valid. He had some money saved; and the funds allocated to him for the voyage had been generous, enough to leave a healthy surplus after he had paid his passage. Perhaps he would make a down-payment on a little wine-shop near the Iron Gate? On reflection, he found the prospect less than enthralling.

* The Gulf of Corinth.

The shock of his abrupt dismissal had given way to a great sadness and concern regarding Theoderic's state of mind. Hadn't some Greek philosopher once said, 'Those whom the gods destroy, they first make mad'?* Assuming it was true, the news that Theoderic had sent troops to Sirmium to take the city and occupy Pannonia was ample confirmation of his fears. Unless they could be changed or ended, Theoderic's ambitions, which now seemed to include recovery of Western imperial territory, would surely end in tears – conflict with the East and dissension in Italy. Anastasius could hardly be expected to look favourably on his vicegerent's plans first to take over and revive a Roman province in an area which the Eastern Empire had come to regard as its own preserve, and second to realize his ultimate dream of being crowned Western Emperor. In Italy, the Romans would never accept a German as their *imperator*, while the Goths would surely resent their beloved 'Dietrich von Bern' changing his title 'King of the Goths' to 'Emperor of the Romans'. Yet Theoderic seemed blind to all of this – as though, simply by believing them, he could bring about his hopes' accomplishment.

By the time he stepped ashore at the Golden Horn (after a short overland journey from Corinthus to Athenae, the voyage had continued from Piraeus to the Bosporus), Timothy, without being consciously aware of having done so, had arrived at a momentous decision. Alone, he could do nothing to help save his old friend and master from himself. But there was a man, probably the only one in Europe, who perhaps could: the Eastern Emperor. Somehow, he would arrange an interview with Anastasius. He would endeavour to make the emperor fully aware of his, Timothy's, concerns about Theoderic's imperial ambitions, while at the same time pleading the king's cause: emphasizing the efficiency of his administration and his essential loyalty towards the emperor. A difficult balancing act? That, for sure. Timothy felt rather like the Colossus of Rhodes, whose legs were said to have straddled the harbour's entrance. (Not, perhaps, the most comforting of similes, he reflected: the mighty statue had been toppled by an earthquake.)

*

* It was actually Sophocles. ('Whom Zeus would destroy, he first makes mad', *Antigone*, *c.* 450 BC.)

Ushered by a *silentiarius* into the reception chamber of Constantinople's Great Palace, Timothy found himself in the same vast colonnaded hall where, thirty-four years earlier, he had been quizzed about Theoderic by Emperor Leo. At the far end of the great space sat an elderly diminutive figure, clad not in imperial robes but in a simple dalmatic. In a most unimperial gesture, Anastasius rose, advanced towards Timothy and, taking him by the shoulders, greeted him warmly. 'Welcome, Timotheus Trascilliseus. My Master of Offices informs me that you have travelled all the way from Ravenna with information concerning King Theoderic, my vicegerent in Italia.' Seating himself on a chair, he waved Timothy to another, and with his own hand poured wine for them both. He glanced at Timothy's uniform of an *agens in rebus* (seldom worn but carefully preserved): pillbox cap, broad military belt, undyed linen tunic with indigo government roundels at hip and shoulder. 'I see you're dressed as an *agens* of the Eastern Empire,' he observed. (No royal 'we', Timothy noted, warming to him.) 'I thought I knew all my *agentes* by sight; you must have been absent from the capital since before my succession to Zeno.'

Anastasius' ancient and careworn face displayed only kindly curiosity. All at once Timothy felt unmanned, close to disgraceful tears. His whole life he had fought and striven, surviving against hard circumstances and harder men, through skills learnt as a boy in the tough school of the Tarsus back streets. It was a contest he had relished all his life. But no more, he realized abruptly. His strength was ebbing; his joy in pitting his wits against others and prevailing had lost its savour. It was this knowledge, combined with the other's unforced cordiality and kindness, that had somehow got to him, filling him with an unfamiliar gratitude mingled with self-pity. No more of this maudlin weakness, he told himself in shame, taking a sharp pull at his morale. If he would help Theoderic, let alone himself, he must stay collected and positive.

'So, my friend,' prompted Anastasius, 'what have you to tell me?'

Timothy held nothing back: his job as Theoderic's bodyguard during the young prince's schooldays; the long journey back to Theoderic's homeland in Pannonia; the migration to Moesia and the years of struggle alternating with alliance, between Zeno and the nation of the Ostrogoths; the rivalry with Strabo; the great exodus to Italy; the wars with Odovacar, and the success of Theoderic's administration following the former's defeat; finally, his dreams of becoming Roman emperor

188

in Italy and – if the rumours were true – of reviving the Western Empire itself. 'When I confided my concerns to him, Serenity, he took it amiss, I fear,' concluded Timothy. 'Hence my presence here.'

Anastasius, who had listened in silence to the long recital, refilled their beakers and murmured, 'Well, we can perhaps turn a blind eye to Pannonia for the moment. After all, it was a Western province once. Before, that is, it became homeland to the Huns, then the Ostrogoths, followed by the Gepids, and now, it seems, returning to its original owners, the native Roman inhabitants. Orestes – Attila's secretary and father of Romulus, the West's last emperor – was Pannonian, you know. Poor little Romulus – pensioned off to Lucullus' villa in Campania. Still alive, I hear.' Anastasius gave a wry chuckle. 'And that could complicate any plans Theoderic may be entertaining to have himself made emperor.' He shot Timothy a keen look, one of unexpectedly steely authority. 'That we simply can't allow. There can only be one Rome, and it is Constantinople – which sounds like an oxymoron, I know.' He smiled, and continued, 'Theoderic is my vicegerent. Nothing more, nothing less. He must, in no uncertain terms, be reminded of that fact – if necessary, by the threat of forced removal from office should be remain obdurate. But hopefully it need not come to that.' He glanced at Timothy appraisingly. 'I am most grateful, Timotheus, for your confiding in me. Knowing what I now do, it may not be too late to mend fences with Theoderic. Perhaps with gentle persuasion he can be made to see where his attitude errs, while being reassured that he remains a valued servant of the empire. It strikes me that you Timotheus, knowing Theoderic better, I suspect, than anybody else, would be the ideal person to take a message to him from myself, couched, of course, in terms of exquisite diplomacy, and peppered with compliments. We could even offer him a second consulship. It would have to be *honorarius* not *ordinarius*,* but it would demonstrate that we hold him in high esteem, and would welcome his co-operation. Perhaps, as with Paul on the road to Damascus, the scales would then drop from his eyes. Will you consider my suggestion?'

* Unlike that of a *consul ordinarius*, the name of an honorary consul, such as Clovis became, did not appear in the *Fasti* (state records, especially consular lists). Western consuls, their appointments subject to ratification by the Eastern Emperor, were nominated by Theoderic.

'How could I refuse, Serenity?' Timothy replied, momentarily over-come. He felt a great surge of hope and gladness. The emperor's proposal offered real hope that Theoderic would be brought to see sense, with the bonus that the rift between himself and the king might be healed. 'My commission from Zeno has never, to my knowledge, been revoked, which hopefully makes me still an *agens* in the service of the Eastern Emperor.'

'It does indeed, my friend. If you still have the document, we will have it updated with our seal, any increments of pay to be made up in full. If not, I will give the order to my *Magister Officiorum* that a fresh commission be—'

He broke off as the door crashed open and a figure in gilded armour burst into the room.

'Julianus!' exclaimed the emperor in surprise and displeasure. 'We assumed our *Magister Militum per Orientem* to be in Persia. What is so urgent that it causes you to enter unannounced?'

'A thousand pardons, Serenity,' declared the other, 'but what I have to tell cannot stand on ceremony. A truce with Persia was the reason I returned post-haste to the capital, to seek your ratification of a provisional treaty. A short time ago, as I was disembarking at the harbour of Phospherion, grave news came in about the latest actions of Theoderic. Not content with taking Sirmium and occupying Pannonia, he went on to invade the empire and has just defeated a Bulgar army commanded by Sabinianus. This, Serenity, is war!'

THIRTY

*A dishonourable victory which Romans snatched from Romans with
the daring of pirates*
Marcellinus Comes [referring to the Eastern Empire's punitive naval raid
on Apulia and Calabria], *Chronicon, c.* 550

To Theodericus Amalo, king of the nation of the Ostrogoths and
our vicegerent in Italia, greetings.

Whereas it has come to our attention that within the months
of Iulius and Augustus of this year present you did knowingly
and without permission from ourselves both capture the city of
Sirmium and occupy the disputed territory of the *civitas* of
Bassianae, commonly known as Pannonia Sirmiensis, being the
eastern sector of the former Roman province of Pannonia
Secunda, and moreover thereafter did proceed without just cause
or provocation to enter under arms into our imperial province
of Moesia Prima, and did there, in alliance with a proscribed
outlaw and criminal, to wit, one Mundo, make war against our
imperial forces commanded by our Magister Militum per
Illyricum, we now desire and demand that immediately upon
receipt of this communication . . .

Timothy looked up from the scroll and in a strained voice asked, 'Do
you really want me to go on, Deric? Why don't I cut to the chase and
tell you in my own words what Anastasius wants? Then we can decide
how best to respond.' His mind flashed back to the meeting with
Anastasius, and the plan that, for a brief moment, had seemed to offer
a happy resolution to the crisis with Theoderic.

Until, that is, arriving from the blue like a *ballista*-bolt, the news
from Julian (now a mature and hardened veteran) had smashed the
plan to smithereens. Privately, Timothy had felt the situation was not

past saving. He was convinced that the 'invasion' of the empire had not been intended by Theoderic, and would peter out as soon as the leaders of the host managed to talk the men out of their madness. He sensed, however, that it would be useless to try to make the emperor and his general see that; Anastasius' attitude had hardened, and Julian was clearly determined to teach Theoderic a lesson. Here was a marvellous opportunity to be revenged on the youthful prince who, thirty years ago, had shown him up at the hunting of the great boar Cambyses, and who later had made him look a fool by countermanding his order to shoot, when charged by Zeno's Excubitors. Recognizing Timothy even after such a lapse of time, Julian had shot him a look of pure malevolence, stemming, the Isaurian had no doubt, from the slap he had administered at the boar-hunt – a blow clearly neither forgotten nor forgiven. Timothy knew that, should Julian ever find the opportunity, he, too, would be singled out for vengeance.

'"Deric"? I know no "Deric",' replied Theoderic in coldly sneering tones. The two men – Timothy standing, Theoderic enthroned – were in an audience chamber in the king's palace in Ravenna. 'You will address me as "*Regnator*" or "Your Majesty". And do not presume to suggest that "we" respond to Anastasius. As far as you and I are concerned, Trasilliseus, there is no longer a "we". You arrive from Anastasius – a *vir spectabilis*,* no less, and his official *nuntius*. No, let all be done according to correct form; then there can be no misunderstanding. Pray proceed.'

Timothy ploughed on wretchedly:

> ... delivered and announced by our trusty and well-beloved servant Timotheus Trasilliseus, you hereby withdraw all troops from our imperial territory and from the other regions aforesaid (a state of war now prevailing between the Regnum Italiae and our Imperium Romanum), which action will suffice to signify the cessation of hostilities, and hereinafter do solemnly swear and promise to limit your activities solely to those proper to the remit of the office of vicegerent, on pain of forfeiture of the said office.

---

* One of the high-ranking titles in the gift of the emperor: *vir illuster*, *vir gloriosus*, and so on.

Given under our seal and hand, the Most Holy the Most Serene Anastasius, Augustus of the Romans, at the Great Palace of Constantinople, IV Kalends October in the year of the consuls Sabinianus and Theodorus.*

'You have betrayed me, Trascilliseus,' accused Theoderic. 'The very fact that you come from Anastasius tells me you have spoken to him concerning myself.'

'I would never betray you!' cried Timothy, hurt to the quick. 'It is true that I spoke of you to Anastasius, but only in your best interests, in an attempt to remedy the misunderstanding that has developed between yourself and the emperor. A dangerous misunderstanding. As things stand at present, you could be in peril, Majesty. Anastasius' senior general is Julian, whom you must remember from your youth. He is to raise an expedition to enforce the withdrawal of your troops from Moesia and Pannonia. Don't tell me he won't exploit his command as an opportunity to settle old scores. For your sake, Majesty, it's vital he be given no excuse to do so.'

'Your concern is touching, Trascilliseus. First treachery, now a warning. You would do better to consider your own position. No doubt you'll be expecting to return to Anastasius bearing my reply. Instead, you will remain here in Ravenna, as . . . let us say as my "guest", pending further developments.'

In other words, a hostage against any tricks that Julian might play, thought Timothy, grim foreboding growing like a cold lump inside him.

In the Senate House, old Festus, the *Caput Senatus*, banged his staff on the floor and called the next speaker: 'Publius Quinctilius Junius Theotecnius Constantius, *Praefectus Urbis Romae*.'

The City Prefect rose from his place on the crowded marble benches and made his way to the rostrum. He was a red-faced, paunchy individual, whose sweating face betrayed his nervousness at addressing the august assembly of 'his betters'. (Oh yes, he'd overheard some of the snide put-downs whispered behind his back by these snobs of Roman

* 28 September 505.

senators. Just because they'd all got pedigrees stretching back to Romulus and owned a few farm-middens in the sticks . . .)

'One of Theoderic's "new men",' whispered Faustus *albus* to Rufius Cethegus seated beside him. 'Jumped-up arriviste – a nobody from Liguria. No family *cognomen*, so makes up for it by giving himself a string of impressive-sounding names. Who does he think he's fooling?'

'He's not one of us, that's for sure,' Cethegus concurred. '"Us", I fear, being very much personae non gratae with our Dear Leader in Ravenna. Have you noticed that, ever since we stood up to him over the Laurentius *v.* Pope Symmachus affair, not a single member of an old Roman family's been given a key appointment? Barring, that is, the Three Wise Men,* whom, for some reason, he seems to trust.'

'You're right. It must go back to that do in Domitian's Palace, where he handed out those silly medals.' Faustus chuckled; 'Mine comes in handy as a paperweight. As I recall, your father got bawled out on that occasion – shocking bad form. Better shush: our country cousin's about to grace us with his views.'

'Honourable Members of this 'ouse,' Constantius began, speaking in a broad north-western accent with a hint of Gallic, 'it is my 'umble opinion that you may not be fully aware of the danger in which our fair City stands.'

A buzz of puzzled speculation rippled round the benches. 'Danger?' whispered Faustus to Cethegus. 'What on earth's he on about?'

'As you all know,' the Prefect continued, 'Theoderic 'as pulled back 'is troops from Moesia and Pannonia to Ravenna, so as to be able to counter possible threats from two directions. Threat number one.' He held up a forefinger. 'In Gaul, Clovis is waiting to pounce on the Visigoths – which 'e can't risk doing for the nonce, because Theoderic, their ally, is too close. Threat number two.' Up came the forefinger again, joined by a thumb. 'A great sea-borne expedition from the Eastern Empire, commanded by General Julianus, Master of Soldiers for the Diocese of Oriens, is presently patrolling off the coast of south-east Italy. Result: Theoderic's in a bind. If 'e marches south to protect the

---

* Symmachus, Boethius and Cassiodorus. Cassiodorus, although a scion of an old Bruttium (toe of Italy) family rather than a Roman one, was very much a part of the senatorial establishment and, as such, definitely 'one of us'.

'eel of Italy, Clovis will attack the Visigoths. But if 'e 'eads for Gaul to
'elp King Alaric, that would leave the Eastern expedition free to strike.'

'But where's the threat to Rome in all of this?' one senator called
out, in tones of mild exasperation.

'From the Adriatic coast to Rome is no great distance.'

'With the Apennines between – good God, man, you'd think this
Julianus was a second Hannibal!' exclaimed another senator. 'The expedition's only there as sword-rattling. Basically, to remind Theoderic to
behave himself.'

'Well, in my 'umble opinion, we can't afford to take no chances.
The walls of Rome need strengthening in places. 'Appen Julianus should
besiege the City, I wouldn't like to bet we'd keep 'im out.'

A chorus of sardonic groans greeted this observation.

'The man's panicking,' Faustus murmured to Cethegus. 'Either that
or he's hoping to curry favour with Theoderic by a flag-waving gesture.'
He stood up and called, 'And where's the money coming from, I'd like
to know? You can be sure the Public Purse in Ravenna's not about to
cough up, and, thanks to the Church lands settlement, most of us are
pretty strapped for cash.'

'We must all do our patriotic bit. A spot o' belt-tightening's 'ardly
going to kill us. 'Sides, Theoderic wouldn't be impressed if 'e 'eard we
was too mean to defend our noble City.'

'Might have known it would come to that,' Cethegus whispered
disgustedly to his friend. 'Fellow's got the ear of you-know-who, unfortunately. We can't afford to hand the king another stick to beat us with.'

And so (reluctantly) the vote was passed to strengthen Rome's defences.

As Clovis's mighty host grew daily greater on the north bank of the
Liger, so Alaric's appeals to Theoderic became ever more frequent
and urgent. Torn between the desire to help his Visigothic kinsmen,
and the need to keep watch from Ravenna on the Eastern war-fleet,
Theoderic set in train a massive warship-building programme. A fleet
of sufficient strength would neutralize the threat posed by Julian's
naval expedition, and the king would then be free to march to Alaric's
aid. The shipyards of Arimimum, of Classis* and Tergeste, rang to

* The port of Ravenna.

the thump of adze and mallet as a steady stream of galleys slid down the ways and into the holding-docks. But before enough could be built, news arrived that Clovis had crossed the Liger and was pushing south, carrying all before him.

In rage and desperation, Theoderic despatched Duke Mammo and Count Ibba with the host, to succour his beleaguered allies. Too late. Before the Ostrogoths reached Gaul, terrible intelligence began to filter through: the Visigothic host had been destroyed* – King Alaric being among those killed – the population scattered and in flight. And to compound a sorry situation, the Burgundians, despite prior friendly overtures from Theoderic, now switched their allegiance to the Franks, laid siege to Arelate, sacked Tolosa and, led by Gundobad, their king, took Barcino† in Hispania.

When Julian (aboard his flagship) heard that Theoderic's host had marched for Gaul, his glee and satisfaction knew no bounds. Now his cup of vengeance would be filled to overflowing, and he would drink deep thereof. Anastasius' orders regarding the expedition's rules of engagement had been specific: it was there purely to make sure that Theoderic adhered to the terms laid down in the official warning conveyed to him by the Isaurian, Trascilliseus. Unless provoked, Julian must not commence hostilities. But what else was Theoderic's warship-building initiative but provocation? Julian knew, of course, that it was nothing of the sort: instead, a desperate measure taken in self-defence, which circumstance had forced upon the king. However, with judicious editing, the facts in his report to Anastasius could be presented in such a way as to constitute a damning indictment of Theoderic, making him, not Julian, appear as the aggressor. With anticipation and excitement rising inside him – like sap in spring within a tree, the general snapped a command to his *navarchus*. The shipmaster relayed the order to the *nautae* – the sailors who tended the sails and rigging, as opposed to the *remiges* who manned the oars. Up to the masthead crept a long red pennant – the signal for the fleet to attack.

*

* Perhaps at Vouillé, near Poitiers.
† Arles, Toulouse, Barcelona.

Tending his flock on the foothills of Mons Garganus* in northern
Apulia, Marcus the shepherd selected a dry stone on which to sit while
eating his midday *prandium* of bread and olives. The early autumn
sunshine was warm, his sheep were grazing contentedly within easy
eyeshot, so Marcus awarded himself a short nap . . .

Awaking, he looked out to sea – and gasped. Emerging into view
around the mighty headland was a mass of sails. Ship after ship hove
into sight; by the time the last had cleared the promontory, Marcus had
counted two hundred – some were big-beamed transports, others sleek
dromons. Abandoning his charges (he could safely leave them for an
hour or two; no wolves had been sighted in the area for many weeks),
he began to run down the hill to spread the news to the villagers of
Bariae bringing in the harvest in the fields below.

In wonder tinged with apprehension, the harvesters watched the
ships drop anchor in the bay fringed by a scatter of lime-washed cottages.
Soon, streams of soldiers from the transports and marines from the
dromons were wading ashore. Orders in familiar Latin (*'Non vos turbatis
sed mandata captate'*†) carried faintly to the workers' ears. A party of
several hundred formed up on the beach (only a small proportion of
the total force, judging from the numbers watching from the decks)
and began to tramp up the hillside in open order, laughing and chatting as though on a spree.

'What lingo's that they're talking?' one young harvester wondered
aloud, stopping work to rest on his scythe. 'Not Latin, that's for
sure.'

'It's Greek, you ignoramus,' muttered a greybeard, shaking his head
in disgust. 'When I was your age, everyone still understood some of
the old tongue, even if they didn't speak it much. Why do you think
this part of Italy's called Magna Graecia? Settled by our ancestors from
across the Mare Ionium‡ centuries ago.'

'Weird-looking bunch,' someone observed, as the strangers drew
near. 'Like ancient legionaries.' And indeed, with their scale-armour

---

* Mount Gargano, a vast, isolated peak on the promontory that forms the 'spur'
above Italy's 'heel'.
† Roughly translated, 'Take it easy, but don't forget you're under orders.'
‡ The Ionian Sea.

*loricae** and classical Attic helmets, and commanded by an officer in muscle-cuirass, they needed only long rectangular shields to resemble Roman soldiers from the time of Trajan or the Antonines. Apart from swords, they were equipped with strange cylindrical bundles which they held in their right hands.

After testing the wind direction, the officer led his men to the upper margin of the fields, along which the soldiers formed a line.

'The bastards are going to fire the crop!' exclaimed a middle-aged harvester. 'See the flashes from their strike-a-lights.' And he raced uphill to confront them. 'Stop!' he shouted, planting himself before their officer.

With a grin, the officer unsheathed his sword and, almost nonchalantly, drew the tip across the other's cheek. With a cry of shock and pain, the harvester clapped a hand to his face to stem the blood pouring from the wound.

No one interfered, as the soldiers flung burning torches into the standing corn. Cowed and silent, the villagers watched in helpless fury as the fruits of that year's labour disappeared in roaring flames.

Their task completed, the soldiers returned to the fleet, which continued its progress down the coast to select fresh targets. The seaboard of Apulia and then Calabria came to be defined by a lengthening wall of smoke from burning crops as the fleet moved south, sacking Sipontum† en route. Rounding the heel of Italy into the Sinus Tarentinus,‡ it prepared to assault the city of Tarentum. But the Tarentines were made of sterner stuff than the Sipontians. Inspired, perhaps, by the defiant spirit of their forefathers, who had broken an alliance forced on them by Rome (to side instead with Hannibal), they made ready to resist. In this they were assisted by topography.

The harbour to the east of the port was sheltered by the twin islets of the Choerades, while the town itself, situated on an island, was connected to the mainland by a bridge and aqueduct – all features which militated against a concerted onslaught. Booms, formed from vessels chained together and joining the Choerades to each other and the mainland, made a defensive necklace across the harbour mouth.

* Cuirasses.
† Now Manfredonia, founded in 1261 from the ruins of ancient Sipontum, by Manfred, king of Sicily and regent of Apulia.
‡ The Gulf of Taranto.

This forced Julian to split his offensive into two separate attacks, one by land, the other from the sea. While the *dromon*s, harrassed by archery from the islets and the shore, attempted to sink the booms by the time-consuming method of ramming each vessel and leaving it to founder, Julian's eight-thousand-strong force of soldiers and marines fought its way slowly along the bridge and the narrow channel of the aqueduct, the Tarentines grimly contesting every hard-fought yard. The end, however, could only be delayed, not prevented. After several hours of bloody hand-to-hand combat as Roman battled Roman, the city fell. It was then subjected to an orgy of pillage and destruction.

The capture of Tarentum marked the culmination of the raid. Getting wind that Theoderic's fleet was now almost strong enough to match his own, Julian, well satisfied with his campaign of retribution, gave the order to make sail for Constantinople. He had paid back Theoderic a hundredfold. As for the Isaurian, the fact that nothing had been heard from him before the expedition left the Golden Horn suggested that the king had detained him as a hostage – preferably in some dank and noisome gaol. How true the saying was that revenge was a dish best eaten cold.

In Ravenna, a mood of black depression settled on Theoderic. Fortune seemed to have deserted him: his dreams of reviving the Western Empire lay in ruins; he had been humiliated by Anastasius – forced to return his conquests in Illyricum, and watch impotently while the south of his kingdom was ravaged by an Eastern fleet. His rival, Clovis, had triumphed in Gaul, destroying the kingdom of his friends and kinsmen, the Visigoths. The Vandals and Burgundians had thrown off their allegiances, the Burgundians by siding with the Franks against the Visigoths, the Vandals (who had a powerful fleet) by withholding aid against the Eastern expedition. Hardest of all to bear, perhaps, was the knowledge that Timothy – who had once been more a trusted friend than a servant – had played him false. To rub salt into his wounds, Anastasius had chosen to honour Clovis, awarding him an honorary consulship – along with the title of Augustus – while his own consular nominee,* Venantius, had been turned down. All this was clearly intended to serve as a

* For the year 507.

reminder that such titles were in the gift of Anastasius, and as a calculated snub designed to put a presumptuous monarch in his place.

In this dark hour, only the counsel of his three Roman advisers,
Boethius, Symmachus and Cassiodorus, provided a modicum of
comfort. Rational and positive, they encouraged him to maintain his
self-belief, pointing out that his present setbacks weighed less in the
balance than his achievements, which were numerous and great. The
darkest hour was followed by the dawn, he told himself; then angrily
dismissed the thought. A king should be above seeking consolation in
such hoary saws.

THIRTY-ONE

It is proper for us, most clement emperor, to seek peace
From a letter of Theoderic to Anastasius, seeking reconciliation
after the hostilities of 507–8; quoted in full by Cassiodorus
(who wrote it), *Variae, c.* 537

Despite Theoderic's rejection of wishful thinking contained in ancient maxims, the Wheel of Fortune spun a full half-circle, and his career, which in the course of his confrontation with the empire had seemed to reach a nadir, began to climb rapidly towards its zenith.

The Ostrogothic army that had failed to rescue Alaric found itself confronted by Clovis's mighty host. In the ensuing battle, Count Ibba was victorious; the loss of thirty thousand of his finest warriors broke the power of Clovis. Mopping-up operations under Duke Mammo pushed the Franks back beyond the Liger and forced their Burgundian allies to withdraw from Provincia.* With their great persecutor defeated, the grateful remnant of the nation of the Visigoths was happy to be incorporated into the realm of its Ostrogothic cousins; thus, almost at a stroke, Theoderic saw his rule extended over southern Gaul and most of Spain.† The Vandals and Burgundians (conscious of their mistake in having roused a sleeping tiger) returned to their allegiance, while the Heruls, Rhaetians and Thuringians eagerly accepted his overtures and became his allies, forming a protective buffer zone to his kingdom, in the north. Finally, the ring of defences was closed to the eastward by an agreement sub rosa with Sabinianus, whereby Pannonia would quietly once more come under Ostrogothic rule – on the understanding that there would be no more incursions into imperial territory.

With the appointment of a Praetorian Prefect of Gaul (in reality,

---

* Provence, where they had been besieging Arelate (Arles).
† Barring its north-west corner, which was Suevic territory, the Hispanic penin-sula had been added to the Visigothic realm of Aquitania, under Euric.

Gaul south of the Liger), and an ecclesiastical vicar for Spain and the *whole* of Gaul – the post was confirmed by Pope Symmachus, so had to be accepted, however reluctantly, by the Catholic Franks – Theoderic set the seal upon his triumph – a victory reinforced by the death of his great rival, Clovis.* A few short years had seen his fortunes change from a state of abject humiliation to one where he could, with justification, claim to have reconstituted much of the old Empire of the West. The time was ripe, he told himself, to begin the implementation of long-cherished plans – plans which would see his imperial dreams at last become reality: the official rebirth of the Western Empire, with himself crowned emperor.

'"It is proper for us, most clement emperor, to seek peace", blah, blah, blah. "Indeed, peace is something to be desired by every state", blah, blah, blah. "And so, most pious of princes, it is in accordance with your power and an honour for us", blah, blah, blah, "to seek concord with you."' Anastasius was in conclave, in his private *tablinum* in the Great Palace of Constantinople, with his two chief generals, Sabinian and Julianus, and Agapitus, the envoy of Theoderic. Anastasius looked up from the king's letter, which he had been reading aloud. 'Well, he sounds contrite enough,' he murmured with a smile, handing the missive back to Agapitus. 'You may tell your master, our vicegerent, that, provided he keeps to the agreement made with General Sabinianus here – never again to cross our frontier in arms – we accept his offer of peace.'

'Hear, hear, Serenity,' enthused Sabinianus. 'I'd stake my reputation that Theoderic will honour such a mutual agreement. When I negotiated with him about the transfer of Pannonia, I felt that I was dealing with a straight and honest man, one whose word could be relied on. In these sorts of situations, I've learned to trust my instinct; I've seldom been proved wrong.'

'Not good enough, Serenity!' exclaimed Julianus. 'Considering Theoderic's outrageous conduct in invading Moesia, he should be made to pay handsomely for reparation, and to come in person to Constantinople and abase himself before your throne. Instead, we hand

* In 511.

him back Pannonia, and are prepared, it seems, to treat him as a friend. Kow-towing to barbarians – it's a disgrace!'

'I think we can say that the harrying of Magna Graecia, to say nothing of the sacking of Sipontum and Tarentum, more than cancels out any debt of reparation,' said Anastasius coldly. A compassionate man, he had been deeply troubled by rumours of gratuitous brutality connected with the naval expedition. As a result, Sabinianus had displaced Julian in favour as well as seniority. 'As for Pannonia,' the emperor went on, 'he's welcome to run it – to him it's a useful buffer zone, to us a drain on our resources, any revenue from taxes far outweighed by the expenses of administration.' He looked sternly at Julianus. 'As Theoderic himself has said, the wars that turned out happily for him were those brought to completion with moderation. A lesson you have yet to learn, it would seem, General.'

And so began a Golden Age for Italy. With peace established, Theoderic's firm and equitable rule ensured prosperity at home, while abroad his status as a father-figure to all Germanic peoples was unchal- lenged. A series of dynastic marriages with women of Theoderic's immediate family helped to create a stability hitherto unknown among the barbarian monarchies of Europe. Under the Pax Theoderica, trade, agriculture and industry flourished to a degree not seen since that happiest of epochs, the near-century from the reign of Nerva to that of Marcus Aurelius. Relations with the East thawed, to the extent that Theoderic's consular nominees, including the once-spurned Venantius, were confirmed in office by the emperor. Supervised by presidents assisted by 'correctors', the administration of Italy's fifteen regions was run efficiently, and a Gothic tendency to violence and an Italian towards corruption were, if not stamped out, at least severely curbed, by the strict enforcement of the law. Public buildings, which had gradually been permitted to fall into decay, were protected and refurbished under a preservation scheme with its own specially appointed architect.

Content to be guided as to policy by his three Roman chief advisers, Cassiodorus, Symmachus and Boethius, and with leisure to cultivate his orchard in Ravenna and take up again his interest in the arts and liter- ature, the king entered on the happiest period of his life. The only touch of sadness was in the loss of his friendship with Timothy, who was under (not uncomfortable) house arrest. Although that friendship was broken, never to be repaired, the king's original anger and feeling of betrayal had faded over time to dull regret. He could afford to make a generous gesture: he would arrange a secret test of loyalty; if Timothy passed, his liberty would be restored, along, perhaps, with a small pension, so that the old Isaurian could see out his days without the fear of penury.

And so, in a glow of serenity and peace, the afternoon of Theoderic's life drew quietly towards its evening. But, unnoticed by him, a cloud had appeared on the horizon, a cloud 'no bigger than a man's hand', which would grow and grow until it filled the sky.

'My friend from Constantinopolis, and your fellow Anular, Lucius Vettius Priscianus,' announced Cethegus, introducing his companion (whose dark skin and tightly curled black hair denoted an African origin) to Cassiodorus, Boethius and Symmachus, ensconced in the *tablinum* of Symmachus' house in Ravenna. 'But I was forgetting, Quintus' – he nodded at his host – 'you two already know each other.'

'Indeed we do,' said Priscianus warmly. 'When we first met in Constantinople, I had to congratulate him on his command of Greek – better than most native speakers'.'

'And showed his appreciation by dedicating three treatises to me,' the senator responded with a smile. He clapped his hands and a slave entered, bearing a tray on which were five goblets and a silver flagon. 'Let's toast this reunion in Falernian.'

'Perhaps later, Quintus,' Cethegus suggested. 'Best we keep our heads as clear as possible while I explain the reasons why I've called this meeting – which must be strictly sub rosa, by the way.' Smiling cheerfully, in a significant gesture he drew a finger across his throat.

'Anastasius is dead at last,'* Cethegus announced, when all were seated, listening, in a silence tinged with apprehension. 'Expect to hear officially in a day or two; my sources usually provide me with intelligence before the government couriers arrive with news.'

'And his death means . . . ?' prompted Boethius.

'That the Acacian Schism, too, is dead. Or, if not yet defunct, shortly to become so.'

---

* He died on 9 July 518, aged eighty-eight.

'Forgive me, Rufius,' said Cassiodorus, looking mildly puzzled, 'but I'll have to ask you to enlighten me.'

'Without elaborating on religious niceties,' Priscian put in, 'it means that peace, theologically speaking, has broken out between Rome and Constantinople. Our new ruler, Justin – another geriatric emperor – is a tough old soldier from a peasant background. The real power behind the throne is his nephew Justinianus – well educated, and highly intelligent, to boot, by all accounts.'

'The point is,' Cethegus observed, picking up on Priscian, 'that they're both fervent Chalcedonians – *id est*, adherents of the doctrine, established by the Council of Chalcedon way back in the reign of Marcian, that Christ has two natures, human and divine. Which, as I'm sure you hardly need reminding, puts them very much in tune with Rome, whose new Pope, Hormisdas, is also strongly Chalcedonian. The Acacian creed, which panders to Monophytism – the belief that Christ has only one, divine, nature, and which, under Zeno and Anastasius, gained ground in Eastern sees – is now almost certainly about to be declared anathema.'

'Your drift, if I've followed you aright,' said Boethius, 'is that, with channels of communication soon to be unblocked between East and West, Romans in both Italy and the empire will shortly be exchanging ideas. Am I right?'

'You are indeed, Anicius Manlius. As I mentioned at our last meeting, there's a growing feeling on both sides of the Adriatic that Italy should be reunited with the empire. That feeling is articulated and given focus by leading Romans: the senators of Rome itself – Laurentians almost to a man – writers, politicians, intellectuals, and more especially by Anulus, the group to which the present company belongs and which, from this moment, will be called upon to help to sway men's minds throughout the Roman world. Justinian himself is thought to be strongly in favour of bringing Italy back into the imperial fold. Not only that, but he's said to harbour ambitions to reconstitute the whole Western Empire.'

'But that would mean . . . the expulsion of the Vandals, the Burgundians and Franks, and the Ostrogoths and Visigoths,' said Symmachus slowly, his fine patrician features set in an expression of concern. 'A momentous step. Could it be done? *Should* it, in fact, be done?'

'The task would certainly be challenging,' replied Cethegus. 'But yes, I believe it could be done. Bear in mind that the barbarians are a tiny fraction – perhaps no more than a hundredth – of the Roman population of the occupied territories. Many are no longer the ferocious warriors they once were. The Vandals have grown soft through the debilitating effects of luxury and a hot climate. The Visigoths and Franks lost many of their finest fighting men in the recent wars. The imperial armies, on the other hand, are strong, well led and well equipped. In a straight fight, Roman troops will always win – thanks largely to barbarian indiscipline and lack of armour. All in all, the odds on us expelling the barbarians are in our favour, I would say. Also, by bringing much of the West's former territory into the Ostrogothic realm, Theoderic may have done us a favour. Reconstituting the Western Empire could be made that much easier. As to your second point, Quintus, I believe it is the patriotic duty of all Romans to rid ourselves of the barbarians – who, let us not forget, are uninvited guests. Look at the tyrannical regime the Vandals have inflicted on the Romans of Africa. And the record of the Franks and the Burgundians hasn't been much better.'

'But under Ostrogothic rule, Italy has prospered,' objected Cassiodorus. 'You can't deny it, Rufius.'

'Theoderic, I grant you, has ruled well – largely through the guidance of you three.' Cethegus nodded at the trio of Roman Councillors. 'But Theoderic's getting on; who knows how much longer his reign will last? I would remind you that on the previous occasion I was here, I warned of the dire consequences of a Gothic dynasty.'

'Obviously Theoderic's successors will be Goths,' Boethius said. 'But . . . a dynasty? Can that be likely? The king has no male heirs, and at his age the chances can't be good that he'll produce any.'

'Ah, but he does have an heir. His daughter Amalasuntha has been married to a Visigoth called Eutharic, for whom an impressive Amal pedigree has naturally had to be concocted. You may well look surprised; the marriage has been kept under wraps, probably because Theoderic suspects that Roman reaction would be less than ecstatic, especially should the couple have a son. But why does all this matter, I hear you ask? Well, the reason is that dynasties are hard to overthrow. Once established, the population tends to tolerate them, even when they're brutal or incompetent, like the Severans or later Theodosians. Smooth transfer of power from one monarch to the next, you see. Lessens the risk of usurpation and civil war, which has always been the curse of Rome. Now, I have it on good authority that scheduled for next year are three events which, taken in conjunction, will reinforce Theoderic's dynastic position immeasurably.'

'Thus making it that much harder to unseat his successors, when the Day of Liberation comes,' added Priscian.

'And these events are?' queried Cassiodorus.

'First,' Cethegus went on, 'Theoderic has nominated Eutharic for a consulship. If it's confirmed by Justin, as it almost certainly will be, the prestige accruing to the house of the Amal will be immense, helping to make Eutharic acceptable as Theoderic's heir. Second, Senator Caecina Mavortius Basilius Decius, who – surprise, surprise – is hoping for a consulship, will, six months after Eutharic takes office, unveil an inscription at Terracina on the Via Appia. Exactly what its wording is, my agents have so far been unable to discover, but I strongly suspect that it's something designed to lend support to item number three.' Pausing for dramatic effect, he looked round at the others.

'Well?' demanded Cassiodorus, at last breaking the tension-building silence.

'A week after Decius unveils his mystery inscription,' Cethegus continued, 'Theoderic intends to present himself in the Basilica of St Peter outside Rome, before Pope Hormisdas – who will then proceed to crown him emperor.'

THIRTY-TWO

Eutharicus was adorned by Justinus with the palm-enwoven robe of the consul

Cassiodorus, *Variae*, c. 537

From his place on the marble benches of Rome's Senate House, Theoderic felt his heart swell with pride as his son-in-law Eutharic, tall, handsome, smiling, advanced towards the rostrum.

With the death of Anastasius and the ending of the thirty-five-year schism between Rome and Constantinople, Theoderic had at first been worried. The religious divide (in a world where prosperity and personal salvation depended on correct belief – an attitude not shared by the sceptical monarch) had meant that his Roman subjects were less likely to look for help and support from an emperor they regarded as a heretic. Now that religious unity had been restored, would these same subjects start conspiring with the Romans of the East, in a move towards political unity? In the event, however, his concern had proved premature. Justin, the new emperor, had been happy to confirm Theoderic and his successors as rulers of the Ostrogothic realm. And when Eutharic visited the emperor in Constantinople, Justin had been so taken with the young Visigoth that he adopted him as 'son-in-arms' (shield-raised according to *Germanic* custom), and had personally nominated him for the Western consulship, along with, and taking precedence over, himself as Eastern consul – an unprecedented honour. In addition, the emperor had designated Eutharic a 'Flavian', a unique privilege reserved for those deemed fit to be associated with the imperial family. Enormously relieved, the Amal king had, to mark the Rome–Byzantium entente, issued three new coins: forty-, twenty-, and ten-nummi pieces, each showing on the obverse an eagle, long a symbol of nobility and power to both Goths and Romans.

'Do you, Flavius Eutharicus Cilliga,' quavered old Festus, 'swear, as consul, faithfully to serve the Senate and the people of Rome, and to reside within the *pomoerium** during your term of office?'

'I do so swear.'

'Then I, in my capacity as *Caput Senatus*, with these symbols of office do hereby invest you as a Consul of Rome, your name, along with that of Justinus, Augustus of the Romans, to be entered in the *Fasti* this Kalends of Januarius, for the year from the Founding of the City the twelve hundred and seventy-third,† to be known hereafter and for ever as the Year of the Consuls Eutharicus and Justinus.'

Two former consuls placed upon the young man's shoulders a robe of cream silk from Serica‡ patterned in a wondrous raised design of squares, lozenges and stylized flowers. Festus handed him an ivory baton topped with a golden finial in the form of a winged figure. Then, to loud and sustained acclamation, the new consul, followed by senators and guests, exited the Senate house and proceeded in procession to the Circus Maximus, there to inaugurate the Games, the expensive duty which every consul was expected to take up and which, for the honour of having the year named for him, could bring about financial ruin.

Within days, Eutharic was the darling of the City, charming all who came in contact with him by his open manner, friendliness and liberality. Generous *sparsiones* – scatterings of coin – pleased the mob, gifts of consular diptychs, waxed writing-tablets with exquisitely carved ivory covers, delighted their aristocratic recipients, while the munificence of the amusements exceeded all expectations.

But Eutharic's charismatic geniality concealed a shrewd and calculating side. Theoderic, intensely interested in the vast and complex systems of aqueducts and drains by which water was conveyed into and removed from Rome, and which, in his fancy, resembled the vessels of a living organism, had arranged for himself and his son-in-law a tour of the city's subterranean sewers. Led by a guide provided by the City

---

* The official city boundary, enclosing a space extending some distance beyond the Aurelianic Walls.
† 1 January 519. Sessions of the Senate were held on the three key dates of the month: Kalends (1st), Nones (5th or 7th), Ides (13th or 15th).
‡ China.

Prefect, the royal pair, after threading a network of dank underground tunnels with deep central gutters along which noisome fluids flowed, paused for a rest inside the Cloaca Maxima, a vast arched channel deep below the Forum Romanum.

'Built by the kings of Rome a thousand years ago,'* Theoderic said wonderingly, pointing to the massive, cunningly fitted blocks of ashlar curving above their heads. 'I wonder, will we ever rediscover such engineering skills?'

'I doubt it, father,' laughed Eutharic, passing over a flask of wine. 'The Gothic kings will have other priorities, I think. War and politics are more our line. Talking of which,' he added lightly, 'I take it my succession – which hopefully will not happen for many years yet – *will* go unchallenged?'

'Have no fear on that score, son. As my heir, Constantinople backs you to the hilt, and Romans in Italy have lost the taste for competing for the purple. Of course, there's poor old Romulus.' Theoderic shook his head and chuckled. 'But nobody remembers him.'

'Romulus?'

'West Rome's last emperor. I'd almost forgotten he existed. He was put on the throne by his father, Orestes, the Roman general who ran Italy at the time, Italy being about all that was left of the Western Empire. When his Master of Soldiers – my predecessor Odovacar – demanded a pay increase for his German federates, Orestes was foolish enough to try to stall him. Bad mistake. Odovacar had him killed, pensioned off little Romulus, who was only a child, and made himself de facto king of Italy, with the tacit consent of Zeno.'

'So where's Romulus now, father?'

'Living in comfortable obscurity somewhere in Campania, I believe. Must be in his fifties – a harmless nobody.' Theoderic laughed. 'Don't worry, son. No one's going to try to get his throne back for him after all these years.'

'I see.' Eutharic took a pull of wine and smiled. But the smile did not reach his eyes.

Before they even sighted her walls, travellers approaching Rome heard

---

* And still functioning.

the roar from the Circus Maximus. Packed into the stands of the vast racecourse – fully a third of a mile long – three hundred thousand people rose to their feet and yelled their appreciation as, according to custom, the Games' *editor*, followed by a procession of mounted dignitaries, rode in a chariot round the *Spina*, the long barrier down the centre of the racetrack. The *editor* was the consul for the year, none other than the son-in-law of Theoderic himself, Eutharic.

The circuit completed, Eutharic alighted from the chariot and joined the assembly in the *Tribunal Judicum*, the raised box where sat the umpires, also privileged spectators. They were: Theoderic, accompanied by his beautiful and learned daughter, the trilingual Amalasuntha, wife of Eutharic; court officials, including the newly appointed Master of Offices, Boethius; Pope Hormisdas, surrounded by a coterie of bishops; and a group of high-ranking envoys from Constantinople. Between box and racetrack, spears in hand, stood a row of flaxen-haired Goths of the royal bodyguard, under the command of Connal the Scot.

Nearby, in an area reserved for senators and their wives, the Anulars (Boethius conspicuous by his absence) formed a compact group.

'Well, we may as well say goodbye to any ideas about reunification with the empire,' sighed Symmachus. 'Now that Justin's given full backing to Theoderic as king and Eutharic as his successor, Ostrogothic rule seems set in concrete. Rufius,' he went on, a hint of bitterness creeping into his voice, 'I thought you said the ending of the Schism was going to change everything.'

Cethegus looked up from studying his racing form for the Greens, engraved on copper. 'Just a moment,' he murmured, bending to his scrutiny once more. 'I'm working out how much to bet on Fuscus. Up-and-coming young charioteer, first in over two hundred races to date. Pomperanus, that's his near-hand horse, is a *centenarius* – over a hundred wins.' He signalled to one of the bet-takers parading below the stands. 'Ten solidi on Fuscus to win.' The man opened his tablets and scratched a note of the bet, along with Cethegus' name, then handed the senator a wooden tally in exchange for ten gold coins.

'*Rufius!*'

Smiling, Cethegus raised his head and put down his racing form. 'Apologies, my dear Quintus. Where were we? The Schism, wasn't it? Not to worry; now that it's over, things should start going our way.'

'Yes, but *when?*' demanded Faustus *albus*. 'Since he accepted the post of Master of Offices, with his sons being tipped for consulships, even Boethius seems to have given up the Cause and gone over to the enemy. It's one thing to act as Theoderic's unofficial adviser, quite another to become his chief minister.'

'Be fair, Acilius. He could hardly turn down the appointment,' Cethegus pointed out. 'Any more than you, Magnus,' turning to Cassiodorus, 'could refuse when Theoderic invited you to deliver an oration in praise of his son-in-law. No, Boethius is simply making the best of things, and marking time until the tide begins to turn.'

'Which it will, gentlemen,' put in Priscian. 'As soon as Justinian takes over.'

'I might be dead by then,' wailed Festus. 'Justin may be old, but who's to say he won't go on for many years yet? Just look at Anastasius.'

'Justin is yesterday's man,' said Priscian. His quiet assurance lifted the prevailing mood of pessimism. And the fact that he was from Constantinople, and presumably had some inside knowledge of the machinations of Byzantine court politics, lent his words an added weight. 'In a sense Justinian has already taken over. Justin may be front of stage, but Justinian's the one who's deciding future policy. And that, take my word for it, is definitely geared towards recovering the Western Empire. Constantinople's full of Roman exiles from Italy who can't wait for the Day of Liberation to come; and they're a powerful pressure group.'

Their conversation was interrupted by a trumpet-blast, the signal for the grooms to lead the four competing teams representing the Red, Blue, Green and White factions, into the stalls from the rear. In the box, Eutharic rose to his feet holding in his right hand the *mappa*, the white cloth to start the race. The *mappa* dropped, the stall gates flew open, and the chariots were off.

Each vehicle, a very light affair with a wide wheel-base, was drawn by four horses, the centre two, selected for pulling power, yoked to the shaft, the outer ones, responsible for turning the chariot, on traces. The drivers, wearing thick leather helmets and short tunics in their factions' colours, had tied the reins round their waists to get more leverage on the turns – a risky procedure in the event of a crash, as their only means of freeing themselves was a sharp knife stuck in the belt. The drivers' strategy was to take the turns as tightly as possible, which meant trying to beat the opposing teams to reach the inside track next to the *Spina*. The race comprised seven circuits of the track, the completion of each lap being marked by the removal of a dolphin from a crossbar at either end of the barricade.

As the chariots flashed round the track, dolphin after dolphin disappeared from the crossbar until only one remained.

'Come on, Fuscus!' groaned Cethegus as the vehicles approached the final turn, with the Blues' chariot in the lead and the Greens' at the rear. Then Fuscus touched his whip to the shoulders of the inside pair; the team picked up speed, and in a magnificent piece of driving Fuscus wove between White and Red to draw level with Blue.

In a desperate attempt to maintain his lead, the Blue driver swung his team as close as he dared round the end of the *Spina*. Too close. His axlerod hit one of the protective bumper cones and broke, the dragging axlebar flung the whole equipage forward with a savage jerk, and down went chariot, horses and driver in a tangle of splintering wood, whipping traces and flailing hooves. Unable to draw his knife in time, the Blue driver died beneath the wheels of Fuscus' chariot, as it ploughed through the wreckage – before hurtling on to win the race.

'Well done, Rufius,' said Faustus *albus* to Cethegus, as the Anulars left the stands. 'You can afford to stand us all a drink from your winnings. In fact, congratulations all round are in order, I think – if you believe in omens, that is.' He smiled at the others. 'Know what that poor Blues' driver called his lead horse? Eutharic. Thought the name might bring him luck, I suppose.'

'If only our beloved new consul had had the accident,' murmured Cethegus, his mischievous tone belying the thoughtful gleam in his eye. 'That would have fouled up the succession nicely. Ah well, we can all dream.'

In the gardens of Lucullus' villa near Neapolis,* the last Western emperor, trowel in hand, knelt to dig a hole. The hole was to receive a young laurel which, when mature, would perfectly set off a mosaic

---

* Naples.

fountain niche, the centrepiece of a series of elaborate waterways spanned by pavilions and pergolas. Romulus looked with pleasure at the contrast that white marble, grey weathered wood and clear running water made with the varying shades of green: box and cypress, plane trees, myrtle and acanthus.

As he tamped the rootball carefully in place, Romulus reflected on his life. At fifty-three, despite being confined – a virtual prisoner within the bounds of the estate – he was not unhappy. In fact, he was probably a great deal happier than he would have been if he had inherited the cares and duties of a Roman emperor. These gardens were his empire, their trees and flowers his subjects, whose tending brought him fulfilment and content. Not many, he supposed, could ask for more.

Preoccupied, he failed to notice a man approaching him from behind. A shadow fell across the grass before him, followed by a sharp, stinging pain across his throat, then a terrible choking sensation. He tried to cry out but no sound came; his mouth filled with warm liquid. Blood sheeting from his neck, the last emperor of the West slumped dying to the ground.

PART IV

THE TOWER OF PAVIA
AD 519–526

THIRTY-THREE

Most glorious . . . Theoderic, victor and conqueror, ever Augustus
Part of an inscription put up at Terracina on the Via Appia, by Caecina
Mavortius Basilius Decius; after 510

'Delicious, Serenity,' pronounced Boethius, after taking a bite from the
pear Theoderic handed to him. 'Truly delicious. I congratulate you;
creating a successful orchard in Ravenna, with its fogs and marshy
exhalations, seems a near-miraculous feat.'

'Well, it was not without problems,' allowed the king, flushing with
pleasure at the compliment. 'I had to grub up the original stock and
replace it with quince for grafting. Then trenching and draining,
building a wall to absorb and reflect heat, judicious pruning from the
second year. Hard work, but worth it in the end, though I say it myself.
But, coming to fruition, I have another crop than pears I would discuss
with you, Anicius.' The king's hand upon the shoulder of his *Magister
Officiorum*, the pair began to stroll beside the fruit trees.

Now approaching seventy, the king was not the man he once had
been, thought Boethius. His hair had changed from gold to silver; aided
by a stick, he walked with a stoop, and his health, formerly robust, had
deteriorated; he was periodically troubled by stomach pains and bouts
of chronic diarrhoea. Also, it seemed to the newly appointed minister
that Theoderic's mind was losing its sharpness and clarity, becoming
susceptible to illusion and irrational suspicion.

However, there was no denying that at this moment Theoderic was
happy. Buoyed up by the glorious hopes of Eutharic's consulship, and
by assurances regarding the succession, Theoderic was in a mood of
expansive optimism, though Boethius felt it had a slightly manic edge.

'I have put back together much of the Western Empire,' declared
the king. 'Italy, Spain, Pannonia and much of Gaul are now a single
realm. Only one thing is lacking.'

'Serenity?'

'What is an empire without an emperor? A building without mortar, which will crumble under stress. I intend to be that mortar; the time has come for me to don the purple and the diadem. Am I right to do so, Anicius?'

Strangely affected by the note of appeal in the king's voice, Boethius felt a rush of concern and sympathy for the tired old warrior. For Theoderic to declare himself emperor would prove, Boethius was sure, to be a step too far. The Hispano-Romans and the Gallo-Romans might (grudgingly) accept a German emperor; but the Romans of Italy, the centre and power base of the resurrected 'empire'? Never. And, from what he had so far gleaned about his character, neither would the emperor-in-waiting, Justinian.

Boethius, however, had no intention of trying to dissuade the king from taking that step.

Much though he liked and respected Theoderic, and appreciated the honour done himself by the appointment as Master of Offices, Boethius' commitment to the Cause overrode his loyalty to the king. If that meant giving the nod to anything that might de-stabilize Ostrogothic rule, so be it – even if what Theoderic proposed could have appalling consequences. Little over a century before, resentment over growing German influence* in the army had spilt over into a terrible massacre of federates' families, and for similar reasons Constantinople had witnessed a bloody pogrom of the Goths.

'I applaud your decision, Serenity,' declared Boethius, feeling like Brutus delivering the final dagger-thrust to dying Caesar. '"Theodericus Augustus", the first in a glorious new dynasty of Western emperors.'

'"Theodericus flamin' Augustus?"' shouted a burly cobbler. Crowds had gathered in the forum of Terracina,† to witness the unveiling of an inscription commissioned by Senator Caecina Decius. "Oo the bleedin' 'ell does 'e think 'e is?' He spat vigorously on the cobbles.

'You ain't 'eard nuthin' yet, mate,' called a man in a blacksmith's apron. 'The buzz in Rome says 'e's to be crahned emperor.'

---

* See Notes.
† A town on the Appian Way between Rome and Naples.

'A Jerry emperor? Over my dead body!' bawled the town drunk.

A storm of boos and catcalls erupted from the crowd. A mudball splattered the gleaming white marble of the plaque, swiftly followed by a barrage of missiles pillaged from the cart of an unfortunate fruit-vendor.

The discontent spread like wildfire throughout Italy. Disturbances broke out in many major cities,* taking the form of serious rioting in Rome and Ravenna. Afraid, perhaps, of the consequences of openly expressing anti-German feelings, the mobs discovered in a half-forgotten piece of legislation a useful screen for their actions.

Earlier in his reign, Theoderic had issued an Edict of Toleration for all faiths.† In practice, this meant freedom of worship for the Jews, 'toleration' being hardly applicable to Nicene Catholicism, the religion of the vast majority of the population. The Gothic conquerors – Arians, and therefore technically heretics – did not need the protection of an edict, since no one in their right mind would dream of persecuting *them*, for fear of armed and instant retribution. An unfortunate consequence of this humane and enlightened decree had been the creation of a smouldering resentment among the Catholic Romans (for whom heresy was an abhorrent aberration) against Jews and Goths alike, the two peoples being vaguely lumped together in the collective consciousness.

Now the Romans had a perfect cover for their anti-German rage. They dared not openly attack the Goths, but the Jews were a different matter. Wealthy and defenceless, they were a convenient (and lucrative) target on which the mobs could safely vent their fury. All over the country an orgy of Jew-baiting exploded, accompanied by robbery, house-breaking and the burning of synagogues.

'*Why?*' exclaimed an anguished Theoderic to Eutharic. 'Surely I don't deserve this? Throughout my reign I have tried my best to rule justly and well. I have bent over backwards to be even-handed in treating my own people and the Romans alike. What should I do, my son?'

---

* Especially Naples, Rome, Ravenna, Milan and Genoa.
† In deference to constitutional sensibilities, Theoderic issued edicts rather than promulgating laws – an imperial privilege. The effects, however, were the same.

'They must be punished severely, these ungrateful dogs of Romans. Perhaps, father, you've been too soft with them in the past. Set up a legal enquiry immediately, so that the perpetrators can be brought to justice. Here, in Ravenna, which saw some of the worst of the rioting, let me make an example of the ringleaders.'

'Very well, my son. Do as you think fit. I put the whole matter in your hands.'

Directed by Eutharic, retribution was swift and harsh. Failure to identify individual offenders resulted in the imposition of collective fines on
whole communities, so that damage to Jewish property could be repaired.
In Ravenna a significant number refused to pay the fines, and accordingly were whipped through the streets by the executioner – immediately
becoming 'martyrs' in the eyes of the populace, their stand applauded
from three hundred pulpits throughout the length and breadth of Italy.
In Verona, in the chapel of St Stephen, a statue of Our Lady, commissioned by Theoderic, for no apparent cause toppled and shattered. Public
jubilation over this 'miracle' soon turned to fury and dismay when the
chapel, in consequence, was ordered to be demolished. As a reminder
that violence would not be tolerated, an edict was issued forbidding all
Romans to carry any arms whatsoever except a small knife for domestic
use.*

Among the Romans of Italy, a spirit of sullen hostility and passive
resistance replaced the rejoicing and euphoria that only a few short
months before had accompanied the inauguration of Eutharic as consul.
Secluded in his palace in Ravenna, the old king, his imperial dreams
shattered, surrendered to a black mood of bitterness and indignation.

In the basilica of St Peter, outside Rome, Pope Hormisdas, Theoderic's
loyal friend and colleague, sadly locked away in a vault the robe and
diadem for the coronation that would never now take place.

---

* Reviving a law passed in 364 by the emperor Valentinian I.

THIRTY-FOUR

*Shortly after that [the riots of 519–20] the Devil found an
opportunity to steal for his own a man who was ruling
the state well and without complaint*
Anonymous Valesianus, *Excerpta: pars posterior, c.* 530

Striding along Ravenna's *cardo*,* Eutharic chuckled to himself as
Romans hurriedly made way for him. The fact that they now feared
and hated him – who had been but a short time before the most popular
man in Italy – bothered him not one whit. That was the trouble with
dear old father-in-law: he wanted to be *liked*, and was hurt and puzzled
when his subjects bit the hand that fed them, so to speak. If you were
a ruler, the only thing that mattered was to be obeyed; if the price of
that was to make those you ruled afraid of you, too bad.

Eutharic had never liked the Romans: an arrogant lot who couldn't
get used to the fact that they'd lost an empire – the Western ones
anyway. This fracas with the Jews had given him the chance to rub
their long noses in it. Not that he had much time for Jews, either – too
devout and cliquish for his liking. But the fact that his own people, the
Visigoths, had tramped around the Roman Empire for forty years before
being granted a homeland, gave him a sneaking sympathy for a people
who had spent the same amount of time wandering the desert before
entering their Promised Land.

Hullo, what was this? A man was standing by one of the newly
repaired synagogues, painting a message on a wall: '*Iudaei spurci*'.†
Delighted to be gifted such an opportunity to make an example of an
offending Roman, Eutharic moved up silently behind the graffitor, who
was so absorbed in his work that he failed to notice the other's arrival.

---

* Main street.
† Filthy Jews.

'Good on you,' murmured Eutharic. 'These Yids need keeping in their place.'

'You're not wrong there, mate,' replied the man, adding a crudely daubed skull to his slogan. Then his smirk faded, as he turned and saw who the commentator was. 'Er . . . just a bit of fun,' he faltered.

'Lick it off,' said Eutharic, smiling pleasantly.

'Sir, y-you don't mean that,' stammered the man, his face suddenly white. He laughed nervously. ''Course you don't. I'll fetch a scrubbing-brush and water. Come off in a jiffy, it will.'

'I said, "Lick it off" you Roman bastard,' reiterated Eutharic, his words all the more menacing for being uttered softly. His voice suddenly cracked like a whiplash: '*Now!*'

Trembling with fright and revulsion, the man began to lick, while a silent crowd, fearful and curious, gathered to watch. Fortunately, the paint was still wet enough to come off fairly easily, and within half an hour a faint smudge was all that remained. The culprit, his lips and jaws smeared with pigment, vomited on to the cobbles.

Chuckling, Eutharic walked on in high good spirits.

In the palace kitchens, Amalasuntha, Theoderic's beloved daughter and wife of Eutharic, supervised the preparation of the evening meal, the *cena*. Fluent in Greek as well as Latin, well versed in classical litera-ture, the princess was an enthusiast for all things Roman, including cooking. Here, her guide and mentor was the great Apicius, his famous cookery book her bible. It was one of his recipes that she was using now. 'Sucking-pig in the manner of Frontinus: fillet, brown and dress; put in a casserole of fish sauce and wine, wrap in a bouquet of leeks and dill, pour off the juice when half cooked; when cooked, remove and dry, sprinkle with pepper and serve.'

Smiling fondly, Amalasuntha anticipated her husband's reaction. Pretending to despise Roman cooking as fussy and pretentious, he had a weakness for any dish which included pork. The dinner-time ritual had become familiar: a show of grumbling, followed by enthusiastic consumption, then (eventually) a compliment on a delicious meal, expertly prepared. Following patriarchal German custom, he preferred to eat alone (seated at a table: none of this effeminate Roman nonsense of lounging on couches).

'The master's ready. You may take this in to him,' Amalasuntha told Prosper, her new young scullion, whom she had taken on after he had repeatedly turned up at the palace asking for kitchen work. Keen and quick to learn, he had emerged with flying colours from a trial period, and was now a valued addition to the kitchen staff.

En route to the *triclinium* with a steaming bowl of 'Frontinus' Speciality', Prosper took a phial from his belt-purse, emptied the contents into the bowl, then proceeded on his way.

'What's this, flamingoes' tongues with mullets' livers, or some such Roman trash?' sighed Eutharic, as Prosper ladled out a small portion onto a plain pewter dish. (No fancy gold or silver Roman plate for a Goth with simple tastes, thank you.)

'Go on, Sire, try some,' coaxed Prosper. 'You'll like it. The *Domina* prepared it specially.'

'Mmm, not too bad,' conceded Eutharic, after sampling a spoonful. He signalled Prosper to fill the dish.

Two days later, Eutharic took to his bed, complaining of violent stomach cramps. Prosper, meanwhile, had disappeared, never to be seen again.

'Greetings, gentlemen,' said Cethegus to the four Anulars awaiting him in Symmachus' house in Ravenna: Boethius, Symmachus, Cassiodorus and, fresh back from Constantinople, Priscian. 'This year of the consul Maximus* bids fair to be an exceedingly auspicious one – an Annus Mirabilis indeed. For the Cause, that is, though not, I fear, for our esteemed lord and master. Quintus,' turning to Symmachus, 'let us for a change, begin with the Falernian. There being nothing to discuss, merely items to report, a toast to Fortuna is in order, I believe. Even the heavens, it would seem, are on our side; a comet, that portent of the death of kings, has appeared in the sky.

'This year has seen three highly desirable deaths,' Cethegus announced when all were seated comfortably in the *tablinum*, goblets brimming with ruby wine. First and most important, Eutharic died recently from a mysterious sickness—' He broke off, when he caught Cassiodorus' eye. 'Don't look at me like that, Magnus. You can't think *I* had anything

*523.

to do with it, surely? Heaven forfend! Plenty of disgruntled Romans in Ravenna willing to do the deed. Anyway, who's to say he didn't die from natural causes? But back to what I was saying. Don't expect to hear the news officially for some time yet. The palace is desperately trying to hush it up – and for good reason.'

'The succession?' suggested Boethius. 'That's bound to be thrown into chaos.'

'Absolutely right, Anicius. The next heir is a child, Athalaric, son of Eutharic and Amalasuntha. Among Germans, for a minor to succeed is unacceptable. Already, powerful Gothic nobles are lining up to try to usurp the throne. Best of all, Justin has refused to recognize the succession.'

'But he seemed only too happy to recognize Eutharic as Theoderic's heir,' protested Symmachus. 'What's happened to make him change his mind?'

'Justinian is what's happened,' put in Priscian, his dark, African face thoughtful. 'Understand that the empire never happily went along with Theoderic's grand pretensions; just made the best of what it undoubtedly saw as a bad job. Remember that when Zeno persuaded him to go to Italy as his vicegerent, it was really a cover to get rid of a dangerous nuisance who was troubling his realm. Granted, Theoderic's turned out better than anyone expected, but the emergence of a Gothic super-state cum Western-Empire-reconstituted on its doorstep was hardly going to be welcomed by the East. Fortunately, Justin – simple, good-hearted old soldier that he is – has had enough sense to let Justinian now take over and make the decisions.'

'And the other deaths?' queried Symmachus.

'Pope Hormisdas – next to you, Anicius Boethius, Theoderic's most loyal and valued colleague,' said Cethegus. 'Undoubtedly, his death will have come as a severe blow. Finally, Thrasamund, the Vandal king, Theoderic's ally, who was married to his sister, Amalafrida. Thrasamund's successor's yet another ancient monarch, a spineless nonentity called Hilderic. Very odd ancestry.' The senator grinned, looking more than ever like a craftier version of Emperor Vespasian. 'Grandson, would you believe, of the Western Emperor Valentinian III, whose daughter Eudocia, Hilderic's mother, was part of Gaiseric's booty from the second Sack of Rome.'

'And the great thing as far as we're concerned,' remarked Priscian, waving a pink-palmed hand in emphasis, 'is that Hilderic has ended the Vandal–Ostrogoth alliance and become – perhaps because of his part-Roman descent – a poodle of Justinian. He's even rumoured to have named him as his heir. If so, Africa could revert to Roman rule without a blow being struck. And just to prove to Justinian that he's really finished with Theoderic, he's clapped Amalafrida in gaol and murdered all her Ostrogothic retinue, who came over with her when she married Thrasamund.'

'It gets better,' the African went on. 'In this same year of the consul Maximus, Justin – Justinian, really – has passed a law declaring Arians to be heretics. Of course, it's only enforceable in the empire, but the implications for Theoderic are enormous. It amounts to the most colossal snub, announcing to the world that Theoderic and his Arian Ostrogoths are spiritual outlaws. In effect it's a rejection of Theoderic by Rome – *id est*, Constantinople – implying that his vicegerency is now held only on sufferance.'

'And there's more,' said Cethegus, rubbing his hands in gleeful satisfaction. 'Theoderic's empire is disintegrating. In Hispania, the honeymoon has soured, thanks to the Ostrogoths behaving to their Visigothic cousins more like conquerors than allies. Encouraged by Justinian, Theudis, a powerful noble, has declared himself king and split Hispania off from Gaul and Italy. In Gaul, the Franks and Burgundians are once again resurgent, threatening the security of Theoderic's outer ring of buffer states: Thuringia, Rhaetia* and Noricum. Even in Italy Theoderic's authority is crumbling. Together, Justinian and Hilderic have dealt him a massive blow. And once a barbarian leader's seen to be weakened, he's in real trouble with his followers. As a result, his nephew Theodahad and a certain Count Tuluin have carved out for themselves huge personal fiefs, virtually independent of central government control. If they're seen to get away with it, others will begin to try it on, and Theoderic's hold on his nobility will slip.'

'I wonder if that's why he's building a fleet?' pondered Cassiodorus. 'Here, down in Classis, and elsewhere, the shipyards are busy night and day turning out vast numbers of *dromons*. Seeing his rule everywhere

---

* Between the rivers Inn and Rhine.

challenged, perhaps this is his response to a perceived threat. If so – unless he's somehow got wind of plans for the Day of Liberation, which anyway is hardly imminent – it's totally irrational and surely points to mental instability. But maybe we shouldn't be surprised. If pushed too far, this is how barbarians behave.'

'Personally I can't help feeling sorry for Theoderic,' murmured Boethius, shaking his head sadly. 'He's always treated me with kindness and consideration, and he's done his best for Italy, according to his lights. It must be terrible for him to see everything he's worked for collapse like an arch whose keystone is removed. I think of a sick old lion surrounded by jackals and hyenas circling for the kill. Rather than pull him down, perhaps we should try to help him.'

'You're not going soft on us I hope, Anicius?' said Cethegus with mock sternness. 'Especially not now. Support for the Cause is growing by the day, with increasing calls from senators, both in Rome and in Constantinople, for Italy to be reunited with the empire. Leading the charge in Rome is a very influential and persuasive senator, Albinus – a name to reckon with, I think we'll find. And talking of sick old lions' – he paused, looking round at the others – 'don't forget they can be dangerous and unpredictable, lashing out when you least expect it. So no loose talk, gentlemen. Our lives could be at stake. Well, enough of politics.' He turned to Symmachus with a smile. 'If you're feeling kind, Quintus, I think we'd all appreciate another flagon of Falernian.'

It had been shipped – with huge difficulty – across from Istria on the other side of the Adriatic. Now, hauled by a double span of two hundred oxen, on a massive sledge moving on rollers, the enormous marble dome, really a capstone of titanic size, approached its destination. This was a vast limestone structure consisting of two cylinders one atop the other, the lower, larger one pierced by arches. Adjoining a section of the building's curving face was an enormous sloping ramp of earth and timber, on to which the dome was eased by a complex block-and-tackle system. This was worked by teams of men astonishingly few in number, thanks to the mechanical advantage obtained from multiple pulleys. Slowly, under the watchful eyes of architects and engineers, the great mass, all five hundred tons of it, crept up the ramp; as it slid home to crown the building, a cheer of triumph (and relief) burst from the workmen and professionals.

Leaning on his stick, Theoderic watched the scene from the top of the Porta Artemetoris in Ravenna's north wall. If they remember me for nothing else, the old king thought sadly, at least they will remember me for this, my mausoleum. What had it all been for? he wondered, reflecting on his long career: his boyhood in Constantinople and the beginning of his doomed love affair with Rome; the epic struggle to find a homeland for his people, culminating in his vicegerency of Italy; his dream of empire with himself becoming emperor, so nearly (it had seemed) coming to fruition; finally, the collapse of his ambitions when all he had striven to achieve suddenly seemed built on sand. What hurt the most was that the Romans, to whose welfare he had tirelessly devoted himself, should have turned against him, with their senators, if rumour could be trusted, in treacherous communication with the empire.

What was the final part of the prophecy that Myrddin, disciple of the saintly Severinus, had foretold for him? Strangely, he could recall the words as clearly now as when he first had heard them: 'After many years the horse dies, to be followed by eight others of his line; the final six of these the eagle of the East attacks, killing the last.' The horse, the totem of the Ostrogoths, must be himself. The eagle of the East could only mean the Eastern Roman Empire. The meaning of the prophecy was clear: his long reign would be followed by a dynasty of eight successors, in whose reigns, barring those of the first two, the empire would attempt to reconquer Italy, finally succeeding with the death of the last.

The sudden tragic death of Eutharic had plunged the succession into confusion. Little Athalaric would become the next king. Assuming the boy was still a minor when he ascended the throne, that spelt trouble, with greedy and ambitious nobles, like Athalaric's relative Theodahad, likely to contest his crown. And after Athalaric . . . Amalasuntha, perhaps? Although gifted and popular, being a woman she would face the same problems as a minor: trying to impose her authority over fierce and independent warriors. Whether or not the prophecy was true, the outlook for his people was not auspicious.

What was left for him, now that his life was moving towards its close? (The increasing severity of stomach pains and attacks of diarrhoea carried a message as stark as it was clear.) Like stranded flotsam left by an ebbing tide, a few things remained that could with profit be attended to. His faithful *Magister Officiorum*, Boethius – the only Roman he had ever truly learnt to trust – should be rewarded with wealth and recognition commensurate with his devoted and unstinting service. Connal, the brave and loyal Scot who commanded his bodyguard, should be permitted to retire with a generous pension, commuted to a lump sum if he wished to return to his homeland. In that event, he could perhaps be asked to seek out news of Myrddin, which could be conveyed back to Italy by a travelling companion. Then there was Timothy, lifelong friend and faithful servant, who had tried to warn him about Roman perfidy and been imprisoned for his pains. Reparation must be made before it was too late.

Finally, and most important of all, he had a duty to defend his own poor people, whom, like Moses, he had led out of the wilderness into their supposed Promised Land. They were beset on every hand by enemies: Vandals, Franks, Burgundians, rebels in Hispania, Romans in Italy, the mighty empire looming like a vast and threatening thunder-cloud beyond the Adriatic. The old king's face clouded momentarily, then brightened. Ships! Ships and yet more ships – great *dromons* no one dared defy; that was the answer. Who could deny that, barring the Amal, the strongest of the German nations was the kingdom of the Vandals? Why? Because it had a navy. (True, a navy built by subject Romans, but the concept was the rulers'.) Rome had beaten Carthage only when she built a superior navy; and the same held for the Greeks in their wars against the Persians. The Ostrogothic navy would become the terror of the seas. Then, all those peoples who had dared threaten his realm would perceive their error and repent.

His mind restored to equanimity, Theoderic descended (with some difficulty) to the base of the Porta Artemetoris and made his way towards his tomb, to thank the men responsible for its completion.

THIRTY-FIVE

King among all the kings of the British people
Nennius, *Historia Brittonum*, *c.* 830

'There she is, Dacore!'* exclaimed Cella to Connal. Far below them
was a distant cluster of timber buildings surrounded by a palisade, near
the head of an immensely long and twisting sheet of water, whose placid
surface reflected the majestic surrounding mountains.

Accompanied by Cella, a full-bearded, jolly bear of a man, one of a
breed of itinerant monks – a familiar sight on the roads of the Empire
and the Christian West – Connal had travelled from Italy through Gaul
and thence by ship to West Cambria in Britannia.† Advised by
Theoderic, who had adopted the same guise himself when journeying
to meet the holy man Severinus, the pair had adopted the distinctive
robe, staff and scrip of pilgrims (bound for Candida Casa in Galweya
and Dun Patricii in Hibernia‡). Thus equipped, they could travel
without fear of molestation in Christian lands, such was the reverence
in which these pious travellers were held.

Skirting the mountains of North Cambria (having learnt that
Artorius was campaigning in the north-west, near the great Vallum
Hadriani), they had walked in fine spring weather through the 'kingdoms' of Dyfed, Ceredigion and Gwynedd, to the port of Bangor. Here,
they had met a holy man of great repute, one Deiniol, who was in the
process of setting up a monastery-cum-centre of learning. Deiniol was
able to tell them the whereabouts of Artorius, who, he assured them,
was accompanied by Myrddin. On his advice, they had taken a ship to

---

* Near the site of the present Penrith, north-east of Ullswater.
† West Wales or Cornwall as opposed to North Cambria, Wales.
‡ Whithorn in Galloway and Downpatrick in Ireland, where the shrines of,
respectively, SS Ninian and Patrick were located.

the mouth of the Deruuentis river in Reged,* in order to avoid raiding-parties of the North Angles which had recently begun to trouble the intervening coasts. From the estuary, they had travelled eastwards through a most beautiful region of tall mountains, waterfalls and silvery streams, studded with tarns and lakes.

Descending to the lakeside, Connal and Cella approached the settlement they had spotted earlier, and, after affirming their credentials (emissaries of Theoderic, king of Italia and vicegerent of the emperor, status confirmed by a sealed royal statement of authorization), were admitted by gate guards into an extensive enclosure. It was thronged with men-at-arms, artisans at work, grooms attending to horses, and was dominated by a massive timber fort overlooking a scatter of lesser buildings – stables, workshops and storehouses. They were escorted to the fort's upper storey; it was furnished as a military headquarters, with maps set out and tables loaded with documents and writing para-phernalia, at which clerks sat working. At the room's far end, deep in discussion with a ring of aides, towered a giant of a man, upright and robust-looking despite being advanced in years, as betokened by a mane of silver hair. He projected authority and confidence.

'Visitors from Italy, my lord,' announced the escort. 'The *Dux Britanniae*,' he murmured to Connal and Cella, then withdrew.

'So, gentlemen, you're here to convey greetings from Theoderic to Myrddin,' said Artorius, when the pair had introduced themselves and explained their mission. 'The King of Italy must think highly of my *medicus* to have sent you all this way. Your timing could be better: we're expecting a major push by the Angles any day.' He shot them an appraising glance. 'It'll get nasty. Once you've seen Myrddin, you have two choices. Either stay and help, as orderlies behind the lines when battle starts; or head for home. I'd strongly advise the latter. You'll probably find Myrddin in the infirmary, mixing up his potions. Now, if you'll excuse me . . .' With a nod, he rejoined his aides.

In an annexe off the infirmary (empty save for one unfortunate who had severed a tendon in his foot while chopping wood), they found, grinding something with a pestle and mortar, a spare elderly man with

---

* The Derwent in Cumberland, then part of the Confederacy of the Britons, which was bounded to the north by Dalriada (Scots) and Alban (Picts).

a gentle face below a cliff of forehead. Introductions over and business stated, Myrddin led them to the refectory, after ordering a meal from the outdoor kitchens.

'King of Italy!' he said when they were seated and his visitors were gratefully demolishing bowlfuls of game stew. He smiled and shook his head. 'When we met – in sad circumstances, at the death-bed of holy Severinus – I sensed that Theoderic would make his mark in the world, but I never dreamt that he would rise so high. Even here, in far-off Britannia, his fame has come to our ears. I'm truly sorry to hear that fortune has treated him less than kindly of late, and that he's in poor health.'

'What news should Cella here take back to him regarding yourself?' asked Connal. 'He'll be travelling alone, as I shall be returning to my home in Dalriada.'

'His message will be brief, I fear. I'm really no more than an extension of Artorius – my function is to help maintain his men in good health, and to tend their wounds sustained in battle.'

'Tell us of Artorius, then.'

'Without Artorius – and before him Aurelianus – by now all Britain would have fallen to the Saxons and their kinsmen the Angles.' Myrddin's face had lit up, his voice become charged with warmth and admiration. 'True, we have given ground, but only slowly, making the enemy pay dearly for every yard of British soil. In West Cambria, North Cambria, Cumbria and Lothian, we hold the line, thanks to Artorius' example and great leadership. Here, the Kymry* are still strong; with the dragon standard at their head, our forces hold their own against the blue-eyed German heathens.' Myrddin smiled and spread his hands self-deprecatingly. 'Forgive me – I got carried away. I was forgetting that it was a "blue-eyed German", Theoderic no less, who suggested we adopt the red dragon as our emblem.'

'That was good,' boomed Cella, pushing aside his empty bowl. 'My congratulations to your cook.' He shot the *medicus* a keen glance. 'The *Dux* said something about an imminent attack.'

'Correct. The Angles are concentrating their advance on the north and north-west. Already, they've pushed far beyond the Humbri river

* From 'Cambroges', fellow countrymen.

as far as the Uure,* from where they're mustering their host for a push westward to Reged here in Cumbria,† where we, of course, intend to stop them.'

'The *Dux* offered us a choice,' rumbled Cella, 'said that if we wanted we could stay and help. I have some skill as a leech, and my friend here is a fighting man.' He looked hopefully at Connal. 'What do you say?'

'I'd say you've made an excellent suggestion,' replied Connal with a grin.

'Well, I won't deny that any extra help is more than welcome, said Myrddin. 'But it's only fair to warn you that the coming battle is bound to be a hard-fought, bloody affair. The Angles are ferocious warriors, also stubborn and determined.'

'I'm not averse to a good scrap myself,' declared Connal. 'If you can use us, we'd be glad to help.'

'Welcome aboard, then.'

Mounted on a grey stallion, and accompanied by his standard-bearer carrying the great red dragon flag, Artorius rode out before the *Exercitus Britanniae*, the Army of Britain. He raised aloft his sword: the short Roman *gladius* that had been the weapon of Aurelianus and before him of his ancestors – back to when the dynasty of Severus had ruled an undivided empire.

'Comrades, fellow Britons,' Artorius called in a deep, strong voice which carried clearly to the waiting ranks, 'here is where we stop them. The mountains of Cumbria shall be a wall on which their heathen host will break and shatter like a wave upon a cliff. Fight now as you have never fought before, and we shall ensure that the western lands of this island will remain for ever – Britannia!'

A moment's silence, then a great cheer arose. It grew in volume to a thunderous roar of acclamation, then slowly died away.

To confront the Angles' advance, Artorius had marched his army from Dacore round the fringes of the Cumbrian mountains to a great

---

* The Humber and the Wear.
† Reged corresponded roughly to the old county of Cumberland. 'Cumbria' covered a far greater area than the present county, extending well into what is now Scotland.

lake on the south-east edge of the massif. Here, on a great plain called Camlan, he had drawn up his troops – infantry in the centre, cavalry and archers on the wings. Behind, on the lake shore, a field hospital had been set up under the supervision of Myrddin, assisted by orderlies (now including Cella) and a group of nuns, whose convent was situated on the largest of the islands with which the mere was dotted.* Heavy horse – the riders clad in ancient imperial-issue mail and helmets (many times patched and repaired) – formed his main strength. The site, level and open, was good cavalry terrain, with wooded rising ground on either side affording security against being outflanked. However, these features, combined with the lake to the rear, ensured that, should the battle go against the Britons, there was no avenue of escape. They must prevail – or die.

In the front rank of the infantry, a mail-clad Connal, his Celtic blood racing at the prospect of the coming battle, leant on the shaft of the great battle-axe he had chosen from the stores; it was a fearsome weapon, whose heavy iron head was welded to a cutting edge of razor-sharp steel. Scouts galloping in gave warning that the Angles were approaching; soon the van came in sight, a dense throng of warriors on foot, big, fair-haired men, most of them unarmoured, bearing spears and shields. With a savage roar, they quickened their pace and rushed to meet the British line. Came a tremendous clash as the battle closed, then the two sides swayed back and forth, each striving to break the other's front.

Filled with the joy of battle, Connal swung his battle-axe, splitting skulls or cleaving limbs with almost every stroke. A trumpet-call rang out, then from either side a mass of armoured cavalry hurtled down upon the Angles, smashing into their flanks to carve red swathes through their close-packed ranks, before withdrawing to let the horses breathe. Desperately, the Angles tried to force a gap in their opponents' line, knowing that, as long as the British centre held, they themselves would be exposed to constant onslaught from those terrible mailed horsemen.

But the centre did hold. Time and again the British cavalry charged, after each attack leaving in their wake windrows of enemy dead – whereupon the archers took their turn to pour in volleys of deadly

* Belle Isle on Lake Windermere.

shafts. Like standing corn in a wheatfield when the mowers have begun their work, the Angle host by slow degrees attenuated, until at last, weakened and fought to a bloody standstill, they began to give ground. Their retreat was no rout, however; fighting grimly all the way, they withdrew in good order from the field.

At length a trumpet-signal called off the pursuit, and the *Exercitus Britanniae* took stock. Though the enemy had been repulsed with great loss, British casualties were high, and one appalling discovery robbed the day of triumph. Artorius was sorely wounded; finding a weak point in his armour, a spear had pierced his lung. His captains gathered round the cot where he lay, tended by Myrddin and the nuns in the field hospital beside the lake.

'Cei, Bedwyr, my faithful *comites*,' gasped the stricken *Dux*, frothy pink bubbles escaping from his lips, 'I leave the army in your charge. Today we have earned a respite, but no more than that. The Angles will return; persistence is in their very bones. You must hold the ground we have won. To ensure that you can do so, I will send for help to the Votadini, our kinsmen to the north-east, who have offered their aid. Myrddin, old friend, will you be my emissary? You know the way, and your skills in diplomacy will prove invaluable. Meanwhile, these holy sisters here have, in their kindness, offered to nurse me – though I fear they will not save my life, only prolong it a little. So now, dear comrades, I will take my leave of you. Vale.'

Watched by his assembled soldiers, many in tears, Artorius was rowed by the black-clad nuns to their island convent in the lake.

Three days after the battle, three travellers came in sight of an arresting spectacle: a mighty ribbon of stone undulating along the horizon. Twenty feet high, studded with turrets and blockhouses, it dipped and rose across the landscape like an endless serpent.

'There she is, the *Vallum Hadriani*,' announced Myrddin. 'Built four centuries ago "to separate the Romans from the barbarians"', as the emperor said. Did a good job for close on three-quarters of that time. But eventually the greater threat came not from the north but from the east, across the German Ocean. As we know to our cost.'

'Makes you wonder how a people who could raise a thing like that could lose an empire,' murmured Connal, awestruck. (A combination of skill, strength, stout mail protection and a modicum of luck had enabled him to survive the battle unscathed, barring a few contusions and minor cuts.)

At Petriana, a fortress near the western end of the great Wall, they requested shelter from the 'commandant'. He was a chieftain of the Selgovae who, with his war-band, occupied the fort, continuing a tradition established by Cunedda, a Romano-British leader who had maintained a military presence on the Wall after the departure of the legions. Myrddin was known by repute among the Britons everywhere. Following the disclosure of who he was and what his mission, the welcome given him and his companions was warm indeed. (As a result of Connal and Cella staying to help Artorius, a strong bond of friendship had developed between them and Myrddin, leading to the pair deciding, for reasons of comradeship and mutual security, to accompany the *medicus* on his mission to the Votadini.)

'Let me see that hand,' Cella said sharply to Myrddin, as the three companions prepared to bed down in one of the fort's old dormitory blocks, which they were to share with members of the war-band. 'I noticed you've been favouring it – at supper you used your left hand to hold your spoon.'

'It's nothing,' murmured Myrddin, holding out his bandaged right hand. 'Caught it on the barb of a javelin I removed from a patient's thigh, during the battle.'

'Infected,' pronounced Cella, after removing the bandage. He shook his head at the sight of the puffy, inflamed flesh that surrounded a ragged gash below the thumb. 'It'll need regular cleaning and dressing – as if you didn't know that. Lucky I'm here to do it for you.'

Next day, the trio headed through the Wall via the fort's North Gate, and pressed on in that direction across open heathery moorland, until intersecting a considerable river flowing to the south-west. This Myrddin pronounced to be the Isca.* Over the next three days they followed the stream to its head, travelling through a desolate landscape of great rounded hills, and sleeping rough at night wrapped in their

* The Esk.

thick woollen robes. The weather kept fine and dry, which was as well, since the condition of Myrddin's injured hand continued to deteriorate, despite constant washing, rebandaging and treating with salves, a supply of which the *medicus* had in his scrip.

From the headwaters of the Isca, they crossed a watershed to pick up a young river flowing north and east, the Tuesis,* according to Myrddin. His hand was now grotesquely swollen, with an ominous red line 'tracking' steadily up his arm. Urgent medical attention was called for, but in this wilderness of moors and barren hills that was a forlorn hope. There was nothing for it but to press on and hope soon to reach a settlement, where rest, and the ministrations of persons skilled in the arts of healing, combined with the patient's own medical lore, might effect recovery.

But it was not to be. After two days following the course of the Tuesis, Myrddin was delirious and could go no further. Making him as comfortable as possible, his companions laid him down on a bed of bracken. For a time he tossed, and muttered incoherently, then he fell into a slumber. When he awoke a short time later, the fever seemed to have left him, for he began to speak in a faint but clear voice. 'My friends, you must complete my mission for me. The way is not hard to find. Follow this river for a further two days; it will take you to Trimontium, a fortress of the Romans beneath a three-peaked hill. There you will meet the great road Agricola built, which will lead you north through a range of hills. From the summit you will see the plain of Lothian stretching to the Bodotria Aestuaria, and in its midst a huge eminence shaped like the shell of a tortoise. That is Dunpender, crowned by a mighty hill fort, the capital of the Votadini.† You know what you must tell them.'

'But we cannot speak the British tongue,' Cella pointed out, his voice breaking.

'You both acquired a smattering when we travelled through the Cambrias. It will be enough for your purpose. Besides, some may have a little Latin. The Votadini were always Friends of Rome, and maintained

---

* The Tweed.
† The three-peaked hill is the Eildon range; Agricola's road (named Dere Street by the Angles) is now the A68; Bodotria Aestuaria is the Firth of Forth; Dunpender is Traprain Law in East Lothian.

contact with the empire to the end. You will manage, that I know. And now, my friends, I must say farewell, for the sands of Myrddin's life have run their course.'

Weeping, they clasped his left hand in their own, and in a little space he breathed his last. With their knives they scraped a shallow grave, and gently laid him to rest.*

---

* And he lies there to this day, at Drumelzier by the Tweed, his resting-place marked by a notice stating simply, 'Merlin's Grave'.

THIRTY-SIX

No man of high and generous spirit will flatter a tyrant
Aristotle, *Politics*, V, *c.* 322 BC

'Paul!' exclaimed Timothy, answering his door to a new *gerulus* or odd-job-man cum janitor for the household guards. 'Last time I saw you, you were a *silentiarius* in the palace. What happened?'

'Creeping Germanization, that's what happened,' replied Paul bitterly, setting down his laundry basket. 'First he got rid of the *protectores domestici*, the Roman palace bodyguard, now it's the turn of the *silentiarii*, both of them replaced by Goths. Gothic gentlemen-ushers – an oxymoron, if ever there was!'

Timothy invited Paul into his *cubiculum* or bedroom, while he looked out dirty tunics and bed-linen to be replaced by the clean items the *gerulus* handed him. The conditions of his house arrest were not oppressive. He had been assigned a small suite in the guards' compound – part of the *civitas barbara* – and shared the soldiers' facilities. This was the zone of Ravenna occupied by the Goths along the *platea maior*,* which also included the palace, court church and Arian episcopal complex. His bodily needs were amply catered for, and, though forbidden to leave the compound, he was permitted to move freely within its spacious confines, and make use of amenities such as the baths and gymnasium.

'If you don't mind my saying so, sir,' observed Paul, rolling up the sheets Timothy passed him, 'you seem to have come down a bit in the world yourself.' His refined face registered concern. 'You used to be Theoderic's right-hand man, as I recall.'

'Past tense is correct,' confirmed Timothy, gesturing Paul to take the room's only chair, then seating himself on his cot. Suddenly, activated by

---

* Now the Via Roma. The 'court church' is S. Apollinare Nuovo.

the Roman's sympathy, a tide of anger, frustration, and resentment – for too long bottled up – welled up, clamouring for outlet.

'The man's paranoid,' he heard himself cry, 'obsessed with crazy notions about becoming emperor. The Romans would never wear it. More to the point, neither would Justin – for which read Justinian, if what I hear's correct. I did the king a favour, pointing out that he was making a big mistake. And what did I get for my pains? Clapped in this hole, with a lot of sweaty Goths for company.'

'How much do you know about what's going on in the outside world?'

'A fair amount. I take my meals in the mess hall with the soldiers; no one's told me I can't use my ears.'

'Then you'll have heard about the riots?'

'Yes, also the death of Eutharic, the succession crisis, the defection of the Vandals, et cetera, et cetera.'

'Common knowledge, sir. There's something else – much bigger – which only a few are privy to. Something which could bring hope to a man in your position. Of course, it's only rumour.'

'Tell me,' demanded Timothy, feeling a stirring of excitement.

'Only if you promise not to breathe a word, sir. If anything got out, it wouldn't just be my job on the line. It would be my neck.'

'You can trust me, Paul. It's the same axe we're grinding.'

'Very well, sir. Some of us *silentiarii* have contacts in the Senate, most of whom would welcome a change of régime. That, of course, could only happen through the intervention of Justinian, a step which some leading senators are urging him to take.'

'Then power to their elbow!' declared Timothy. 'I never thought I'd hear myself say it – I who used to count myself Theoderic's friend – but for his own good and that of Italy it's time his rule was ended, hopefully without bloodshed. Honourable retirement with a consulship would be a kind end to a career which in many ways has been a great one.'

'Unfortunately, that isn't the Roman way,' said Paul, shaking his head sadly. 'More likely, he'd share the fate of Stilicho.'

'Better that, perhaps, than dragging out the remainder of his days in discord and disappointment.'

'That's true.' Paul rose and picked up his basket. 'Well, I must be on my rounds; would you mind opening the door for me? Keep your spirits up, sir. Change may happen sooner than you think.' And with a smile, he slipped out and was gone.

Struggling muzzily from sleep in response to the knocking on his door, Timothy glanced at the window; grey dawn light was filtering through cracks in the shutters.

Opening the door, he found himself confronted by Fridibad, the *saio** in charge of messages between the palace and the military compound.

'My apologies, Herr Timothy, for waking you at such an hour,' said Fridibad, a tough-looking Goth of middle years. 'You are to come with me.'

'What's all this about?' asked Timothy, alarm churning in his stomach as he donned leggings, tunic and shoes. A dawn call could only betoken bad news.

'My orders – from the king himself – are that you be taken under escort to Ticinum† and lodged in that city's tower.'

'On what charge?' Timothy seemed to feel a cold hand squeeze his heart. The Tower of Ticinum! That was one place you didn't want to end up in. It had a sinister reputation as the final destination of those who had offended against the state.

'I was not told, Herr Timothy,' replied the *saio* with gruff sympathy. He shifted his stance awkwardly, and spread his hands in an apologetic gesture. Timothy had been a popular 'guest' in the compound, his store of racy anecdotes going down well with the Gothic soldiery at meals in the mess. Whereas, in similar circumstances, Romans would have shunned him as persona non grata, the Amal had taken Timothy to their hearts as a fellow warrior and teller of stirring tales, his status enhanced by their Teutonic respect for grey hairs.

As he accompanied Fridibad across the compound's great *quadratum* towards the guard-room, it was suddenly clear to Timothy what had happened. Paul had been a 'plant', sent by Theoderic to sound out Timothy for his real views about the king. How could he have been

* Crown agent (see Notes).
† Pavia.

so gullible as to fall for such a ruse? Timothy asked himself with bitter self-recrimination. It seemed that, like a thief in the night, his dotage had crept up on him, eroding his customary guardedness. No fool like an old fool, somebody had once said. Well, they certainly got that right, he thought savagely, all at once feeling every one of his eighty-four years. This would never have happened with Timothy the gang-leader of Tarsus, Timothy the prince's minder in Constantinople, Timothy the king's resourceful friend and right-hand man of the great migration and the glory days in Italy – before everything turned sour. Like the leader of a wolf pack past his prime who finds his supremacy usurped by a younger rival, he had lost his edge and must therefore pay the price.

A few hundred yards away, his mood alternating between rage and sorrow, Theoderic wandered the pathways of his orchard, trying to come to terms with the information that Paulus, *silentiarius* turned informer, had brought to him concerning Timothy. In his mind he had rehearsed, with joyful anticipation, the scene when he and Timothy (freed from house arrest following a little test of loyalty – which surely would prove no more than a formality) would at last be reconciled. Instead, there had come the revelation that his once loyal friend and mentor had turned against him. Wounded to the heart, his mind clouded by fits of fury followed by depression, the old king had blindly paced the palace corridors and grounds – none daring to intervene – finally coming to himself as the shapes of his beloved fruit trees emerged slowly in the first pale rays of dawn. Timothy's rejection meant that he was now alone, Theoderic told himself, the storm of his emotions resolving itself into an overwhelming sadness.

No, wait; there was still Boethius, his loyal Roman servant and adviser. The description could also apply to Symmachus and Cassiodorus as well, but Boethius was more than that. He was a true friend, whose unfailing sympathy and understanding had helped the king before in many a pass. Now, in this time of trouble and distress, he would surely prove a strong staff on which to lean. Comforted, his steps now steady and assured, Theoderic began to make his way back towards the palace.

THIRTY-SEVEN

Cyprian's charge is false, but, if Albinus did it, both I and the entire Senate have done it acting together
Anonymous Valesianus, *Excerpta: pars posterior, c.* 530

From Rufius Petronius Nicomachus Cethegus to Anicius Manlius Severinus Boethius, *Magister Officiorum*, greetings.

Dear friend and fellow Anular, I write to warn you of a very real and pressing danger facing many in the Senate, and especially yourself.

Theoderic has long nurtured suspicions that correspondence between senators in Italy and the court in Constantinople has been of a treasonable nature. Alas, he now has proof. You may remember that at our last meeting I mentioned a leading senator, one Albinus. It has come to my attention (I have 'ears' in the corridors of power here) that a letter of his to Justin has been intercepted by Cyprian, the *Referendarius*, or head of security. The contents could scarcely be more damning: it openly invites the emperor (he infers Justinian, of course, as opposed to Justin) to free Italy from the Ostrogothic yoke! Now, had the letter been written by some naive aristocratic youth indulging in a spot of wishful thinking, Cyprian might conceivably have let it pass. However, Albinus being a pillar of the Senate and from the great family of the Decii, the matter could not be overlooked.

If Cyprian could be portrayed as acting out of malice, it might help Albinus' case; but I fear it would be unproductive to pursue that line. Cyprian, unfortunately, is one of that dreadful tribe of 'honest plodders' – not overendowed with brains but thorough, and conscientious to a fault. Two years ago he was sent on a mission to Constantinople; it would be surprising if, while there, he failed to overhear some of the talk swirling about concerning change of régime in Italy. If he goes ahead and gives evidence – which he is virtually bound to do – it will be in a full session of the Consistory which you, Anicius, as Master of Offices will be required to attend. In that event, little short of a miracle can save Albinus.

I come now to a second matter, which concerns yourself. Bad news, I'm afraid. Another letter has been intercepted, this time one of yours, also addressed to Justin. In it you say you hope for '*libertas Romana*' – which is code, of course, for Byzantine intervention in Italy. Dear boy, your indiscretion passes belief; I need hardly point out that you now stand in the very greatest danger, should Cyprian disclose the letter's contents. There is, however, one glimmer of hope. Thanks to my network of *inquisitores*, I have managed to, let us say, 'liberate' the original epistle. (So you owe me one, my friend.) Cyprian's team will undoubtedly attempt to reproduce a copy from memory, but comparison of hands will enable you to claim it to be a forgery. That *may* be enough to put you in the clear. Let's hope so; our old enemies in the Senate – Faustus *niger* and the rest of the anti-Laurentius brigade – will be salivating at the chance to pull you down. Your friend and colleague Symmachus, our new *Caput Senatus* (old Festus at last having gone to claim his Heavenly reward), will naturally speak up for you, and his views do carry weight.

As soon as you have read this letter, burn it. Now is a time for keeping heads down and saving skins. So, please, no outbreaks of Roman *nobilitas* or soul-baring, weaknesses to which I feel you may be prone. Meanwhile, as it says in the Bible, 'be strong and of a good courage'. Vale.

Written at the Villa Jovis, Caelian District, Roma, *pridie Kalendas Octobris*, in the Year of the Consuls Justinus Augustus and Opilio.*

Shaken, barely able to absorb Cathegus' chilling revelations, Boethius set about reducing the letter to ashes.

*

* 30 September 524.

In the great reception hall of Theoderic's palace in Verona, the *consistorium* awaited the arrival of the king. This court, which dealt with important matters affecting Romans as opposed to Goths, was made up of *Comites Primi Ordinis*, Counts of the First Order, mostly Romans, none of rank below *Spectabilis*. Chief among them, by virtue of his being the *Magister Officiorum*, was Boethius. Facing each other in front of the court stood the tall, commanding figure of Albinus, his senatorial toga lending him an air of dignity, and his accuser, Cyprian, a bluff-looking individual with a weatherbeaten face.

Looking angry and upset, leaning on a stick, Theoderic shuffled in and seated himself on a throne-like chair to one side of the chamber. At a signal from the king, an official invited Cyprian to declare the charge.

'Your Majesty, honourable members of this court,' declared the *Referendarius*, his voice still showing a trace of the clipped vowels of the Aventine slums where he had been raised, 'the charge is treason, as this letter will make clear.' He handed a small scroll of vellum to a steward and instructed him to show it to Albinus. 'You do not deny that this is yours, Senator?' Cyprian enquired politely.

Albinus glanced briefly at the document and shrugged. 'Certainly I wrote that,' he affirmed carelessly, as though the letter were of little consequence.

'With Your Majesty's permission,' continued Cyprian, 'I shall read the relevant section to the court. Then you may all judge its import for yourselves. In the following passage, Albinus is directly addressing the emperor.

'"... most honoured Augustus, all Italy cries out for your assistance. Only let the sun of your presence shine upon this benighted land, and her present afflictions would dissolve and vanish like mist at break of day."' He looked round at the rapt faces of the *Spectabiles*. 'If that ain't—is not treason, gentlemen, I don't know what is.'

Theoderic leant forward, a hectic spot burning in each cheek. 'Albinus,' he said in a low, hoarse voice, 'have you anything to say?'

Drawing himself up to his full impressive height, Albinus bowed to the king. 'Your Majesty, members of this court,' he began in an urbane and reasonable tone, 'take any sample of the contents of the diplomatic bag of correspondence destined for Constantinople. I guarantee it would contain many phrases of polished flattery such as diplomacy requires, which – taken out of context – could be made to appear just as "treasonable" as the excerpt you have just had read to you. I was merely suggesting to the emperor that a state visit would prove of inestimable benefit in smoothing away the unfortunate misunderstandings that have recently arisen between Ravenna and Byzantium. If *that* is treason, I am happy to plead guilty to the charge.'

Boethius, who had listened with growing admiration, decided that, notwithstanding Cethegus' sensible advice, he must speak up in the senator's defence, or he would not be able to live with himself. Was it Roman patriotism that prompted him, or merely a sense of solidarity with, and loyalty to, his own class? He could not be sure. All he knew was that silence – prudent but cowardly – was not an option. Rising to his feet, he heard himself exclaim, 'The charge is false, Serenity! If Albinus is guilty, then I and the entire Senate are also guilty. If men can be condemned on such a trumped-up accusation, it is a sorry day indeed for Roman justice.'

A stunned silence followed his outburst. Theoderic stared at his Master of Offices with shocked incredulity. 'Anicius Boethius, are you blind as well as deaf?'

'Neither, Serenity,' declared Boethius, the enormity of his declaration beginning to sink in. Well, it was too late to row back now. He must continue on the course he had set himself – even though it might be destined for the rocks. 'My only concern is that the light of truth should so illumine the minds of all present that they do not, through a misunderstanding of the sense of a few phrases, condemn a noble Roman who is innocent.'

'Then, *Magister*,' broke in Cyprian, sounding uncomfortable, 'you force me – reluctantly, I may say – to disclose the contents of a letter you yourself wrote to the emperor. I had hoped, as it is not strictly germane to the case we are here to examine, that I could avoid doing so, but you leave me no choice.' Producing another letter, he read aloud, '"It is my hope, and also that of many senators, that *libertas Romana* may soon be restored to Italy."'

'It is a forgery!' declared Boethius, his heart beginning to pound and his palms to sweat. 'Anyone familiar with my hand will testify to that.'

'It is a *copy*,' countered Cyprian, 'written admittedly from memory.'

An edge of anger entered his voice as he continued, 'The original was stolen from my office. And you, *Magister*, dare talk about the light of truth.' He looked round the assembly, then at Theoderic. 'Your Majesty, members of this court, I rest my case.'

Theoderic cast a stricken gaze on Boethius. 'Et tu, Anici,' he whispered brokenly.

Maddened by grief and a feeling of betrayal, racked by bouts of a sickness soon to become terminal, the old king – all pretensions to *dignitas* and *civilitas* thrown to the winds – succumbed to a protracted fit of blind fury, striking out at all who might be considered enemies. Albinus was the first to die. Then the *Caput Senatus*, Symmachus – who dissolved a cowed and apprehensive Senate to prevent it from condemning in absentia his friend and son-in-law Boethius – was arrested and excuted. Pope John, Hormisdas' frail and elderly successor, was thrown into gaol after a papal mission to Constantinople failed to persuade the emperor to relax his anti-Arian laws; still incarcerated, the pontiff died soon afterwards. In revenge for the Eastern legislation against Arians, Theoderic prepared a mandate for the enactment of laws prohibiting Catholic worship – practised by the vast majority of his subjects. And a special court – the *judicium quinquevirale* of five (carefully selected) peers of Boethius, presided over by Eusebius, the City Prefect of Rome – found Boethius guilty of treason while yet in custody. The verdict was facilitated by the testimony of several witnesses: Faustus *niger* and his coterie, also some of the provincial parvenus in government who felt their position threatened by Boethius and his aristocratic circle. (They even utilized his interest in philosophy to have sorcery included in the charge.) Conveyed in fetters to the grim fortress-city of Ticinum, he was imprisoned in its forbidding keep, where he finished writing his magnum opus, *The Consolation of Philosophy*.*

United in fear and hatred of Theoderic, and freed from any loyalty to him, the senators of Italy resumed their plotting with Justinian, their hopes reciprocated by the emperor-to-be.

* See Notes.

THIRTY-EIGHT

By whose accusations did I receive this blow?
Boethius, *The Consolation of Philosophy*, 526

'Timotheus Trascilliseus, former royal servant, hear the sentence of Eusebius, Count of Ticinum',* acting under orders from the king.' The *saio* delivering the message looked up briefly from the warrant, his impassive blue eyes beneath the studded *Spangenhelm* connecting momentarily with Timothy's. Then he continued, 'At the first hour of the day of six Kalends September in the Year of the Consul Olybrius,† you are to be taken to the place of execution within the bounds of this prison, there to suffer death by the sword.' His business done, the *saio* turned on his heel and departed; Timothy heard the key of his cell turn in the lock.

Well, at least he now knew the worst – which was a relief of sorts. He consulted the tally of the time of his imprisonment that he had scratched on the wall. In ten days! Which was worse, to have the inevitability of death confirmed, or to suffer the suspense of uncertainty about one's fate? At least the latter allowed one still to hope. At his age, having long outlived his biblical span, death should hold no terrors for him. But the truth was that it did. Despite the Church's assurance of an afterlife, reinforced by the vast panoply of a glittering clerical hierarchy and glorious ecclesiastical buildings, there lurked a gnawing doubt that beyond the end of life lay ... nothingness, a terrifying oblivion where consciousness ceased for ever to exist. Life, even in the confines of this bare cell, was sweet, thought Timothy, appalled at the prospect of departing from it.

*

* Not to be confused with Eusebius the City Prefect of Rome.
† 6 a.m., 27 August 526.

Roused by footsteps in the yard below the tower, Timothy rose from his straw-filled pallet and looked down from the small barred window of his cell. Into the grassed enclosure – rather grandly known as Ager Calventianus – a prisoner was being led by two warders, who proceeded to secure him by stout straps to a chair in the middle of the green. Beside the chair, long clubs protruding from their belts, stood two brutal-looking men, one of whom held a length of cord. With a start, Timothy recognized the prisoner: Boethius, whom he remembered as an adviser and close confidant of Theoderic. He recalled that the Roman had been prominent among those rumoured to be plotting with Constantinople for Italy to be reunited with the empire.

Tying the cord in a loop round the prisoner's head, one of the executioners, inserting a stick below the ligature, began to twist and tighten it. As the cord bit deep into the prisoner's flesh and started to compress his skull, he jerked against his bonds and cried out in agony. Horrified, Timothy watched Boethius' eyes begin to start from their sockets, while his cries changed to a continuous high-pitched scream. With their clubs, the executioners rained violent blows on the prisoner, the thumps, like wet laundry being pounded, carrying clearly to Timothy's ears. At last, with a horrible crunching, the victim's skull was stove in and he slumped against the straps, released by death from further torture.

Shaking with revulsion, Timothy drew back from the window; death by the sword would at least be mercifully quick. Although liable at times to fits of violent fury, Theoderic was not a cruel or vindictive man. The only explanation for his condemning Boethius to such a dreadful fate must lie in some terrible betrayal on the Roman's part – a betrayal clearly far more heinous than Timothy's had been.

Awaking from a brief and troubled sleep on the morning scheduled for his execution, Timothy watched with dread as the window of his cell slowly took on definition as a pale rectangle. The key squealed in the lock and the door creaked open to reveal, flanked by two warders, a tall figure wearing *Spangenhelm* and military belt – not the official who, ten days ago, had announced his sentence.

'I see I have arrived in time,' said the *saio*; his voice seemed strangely familiar. 'Good news, Herr Timothy. The warrant for your execution is revoked, and you are a free man.'

'*Saio* Fridibad!' exclaimed Timothy, recognizing him in the growing light. Relief swept through him, making him feel faint and giddy.

'The king is dying,' the Goth continued sadly. 'He would make his peace with you, Herr Timothy. The end is not far off, so we must make haste. I have fresh horses waiting, if you are able to ride.'

On the previous day, as the king sat at dinner, the meal's main dish was placed before him and the cover removed.

'Take it away!' shouted Theoderic, gazing in horror at the thing that confronted him with blank staring eyes, its mouth, fringed with long, sharp teeth, agape in silent accusation. 'It is the head of Boethius!'

Bowing, the servitor removed the great fish's head, while the king stumbled from the table and retired to his bed-chamber. Soon, in a recurrence of the aguish fever afflicting him of late, he lay trembling with cold beneath a weight of blankets.

'If only I could take back the past,' the king murmured brokenly to his physician, Helpidius, and his daughter, Amalasuntha, in attendance at his bedside. 'I have cruelly wronged my two most loyal servants, Symmachus and Boethius – both dead at my command. Also Timothy, once my dearest friend, who is to die tomorrow. Their betrayal of me I brought upon myself; I see that now. Too late to save Timothy, alas. If only the *cursus publicus* were still working, there might have been a chance . . .'

As the king drifted into a fitful slumber, Amalasuntha set her powerful intelligence to work. How far from Ravenna was Ticinum? Two hundred miles at most. But still an impossible distance for even the swiftest and most powerful steed to cover in twelve hours, the time remaining before the Isaurian was due to die. Granted, the *cursus publicus* – the old imperial post service with relay stations every eight miles where fresh mounts were available – had been defunct for years; but there were towns along the Via Aemilia: Bononia, Mutina, Placentia* and others, where horses could be requisitioned. Provided the rider knew his business, at a pinch a good horse could cover twenty miles in an hour – which rate could be maintained throughout the journey, given sufficient changes of mount. She made a swift computation; there was

* Bologna, Modena, Piacenza.

still time – just – for Timothy to be reprieved. When her father died, which must be soon, she would assume the regency for her son, little Athalaric. Was that enough to let her act now in Theoderic's name? Well, she would soon find out. Unthinkable to wake her dying father; this was something she must manage on her own. Sending for her secretary, for *Saio* Fridibad (an excellent horseman) and for Cassiodorus, the new Master of Offices, whose countersignature on the documents would reinforce her authority, she began to draft the pardon for Timothy and the requisition orders for fresh horses.

Weakened by dysentry and fever, Theoderic felt the end fast approaching. He had made his final dispensations to the Gothic chiefs and Roman magistrates who filled the chamber, entreating them to keep the laws, to love the Senate and to cultivate the friendship of the emperor. One last thing remained: to be reconciled with the friend who knelt beside his bed.

'Forgive me, Timothy,' he whispered, stretching out his hand.

Tears blurring his vision, Timothy took it. He felt its grip tighten, then suddenly relax. Theoderic was dead.

AFTERWORD

The true measure of Theoderic's stature lies, perhaps, not so much in his transmutation from semi-nomadic warlord to the enlightened ruler of Italy, as in his feat of successfully balancing and controlling two diametrically opposed social systems. He had, on the one hand, to govern his own people – a shame-and-honour Iron Age society based on *personal* allegiance to a warrior-leader – and, on the other, to rule what in some ways was almost a modern capitalist state, held together by a complex web of laws, bureaucratic institutions and property rights, geared to the acquisition of wealth. Two such differing regimes could never be synthesized, and Theoderic did not try. But the fact that he succeeded throughout most of his long reign (despite allowing himself to be distracted by imperialist dreams) in maintaining a benevolent *apartheid* between these powerful centrifugal forces, was a very great – indeed, a unique – achievement. As Robert Browning (in *Justinian and Theodora*) says, quoting an unnamed scholar, 'he was certainly one of the greatest statesmen the German race has ever produced, and perhaps the one who has deserved best of the human race'.

In the end, however, the experiment was a failure, though a noble one. His feeble successors, with the possible exception of Totila, could never hope to emulate his example, and the 'Ostrogothic century' (from the emergence of the tribe into the light of history as allies of Attila at the Catalaunian Fields in 451 to its political extinction by Justinian's generals in 554) ended in the Amals' defeat and their disintegration as a people.

For anyone attempting to write a story based on the life of Theoderic, it is extraordinarily fortunate that his lifespan covers a period rich in contemporary or near-contemporary sources. Cassiodorus, *quaestor* and Theoderic's Master of Offices after Boethius, provides the most significant material, a vast collection of official correspondence on behalf of the Gothic administration, which was published under the title *Variae*. Another, less-known author is Ennodius, a bishop, whose numerous letters, mainly to clergy, throw considerable light on Theoderic's reign. Perhaps the most interesting writer, from a human and dramatic point of view, is the splendidly named Anonymous Valesianus. The sonorous appellation is not, alas, that of some distinguished scholar of late antiquity, but was coined to designate an unknown Roman author whose work (the second part of an anonymous document) was edited by Henri de Valois in 1636. Another useful source touching on Theoderic is *Gothic History*, an abridged version of a lost work by Cassiodorus, written in the mid sixth century by Jordanes, a Romanized Goth living in Constantinople. Procopius, a Greek writer who accompanied Justinian's general Belisarius on part of his Italian campaign, provides an account of Theoderic in the opening pages of his *Gothic War*.

Regarding modern sources, I am greatly indebted to my publisher Hugh Andrew for kindly lending me the following: *Theoderic in Italy* by John Moorhead, *The Goths* by Peter Heather, *A History of the Ostrogoths* by Thomas Burns, *History of the Goths* by Herwig Wolfram, and Robert Browning's *Justinian and Theodora*. Other sources I found useful were Gibbon's matchless *Decline and Fall*, Peter Heather's *The Fall of the Roman Empire*, Richard Rudgley's *Barbarians* and *Theoderic the Goth: The Barbarian Champion of Civilization* by Thomas Hodgkin, a Victorian scholar who wrote about his subject with insightful empathy. Details about chariot-racing and beast-hunts in the arena were quarried from a racily written but absorbing little book, Daniel P. Mannix's

Those About to Die, crammed with fascinating facts and colourful vignettes.

In the interests of drama and clarity, I have (as mentioned in the relevant sections in the Notes) gone in for some telescoping and abridging of events, hopefully without distorting essential historical truth. Anyone who has ever wrestled with the arcane complexities of the Laurentian Schism, or the Ostrogoths' tangled *Völkerwanderung* throughout the Balkans, will understand my reasons for doing so.

Bar some minor characters and the obvious example of Timothy, the Dramatis Personae are based on real people. Many – such as Rufius Cethegus, who features as an arch-schemer – needed considerable fleshing-out to make them come alive. This hardly applied in the case of Theoderic, whose richly complex character was able to speak for itself in almost every situation. The tension between his natural tendency to *furor Teutonicus* and desire to achieve Roman *dignitas* and *civilitas* generated much of whatever claim to drama the story possesses.

The War Between Theoderic and Odovacar, 489–93

Suspecting that a detailed résumé of the campaign would test the patience of most readers if encountered in the text, I append here a summary of the main events.

Advancing from Isonzo Bridge in the summer of 489, Theoderic defeated Odovacar's forces at Verona, causing the Scirian king to retreat to Ravenna, which, being surrounded by marshes, was notoriously difficult to attack. When Tufa, one of Odovacar's chief generals, deserted to Theoderic, the game seemed up for Odovacar. However, on being despatched by Theoderic to attack his old commander, Tufa again switched sides, enabling Odovacar to sally forth from Ravenna.

Now on the defensive, Theoderic took shelter in the heavily fortified redoubt of Pavia, from which precarious position he was rescued by the fortuitous arrival of a force of Visigothic allies. Now strong enough to take the field again, Theoderic was able to defeat Odovacar at the River Adde on 11 August 490, forcing him to return to Ravenna, which Theoderic then besieged. (Tufa, meanwhile, had split from Odovacar – again! – and was operating independently in the Adige valley region; he was finally brought to bay and killed in 493.)

Theoderic's capture of Rimini in 492, enabling him to tighten the blockade of Ravenna, spelt the beginning of the end for Odovacar. In February 493 he was forced, under pressure from the effects of famine, to make terms with Theoderic, Bishop John of Ravenna acting as intermediary.

His subsequent murder by Theoderic, condemned by some as treacherous and barbaric, was in truth an act of political necessity, forced on the Amal king in the interests of his own survival. In the ancient world, power-sharing was always fraught with hazard for the parties involved. Even Diocletian's radical experiment, the Tetrarchy, designed to ensure the smooth functioning of the machinery of rule and succession, can hardly be accounted a success story. Once that emperor's cold and powerful personality ceased to control the system he had devised, its inherent strains began to show, soon to result in the old cycle of murderous rivalries and usurpations starting up anew.

APPENDIX II

The Laurentian Schism

Like the Schleswig-Holstein Question, or Fermat's Last Theorem, the Laurentian Schism has caused strong men to weep in the attempt to unravel its complexities. It came about for the following reasons. After the death of Pope Anastasius on 17 November 498, two men were simultaneously ordained Bishop of Rome, the deacon Symmachus and the archpriest Laurentius. Theoderic's finding in favour of Symmachus, however, failed to resolve the controversy. Laurentius' supporters brought a number of grave charges against his rival, the main ones being: that he had miscalculated the date of Easter; that he consorted with disreputable women; that he had squandered the wealth of the Church; and that he had produced forged documents to support his claim. Theoderic accordingly ordered that a synod be held in Rome to settle the matter by giving judgement concerning these charges against Symmachus. However, as Symmachus was proceeding to the basilica of Santa Croce in Rome, where the synod was to be held, he was roughed up in a clash (in which several priests were killed) between the rivals' followers. Subsequently, he declared his refusal to be judged by the bishops making up the synod, claiming that, as Pope, he was [conveniently] above jurisdiction. The bishops, uncertain as to their powers to proceed in judgement, dithered; but Theoderic finally unblocked the logjam by ordering that the churches of Rome be handed over to Symmachus, and that Laurentius go into compulsory retirement on an estate belonging to his patron, Festus.

The schism had wide ramifications, especially concerning senatorial families whose estates had suffered losses because of barbarian invasions, and confiscations to reward the followers of Odovacar, then of Theoderic. One result of Theoderic's fiat in favour of Symmachus was that lands previously granted to the Church by senatorial families should remain in the pontiff's possession. Despite doubts as to the strict legality of some of these grants or whether they had been gifted in perpetuity, alienation of land to the Church was allowed to stand – much to the dissatisfaction of most Roman senators. At the other end of the social scale, the plebs were assiduously wooed by Symmachus (quite possibly in a cynical move to reinforce his power base), who made available generous supplies of free food in a series of lean times, a stance with parallels to that of Caius Sempronius Gracchus regarding the poor of Rome, in Republican times.

As an Arian and an outsider, Theoderic was well placed to take a detached and impartial view when it came to ruling on the controversy. This was no doubt on the whole a good thing, as neither side could accuse him of bias. However, one drawback was that Theoderic's likely impatience with the minutiae of the schism's implications may have led him to overlook the problems arising from the disposition of Church lands. His fiat on the matter must have cost him the support of many distressed senators anxious to claw back some of the property their ancestors had gifted to the Church prior to the barbarian invasions.

The points covered by the above are what we may call the social and political aspects of the Schism – all pretty clear and straightforward. But when we turn to the theological issues behind the rift (which is ultimately linked to relations with the Eastern Empire) things become impenetrably obscure and complex. A brief passage from the *Liber pontificalis* gives a hint of what anyone brave enough to try to make sense of these issues is up against: 'Many clergy . . . separated themselves from communion with him [Pope Anastasius] because, without consulting the . . . clergy of the whole Catholic Church, he had entered into communion with a deacon of Thessalonica named Photinus who had been in communion with Acacius,* and because he secretly wished to call back Acacius and was not able. This man was struck down by the Will of God.' In contrast to Moorhead, who struggles manfully in his *Theoderic in Italy* to explain the religious issues behind the schism, Gibbon's disdain for Christological hair-splitting allows him to dismiss the controversy in the following delicious put-down: 'without condescending to balance the subtle

---

* The subject of yet another division in the Church, the Acacian Schism, the progenitor of the Laurentian Schism.

arguments of theological metaphysics . . . his [Theoderic's] external reverence for a superstition he despised may have nourished in his mind the salutary indifference of a statesman or philosopher.' (You know you're trawling in deep waters when Moorhead summons a word like 'eirenic' to comment on theological niceties!)

Peeling back several layers of theological onion skins, we come at last to the religious nub at the heart of the Acacian and Laurentian schisms: the Henotikon. This was the Edict of Union issued in 482 by Zeno to the Churches of both East and West, intended to resolve a dispute which had broken out subsequent to the Council of Chalcedon of 451. That Council had decreed that Christ had two natures, human and divine (*una persona, duae naturae*), a doctrine fiercely opposed by the monophysites (strongest in the Eastern sees of Jerusalem, Antioch and Alexandria), i.e., those who believed that Christ had only one nature (divine), but happily accepted by most Western bishops; after all, the Chalcedonian formula had been devised by none other than Pope Leo in his famous *Tome*. The dispute (with strident personalities such as Timothy 'the Weasel' and Timothy 'the White Hat' throwing oil on the flames) flared up again when one Peter Mongus, an opponent of Chalcedon, gained control of the See of Alexandria and began to correspond with Acacius, the new philo-monophysite Bishop of Constantinople, who devised the wording of the Henotikon. In the West, the Henotikon (full of crafty circumlocution surely designed to obscure the fact that it was pro-monophysite) was seen as a fudge, hostile to Chalcedon, and as a result rejected wholesale. Then Pope Anastasius (496–98), at first cool towards the Henotikon, seemed – in a volte-face which cost him the allegiance of many Western clergy – to be veering towards acceptance of it by the time Festus returned from his mission to Emperor Anastasius.* (Pay attention!) As part of Festus' mission was to secure acceptance of the Henotikon by the West, and as Festus was Laurentius' patron, it can be assumed that Laurentius was pro-Henotikon, an assumption reinforced by passages in the *Liber pontificalis* which state that Laurentius' supporters favoured Pope Anastasius when he wavered towards acceptance of the Henotikon. The same source is uncompromisingly hostile to Pope Anastasius

---

* On 17 November 498, the very day Pope Anastasius died.

('struck down by the Will of God'), but extremely favourable to Pope Symmachus. The clear implication is this: Laurentius was pro-Henotikon and therefore anti-Chalcedon, Symmachus the opposite; thus, by a process of theological osmosis, the Acacian Schism was incorporated into, and continued by, the Laurentian Schism.

In practical terms the effect of the Acacian/Laurentian Schism was to create a rift between Rome and Constantinople, which was not healed until the death of Anastasius (the emperor, not the Pope) in the latter part of Theoderic's reign. Also, it enabled both Odovacar and Theoderic to establish their regimes largely free of pressure from the East. However, with the formal resolution of the Schism in 519 came reconciliation between Rome and Constantinople. (The new emperor, Justin, aided by his nephew, Justinian – both were rigorous Chalcedonians – established an entente cordiale with Pope Hormisdas, resulting in the absolute condemnation of Acacius, and even of the emperors Zeno and Anastasius, as fellow travellers.) Peace having broken out between the two capitals (theologically speaking), forces inimical to Theoderic began to emerge from the shadows throughout the Roman world. The Ostrogothic occupation became increasingly viewed as an unwelcome interlude, its unwitting function to provide a caretaker government for Italy against that country's reincorporation into the Roman Empire.

The above résumé, stripped of all finer points of theology (which, I confess, defeat my comprehension), presents the bare facts of the Laurentian Schism. The omission of theological minutiae hardly matters, I think, as it was the Schism's *effect*, rather than its religious content, that had a bearing on Theoderic's career.

APPENDIX III

Romans and Barbarians

Throughout the text, I have used the term 'barbarian' not, I hope, in a pejorative sense, but simply to designate the Germanic peoples who overran the Western half of the Roman Empire and for a time (the Ostrogoths in particular) caused considerable trouble within the surviving Eastern half. The main and most obvious difference between Romans and barbarians was about culture and literacy. Especially literacy. In recent times there has been a movement to rehabilitate the barbarians: the Vikings were explorers and traders, rather than blood-thirsty marauders; Saxons intermarried peaceably with Romano-Britons instead of going in for ethnic cleansing; the exquisite craftsmanship of Celtic and Teutonic jewellery and weaponry puts these peoples on a par with the Romans; and so on. Recently, Richard Rudgley and Terry Jones, in their identically titled books, *Barbarians*, put up a well-argued case for the defence. Both, however, in my view, ignore the elephant in the sitting-room: *the barbarians were illiterate*.

Writing alone enables ideas to be recorded and transferred, which in turn allows them to grow and develop. Without writing, sciences, philosophy, literature, etc. – the very building-blocks of civilization – would be inconceivable. All of which is rather stating the obvious. Without writing, societies are prisoners of the immediate, limited by memory and experience as to how to shape their plans and actions. Oral transfer of knowledge can't compete with libraries.

The virtues and defects of shame-and-honour barbarian warrior societies compared to those of Graeco-Roman civilization need not be examined here, as they have been touched on fully in the text.

The popular image of the barbarian as ferociously brave, but with mind and emotions at the mercy of physical urges, in contrast to the rational Roman, whose ordered intelligence was always firmly in control of his body, is over-simplified and something of a cliché. (Shades of Bonnie Prince Charlie's Highland warriors, and the polite society of Georgian England that was given such a fright by them!) Nevertheless, although based to some extent on Roman propaganda, it does contain a useful grain of truth. However, it's perhaps worth reminding ourselves that barbarian societies weren't static, and could evolve quite quickly into ones that could in no way be described as such. The heroic savages described in *Beowulf* are separated by only a few generations from that great polymath the Venerable Bede.

Prologue

the army of the Romans

That this was an *East* Roman army doesn't make it any less Roman. The term 'Roman' was flexible and inclusive, referring initially to the inhabitants of a small city on the Tiber, then to those of Latium, then Italy, and finally, in AD 212, to all free inhabitants of the empire. Roman emperors could be from many races – Spaniards, Illyrians, Africans, Arab, et al., though never, strangely, German. (The reason, perhaps, was because Germania, never having been conquered by Rome could not be fully accepted by her. An academic once seriously suggested that the rise of Nazism was ultimately due to the fact that, unlike most of the rest of Europe, 'Germany had never been through the public school of the Roman Empire'!) Claudian, one of the most celebrated late Latin poets, was a Syrian whose mother tongue was Greek. Writing *c.* 400, he rejoiced that the inhabitants of the empire, though of diverse origins, 'are all one people'. There exists a mindset which defines East Romans as 'Byzantines' – i.e., as different in some way from 'real' Romans. But when the Western Empire fell in 476, a fully Roman state continued in the East for nearly two more centuries (after which much of its territory was lost to Arabs and Avars), and its citizens certainly thought of themselves as Romans. ('Byzantine' was a term invented by Renaissance scholars and would have had no meaning for contemporaries of the late Ancient World – bar as an alternative to 'Constantinopolitan'.)

converted to Christianity

According to Joseph Vogt in his *The Decline of Rome*, 'it seems probable that the tribes of the great federations were already [Arian] Christian at the time they entered the empire'. Arianism differed from Orthodox Christianity in one key respect: Arians held that, as the Son, Christ was inferior to God the Father, and was therefore excluded from His divinity, a concept which appealed to Germans with their patriarchal society. To Catholic Romans, however, this made Arians heretics as well as barbarians – doubly beyond the pale. Christianity was introduced to Ethiopia at the beginning of the fourth century, but mass conversion of German tribes began only in 341 with Ulfilas' mission to the Goths.

the blazing hulks . . . swept down

The expedition of 468 shows striking parallels with the Spanish Armada. In both cases, the plan was not to engage in a sea battle but to enable a powerful invading force to land. In both cases, the outcome was decided by the use of fireships. In 1588 the Spaniards did at least have sea room to escape downwind. But for Basiliscus' fleet escape was complicated by the difficulty of avoiding being driven on to the lee shore of the long Cape Bon peninsula. The effects of the disaster were decisive and immediate. In the West the Vandals were reprieved, while Visigoths, Burgundians and Suevi – realizing that there was no longer any central force strong enough to stop them – started carving out independent states from imperial territory. In less than a decade, the empire went from somewhere to nowhere. In 468 much of the Western Empire, though tottering, was still intact and owed allegiance to the Italian centre, an allegiance fortified by the arrival of Anthemius, who inspired genuine hopes of a revival. By 476 the bonds had all dissolved, and in that year the Western Empire came to an end.

vessels piling up on the rocky shore

Square-rigged Roman ships were a good deal less manoeuvrable than modern sailing-vessels. With a following or side wind they could make good progress, but against contrary winds, making seaway was much harder. Of course, galleys (rowed *not* by slaves, as depicted in the film *Ben Hur*, but by *remiges*, a category of seamen separate from the *nautae* who managed the sails and rigging) could move independently of the wind. According to Adrian Goldsworthy (*The Complete Roman Army*), experiments with a full-scale replica Roman galley showed that such a vessel could maintain a cruising speed of four knots, twice that if under sail or for short bursts as in a ramming attack.

the Vandals struck
The Vandal fleet consisted of captured Roman ships or vessels constructed by subject Roman shipwrights, sailed and navigated by indigenous north Africans. From these craft, Vandal warriors would board other ships or put ashore as raiding parties.

limped back to the Golden Horn
Procopius lays the blame for the outcome of the great adventure squarely on Basiliscus. But the simple explanation may well be just bad luck with the wind. To accommodate both possibilities, I have portrayed Basiliscus as being willing to fleece Gaiseric (who, according to Procopius, bribed the general to agree to a five-day truce in the hope that the wind would change), while not, consciously, at least, allowing this to affect his strategy.

a fourteen-year-old hostage
In the ancient world, the giving of hostages was more about diplomacy than yielding to punitive coercion. The hostage was often a junior royal, handed over as a pledge of good behaviour or adherence to a treaty. To Rome, the practice provided an opportunity to turn barbarians into lovers of the Roman way of life, therefore less likely to prove hostile.

Chapter 1
styluses and waxed tablets
Known as *codices*, pairs of hinged waxed boards were the notebooks of the Roman world. Writing, scratched on the waxed surface, could be readily erased by the flattened end of the pointed writing-tool, the *stylus*.

betting on the Blue or Green team
Blue and green were the respective colours of the rival chariot-racing teams competing in the Hippodrome. These teams inspired fanatical support from their fans, support which had a political dimension (the Blues championed the Establishment, the Greens the people) and could lead to serious rioting, as happened in the Niké riots of 532 which nearly toppled Emperor Justinian.

Aristotle on the subject of the young Alexander
The famous philosopher was the tutor of Alexander aged thirteen to sixteen. Aristotle's image of the 'great-souled man' gave the future king a model for the role he wished to emulate.

Basiliscus . . . has taken sanctuary in Hagia Sophia
He was eventually reprieved, thanks to his sister's intercession with the (justifiably furious) emperor, Leo I. Hagia Sophia/Sancta Sophia (Holy Wisdom) was the predecessor of the present building erected in the sixth century by Justinian. The great cathedral is now a mosque.

Anthemius might . . . be the last Augustus of the West
Not quite. Like almost all failed emperors, Anthemius was 'disposed of', to be followed briefly by: Olybrius, Glycerius, Julius Nepos and Romulus Augustus. Ricimer's successor, Odovacar, another barbarian Master of Soldiers, deposed Romulus in 476 and sent the imperial regalia to the Eastern Emperor, Zeno, as the sole remaining ruler of the 'One and Indivisible Empire'. In reality, the Western Empire was no more, and Odovacar had become an independent German monarch in Italy, like Gaiseric in Africa and Euric in Gaul and Spain.

a tough Isaurian
Rather like the Highlanders in early modern Britain, the Isaurians, an independent-minded people from south-west Anatolia, were a constant thorn in the flesh of the imperial government. So much so, that the term 'Isaurian' was to become virtually synonymous with 'insurgent'.

Walls of Theodosius . . . aqueduct of Valens
Both these colossal structures are still standing, testament to the strength and durability of Roman architecture. Inviolate for a thousand years until breached by Turkish cannon in 1453, the Walls are being restored to their original glory.

a tall marble column
The Column of Arcadius was modelled on the Columns of Trajan and Marcus Aurelius in Rome. The imagery of the latter pair, though triumphalist, is not altogether devoid of a spirit of compassion and humanity. The Column of Arcadius – an ugly example of state-sanctioned

chauvinism – was redeemed by no such sentiments. The monument no longer exists, bar its base; but a drawing, showing a lynch-mob unleashing a pogrom against the city's Goths, was made before its demolition in 1715.

Cambyses. The legendary wild boar
An appropriate soubriquet. Cambyses, king of the Medes and Persians from 529 to 522 BC, was notorious for aggression and ferocity.

Chapter 2
outside the Charisius Gate at the second hour
Constantinople is built on a peninsula surrounded on three sides by sea or arms of the sea, the landward side being sealed off by the massive bulwark of the Theodosian Walls. These were pierced by six principal gates with subsidiary military gates between each pair. The Charisius Gate in the north marked the egress of one of the principal thorough-fares of the city, the Mesé; the name was also given to the main street in the south, which exited via the Golden Gate. The Roman day, from sunrise to sunset, was divided into twelve hours which varied in length according to the season. Midday corresponded to the sixth hour.

a celebrated local martyr
At the Council of Chalcedon in 451, the mummified corpse of St Euphemia, according to the seventh-century chronicler Theophylact, 'stretched out her dead and lifeless hand to take the tome'. The 'tome' in question was a tract written by Pope Leo, arguing that Christ's nature was both human and divine. This was hotly contested by the opposing faction, the Monophysites, who believed that Christ had only one nature: divine. At the Council, the dispute was resolved in favour of those supporting Leo – no doubt helped by Euphemia's posthumous sign of approval.

Tempered steel with razor edges
Steel is simply wrought iron (i.e., iron with the impurities removed by beating when white-hot) made to absorb a little carbon. This was achieved by heating the iron in a bed of charcoal. The resulting steel could then be tempered by a process of annealing. Chemical analysis of a selection of Roman swords (e.g., the Mainz 'Sword of Tiberius',

cited by Bishop and Coulston, *Roman Military Equipment*) has shown them to consist of high-quality carburized steel with a soft/wrought-iron core. The best Roman steel was manufactured in Spain.

For all your courage, Goth, you'll never be one of us
In AD 376 the Gothic nation, attacked by a terrible new enemy, the Huns, were granted sanctuary within the Eastern Empire. But, owing to ill-treatment by corrupt Roman officials, they rebelled against their hosts and defeated a huge Roman army sent to crush them, at Adrianople in 378. While one great division of the tribe, the Visigoths ('Wise Goths'), eventually sought their fortune in the West, the remainder, the Ostrogoths ('Bright Goths'), after a sojourn in Pannonia were suffered to settle in the East – troublesome and unwelcome guests, assigned a 'reservation' in the Balkans.

Chapter 3
Leo and his top general, Zeno
Leo (457–74), often referred to, most inappropriately, as 'Leo the Great', purely to distinguish him from his grandson and successor Leo II (474), 'Leo the Small', was an undistinguished Dacian officer who succeeded Marcian, the emperor whose defiance of Attila persuaded the Hun king to switch his attack to the West. Dominated by Aspar, the great general who had been instrumental in securing the purple for Marcian, Leo resented his subservient status and tried to counteract Aspar's influence by enlisting in the imperial army a force of Isaurians. These were a wild tribal people from the Taurus Mountains, ruled by a chieftain called Tarasicodissa. Changing his name to Zeno, Tarasicodissa became the commander of the Excubitors, as the Isaurian unit was named. In about 471, in the course of settling an insurrection, Zeno had Aspar murdered, taking his place as Leo's *éminence grise*. By this time Zeno had married Leo's daughter Ariadne, thus putting himself in line for the throne, as Leo had no sons. On Leo's death in 474, he was succeeded by his grandson Leo, a child of seven, son of Zeno and Ariadne. Soon afterwards, Leo II died in mysterious circumstances (his father being suspected of his murder), to be succeeded by Zeno (474–91). Zeno's reign was briefly interrupted by a usurper, Basiliscus, the

general whose incompetent handling of the 468 expedition against the Vandals ensured the collapse of the Western Empire eight years later. Intrigue, jealousy and murder – classic Roman politics!

look what he [Alaric] did to Rome
In 408 Alaric, king of the Visigoths, laid siege to Rome in an attempt to force the Western Emperor, Honorius, to grant his people a homeland and recognized status within the empire. Negotiations seemed to begin well, and the siege was called off. However, provoked by endless vacillation on the part of Honorius, Alaric lost patience and in 410 sacked the city. Although little damage was done and few lives lost, the sack had huge symbolic importance, sending shock waves reverberating round the Roman world.

Pridie Kalendas Junii, in the year of the consuls Leo . . . and Probianus
The Romans dated important events 'from the Founding of the City – *ab urbe condita*' or AUC (753 BC) – but for most dating purposes the names of the consuls for any given year were used, one from Rome, the other from Constantinople. Dates within any given month were calculated by counting the number of days occurring *before* the next of the three fixed days dividing the Roman month: Kalends, the first day of the month, the Nones on the 5th or 7th, and the Ides on the 13th or 15th. (In March, May, July, and October, the Nones fell on the 7th and the Ides on the 15th, in the remaining months on the 5th and 13th respectively.) Thus, the Ides of January happening on the 13th of that month, the next day would be termed by a Roman not the 14th, but the 19th *before the Kalends of February*, reckoning inclusively, i.e., taking in both the 14th of January and the 1st of February; and so on to the last day of the month which was termed *pridie Kalendas*.

the Golden Gate
This began life as a huge triumphal arch erected *c.* 390 by Theodosius I. Originally outside the city, it was incorporated into the new Walls built by Theodosius II. The gates themselves were originally covered in gold plate, hence the name.

Legio Quinta Macedonica
Egyptian carvings of the fifth and sixth centuries show soldiers of this unit, identifiable from the sunflower-like design on their shields, in graphic detail. They are portrayed wearing very traditional gear that would not have looked out of place on Trajan's Column: scale armour with pteruges (protective leather strips) at the shoulders and between the groin and knees, and classical 'Attic' helmets complete with brow reinforcements and cheek-pieces. (In the Eastern Empire, uniforms tended to be more conservative than in the West, perhaps because of the influence of Hellenic tradition – the conquests of Alexander, the Persian Wars, etc.)

Chapter 4
a line of figures performing a processional dance
These dances, known as *Kukeri*, are still performed in some places in Bulgaria, always by male dancers. Dressed in animal skins, including masks often made from the heads, they parade in a trance-like state through towns and villages, chanting and shouting, to drive away evil spirits. The dances are thought to have originated from the ancient Thracians.

the monastery of St Elizabeth
Elizabeth the Thaumaturge, or Miracle-Worker, was a popular saint who arose in Constantinople during Leo's reign. She reputedly killed a dragon, after first 'sealing' it in its cave with her crucifix. For this and various miracles of healing she was canonized, her feast-day being 24 April – the day after that of St George (coincidence, or what?). The monastery described in the text is loosely based on Bulgaria's famous Rila Monastery, dating originally from 927 (though since heavily restored), so not *too* remote in time from my fictional one.

Chapter 5
such blades were lethal
German master-swordsmiths of the Migration Period (Frankish ones especially) were capable of producing blades whose construction involved a very high degree of craftsmanship. The best ones were made by 'pattern-welding', in which several iron rods were twisted together, beaten flat, then edged with steel. When washed with acid, the sword's flat surfaces

displayed beautiful patterns rather like those of watered silk. Naturally, weapons of such quality were time-consuming to produce and therefore expensive, so were possessed only by individuals of high status.

The Norns who weave the web
Strictly, the Norns belong to Scandinavian rather than Teutonic mythology. But as the pantheon of these ethnically virtually identical peoples was intimately entwined (Odin/Woden/Wotan et al.), I felt I could legitimately mention them in this context. Although the Goths' were now Christian, lingering adherence to the old warlike deities must have persisted just below the surface, especially with people nurtured on heroic myth.

Chapter 6
Thiudimer's 'gards' or palace
Gothic words such as *baurg* (town), *kind* (kin), *gards* (large house) and *haims* (village) show close affinity with *burg/burgh, cyn, garth, ham* from our own Anglo-Saxon and Viking linguistic heritage – showing that Germanic and Nordic languages have common roots, even when spoken by peoples widely separated by geography. That we have a comprehensive knowledge of the Gothic language is thanks to one Ulfila or Ulfilas, a Gothic missionary who, from 340 till his death in 381, was largely successful in converting his people to (Arian) Christianity, and whose translation of the Bible into Gothic we still possess.

his concubine not his wife
Ancient sources – Jordanes, Anonymous Valesianus, et al. (they refer to Erelieva as *concubina*) – confirm that her marriage to Thiudimer was invalid. That Thiudimund could entertain realistic hopes of succeeding Thiudimer is suggested by Jordanes in *Getica*, where he points out that, on his father's death, Thiudimund was completely passed over as heir, *contrary to traditional practice* (my italics). If his birth were legitimate (in contrast to Theoderic's), this of course would provide a strong basis for such hopes. To reinforce this possibility, I have given Theoderic and Thiudimund different mothers, with Thiudimund's being married to Thiudimer. Speculation, admittedly, but, in the interests of giving a dramatic twist to the story, hopefully legitimate.

Chapter 7

striped with reinforcing layers
This curious feature, known as 'brick-banding', is typical of the late Roman walls of many cities, e.g. Ankara, Diocletianopolis (Hissar, Bulgaria) and, most famously, Constantinople. The last example was the inspiration, nearly a thousand years later, for the variegated layering of the ramparts of Caernarvon Castle.

above them rose the citadel
Nothing Roman remains today of Belgrade's Kalemegdan Citadel – hardly surprising, as it was razed and rebuilt many times in its long history, which stretches back to Celtic times. What can be seen today is mainly of Austro-Hungarian and Turkish (e.g., the Stambol Gate) construction from the eighteenth century. For lack of evidence on the site itself, I based the appearance of the gatehouse partly on Trier's late Roman Porta Nigra.

a 'ladder' of axes raced up the face of the gate
This was suggested by an incident in the film *The Vikings*, starring Kirk Douglas.

Alexander, Caesar or Aetius
Nearer our own time, leaders of this stamp – charismatic personalities with the power to inspire others to *want* to follow them, include – Robert the Bruce, Henry V, Joan of Arc, Nelson, Napoleon (unfortunately), Shackleton and Churchill. There is evidence that, *c.* 471, Theoderic underwent something of a personality change (see Richard Rudgley's *Barbarians*) from the timid recluse of Constantinople to the young Alexander of Singidunum.

to ferry the rest . . . across the Danube
Jordanes is specific in stating that Theoderic crossed the Danube with his army, but does not explain how. He couldn't have used Constantine's great stone bridge at Oescus (even supposing it was still intact), as that was many miles downstream from Singidunum. Getting six thousand men across a wide river was the sort of thing Roman generals took in their stride. But for a teenage lad in charge of a large force of unruly barbarians . . . ? However it was done (and I've had to fall back on imagination here, for a solution), it was a remarkable feat.

Down crashed the massive iron grille
A Roman portcullis? An anachronism, surely? This clever device was
not, however, a medieval invention. According to Peter Connolly in
his magnificent *Greece and Rome at War*, it is first mentioned during
the Second Punic War; he also states that the channels for these gates
can be seen at many Roman sites, including Nîmes, Aosta and Trier.
The stratagem of using a stalled wagon to enter the gateway is based
on a ruse by Scottish freedom fighters to take a castle in English hands
(Linlithgow), during the Wars of Independence.

'Keep Singidunum for the moment'
And keep it he did – the first incident (in 471) in an on–off relationship with the Eastern Empire which was to seesaw until 488 (when
Zeno invited him to take over Italy from Odovacar), and re-emerge in
the final decade of his life.

Chapter 8
Sidonius Apollinaris, former bishop of Arverna
Sidonius Apollinaris – distinguished man of letters, aristocrat, bishop
(of Arverna, 471–5), son-in-law of an emperor (Avitus) – was one of
the few Gallo-Roman nobles who forcibly resisted the encroachments
of the barbarians. Others of his class tended to make the best terms
they could with their uninvited 'guests' (a Roman euphemism for the
German invaders!).

Chapter 9
Ambrosius Aurelianus, son of a Roman senator and resistance leader
Mentioned briefly by Gildas and Nennius, little is known about
Aurelianus beyond the fact that he was of Roman descent and headed
British resistance against the Saxons some time in the fifth century.
S. E. Wibolt in *Britain under the Romans* places him early in that century;
Neil Faulkner in *The Decline and Fall of Roman Britain* dates his
campaigns to *c.* 475–500.

venerated as a 'holy man'
In his *Vita Severini*, Eugippius (a monk who had been present at his

subject's death and gathered stories about him from his close companions) mentions the meeting with Odovacar, and describes in detail both the soldiers' expedition to draw their final pay instalment, and Severinus' organizing centres of defence. As Severinus refused to disclose anything about his origins, except some training as an ascetic in the eastern deserts, I felt at liberty to fill in the blanks. As he apparently spoke beautiful Latin, I thought it safe to assume that he was a cultured man of considerable education. In his account of the Batavan soldiers' journey, Eugippius implies that they were ambushed before they reached their destination; for dramatic reasons I have had this happen as they returned.

Chapter 10
a bloodstained 'gladius'
Aurelianus is historical, but Artorius – Arthur – belongs firmly in the realm of myth. Legends (first recorded *c*. 830 by a Welshman, Nennius) abound, but, so far, no hard evidence has come to light. However, the fact that the Arthur stories are known 'wherever Celts have spoken a Brythonic tongue', suggest that his existence may be more than merely fabulous.

Chapter 11
the highs and lows of his career
To say that the movements of the Amal branch of the Ostrogoths throughout the Balkans and Thrace in the decade 471–81 were convoluted would be like describing the ascent of Everest as a challenging hill-walk. For we're dealing with a tangled web of marches and countermarches, double-dealing, promises made and broken, treaties signed then ignored, shifting alliances, negotiations running into the sand, etc., involving the relationship between, on the one hand, Thiudimer and then his son Theoderic and, on the other, Leo then Zeno, with the manoeuvrings of Strabo thrown in to muddy the water. To attempt a fictional version of all this without some radical abridgement would stretch the patience of most readers beyond snapping-point. So, following the example of Howard Fast in his novel *Spartacus*, I've gone in for a good deal of pruning and telescoping. For example, the confrontation between the two Theoderics at Mount Sondis in 478, and Thiudimund's abandoning of his wagons near Epidamnus in 479, I've

presented as two connected incidents in a single event. Also, I've moved Theoderic's route across the Balkan Mountains slightly to the west: from Marcianople (Mt Sondis) to Novae (Shipka Pass) as the latter feature makes an appropriately dramatic setting for the face-off between the two rivals.

the last Western Emperor

So ended – with a whimper rather than a bang – five hundred years of empire (and, before that, five hundred years of the Roman Republic). The orthodoxy among some historians is that the collapse of the West was an organic process rather than an event, the date of its official end, 476, simply a marker for something that had in fact been going on for a considerable time. If, however, we put the date of the fall of the West back a few years, from 476 to 468, it *can* be seen as a single catastrophic event; before 468, the West was still salvageable after that date, its collapse was inevitable and swift (see Notes for the Prologue).

facing each other across a river

This time-honoured tradition – with its inherent sense of drama and occasion – held a special appeal for the Goths, for whom it seems to have been a favoured way of staging 'summit meetings'. Other shame-and-honour societies have exhibited a similar penchant for dramatic panache when holding grand assemblies – Native American 'pow-wows' or Highland clan gatherings, for example.

Chapter 12

a Hun great horse and a chunky Parthian

Contrary to popular belief, Hun horses were not shaggy little ponies but huge, ill-conformed brutes, inferior perhaps in intelligence and speed to the smaller north African and Arab strains, but powerful and capable of great endurance. The Parthian horse – chunky and solid, large of cheek and muzzle, with strongly arched neck and rounded haunches – was a good all-round war-horse and the favourite breed of stablemasters for the Roman cavalry. This was perhaps more for aesthetic than practical reasons; for example, it performed less well in hot conditions than the Arab or African. In imagining a Hun–Parthian cross, I've combined the size and power of one with the pleasing looks of the other. I thought Sleipnir should be huge – but twenty hands was perhaps stretching things a bit.

going back to Xenophon
Moves first recorded in the Greek commander's *The Art of Horsemanship*, and still performed today by the famous Lipizzan stallions of the Spanish Riding School in Vienna, which are direct descendants of horses bred for the Roman cavalry. Their movements and figures, especially the marvellous 'airs above the ground', are derived from those that Greek and Roman cavalry mounts were made to practise.

an unheard-of honour for a barbarian
Well, not quite. Stilicho, the great Vandal general of West Rome's armies in the reign of Honorius, was made consul for the year 400, in recognition of his services. Despite this, he fell from grace and was put to death for failing to prevent the invasion of Gaul in 406–7 by a huge barbarian confederacy.

Chapter 13
Myrddin, from Cambria in Britain
Myrddin: Welsh personal name which Geoffrey of Monmouth Latinized into Merlinus (Merlin) in tales of Arthurian romance. For obvious reasons I have associated him with Artorius (Arthur); in some legends he is confounded with Ambrosius Aurelianus. Two distinct Merlins emerge from the stories – a fifth-century Welsh Merlin (cited by Geoffrey of Monmouth in his *Vita Merlini*), and a sixth-century Caledonian Merlin. A medieval tradition ascribes to Merlin the gift of prophecy.

I have arrived at my own Rubicon
The stream separating Cisalpine Gaul from Italy proper, which Julius Caesar crossed with his legions, thus precipitating a bloody civil war with Pompey, has become synonymous with a personal moment of truth or point of no return. In Theoderic's case, this was a consequence of Strabo's death in 481. The demise of their leader persuaded the Thracian Goths to unite with the Amal Goths under Theoderic. This apparent stroke of luck was in reality a major headache both for the Amal king,

and for the Eastern Empire. Instead of two rival Gothic factions effectively neutralizing each other, the Eastern Empire was now faced with a huge, undifferentiated, potentially hostile barbarian mass. Could it afford to tolerate such a volatile presence within its borders? If not, what stance would Theoderic be forced to adopt?

solve the problems of the Noricans
Odovacar's 'solution' (which could be interpreted as an admission of failure) was to resettle the 'Romans' (i.e., the populations of towns and their garrisons) of Noricum within Italy. If the majority of country-dwellers had been sheltering in the towns, this would imply a mass emigration of refugees to Italy. It seems unlikely that the entire population of Noricum would have decamped, but what proportion remained behind can't be ascertained.

it is the red dragon which prevails
The ninth-century Welsh chronicler Nennius alludes to a prophecy in which the red dragon (i.e., the Britons – the ancestors of today's Welsh) would one day overcome the white dragon (the Anglo-Saxon forebears of most twenty-first-century English people). If there's any truth in the prophecy, that would imply Welsh independence some time in the future. That is perhaps (some would say unfortunately) unlikely, despite the halfway house of the present Welsh Assembly. Though ethnically and linguistically far more distinct from their English neighbours than are the Scots – that 'mongrel nation' – Wales has been politically joined to England for four hundred years longer than Scotland, with the result that habit and conditioning have perhaps done their work too well. (A recent experiment involving DNA sampling showed the Celtic gene, as opposed to the Teutonic, to be much more prevalent among Welsh people than among Scots.) Now, if instead of dragons the prophecy had said lions . . .

Chapter 14
a revolutionary new weapons system
I couldn't resist the temptation to put back the use of Greek fire from the seventh to the late fifth century. Supposedly invented by Callinicus of Heliopolis in 668, its first recorded use was in 674 against the Arabs, then

besieging Constantinople. Creating terror perhaps disproportionate to its effect (its nearest modern equivalent is napalm), it was undoubtedly the most effective form of ordnance prior to gunpowder. As with that composition, its precise origins are shrouded in mystery – sufficient licence (excuse?) I thought, to allow me to include it in the story. After all, if James Clavell in his novel *Shogun*, can equip troops with Elizabethan bayonets . . .

the order . . . for his recall
With suspicion of Theoderic's motives at times verging on the paranoid Zeno seems to have been genuinely worried that the Amal king 'could prove disloyal' (to quote the chronicler Ioannis Antiochenus), and join forces with Illus against him. Hence Theoderic's recall – a U-turn which provoked him to understandable fury, causing him to wreak revenge by (once again) beating up Thrace, then attacking Constantinople. It never seems to have occurred to the Romans that, by dealing with barbarians honestly and fairly, they might have succeeded in establishing a harmonious modus vivendi with them. This blind spot may have stemmed from a deep-seated concept of barbarians as 'subhuman', therefore hardly deserving of humane treatment. Perhaps the attitude was linked to an atavistic fear originating in incidents like the occupation of Rome by the Gauls in 390 BC, and the destruction of Varus' legions by Hermann's Germans in AD 9.

I need someone to take over in Italy
Who initiated the move to Italy, Zeno or Theoderic? Among ancient writers, Procopius, Jordanes (in his *Romana*) and Anonymous Valesianus come down firmly on the side of Zeno, while Ennodius and Jordanes (this time in his *Gothic History*) plump for Theoderic (it seems that Jordanes wanted to have his cake and eat it!). Considering that in 488 Theoderic had become a real danger to Zeno, it seems only natural that the emperor would seek to be rid of him by holding up Italy as a desirable carrot. With the notable exception of Gibbon, this is the view that most modern historians subscribe to.

threatening to send warriors
Nothing, but nothing, in the dealings of Constantinople with barbarians was ever simple. Perhaps over-reacting to Odovacar's bellicose stance

(which may have been more bluster than a real threat), Zeno mobilized the Rugians in the west to block any hostile moves by the Scirian king. This resulted in a chain reaction of retribution and misery: in 487 Odovacar attacked and destroyed the Rugian kingdom, capturing and executing its king; caught up in the conflict, the wretched inhabitants of Noricum emigrated en masse to Italy (see the Notes for Chapter 13); the son of the Rugian king escaped, and with a band of pro-Ostrogothic followers marched downstream along the Danube to join Theoderic in Moesia, as he was about to set out for Italy. Theoderic was under instructions to overthrow Odovacar and rule Italy 'until the emperor arrived in person' (Anonymous Valesianus). This quotation is an example of the elaborate fiction which maintained that the de facto barbarian kings of Italy were actually the appointees of the Eastern Emperor! Back to Illus: the Isaurian pretender was cornered, captured and executed in 488, the year of Theoderic's commission to invade Italy.

the comforting illusion
In 476, Odovacar, the Scirian adventurer who had risen to become commander of the Army of Italy, was short of money to pay his (barbarian federate) soldiers – hardly surprising, as the state revenues had virtually dried up. Payment in land being the only viable alternative to cash, Odovacar applied for permission to distribute land grants, from the imperial government, which was controlled by the Patrician Orestes who had installed his son, the boy Romulus, as Western Emperor. When permission was refused, the Scirian acted swiftly. Showing a sure grasp of *realpolitik*, he captured and killed Orestes, rewarded his soldiers with land – either public or confiscated from Romans, sent young Romulus into exile and, to give his actions a cloak of legality, persuaded the Senate to send the imperial robes and diadem to Zeno in Constantinople 'as one shared Emperor was sufficient for both territories' (Malchus). They also requested that Odovacar be given the rank of Patrician and entrusted with the government of Italy. Though Zeno's reply was carefully ambiguous (after all, Julius Nepos – the Eastern nominee, though he had been forced into exile – was anxious to reclaim his throne), behind its polished phraseology lay an acknowledgement of the truth: Italy, like Gaul, Spain and Africa, was now ruled by a barbarian king, and the Western Empire was over.

Chapter 15
crossing the Mare Suevicum

In his *Gothic History* (based on an earlier, more detailed work by the Roman Cassiodorus) Jordanes, a Goth living in Constantinople in the sixth century, developed three main points: a) that the Goths originated in Scandinavia, b) that they migrated south-east across what is now Poland and the Ukraine until they reached the Black Sea, and c) that they eventually divided into two groups, the Visigoths and the Ostrogoths, ruled by ancient royal lines, the Balthi and Amal respectively. Although his conclusions are based on oral tradition, archaeological evidence tends broadly to support them. Two cultures associated with the Goths (from grave-goods etc.), the Wielbark in Poland and the Æ ernjachov north of the Black Sea, have been identified along the migration route described by Jordanes. It would be an over-simplification to identify the fourth-century groupings of the Tervingi and the Greuthungi with the Visigoths and the Ostrogoths, but certainly in the fifth century these two great branches developed distinct and separate identities, each under its own ruling family.

a time of gods and heroes

The Goths seem to have shared certain ideals and aspirations with other Germanic groups, especially the linking of a man's status with brave deeds, and a king's sacrificing himself for his people – a tradition enacted in historical times by Ermanaric's suicide following his defeat by the Huns. (The Goths, by this time converted to Christianity, may have been torn between admiration for a traditionally heroic act and disapproval, as suicide was condemned by the Arian Church, as well as by the Catholic.) Nordic/Teutonic mythology with its pantheon (Odin, Thor et al.), ideas of good versus evil (Balder *v.* Loki, Ragnarok), and the marvellous poetical and significant image of the ash tree, Yggdrasil, the Tree of Life, after being handed down orally for untold generations, was eventually permanently recorded in written works such as the seventh-century Anglo-Saxon poem *Beowulf*, the *Gesta Danorum* by Saxo Grammaticus in the twelfth century, the Icelandic *Prose Edda*, and the *Heimskringla* of Snorre Sturlason, completed *c.* 1230.

Chapter 16

list of Things to be Done

The migration of a whole people necessarily involved planning and preparation on a massive scale: wagons, of course, were the *sine qua non* of such ventures, but archaeology is little help in visualizing what Gothic wagons were like. (With the exception of a beautifully constructed and sophisticated wagon as part of the furniture for the afterlife in a high-status barbarian grave, there is virtually no surviving evidence.) However, remains of ancient chariots show that wheel construction was highly efficient, involving spokes, hubs, axle-pins, and iron tyres; it's safe to assume that similar technology would apply in the case of wagons. Similar problems (migration on an epic scale involving the crossing of rough terrain, especially difficult mountain ranges) tend to produce similar solutions. So, boldly sticking my neck out, I have assumed that the basic construction of Gothic wagons must have resembled in essentials that of Boer and Conestoga wagons if they were to cope successfully with the rigours of the journey. The same principle would apply with draught animals, provisioning, etc. In connection with the tools I've enumerated (augers, chisels, tongs, etc.), Roman and barbarian toolkits have been found, which are virtually identical to their modern counterparts.

the last day of September

I can find no source which gives an exact date for the start of the expedition. Moorhead (in *Theoderic in Italy*) says, 'probably towards the end of 488', Heather (in *The Goths*) states, 'in the autumn and winter of 488/9, Theoderic . . . set out', while Wolfram (in *History of the Goths*) says only that 'the Goths waited for the harvest before they left the Danubian provinces'. Gibbon's statement that the march was 'undertaken in the depths of a rigorous winter' must, I think, err on the side of lateness. All in all, the end of September seems a credible date for the migration to begin. By then the harvest would be in, and they would still have time to break the back of the journey before the onset of winter. From Novae to the River Ulca – where they encountered the Gepids – via the route I've described (which we know is the one they took) is nearly six hundred miles. Assuming an average rate of travel of ten miles a day (which allows for inevitable delays and stopovers), they would accomplish this stretch in two months, arriving at the Ulca about the end of November. This would still give them time to push far enough up the valley of the Drava before wintering, to be able to cross the Julian Alps into Italy the following spring.

two hundred sections altogether
The wagon trains of American pioneers or Boers on the Great Trek set out not as amorphous mobs but as organized mobile communities made up of separate groupings, and operating under strict codes of discipline, with a hierarchy of command. It is fairly safe to assume that the emigration of the Ostrogoths (to which must be added Fredericus' Rugians) must have been run on broadly similar lines. As no sources give any details, however, I've had to fall back on invention. How many did the Ostrogoths number? Again, no precise figures are available. Burns (in *History of the Ostrogoths*) suggests forty thousand, which seems far too low; Wolfram estimates one hundred thousand, a figure with which Moorhead agrees, while Richard Rudgley (in his fascinating *Barbarians*) suggests three hundred thousand. As a compromise, perhaps two hundred thousand would be a realistic total.

Chapter 17
To put on such a show of force
Exactly why the Gepids chose to offer battle remains a mystery. On the face of it, they had nothing to gain and everything to lose by taking on such a powerful nation. Wolfram (in his impressive and synthe-sizing *History of the Goths*) says, 'Whether the Gepids were in league with Odovacar or whether they were doing this on their own is unknown.' He goes on to wonder if Odovacar may perhaps have enlisted the Gepids as allies, but admits that this is only speculation. Jordanes claims that the Gepids were old enemies of the Ostrogoths – hardly in itself a valid reason for confronting them at a juncture when they were merely transients and not acting in the least aggressively. I can find no other source which offers an explanation for the Gepids' conduct. Of course, all this uncertainty provides a splendid opportunity to devise a fictional reason, one which ties in with Thiudimund – concerning whom the records are largely (and conveniently!) blank. From the scanty information we do possess, we know that his claim to the throne was

passed over (because he could offer, Wolfram says, 'no evidence of his fitness for the kingship') in favour of Theoderic's; also that in 479, when leading a column assigned to him by Theoderic, he was outmanoeuvred by the Roman general Sabinianus, only escaping by abandoning his people – resulting in many being taken prisoner, and hundreds of wagons being lost. This allowed me, without distorting known historical fact, to present him as a jealous sibling who was also cowardly and incompetent. (All very useful for dramatic purposes.) As history is silent about him after 479, I was able neatly to kill him off in the battle at the Ulca, he having fulfilled his fictional raison d'être.

you will lead the Forlorn Hope
Despite having a modern – well, early modern – ring, being chiefly associated with wars from the seventeenth to the early nineteenth centuries, the term 'Forlorn Hope' (from the Dutch *verloren hoop*, 'lost troop') doesn't mean that the phenomenon itself is anachronistic in the context here. Ancient history abounds with examples of intrepid volunteers leading desperate sorties to carry a breach etc. (e.g., Tiberius Sempronius Gracchus was awarded the *corona vallaris* for heading a scaling-party over the walls of Carthage). With their reputation for reckless courage, acts of self-sacrificing valour by barbarians were doubtless even more common than those by Romans. But, as history was written by the Romans, such incidents were seldom recorded. An exception was made in the case of Theoderic at the battle of the Ulca. The Roman panegyrist Ennodius wrote (in *Panegyricus dictus Theoderico*) that he turned the tide of battle by heading a counter-attack 'like a lion in the midst of a herd', just when it seemed that the Gepids were gaining the upper hand. But of course on that occasion, Theoderic, acting in the capacity of Zeno's vicegerent-to-be, was fighting on the 'right' side.

Chapter 18
the West's finished
Except that it wasn't. In the 530s, Justinian, the Eastern Emperor, began a long campaign to restore the Western half of the 'One and Indivisible Empire'. His brilliant generals Belisarius and Narses succeeded in clearing Africa, Italy and southern Spain of Vandals, Ostrogoths and Visigoths respectively, so that by the end of his reign, in 565, the Roman

Empire had almost regained the same dimensions it possessed just prior to Julius Caesar's conquest of Gaul. A truly remarkable achievement, but one that was destined not to last. By the end of the century Germanic Lombards had taken over much of Italy, and in the next, Avars, along with militant Islam, were to reduce the empire to an Anatolian rump, with an archipelago of tiny imperial possessions alone surviving in the West. (The Eastern Empire survived, though in increasingly attenuated form, until 1453 when Constantinople finally fell to the Turks.) Although, in a physical sense, the Roman Empire may have passed away, it is astonishing how the *idea* of Rome has continued to grip the minds of rulers and statesmen: from Charlemagne crowned emperor in Rome in 800 to the failed attempt to create a European Constitution, whose aims were prematurely carved in Latin in splendid Trajanic capitals on a marble plaque in Rome.

chatting easily with the Franks
Sidonius Apollinaris wrote to Syagrius congratulating him on his ability to communicate with barbarians. 'I am . . . inexpresibly amazed,' he commented, 'that you have quickly acquired a knowledge of the German tongue with such ease . . . The bent elders of the Germans are astounded at you when you translate letters, and they adopt you as umpire and arbitrator in their mutual dealings.'

Clovis . . . inspiring respect
For most of the fifth century, the pre-eminent barbarian power in Gaul was the Visigoths, with Frankish influence west of the Rhine tenuous at best. Following the death of the great Euric in 484, that situation rapidly went into reverse. By the time of Clovis's death in 511, the Franks had become the dominant power in Gaul – whose name in consequence changed to Frankia/Francia (France).

Chapter 19
the Forts of the Saxon Shore
To counter Saxon raids, an increasingly serious threat from the late third century on, a chain of ten massive forts was built from the Wash to the Isle of Wight, under the command of the *Comes Litoris Saxonici*, the Count of the Saxon shore, the second highest military post after

the *Dux Britanniae*. When the usurper Constantine (self-styled III) with-drew the regular troops from Britain in 407, the *limitanei* continued to function, even after the collapse of the Western Empire in 476. The last of them, the Numerus Abulcorum stationed at Anderida (Pevensey), were finally wiped out by the Saxons in 491.

his headquarters near Castra Gyfel
Despite Ilchester's obvious Roman ancestry, I've been unable to trace its Roman name. In the Domesday Book it's Givelcestre, 'Roman town on the Gifl'. Gifl, being an earlier name for the River Yeo on which the town stands, would have been a Brythonic appellation. In the same way that the Romans called Chester (on the River Dee) Castra Deva, I've guessed that they might have called Ilchester Castra Gyfel.

a magical landscape
The grassy chalk uplands of southern England (mainly in Surrey, Sussex and Thomas Hardy's 'Wessex') are rich in man-made features dating from neolithic times to the Iron Age: ridgeways along the crests of the various downs, chalk-cut giants and horses, barrows, stone circles of which Avebury and Stonehenge are the most famous, hill-forts, and that amazing eminence Silbury Hill (alluded to by Myrddin in the text). A few of the above are, or may be, imposters. All the extant White Horses, bar the one at Uffington (probably first-century BC), are eigh-teenth- and nineteenth-century, though two others, now destroyed, are known to have existed anciently. The Long Man of Wilmington is presumed to be ancient, as is the famously priapic Cerne Abbas Giant – though there's a theory that the latter is an eighteenth-century forgery by an aristocratic joker poking fun at antiquaries.

an extraordinary edifice
Known today as Cadbury Castle (officially South Cadbury hill-fort), this Iron Age hill-fort with late-fifth-century additions has long been held to be King Arthur's Camelot. This theory is reinforced by 'Camel' place-names in the vicinity: West Camel and Queen's Camel; while the second name-word re the nearby Chilton Cantelo becomes 'Canelot' by switching round the letters. The Cadbury site, along with

Glastonbury a few miles to the north, is a happy hunting-ground for Arthurian enthusiasts, with Glastonbury proving an especially copious fount of associated legend – the Holy Grail, Avalon, Excalibur, the Round Table, Arthur's Grave ('discovered' in 1191), etc.

Artorius' great victory at Mons Badonicus
'Mount Badon', in Arthurian legend, is where Arthur won a great victory against the Saxons. Two sites have been suggested for the battle, one at Liddington Castle, an Iron Age hill-fort six miles north of Marlborough in Wiltshire (the one I've chosen), the other at Badbury Rings, near Wimborne Minster in Dorset.

Chapter 20
which route to follow
Sources differ as to what route through the Julian Alps Theoderic took to reach Italy. Heather in *The Goths* and Wolfram in his *History of the Goths* both say he reached his goal via the valley of the Vipava (through the southern part of the Julian Alps), whereas Burns in *History of the Ostrogoths* states that Theoderic advanced up the Drava River (well to the north of the Julian Alps), then crossed the Julian Alps to the Isonzo River and on to Italy. Clearly, these two routes are mutually exclusive. I've settled for the Drava route as being perhaps strategically preferable to the other. Also, it enables one to exploit the dramatic bonus provided by the arresting Luknja Pass (which Theoderic would have had to use), the col below the awesome cliffs of Triglav's north face.

its junction with the Sorus
I've been unable to find the Latin name for the River Sora, but as the Romans called the Drava 'Dravus' and the Sava 'Savus' ...

the highest summit of the Alpes Juliae
Having had no luck tracing the three-peaked Triglav's Latin name, I've resorted to invention, following the example of 'Trimontium', the name the Romans gave the three-peaked Eildon Hills in Roxburghshire, where Agricola established a great military camp. (Spik, Triglav's sister peak, I've christened Spica, Latin for 'spike': appropriate, considering the mountain's shape and present name.)

a vast stony trough

This is Vrata, the long valley that leads from the Sava up to the pass of Luknja, overlooked by the towering cliffs of Triglav's North Face. The waterfall described in the text is the upper one at Slap Periœ nik; I've moved it nearer the stream (which does indeed disappear underground) to enable Theoderic's wagons to pass beneath it. The terrain on the far side of the pass I've described as less steep than it actually is, in order to point up the rigours of the ascent by contrast.

Odovacar . . . had withdrawn

Wolfram, Burns and Heather say that an inconclusive battle was fought between the two rivals at Isonzo Bridge, resulting in Odovacar retreating to Verona. However, Moorhead suggests that Odovacar, alarmed by the size of Theoderic's host, withdrew from the Isonzo without giving battle. (7Ennodius, in *Panegyricus dictus Theoderico*, describes Odovacar as summoning all the nations against Theoderic, with very many kings coming to fight for him. Whoever these kings were – and it's tempting to dismiss them as hyperbolic – they were conspicuous by their absence when Odovacar did eventually confront Theoderic in battle.)

Chapter 21

he had been . . . entombed – alive

Rumours that Zeno had been heard crying for help from within the tomb (cries that were ignored, due to his being a hated Isaurian), gained wide circulation in Constantinople, and were long believed. Even a hundred and fifty years later, the emperor Heraclius gave orders on his death-bed that his corpse should lie in state until corruption had set in, lest he suffer the same fate.

an undistinguished . . . palace official

Despite his being elderly at his accession, the twenty-seven-year reign of Anastasius was one of the Eastern Empire's longest. It was also, despite being comparatively uneventful, one of the most successful and enlightened. A mild and by all accounts rather colourless individual, Anastasius suppressed the barbarous fights between men and wild beasts, abolished the sale of offices and an ancient tax on domestic animals, constructed aqueducts, harbours and the Long Wall to the west of the capital as an extra defence against barbarian incursion, and campaigned effectively against Persians and Isaurian insurgents. A not unimpressive record, which compares favourably with those of many Eastern emperors.

Chapter 22
Rome's Senate House
Despite what, in the story, Cassiodorus seemed to believe, this was not the building that Scipio and Caesar knew, but an Imperial replacement dating from the reign of Diocletian and today known as the Curia.

you must have contact with the Sibyl
A reference to the authoress of the Sibylline Prophecies (foretelling the future destiny of Rome), the Oracle of Cumae.

he's no Sulla
Lucius Cornelius Sulla, successful general and ultra-reactionary politician, became Dictator of Rome in 81 BC. There followed a reign of terror, which saw several thousand 'enemies of the state' proscribed and executed. The young Julius Caesar very nearly became one of Sulla's victims, but saved himself by the coolness and courage of his deportment when interrogated.

Chapter 23
a careful sale and redistribution of land
Liberius implemented a system of parcelling out called 'thirds'. The term is surely misleading. Given the tiny number of Goths compared to Romans, this could hardly mean that the native Italians were to be deprived of one-third of their land and property. The fact that the final settlement seems to have satisfied Theoderic's followers, without causing undue hardship to their Roman 'hosts', argues that Liberius pulled off an astonishing coup, squaring the circle of conflicting interests. (See Moorhead's *Theoderic in Italy*, Chapter 2.)

one young female . . . called 'Spicy'
One of the charges brought against Pope Symmachus (who seems, like some of his Renaissance successors, to have been as much worldly

politician as spiritual leader) by his opponents, was that he consorted with loose women, especially one who rejoiced in the nickname 'Conditaria', which translates as 'highly seasoned', or indeed 'spicy', as Chadwick renders it in his *Boethius*.

Laurentius, must . . . retire

For the sake of dramatic clarity I have telescoped Theoderic's confirmation of Symmachus as Pope, his fiat concerning Church lands, and his decision as to the fate of Laurentius, into a single incident. In fact, final settlement of these matters was not reached till some time after 500.

he was able to back his claim

Displaying a breathtaking combination of inventiveness and lack of scruple, Symmachus produced a formidable battery of forged documents to support his claim: *Synodi sinuessanae gesta*; *Constitutio Silvestri gesta Liberii*; *Gesta de Xysti purgatione*; *Gesta Polychronii*. Anyone interested in their contents will find them admirably summarized in Chapter 4 of Moorhead's *Theoderic in Italy*.

the five hundred and first

Our present system of dating from the birth of Christ, devised by Dionysius Exiguus, was only officially adopted in 527, the year after Theoderic's death. However, it's not unreasonable to suppose its periodic use for some time prior to that date. Official acknowledgement of any important change often lags behind a ground-swell of popular usage or opinion; e.g., the adoption in Scotland of Christmas Day as a public holiday, which, for four hundred years following its prohibition as a pagan festival by John Knox, it had not been.

The beautiful discs

This is the famous Senigallia medallion, named after the town near which a surviving example was discovered in 1894. The medallion has generally been dated to 500 and associated with Theoderic's visit to Rome on the occasion of his *tricennalia*. However, my old tutor Philip Grierson has argued for a date of 509 (see 'The Date of Theoderic's Gold Medallion', *Hikuin*, 1985).

yet were themselves still here
And, in some cases, still are: the Massimo (Maximus), Colonna and
Gaetani families have pedigrees stretching back to the Roman Republic.
(The consul Fabius Maximus was famous for adopting 'Fabian' tactics
against Hannibal.)

Chapter 24
the bowels of the amphitheatre
Like one of those clever cutaway models designed to show the inner
workings of the human body or the internal structure of a building, the
Colosseum, in its present plundered state, shows clearly the honeycomb
of passages under the arena where the animals were caged and then
transported to the surface by means of a complex system of lifts and
ramps.

Thrasamund's . . . hunters
The excavated Roman villa at Piazza Armerina in Sicily boasts a magnificent series of mosaics, dating from *c*. AD 300, showing how animals
for the Roman Games were captured and transported. There are
mounted men driving stags into a circle of nets; men loading elephants
onto a galley; a Roman animal-catcher directing Moorish assistants to
surround and net a lion; an ox-drawn cart with a shipping-crate
containing one of the big cats; etc.

he strained to twist the creature's horns
I hold my hands up; the incident's a shameless crib from a scene in the
film *Quo Vadis?*.

can have terrible consequences
There is ample evidence that *seditio popularis* (the expression surely
needs no translation) at this time caused Theoderic considerable concern.
The *Liber pontificalis* paints an alarming picture of fighting between
Laurentian and Symmachan mobs (egged on, respectively, by Festus
and Probinus, and by Faustus *niger*); of clergy put to the sword, and
nuns taken from convents and clubbed; and fighting in the streets of
Rome a daily occurrence. Pope Gelasius (492–96) reported that two

successive bishops were murdered in Scyllaeum (Squillace), and the *Fragmentum Laurentianum* uses the expression *'bella civilia'* to describe the rioting in Rome. Things got so bad that on 27 August 502 Theoderic wrote to the bishops assembled in Rome to use their influence to curb the prevailing disorder.

Chapter 25

to hold administrative posts

Under Theoderic, the administration of Italy continued virtually unchanged from imperial times. There were a few (a very few) deviations from his principle whereby the bureaucracy would be manned by Romans, the army by Goths. Count Colosseus, in charge of Pannonia Sirmiensis with troops under him, Servatus Dux Raetiarum, and one Cyprian, who served Theoderic in a military capacity, were all Romans; while Wilia the *Comes Patrimonii*, Triwila the *Praepositus Sacri Cubilici*, and the senator Arigern, were all Goths. They were, however, exceptions. To a contemporary, unless they lived in the Gothic heartland of north-east Italy with its capital at Ravenna, it would have been difficult to tell that the country was no longer part of the Roman Empire.

a panegyric . . . welcoming refugees

Who were these people? Priscian is not specific, but Zachariah of Mytilene (*Historia ecclesiastica*) wrote of one Dominic 'who had a quarrel with the tyrant [Theoderic] and took refuge with King Justinian'. The reference to Justinian (who was not, of course, emperor in Theoderic's lifetime, but who might loosely be described as 'king' in his capacity of virtual co-ruler with Justin) means that the event occurred towards the end of Theoderic's reign, when the label 'tyrant' might be held to have had some justification. Priscian however (as mentioned by Ennodius in *Panegyricus dictus Theoderico*), was writing at the very beginning of the sixth century, when Theoderic's popularity was (with the exception of the Laurentian senators disgruntled by the alienation of Church lands) as yet undimmed. Perhaps it was this senatorial clique (expanded by wishful thinking into a larger and more representative group) that Priscian had in mind.

send him an expert harpist

As elsewhere, for the sake of clarity and conciseness, I've gone in for some telescoping of events – without, I think, compromising essential historical truth. The Alamanni were defeated by Clovis twice – in 497 and again in 506, when they sought refuge with Theoderic. A little later, we find Theoderic writing to Clovis warning him against attacking the Visigoths: 'Put away your iron, you who seek to shame me by fighting. I forbid you by my right as a father and as a friend. But in the unlikely event that someone believes that such advice can be despised, he will have to deal with us and our friends as enemies' (Cassiodorus, *Variae*). As Theoderic had already warned Clovis not to prosecute his war against the Alamanni any further, it seemed opportune to represent these events as happening more or less simultaneously, and to refer to them in a single letter, with Clovis's appeal for a harpist thrown in for good measure.

the diptych . . . presented to him

Such diptychs – among the most attractive minor works of Roman art – were often exchanged as gifts on appointment to high office, especially when someone was named as consul. Celebrated examples from *c*. 390–400 are: the diptych of the Symmachi (the family of the grandfather of the Symmachus in the story), defiantly displaying classical figures engaged in *pagan* ritual, at a time when such practices were being rigorously suppressed; that of Stilicho, the front cover showing the Vandal general, the back his wife Serena with their son Eucherius; and the consular diptych of Honorius, showing the emperor arrayed in the full panoply of a Roman general.

Chapter 26

son of . . . Sidonius Apollinaris

Although Apollinaris' visit to Clovis is fictional, it is consistent with his known behaviour. When Clovis launched his next attack on the Visigoths, Apollinaris led a contingent from the Auvergne to help Alaric II, only to be killed fighting at the battle of Vouillé, along with Alaric himself.

despised for their barbarism
An opinion attested by Cassiodorus (*Variae*), Ennodius (*Opera*) and Jordanes (*Getica*).

The sole authority we need
A view astonishingly seeming to predict a central tenet of Wyclif, Luther, Tyndale and other early Reformers a thousand years later. The evangelizing success of the Iro-Christian Church (Armagh, Iona, Lindisfarne, Luxeuil, etc.) was soon to be eclipsed by that of Rome. Beginning with Pope Gregory the Great's sending of Augustine to convert King Ethelbert of Kent in 596, a wave of Roman Catholic missionaries (many of them Anglo-Saxons, such as Wilfrid, Willibrord and Winfrid) had great success in converting non-Catholic areas of Europe, especially in Germany and Scandinavia. In England, in 664 at the Synod of Whitby, the differences between the Celtic and Roman Churches (concerning Easter, tonsures, the role of Scripture, etc.) were thrashed out and finally settled in favour of Roman practice.

hurled them into the flames
Clovis's barbarous feat of throwing both the donkey and its load into the fire is a retelling of an incident which my old tutor Philip Grierson (see Notes for Chapter 23) relished recounting at tutorials, to illustrate a certain barbarian leader's (Merovingian king's?) jocular way of demonstrating his physical prowess.

Chapter 27
Cassiodorus' History of the Goths
This unfortunately has been lost, but an extant one-volume summary of it was made in the mid sixth century, entitled *Getica*, by Jordanes, a Romanized Goth living in Constantinople.

a sort of Debatable Land
A term borrowed from Scottish Border history. For centuries, a small strip of land straddling the present Dumfriesshire/Cumbria boundary was disputed between the Scots and the English – a situation tailor-made for exploitation by the Border reivers, with their endless capacity

for guile and manipulation. In 1552, with tremendous ceremony, the French Ambassador presiding, the matter was finally settled. A trench and bank (still known as the Scots' Dike) was driven through the middle of what was now no longer the Debatable Land, following the present Border line between the two countries.

Theoderic wearing . . . a diadem

The mosaic head and bust, showing Theoderic wearing an impressive diadem, was uncovered during building work in Theoderic's great church in Ravenna, St Apollinare Nuovo. Thought at first to represent Justinian, it is now generally accepted as portraying Theoderic.

construction of a water-clock and sundial

These, like the selection of a harpist for Clovis, were important and prestigious commissions, indicative of Boethius' high standing in Theoderic's court. Cassiodorus demonstrates this when he places them in positions of honour in *Variae*. Apart from his official work, Boethius – still only in his twenties – was tackling numerous demanding scholarly projects, such as translating from Greek to Latin all the works of Aristotle and the Dialogues of Plato.

based on the one Diocletian had built

Theoderic's palace has gone, but is represented in mosaic in the church of St Apollinare Nuovo. Diocletian's palace at Split (Spalato), on which it is thought to have been modelled, is immense, dwarfing the present town, which has grown up partly inside its well-preserved shell.

my noble Roman with a Gothic heart

To some scholars (e.g., Ensslin, *Theoderich*) it's an article of faith that no Roman was employed in a military capacity in Theoderic's army. Ever. However, this was not a rubric carved in stone; the example of Cyprianus adds further proof. We learn from Cassiodorus (in *Variae*) that Cyprianus' father Optilio was an 'old soldier', and that the entire family was steeped in military tradition – presumably from imperial times. The expression 'with a Gothic heart' was formed as a counterpart to Sidonius Apollinaris' *cor Latinum* (*Epistulae V*).

Chapter 28

Sabinianus . . . son of a famous general

Sabinianus senior was one of Zeno's most effective generals. In 479, during one of the interminable on/off series of campaigns waged by the empire against the Ostrogoths, he almost finished Theoderic's career. Intercepting one of Theoderic's columns headed by Thiudimund, he captured all the wagons and took a large number of prisoners – an incident which I've transposed in the story to the Ostrogoths' crossing of the Haemus range. In 481, Sabinianus senior (aka Magnus) fell victim to intrigue and was murdered by order of Zeno – an act of senseless folly, no evidence of guilt being produced against the general. That the son's career (he rose to become *Magister Militum per Illyricum*) was not adversely affected, suggests tacit acknowledgement on the part of the Eastern establishment that the murder was unjustified.

Mundo, a renegade warlord

This leader of 'prowlers, robbers, murderers, and brigands' (Jordanes, *Getica*) was enlisted by the Goths because they 'were in desperate need of help', according to Wolfram (*History of the Goths*). Moorhead (*Theoderic in Italy*), on the other hand, states that the Goths responded to an appeal by Mundo for help against Sabinianus. Moorhead also says that Mundo was 'probably a Gepid', whereas Wolfram describes him as 'Hunnic-Gepidic'. Burns, however (*A History of the Ostrogoths*) has him as 'a Hun by ancestry'. One pays one's money and one takes one's choice. Moorhead implies that Mundo was already a federate of Theoderic *before* the Sirmian campaign. But as Mundo's base, Herta, was a hundred miles east of the empire's western boundary (and therefore surely coming under Eastern suzerainty), I presume to question this. It seems inherently more likely that Mundo became a federate only *after* the Ostrogoths had occupied the area, perhaps partly to annul his outlaw status in a move aimed at self-protection.

his eyes are upon you

The idea that the Ostrogoths' natural unruliness could be curbed by the thought that Theoderic was watching them from afar was suggested by some lines in Ennodius' *Panegyricus Dictus Theoderico*. Just before the commencement of the battle against the Bulgars, Pitzia reminds the Goths that the eyes of Theoderic are upon them, and tells them to think of Theoderic should the battle ever seem to be going against them, when their fortunes will surely revive. Gibbon reinforces Ennodius: 'in the fields of Margus the Eastern powers were defeated by the inferior forces of the Goths and Huns . . . and such was the temperance with which Theoderic had inspired his victorious troops, that, as their leader had not given the signal for pillage, the rich spoils of the enemy lay untouched at their feet'. The phrase 'Big Brother is watching you' springs to mind; in this context however, its significance is entirely benevolent.

slaughtered to a man
Moorhead (*Theoderic in Italy*) states that 'In 514 Theoderic . . . put to death a man described as Count Petia', and goes on to say that 'there were two, and just possibly three, counts with similar names, but it is not at all clear whether the general of 504–5 was put to death in 514'. This uncertainty, plus the fact that the records are silent regarding Pitzia after 504–5 (assuming that he was not 'Count Petia'), allowed me to have him die fighting in a desperate last stand against the Bulgars.

Chapter 29
the 'navicularii'
The guild reached its peak under the late empire, during the fourth century, its security and continuity set in concrete, thanks to imperial legislation. We know that trade between Italy and the Eastern Empire, also with southern Gaul and parts of the Mediterranean littoral of Spain, continued (doubtless considerably attenuated) after the fall of the West. I've therefore hazarded the assumption that – being so firmly established even towards the West's last days – the shippers' guild survived that empire's demise, a supposition reinforced by the fact that under Odovacar and Theoderic Roman administration and institutions continued largely uninterrupted in Italy.

Chapter 30
'One of Theoderic's "new men"'
Of a sequence of five men appointed to the post of City Prefect after 506, not one became consul or was from any of the great families of

Rome. From this time, when making key appointments Theoderic turned decisively towards '*novi homines*', men who were court apparatchiks, not aristocrats. Moorhead (in *Theoderic in Italy*) says, 'it is possible that his [Theoderic's] change of policy was connected with his final decision against Laurentius, who enjoyed widespread senatorial support in 507; perhaps a degree of punishment, and conceivably fear, were [*sic*] involved'.

to strengthen Rome's defences
Refurbishment of Rome's *moenia* at this time is confirmed by Cassiodorus (in *Variae*), who also records the burning of crops and the attack on Sipontum by the Eastern naval expedition.

a massive warship-building programme
'Their [the Eastern expedition's] retreat was possibly hastened by the activity of Theoderic; Italy was covered by a fleet of a thousand light vessels, which he constructed with incredible despatch' (Gibbon).

The shipyards of . . . Tergeste
Dalmatia, which then included Trieste (Tergeste), was annexed by Odovacar to his kingdom of Italy, following the death of Nepos.

friendly overtures from Theoderic
A diplomatic mission to the Burgundians had been accompanied by prestigious gifts: a sundial and a water-clock (see Chapter 27).

this part of Italy's called Magna Graecia
Between the eighth and sixth centuries BC, a number of flourishing Greek colonies (Metapontum, Tarentum, etc.) was established in southern Italy, which thus (by the time of Pythagoras, according to Polybius) acquired the name Magna Graecia. Arriving at Crotona c. 530 BC, the great philosopher and mathematician soon exerted supreme influence in Megalē Hellas, as the region was called in Greek.

Like ancient legionaries
Simon MacDowall's *Twilight of the Empire* (one of the splendid Osprey series about armies and campaigns) contains graphic descriptions, together with illustrations (based on contemporary evidence) of the

appearance of sixth-century East Roman soldiers. Exchange their oval shields for long rectangular ones, and they would be practically indistinguishable from legionaries of the classical period. The example of orders (still given in Latin in East Roman armies at this time) in the text, is taken from Mauricius' *Strategikon*, a sixth-century training manual.

The seaboard of Apulia and then Calabria
Calabria, the ancient 'heel' of Italy, has since (at some time prior to the eleventh century) moved westwards, to become its 'toe'! The 'toe' was anciently the region known as Bruttium.

along with the title of Augustus
'Honorary consul' was an established title, but 'honorary emperor' would be a constitutional absurdity. 'Augustus' admits of only one interpretation: emperor; and that Clovis certainly was not, in any sense except, perhaps, the complimentary. Yet Gregory of Tours (in *Historia Francorum*, *c.* 560) is unequivocal: 'from that day [i.e., Clovis's victory over the Visigoths] he was called consul or augustus'. Procopius probably had these titles in mind when he says (in *Opera*) that the Franks looked for Anastasius' 'seal of approval'. The conundrum is perhaps best explained by seeing the titles as ammunition in Anastasius' campaign to put Theoderic very firmly in his place after the king's Pannonian/Moesian adventure in 504 and 505, a campaign of which the naval expedition against south Italy formed a major part. In this context the award of the title 'Augustus' to Clovis can be interpreted as constituting a snub to Theoderic, designed to puncture any imperial pretensions the king may have entertained, reminding him that only Anastasius had the power to dispense such appellations. There can be no doubt that Anastasius intended 'Augustus' to be purely titular. Yet it seems rather to have gone to Clovis' head. Gregory describes him wearing purple and a *diadem*, and, in imitation of Emperor Constantine, dedicating a church to the Holy Apostles (viz. Saints Peter and Paul).

his own consular nominee
This has to be yet another example of Anastasius' determination to

punish Theoderic for invading imperial territory. The sole consul for 507 was Anastasius himself, making him consul for the third time.

Chapter 31

once more come under Ostrogothic rule
The only source that I can find that disagrees with this is Wolfram's *History of the Goths* wherein he says, 'Probably in 510 Theoderic . . . ceded to Byzantium . . . the eastern part of Pannonia Sirmiensis'. But Burns (in *A History of the Ostrogoths*) states, 'Sabinianus accepted the restoration of Ostrogothic control at Sirmium, and the Ostrogoths gave up any designs on expanding their power beyond Sirmium' – a conclusion backed up by maps of Theoderic's realm, as shown in historical atlases.

the wars that turned out happily for him
From a letter of Theoderic to Clovis, quoted by Cassiodorus (in *Variae*).

a father-figure to all Germanic peoples
Theoderic emerges as a heroic figure, of immensely prestigious status among Germanic peoples, in early mediaeval legends such as those appearing in the *Hildebrandslied*, which dates from the time of Charlemagne.

dark skin and tightly curled black hair
These features were probably inherited from Berber rather than negro ancestry. Though black people were by no means unknown in Roman Africa, their presence was accounted for by slavery, or by immigration via Nubia, Ethiopia and Axum (Sudan). The appearance of native North Africans is well represented in busts of Emperor Septimius Severus and his son Caracalla. Moorhead (in *Theoderic in Italy*) confirms that Priscian 'was probably an African'.

dedicating three treatises to me
These tracts were *De figuris numerorum*, *De metris fabularum Terentianis*, and *Praeexercitamina*.

another geriatric emperor
It was an age of redoubtable old men living active or productive lives extending far beyond the biblical span: Anastasius, who died aged eighty-eight; Justinian, at eighty-two still working in his study; Liberius, commanding troops not long before his death at eighty-nine; Cassiodorus – still writing at *ninety-three* – who lived to be a hundred, and whose life (468–568) encompassed both the Western Empire's fall and its partial restitution under Justinian; Narses, Justinian's general, who, aged eighty, took Verona from the Ostrogoths, and who died in 575, aged ninety-five.

Amal pedigree has ... had to be concocted
This was actually carried out by Cassiodorus (not acknowledged in the text for reasons connected with plot development), who, digging in Ammianus Marcellinus, barefacedly added the heroic Ermanaric (who ritually committed suicide following his defeat by the Huns) to the Amal family tree, then attached Eutharic's line to him. Ermanaric was actually a Visigoth, not an Ostrogoth, but Cassiodorus was not going to let a piffling distinction like that deter him. 'Creative genealogy' is not, it would appear, a modern phenomenon, but was alive and well in the sixth century.

especially should the couple have a son
Which they duly did. Their offspring, Athalaric, succeeded Theoderic while still a child, Eutharic having already died in mysterious circumstances.

Chapter 32
Theoderic felt his heart swell with pride
There is no evidence that Theoderic visited Rome again subsequent to his extended stay in 500. But, considering the symbolic importance of Eutharic's consulship as a gesture of imperial approval for Theoderic's own rule and his son-in-law as his successor, it would have been fitting, to say the least, for him to have been present at the investiture. So having him attend is not, hopefully, stretching possibility too far. As for Eutharic himself, the records are scanty and contradictory. According to Cassiodorus, he was old; but Jordanes maintains he was youthful and attractive ('wholesome in body'). Some sources say he was a Visigoth,

others an Amal (i.e., an Ostrogoth), while Wolfram refers to him as a 'Visigothic Amal' – a contradiction in terms, surely. Eutharic is certainly a Germanic name, but Cilliga is not; so his ethnic origins seem far from clear. Altogether, a man of mystery. Taking all this into account, I think it was legitimate for me to select those components which seemed best suited to the story.

patterned in a wondrous raised design
Pop-eyed, they stare out at us, those late Roman consuls, from the ivory covers of their consular diptychs, with their page-boy bob haircuts and robes of 'wondrous design', consular baton in left hand, *mappa* raised in right, ready to start the Games. (Cassiodorus' description of the robe as 'palm-enwoven' may refer to the raised lines of the patterns of rectangles, flowers, etc., perhaps suggestive of the ribs and stem of palm-fronds?) Could their expressions of stoic alarm hint at uncertainty about the survival of their institution? (The last Western consul was appointed for the year 530, the last Eastern, nine years later.) Or perhaps they merely indicate concern about their ability to pay the enormous expenses incurred by giving the Games.

the roar from the Circus Maximus
Roman chariot-racing was big business, involving a vast network of organizations run by huge corporations with thousands of stock-holders. It's ironic to think that the colossal enterprise survived (in attenuated form) the collapse of the Western Empire, only to fizzle out (in Rome, not Constantinople) under that empire's partial restitution by Justinian.

the last Western Emperor
What happened to Romulus – nicknamed, with affectionate contempt, Romulus 'Augustulus' – little emperor' – after he was compulsorily retired with a generous pension (an act which reflects most creditably on the 'barbarian' Odovacar)? If a letter written to 'Romulus' by Cassiodorus in the period 507–11 refers to the ex-emperor, that means he was still alive more than thirty years after his deposition. Other than this, we can only speculate as to how long he may have survived, which allows me to have him still living (imagined as a gentle recluse) in

Lucullus' villa near Naples in 519. The villa, constructed by a famous general of the late Republic, was a celebrated beauty spot. (Gibbon gives a good description of the place and its history).

Chapter 33
a successful orchard in Ravenna
'After the example of the last emperors, Theoderic preferred the residence of Ravenna, where he cultivated an orchard with his own hands' (Gibbon).

the newly appointed minister
Boethius became Master of Offices (comparable in some ways to our rôle of Prime Minister) in 523. In the interests of the story, I have put this date back a little without, I think, distorting the sequence of historical events.

resentment over growing German influence
Germans had never been acceptable as emperors. Though it was never put to the test, there are good reasons for supposing that overstepping such a 'red line' could have had dire consequences. For example, in Constantinople in 400, as an indirect result of Alaric's Goths going on the rampage in the Balkans, anti-German violence flared up and several thousand Goths were massacred. And in Italy, following the execution of the Vandal general Stilicho in 408, suspicion of the Germans in the army had led the Roman element to launch a pogrom against the families of the German troops. Despite such precedents, did Theoderic attempt to cross that line?

The rioting of 519–20, which I have suggested could well have been a cover for anti-Arian (i.e. anti-Gothic) resentment, was not an immediate consequence of any measure enforcing religious toleration, which had long been in force. ('They respected the armed heresy of the Goths; but their pious rage was safely pointed against the rich and defenceless Jews' – Gibbon.) So what could have sparked it off? Cassiodorus, according to Moorhead (in *Theoderic in Italy*) suggests that the disturbances were not specifically anti-Jewish but were rooted in some other cause. Is it too fanciful to suggest that the Terracina inscription proclaiming Theoderic emperor, which may well have been contemporary with the riots, could have been that cause? The planned coronation in St Peter's is invention, but the fact that nearly three centuries later a German monarch (Charlemagne) *was* crowned there as (Holy) Roman Emperor, gives food for thought. Was the idea behind the coronation of 800 original, or was it perhaps inspired by a memory of Theoderic's unfulfilled dream?

retribution was swift and harsh
This is confirmed by Anonymous Valesianus, who ascribes to Eutharic the punishments meted out to the Romans of Ravenna. To quote Wolfram (in *History of the Goths*), 'Eutharic's popularity among the Romans must have declined quickly for during the unrest of 520 he advocated stern countermeasures'.

his imperial dreams
The wording and imagery of the Senigallia medallion, the Ravenna mosaic portrait head crowned with a diadem, the Terracina inscription: these are but the most telling manifestations of Theoderic's ambition to become a Roman emperor, occasions when, as Heather (in *The Goths*) says, 'the mask slipped'.

Chapter 34
a sneaking sympathy for a people
Like the Visigoths (and indeed the Ostrogoths), the Jews were forced to become a wandering people, especially when (after several failed and bloody insurrections against Roman rule) they were finally expelled from Palestine by Hadrian, thereafter to encounter varying degrees of persecution in the countries where they tried to make a home – culminating in the Holocaust. 'Nowhere is Theoderic seen more attractively than in his policy towards the Jews', says Moorhead. Compared to zealots like the emperor Theodosius I and his partner in bigotry Bishop Ambrose of Milan, who stamped out the slightest deviation from orthodox Catholicism with fanatical thoroughness, Theoderic comes over as a model of enlightened tolerance, rare for his time and indeed for any subsequent period. When Pope Hormisdas was all for putting pressure on Justin to whip the Monophysites of Egypt into line, Theoderic may well have played a part in ensuring that moderate policies prevailed,

which, by turning a blind eye to Egyptian 'heresy', may have averted another Schism. The conclusion of his letter to the Jews of Genoa, giving them permission to rebuild their synagogue, says it all: 'We cannot command adherence to a religion, since no one is forced to believe unwillingly'. What a tragedy that such a gifted, courageous and resilient race, who have produced, inter alios, David, Jesus, Paul of Tarsus, the historian Josephus, the philosopher Spinoza, Mendelssohn, Einstein and Menuhin, should have suffered 'the slings and arrows of [such] outrageous fortune'. If only they could have taken a more accomodating stance towards the Romans, the present agony of Palestine might have been avoided.

that portent of the death of kings

This is mentioned by Anonymous Valesianus, also by various Byzantine authors who date it as occurring *c*. 520. (The association with the death of kings comes from the Roman author Suetonius, whom the Anonymous may have read.)

named him [Justinian] as his heir

Whether Hilderic went quite as far as this is doubtful, but he certainly established a very cordial entente with Justinian, who avidly cultivated his friendship – to the extent that, according to Browning (in *Justinian and Theodora*), 'For a time it looked as though Africa might be returned to Roman sovereignty without a blow being struck.' When Justinian eventually invaded, Hilderic was murdered by the Vandal nobles, on suspicion of being a fellow traveller.

the shipyards are busy night and day

Compared to his hasty construction in late 507 or early 508 of a fleet of light vessels to counter an Eastern naval expedition against Italy, Theoderic's building of an armada in the last years of his life (probably starting in 523) was a vast project involving the launching of a thousand mighty warships or *dromons*. Whereas the first was a sensible and timely response to a very real and pressing emergency, the second seems to have been an inexplicable over-reaction to largely illusory threats: a perceived Rome–Constantinople senatorial conspiracy to overthrow him; and Hilderic's pro-Byzantine policy following his accession in 523. (Theoderic's attitude towards Hilderic must have been coloured by the fact that the new Vandal king had thrown Thrasamund's widow, Amalafrida, Theoderic's sister, into prison, where she later died, and had her Ostrogothic bodyguard slaughtered.) To create such a massive armament in case 'The Greek [i.e. the East Roman Empire] should ... reproach or ... the African [i.e. the Vandal king of Africa] insult', as Cassiodorus put it, seems a disproportionate response, suggesting a state of mind approaching paranoia. True, the invasion did eventually materialize, but it was hardly imminent in Theoderic's lifetime. In *Theoderic in Italy*, Moorhead suggests that 'the building of the fleet may have been in response to the death, perhaps not of natural causes, of Amalafrida', which some scholars date as occurring in 523, others in 525 or 526. Such a response surely belongs more to some distant heroic age (shades of Helen of Troy – 'the face that launched a thousand ships') than the cold realpolitik of late antiquity. If true, it suggests that Theoderic may have been suffering from some kind of mental breakdown.

they will remember me for this

No fear of that not happening! Massive, austere, uncompromising, the Mausoleum of Theoderic dominates the landscape and is impossible to ignore. The workmanship is superb, the limestone blocks of its construction fitting so exactly as to need no mortar. How the dome was transported across the Adriatic and manoeuvred into position remains a mystery. Even with today's sophisticated technology, the undertaking would present a daunting challenge. Regarding its design, varying theories abound. Some claim Gothic inspiration, others classical, while one scholar (Professor Sauro Gelichi, of the University of Venice) maintains that the dome was modelled on a yurt, the circular tent used by nomads: a fascinating theory of whose validity I remain to be convinced. Overall, opinions regarding design seem to settle for a classical late-Roman structure with a few Gothic touches, especially in the decoration of the outside walls of the upper storey. Within that storey lies Theoderic's sarcophagus of Egyptian porphyry – significantly, the material reserved for the use of emperors. Today, it lies empty, his body probably removed, at the time of Justinian's re-occupation, by zealous Nicene Catholics.

Chapter 35
the 'kingdoms' of Dyfed, Ceredigion and Gwynedd
According to Winbolt (*Britain under the Romans*), native rulers – called *gwledig* – undertook the defence of Britain after the departure of the legions. In this context he mentions Ambrosius Aurelianus (actually of Roman rather than British origin), one Cunedda, who maintained a force of nine hundred horsemen on the Roman Wall, and Cunedda's descendants who ruled in Wales, such as Keredig and Meirion who gave their names to the areas they ruled (Ceredigion and Merioneth). Arthur is referred to as a semi-mythical 'king' leading a British resistance movement against the Saxons.

a holy man of great repute, one Deiniol
Deiniol (later canonized) founded a college in Bangor in 525, and became the town's first bishop in 550.

a most beautiful region
Known today as the Lake District.

Here, the Kymry are still strong
At the time of the Roman invasion of AD 43, there were two separate Celtic peoples in Britain: the Picts living to the north of the Forth–Clyde valley, and the Welsh-speaking Britons who inhabited the rest of the island. After the departure of the legions *c.* 407, German tribes – Jutes, Angles and Saxons from coastal northern Germany and the Jutland peninsula (who had been raiding eastern Britain for more than a century) – began to arrive in ever greater numbers, to settle south of Hadrian's Wall. The invaders (Saxons in the south, Angles in the Midlands and the north) gradually pushed the Britons into the far west, mainly Wales and Cornwall, where they continued to live in freedom, speaking their own language. (Cornish died out about two hundred years ago, although efforts are being made to revive it; Welsh not only survived but is flourishing.)

Undoubtedly, the Romans were responsible for creating a feeling of unity among the Britons, who were a collection of disparate tribes at the time of the invasion. After the legions had left, this 'Britishness' was almost certainly strengthened by resistance against a common

Anglo-Saxon enemy – to the extent that Ambrosius Aurelianus seems to have been a genuine national leader rather than a local warlord. That Cunedda could rule in Cumbria, and his descendants in Wales, reinforces the idea that the Britons saw themselves as a single people, the 'Kymry', as does a tradition (which I've made use of in the story) that the Votadini moved south (perhaps to Wales, but we can't be sure) to assist their hard-pressed kinsmen in their struggle against the invader.

a great plain called Camlan
In legend, Arthur was mortally wounded at the Battle of Camlan (site unknown) and was then rowed to an island in a lake (Avalon?) by six black-clad queens. Slightly adapted, I've incorporated this account into the story.

an arresting spectacle
The imposing remains of Hadrian's Wall, which crossed England from the Tyne to the Solway (a distance of seventy-three miles), are testimony to the power and organizing ability of Rome. That such a massive undertaking (not just a wall, but a complete frontier zone including huge fortresses, 'milecastles' and turrets, and a complex infrastructure of roads, supply depots and a port) could happen in a remote and comparatively unimportant province, speaks volumes about the empire's vast resources and terrifying efficiency.

The term *Vallum Hadriani*, which is what the Romans called the Wall, is slightly misleading. Strictly, the 'Vallum' was the broad ditch fronting the inside of the Wall and demarcating the military zone, not the actual barrier itself.

Chapter 36
Creeping Germanization, that's what happened
Despite Paul's fears, it didn't creep very far. Unlike Normanization in post-Hastings England, or Africanization in post-colonial Rhodesia, Germanization in Theoderic's Italy was very limited, being essentially confined to manning the army with Goths – hardly a radical step, as the Army of Italy in the last years of empire had been largely made up of federates. Otherwise, the phasing out of the Roman palace bodyguard, together with sundry palace officials and the *silentiarii*,

and replacing them with Goths, seems to have been the only other significant change. The administration continued to be run almost exclusively by Romans.

Fridibad, the 'saio'

Theoderic's power ultimately resided in his ability to *persuade* his Ostrogothic fellow tribesmen to accept his authority; unlike Roman emperors, German kings ruled by consent. Gothic nobles (*comites*, or counts) saw themselves as a warrior élite, the risk of them becoming 'overmighty subjects' always present, as men like Theodahad and Tuluin graphically demonstrated in Theoderic's closing years. Between the nobles and the mass of the Ostrogothic people were the *saiones*. The term's meaning is hard to define exactly; perhaps the English 'sheriff' (in the mediaeval sense) comes closest. Intermediaries, and enforcers of the king's writ, representing the *personal* leadership invested in the royal power, they eschewed lofty ranks and titles. Burns (in his scholarly and highly readable *A History of the Ostrogoths*) is most enlightening: 'the actual royal 'firefighters' were the *saiones* . . . the king's men [taking] charge for the king himself, wherever they went. Unless the king retained their loyalty and obedience and the respect they inspired, he could not rule.'

Chapter 37
a leading senator, one Albinus

Son of a consul (Basilius in 480) and himself a consul (in 493), Albinus was a scion of the very powerful and distinguished family of the Decii, had been connected with the negotiations to end the Acacian Schism, and was a leading member of the Senate. That he had been engaged in correspondence with Constantinople is not in doubt, though whether this was treasonable cannot be confirmed.

Cyprian, the Referendarius

He charged Albinus with having sent Justin a letter hostile to Theoderic's kingdom. Unfortunately, we have no details about what precisely this implied. Cyprian was an interesting character and, as far as we can tell, an honest official. He had served in Theoderic's army – one of the few Romans to have done so – and, almost uniquely among

Romans, could speak Gothic. A riding-companion of Theoderic, he was, according to Cassiodorus, a man of action rather than reading. Burns asserts that in charging Boethius Cyprian 'was just doing his job', and cites his subsequent promotion to *Comes Sacrarum Largitionum* and *Magister Officiorum* as evidence of his probity. Given this, it is at least open to question whether Boethius was telling the truth when he claimed that the letter written supposedly by him that contained the damning words *'libertas Romana'* was a forgery. However, as Gibbon – with the splendours of the English justice system in mind – said, 'his innocence must be presumed, since he was deprived by Theoderic of the means of justification'.

Written at the Villa Jovis
Coming hot on the heels of the political catastrophes that afflicted the late years of Theoderic's reign – the urban riots, defection of allies, Constantinople's anti-Arian laws, etc. – the apparent treachery of Albinus and Boethius (just the presumed tip of a senatorial iceberg) must have been particularly cruel hammer-blows. I have taken advantage of the uncertainty regarding dates for this period to present the events covered by the chapter (which have a real sense of nemesis following hubris, befitting Greek tragedy) as occurring in rapid sequence, in order to heighten the dramatic tempo. As Moorhead says, 'The timetable of these events is not as clear as we would like, especially as there are problems in the chronology of Anonymous Valesianus'.

imprisoned in its forbidding keep
As the tower of Pavia no longer exists (it was demolished in 1584), we can only speculate as to its appearance and function. Gibbon mentions a Pavian tradition that it was a baptistery.

The Consolation of Philosophy
Although written by a committed Christian, this celebrated work (which takes the form of a dialogue between the author and a personified Philosophy) contains not a single reference to Christianity, its tone throughout reflecting a Neo-Platonist cast of mind. Its theme is that all earthly fortune is mutable, and everything save virtue insecure. Of impeccable Latinity, its style imitates the best models of the Augustan

age. It was translated into Anglo-Saxon by King Alfred, and translated into various languages throughout the Middle Ages, when it achieved something of the status of a 'best-seller'.

The death of Boethius (and thus the termination of his last work) is usually dated to 524. Moorhead, however, argues convincingly for a date of 526. As he says, 'the later we date the execution of Boethius the easier it is to account for the perfection of the work he wrote in prison'.

Chapter 38

Ager Calventianus

Suggestions as to the exact location of the scene of Boethius' execution vary: 'the distant estate of Calventia' (Burns); 'Agro Calventiano . . . between Marignano and Pavia' (Gibbon); and 'agro Calventiano, almost certainly a part of Pavia' (Moorhead). These differences, I felt, gave me the freedom to make the place the Pavian equivalent of 'Tower Green'. The method of despatch is given in ancient sources as either by cord and club (Anonymous Valesianus), or alternatively by sword (*Liber pontificalis*). Most modern scholars go for the cord-and-club version. Gibbon gives a gruesomely graphic description of Boethius' death by this latter method, also of the scene where Theoderic sees in the head of a fish the avenging spectre of Symmachus – which I've taken the liberty of changing to that of Boethius, for obvious dramatic reasons.

an impossible distance

But not if the story of 'Swift Nick' Nevison (on which the Dick Turpin myth is based) is true. In 1676, he established an apparent cast-iron alibi for a robbery he committed at Gadshill near Gravesend, at four in the morning. Taking the ferry from Gravesend to Tilbury, he then rode to York via Chelmsford, Cambridge and Huntingdon, and 'then holding on the [Great] North Road, and keeping a full larger gallop most of the way, he came to York the same afternoon' (Daniel Defoe, *A Tour through the Whole Island of Great Britain*).

The distance from Gravesend to York is almost exactly two hundred miles, the same as that from Ravenna to Pavia. Given that the Via Aemilia in 526 would have been in far better condition than the Great North Road in 1676, that the terrain of the Po valley is even flatter than that of eastern

England, and that Fridibad had the advantage of changes of mount, the *saio* could well have completed the journey within twelve hours. As Roman dinners started considerably earlier than ours, Theoderic could have taken to his bed by 5 p.m., and Fridibad been on the road by 6 p.m.

Theoderic was dead
He died on 30 August 526 (shortly after the execution of Boethius, Moorhead suggests), the very day on which his anti-Catholic legislation, which included the surrender of churches to Arians, was due to come into force.

1/1/100